CW01642364

ON THE RIVIERA

To George,

plod on canny,

Nicky Moan

x

PONIES ON THE RIVIERA

A kitchen sink drama set in Sunderland in the 80s and 90s

Nicky Moon

Copyright © Nicky Moon 2025
All rights reserved.

All characters are fictitious, and any resemblance to persons, living or dead, is coincidental, apart from some of the teachers. The events described in real places are fictitious, and any resemblance to real events is coincidental.

This book is sold subject to the condition that it shall not, by way of trade or otherwise, be hired out, lent or resold, or otherwise circulated without the author's/publisher's prior consent in any form of binding or cover other than that in which it is published and without a similar condition including this condition being imposed on the subsequent publisher.

The moral rights of the author have been asserted.

Front cover illustration by Nicky Moon
Cover design by Jac Lee, UK
Art scanning and retouch by R Young Art Gallery, Wokingham, UK
Proofreading by Michelle Emerson (michelleemerson.co.uk) and Moon Medical Communications (moon-medical.com)

Thank you to Katharine Stenlake, Rowena McMenamin, Rosalind Byrne, Hela Giddings, and Sylvie Hickman. Special thanks to Jac Lee for designing the cover and marketing materials. Special thanks to Michelle Emerson – it was great to work with a literary professional and fellow northerner who survived the 70s.

Skiderp Marras!

I was born in 1972 and grew up on Grindon where I was the only kid called Annick, so was glad to be known as Nicky. I went to Grindon Infants, Broadway Juniors, and Bede Comp, and ran for Sunderland Harriers (1986–90).

I worked in the night-time economy (1990–95), including the Blue Monkey when it changed from regular club to rave club (whoa), and Idols, which was normal for the 90s. During the day, I went to Wearside College, then did a degree and PhD in physiology at Newcastle, followed by post-doctoral research at Oxford and Manchester. I didn't meet anyone from Sunderland at Oxford, so if you could all try harder, that would be good.

I work as a science writer and have lived down South for over two decades. I still have a Mackem accent and dream of living over the seafront, obviously (dolphins!).

When my kid started school, she had a toilet accident, 'I got to the bathroom, but the cubicles were full.' My advice was, 'Next time, bang on the door, and shout, ha'way lasses, stamp yer feet!' She looked at me in horror and said in her little posh voice, 'Oh Mummy, you're so Northern.' I thought, thanks very much, I am Northern. To prove it, I wrote this book.

Nicky Moon

There's no point having dreams if you're poor (but no one can stop you)

In 1976, seven-year-old Paula has a donkey ride along Seaburn beach and falls in love with horses. She dreams about owning one, or riding one, or stroking one would do, but there's no danger of that when you're living down the maisonettes. It was ellish when she lived at Thorney Close, like in the photo with the silver Christmas tree. That was before Dad went away and Mam met a miner called Billy who spends more time in Steels than down Herrington pit.

Paula can't wait to leave school and get a job sewing clothes for Marks and Spencer. In Maggie's Britain of record unemployment, the Dewhirst factory offers a steady job and canny money for a lass. But when Billy hoys a dicky radge, and they have to run, things go from bad to great when she's fostered by a rich family. But then there's Dad and everything else.

Dedicated to Mr Howe

Chapter 1

August 1976

She balanced on the arm of the chair, singing, '*Here we come into town, gettin up, fallin down*,' while David chased himself around the living room with her knitted Dougal. He whirled it in the air and smacked it off her face, '*Ecky thump!*'

'Here-man,' she said, diving on him. His legs buckled as she hooked her arm round his neck, dragging him to the floor in a headlock.

'Ah cannet breathe,' he rasped, clawing at her arm. His hand dropped and he went still.

She slackened her arm, and he slumped on the carpet. His chest wasn't moving. She prodded him in the side. 'David, wake up, will yer?'

'Ahhh!' he said, jumping to his feet. 'Had yer gannen. Did yer think ah woz deed?'

'Shhh, man! We'll get wrong.'

There was a bang on the ceiling and Mam shouted, 'Keep the bloody racket down.'

Mam had rolled their cossies into towels and put them in a placker bag because Dad was taking them to the beach today. They didn't see Dad for ages when they first moved to Pallion, but now he lived at Pennywell, they saw him most weekends.

She picked up the bag of towels, 'Should uz wait for Dad at the top of the road?'

'Aye, good idea, ower kid.'

'Ah'm not a kid, ah'm seven,' she said, swinging the bag at David's head.

'Gis it here. Mam said ah had ter carry the towels.'

'Nor.'

'Aye.'

He pulled the bag and after a tug-of-war, yanked it from her grip, sending her flying into the wall, knocking the keys off the brass gun.

Mam thudded her foot 'Gan wait outside, or yer'll be forrit!'

The maisonettes went down one side of the road and on the other side, there were garages and fences and a car place with tyres outside. When they got to Steels, David said, 'Let's stop here.'

She watched the big and little lasses walking up the main road towards the building with the see-through front that showed the stairs zigzagging between the floors. Some of the lasses were wearing purple leotards with a white cat on the front.

It wasn't long before a green car turned the corner and slammed the brakes on. Uncle Jimmy and Dad were in the front, and cousins Julie, seven, Mark, ten, and Gavin, thirteen, were in the back. Dad got out. He was wearing a red t-shirt with green oblongs on the shoulders and cut-off jean shorts. He put his hands on his hips. 'Wot der yers think?'

'Mark four Cortina estate, R reg,' said David, 'wait until ah tell me mates about this.'

Uncle Jimmy opened the boot, and they climbed in amid cries from Mark and Gavin about also riding in the boot.

'Yers can gan in on the way back, now turn rund and sit down,' said Uncle Jimmy to the heads popping over the back seat.

All aboard, Uncle Jimmy lit two fags, gave one to Dad and said, 'Let's away.' The engine growled and the floor shook. He turned the radio up to blasting and they set off. The car went fast down Hylton Road and it felt ellish seeing the shops fly by.

Then Mark punched Gavin, and said, 'Have yae let one rip?'

'Here-man, it wozn't me,' said Gavin, punching him back.

'He who smelt it, delt it,' said David, pointing at Mark, who grabbed his finger and bent it back and said, 'Beg for mercy,' while Gavin leaned out of the window and took gulps of air.

Uncle Jimmy turned the radio down. 'If yers dinnet pack it in, yers can get out and walk. Nor speakin till wer see the bridge, reet?'

She lay down with her head under the back window and looked at the clear blue sky that went on forever. Today was going to be topper, much better than normal days.

After a while, Gavin shouted, 'Bridge!'

The car went dark as the sky was covered with metal beams held together with wass bolts like from the biggest Meccano set ever.

'Ten points for the first person ter see the sea,' said Dad.

She sat up and looked down the river, which disappeared as they reached the other side of the bridge, where all she could see were maisonettes like the ones she lived in. They went past shops and pubs and houses that looked like they were built in the olden days, and then there was a huge square building with a ramp going up to it and a skittle on the side. After that, there was a huge brick building with arched windows down the side and the front had grand windows and tall wooden doors with wet people coming out. Along the top, in letters like from the Romans, she read, PUBLIC BATHS. There were houses with arched doorways, then shops with arched windows above, and next a church with arched windows, so she reckoned that arches were all the rage along this road.

'Windmill!' shouted Gavin.

Three heads leaned through the gap in the front seats, blocking the view.

When Mark turned to punch David, she leaned into the space to see the sails going round and Windy Miller stepping out at just the right time not to be hit on the head. Instead, behind a tumbled-down wall, there was a wrecked windmill with broken sails. Uncle Jimmy made the car stop and she was thrown backwards onto her bum.

The car shuddered and smelled of petrol as they watched the red traffic light. The boy in the next car was hanging his body and arms out of the window so she stuck her tongue out at him. When the light went green, everyone cheered, the car lurched forward and turned the corner, and there in the distance, above the chimleys and spires, was a line of glistening blue.

'Sea!' she shouted, winning the points.

She was glad to get out of the boiling car and sit on the wall. Dad took his t-shirt off and wrapped it round his head and stuck his ciggies half down the front of his shorts.

'Reet, wee's carryin wot?' said Dad, as Uncle Jimmy unloaded the car.

Gavin shouted, 'Top,' and darted off, followed by the lads, while Uncle Jimmy shouted after them, 'Ow! Get back here and help!'

Dad gave her the wireless. 'Carry it by the handle and dinnet drop it.'

Uncle Jimmy carried Julie and two bags of rolled-up towels, and Dad carried two sunbeds and a red coolbox.

The sand was scadden and the fresh air was full of laughter and screams.

'How's about here?' said Dad, dumping his stuff down.

'It's fillin up,' said Uncle Jimmy, looking down the beach.

'Aye,' said Dad, 'gis the towels.'

He unrolled the orange towel with a flick and she helped him unroll the others and arrange them on the sand in two rows.

'Reet then lasses, get yer cossies on,' said Dad.

Julie took her dress off and underneath she was wearing a pink bikini which had a frilly top that went across her chest above her nipples.

Dad held up a towel while she changed, and when she stepped out in her cossie, he said, 'Last one in the sea's a rotten egg!'

They sprinted towards the water that was twinkling in the distance – soft sand, grassy sand, soft sand, damp sand – it was miles down the beach – pebbly wet sand, wet sand – she kept running until her feet hit the sea and she was swept under the freezing water. As she tumbled in the waves, she didn't know if she was upside down or the right way up, and there was water in her ears and mouth, and then she was dumped on the wet sand. She rubbed her stinging eyes, and as they cleared, she made out the shape of Julie, dumped on the sand next to her. They held hands and ran into the waves again, losing grasp of each other's fingers as they went thrashing into the foam.

They played in the waves for ages until Julie slied off with some lasses with a beach ball, so she played in the sea on her own and then joined a family who were scratching a river with a stick. It was a good game, but when she got thirsty and hot, she wandered up the beach, searching for a familiar face between the deck chairs and windbreakers.

'Ow, Paula, ower here.' Dad was waving his arms miles up the beach.

Glad to finally reach camp, she plonked her wet bum on the towel.

'Where's Julie?' said Uncle Jimmy.

'In the sea,' she said.

'Der yer think ah should gan and get ah?' said Uncle Jimmy to Dad.

Dad held a pretend telescope to one eye and pointed it at the shore. 'There's hods of bairns down there. She'll be reet.'

Dad and Uncle Jimmy lay on the sunbeds while she made holes in the sand with her finger. The sun was a tiny red circle in the vast blue sky, and soon, her back was burning, so she moved the towel and burrowed the sand underneath to make a shallow pit. She wiggled into the deep, damp sandpit and lay facing up, pulling the towel over the top of her body and head. She gazed at the sky through the towel and the sun turned into hexagons that went rainbow colours when she squinted.

Above the hazy noise she could hear familiar voices, far away at first, and then, 'Ah won like,' said Gavin. She peeped out of the towel to see David and Gavin stripped to their cowies and Dad and Uncle Jimmy adjusting their sunbeds from down to up.

Dad opened the coolbox: crisps, half a loaf, apples, milk, and ice cubes.

'Sarnie, anyone?'

'Me.'

'Me.'

'Ah dinnet like cheese,' said Gavin.

'There's nor cheese, son,' said Dad.

They sat on the towels and passed warm lemonade between them and then they had a competition to see how far they could hoy their gowks. The lads changed into their trunks and they ran down the beach and into the sea. She walked out as far as she could until she was on her tiptoes. David and Gavin could swim, so they went even further out.

They were playing in the sea and having a right laugh until David got half drowned under a yellow dinghy and started a fight with a kid from the dinghy family. David punched the lad in the chest before the older kid pushed him away, and then David stormed out of the sea in a right mood followed by Mark and Gavin. She tried to play with some younger lasses who were building a skyscraper sandcastle, but an older lad came over and said,

'Gan and cause trouble somewhere else.'

Back at camp, Dad and Uncle Jimmy were lying on the sunbeds.

'Where's ower Julie?' said Uncle Jimmy.

'Dunnar,' said Gavin.

'Well, gan find her, for fuck's sake.'

'She knars where we are,' said Dad. 'She'll come back when she's bored.'

The lads put their clothes on, so she put her green dress on. She remembered when it was down to her shins and now it was up past her knees, which was just as well on such a hot day.

'Can uz gan ter the fair?' said Mark.

'Haddaway and shite, ah'm not made of money,' said Uncle Jimmy.

'Yers could sneak on the ghost train like we used to,' said Dad, opening his fag packet and tipping out some change. He gave David a fifty-pence piece. 'Share it wer yer sister.'

Uncle Jimmy pulled his wallet out of his trunks. 'Look for yer sister on yer way ter the fair,' he said, giving Gavin a wrinkled pound note.

She carried her flip-flops, trying not to get her dress wet as she followed the charge along the sea's edge, which was quicker, said Gavin, than taking the road. The sea was coming in and was touching the pebbly wet sand, squashing everyone up the beach.

'Look!' said Mark.

They turned, thinking that he'd seen Julie, yet instead, coming along the shore was a bunch of donkeys. They kept walking, not interested in the jingling bells and he-haws. She was hopeful that Mark would stop, but he shrugged and followed the others. She shouted after them to stop and then they were lost in the hazy crowd. She'd have to catch them up because she had no choice other than to walk toward the lovely donkeys.

They smelled like a pet shop, only much nicer. She went up to the grey one with the black ears and stroked her nose. She was the best one. She had kind eyes with long lashes. The donkey smiled when she stroked her, and she got butterflies in her belly.

'Twelve pence,' said the lad.

'Ah haven't got any dosh,' she explained. 'Can ah gan on this one?'

An old gadgie came over. He was wearing a sweaty vest and had a leather money sack hanging from his fat belly. She put her nose on the donkey to block his stink.

'Where's yer mam, luv?'

'Ah'm here wer me dad.'

'Yer'll have ter get him. Yer need a grown-up ter ride.'

As the lad led the donkey away, she kept stroking. 'Can ah stroke for nowt?'

'Gan and get yer dar.'

She put her arms around the donkey's neck and rubbed her cheek on hers.

The smelly gadgie came back and shook his head. 'If ah dee it for one, ah'll have ter dee it for them all.'

The lad put his arms around her middle and pulled. She clung on the best she could until her fingertips slipped down the fur and off the nice donkey.

The sea was coming in fast, and people were shifting their stuff as the empty camps were eaten by the lapping waves, a blanket, some shoes, a football. It was the opposite to this morning when the beach was full and the sea was empty. Now there was nobody on the beach, and the sea was full of grown-ups bobbing up and down, some of them really far out.

She kept running and when she caught up with the lads, she said, out of breath, 'Can wer gan on the donkeys?'

'Nor,' said David. 'Wer garn on the bandits.'

'Ha'way man, wer can gan ter the bandits after,' she pleaded.

'The donkeys are miles away; look, yerv missed them,' said Gavin.

'Will yers wait for uz while ah gan on them?'

'Yerv missed them,' said David.

The donkeys were a brown blur in the distance, and it felt like one end of some gowie was stuck to her heart and the other end was stuck to the donkey.

'Ah'm not comin wer yer, ah'm gannen on the donkeys,' she said.

'Will yer see if yer can find Julie?' said Gavin.

She ran along the shore in the direction she'd come from, jumping tons of broken sandcastles. The massive one with the lolly sticks on top had about ten kids booting into it. In the distance, she could see the yellow dinghy like a gigantic banana on the grassy sand, so she ran over some peoples' blankets towards it. As she weaved between deckchairs she heard a two-finger whistle, like a secret code through the air. She turned to face the sound and saw Dad waving his arms.

'Paula, ower here.'

Dad was by himself.

'Where's Uncle Jimmy?' she said.

'He's lookin for Julie. Wot yer deein here?'

'Can ah have twelve pence for the donkeys?'

'Why-aye, man.'

She held his hand as they walked. 'Can wer gan ter the fair after the donkeys?'

'Aye, if yer like.'

The donkeys were standing still and drinking water so she counted them: six. It must have been baking with all that fur and then there was the blanket and saddle.

She was boiling and she was only wearing a dress. Dad waved at the smelly gadgie and he came over.

'Alreet, Eddie lad? This yer nipper?'

'Aye, this is Paula.'

'Yer wanna gan on a donkey, sweetheart?'

She looked at Dad as if to say am I really going to get a ride? Nothing this good was ever certain.

'Which one?' said Dad. She pointed to the one with the long lashes.

The lad brought the donkey over. 'This is Polly.'

She stroked her lovely nose.

Dad winked. 'Ready?' He lifted her up and plonked her on Polly.

Mr Smelly said to the lad, 'Tack her ter the headland.' Then he said to her, 'An extra lang ride for me marra's princess.'

The lad started running and so did Polly, bells jingling. She jigged up and down and slipped from side to side, but once she got used to it, it was easy. The salty air blew in her face and she was so high that she could see to the end of the sea. She'd never felt so free and full of sparkles. She didn't want it to end ever, ever, ever.

She held Dad's hand as they crossed the road on the way to the fair.

'Are yer sure yer cannet hold it in, man?'

'Ah'm burstin,' she said.

'Ah wish yer'd telt uz yer needed a wee before wer left the beach.'

'Sorry, Dad.'

He took her into the Bay Hotel, which was dark and smelled of beer and smoke.

'Ah'll wait here,' he said. 'Yae get yersel in the loo, there's me good lass.'

When she came out, he was gone, so she wandered into the big room with a bar that was chocka with men drinking pints of beer and smoking.

'Can ah help yer, pet?' said a bright-red man.

'Ah'm lookin for me dad. He's called Eddie.'

A cold hand landed on her arm. It was Dad. They went outside and down the side of the pub, past the carpark, and stopped at three white posts next to a square of cobbles.

'Wait here,' he said. 'Ah have ter gan see a man about a dog.'

'Wot type of dog?'

'A big fluffy one like the Dulux dog.'

'When will yer be back?'

'Soon.' He pointed along the four sides of the square. 'Stay on the cobbles.'

'When's soon?'

'Dinnet gan near the cars or the road.'

'When will yer be comin back?'

He gave her a cuddle. 'See yer in a bit. Dinnet move from here.'

She sat on the middle post, or as it was now known, White Beauty, a horse with a white body, white mane, and white tail. The posts to either side were Red Rum and Yellow Whiskey; both were black with black manes and black tails. She click-clacked her tongue and lifted her body up and down as White Beauty crossed the field of long grass with red poppies. Red Rum chased ahead and jumped the hedge and she had to cling on as White Beauty chased after him and jumped the hedge, higher and longer than any horse ever before.

Her bum was killing so she got off White Beauty and went to the bushes to pick some pretend apples to feed the horses. This meant going outside of the cobbled square, but they were hungry so she thought it would probably be okay. She filled her basket with apples and took them to the horses. Her belly felt like an empty bucket, and she could smell fish and chips. She went back to the bushes and stood on the wall. Where was Dad? It must be a git important dog to take this long. She went to the horses and sat on White Beauty.

'There's a little lass playin on the bollards.' A group of people on the pavement looked over the bush, and then a bright-red man hopped over the wall. 'Wot yer deein here by yersel?'

'Ah'm waitin for me dad. Can ah have a chip?'

'Aye.' He held out a carton of fat chips and she took a greasy handful. They were really nice, so she took some more.

'He'yar, have them,' said the red man.

She took the chips, and he jumped back over the wall as his friends cheered.

Her nostrils tingled with vinegar and her lips stung with salt, and as she chewed, her mouth flooded with soft, warm yumminess. The best chips ever. Where was Dad? She wandered to the front of the carpark and put the carton in the bin, then climbed onto the wall. She walked along like Professor Yaffle, stepping down like he steps down the books, ding, ding, then she walked a bit more, ding-ding, ding-ding, and stepped down some more books.

'Ow!'

An arm flew across her chest and pushed her backwards, and when she looked up, she was on the kerb next to where the cars pull in.

'Yerl get knocked ower playin here,' said a woman with a red face, pink arms, and white legs, like a space rocket ice lolly. 'Where's yer mam and dad, pet?'

'Ah'm waitin for me dad,' she said, running off to where she should be.

She sat on White Beauty and stroked her mane. They were safe now. Clip-clop, clip-clop.

'Excuse me. Did yer say yer were waitin for your dad, luv?'

It was ice lolly woman.

'Aye. He said dinnet move off the cobbles.'

'Where did he gan?'

'Ter see a man about a dog.'

'Ah, reet, ah see. Yer better come wer me, pet.'

'Where tee?'

'Ter find him; ah bet he's inside the pub lookin for yer.'

She held ice lolly woman's hand, and they went inside and up to the bar where the woman started talking to the barmaid. This was much closer to the bar than she was allowed in the Mountain Daisy. From this close, she could see the upside-down bottles and a shelf full of crisps.

The barmaid came over. She had smooth brown hair and a necklace made from red beads like sarsaparilla tablets. 'Where's yer dad, pet?'

'Ah dunnar.'

'Come on, let's look for him.'

They went all over the downstairs and she couldn't see him, so they went upstairs, and the barmaid asked the people sitting at the tables along the windows if they'd seen Eddie Hasting.

None of the people had seen him, but hods of them offered her a crisp, which she took, apart from the nasty prawn cocktail ones.

'Can she sit at the end of yer chabble while ah mack a phone call?' said the barmaid.

'Why-aye.' A red man stood and offered her his chair. 'Sit down, pet, wot's yer name?'

'Paula.'

'Wot flavour crisps der yer want, Paula?'

'Beefy please, thank you.'

The red man went away with the barmaid and she wondered who she was going to speak to on the telephone. Maybe her nana; apart from it wasn't Sunday, which is the normal night to talk to nanas on the phone. The people at the table were holding ciggies out to the side or high in the air or down under the table and her eyes were stinging.

'John, open the winda for the bairn, will yer?' said a woman.

A man opened the open window wider. 'He'yar pet, stick yer heed owt.'

She leaned out and looked up and down the road to see if she could see Dad. The cool sea breeze felt nice on her face. It was getting dark and there was a tiny ship with twinkling lights far out to sea and she wondered if the sailors were looking through the portholes at the faraway lights of the Bay Hotel. She watched the twinkly ship sail away until it was a tiny speck on the dark sea.

She'd long finished her beefy crisps and lemonade when the barmaid appeared from the smoke and said, 'Ha'way, Paula, come wer me.'

She held the barmaid's hand as they went down the stairs and outside, where there was a policeman. He must have been inside all day because he was as white as a bottle of milk.

'Are you Paula?'

'Aye.'

'I hear you've lost your dad.'

'Nor, ah'm not lost, he's comin back.'

'Where did he say he was going to?'

'Ter see a Dulux dog.'

'A big fluffy one?'

'Aye, der yer knar where he is?'

She held the policeman's hand as they walked down the side of the pub past the stables where the three horses were sleeping. She pointed, 'That's where me dad telt uz ter wait.'

'Have yer ever been in a police car?'

'Wot? A jam sandwich?'

'Shall we go and see?' The policeman took her to a white car with a red stripe down the middle that looked exactly like a jam sandwich.

'Can ah have a ride?'

He opened the back door and she got in. It smelled like gowie, and mini traffic lights were hanging from the mirror. The policeman was in the front talking on his crackly radio and she heard him say Dad's name. He turned round. 'Where's yer mam, Paula?'

'At home.'

'Where's that then?'

'Peacock Street West.'

'Pallion?'

'Aye.'

The police car was speeding along much faster than Uncle Jimmy goes, and every time he turned a corner she went fleeing along the seat, like on the back of the Jolly Bus. The car window was open, and she closed her eyes and imagined she was riding a black horse beside the dark sea.

They were driving down her road when she saw David walking past the tyre place. 'There's me brotha,' she called out.

The policeman stopped and opened the door for her to get out.

'Where've yer been?' said David. 'We woz lookin all ower for yer.'

'Is this your sister?'

'Aye,' said David, standing up straight.

'How old are you, son?

'Thirteen.'

She bit her lip; he was ten.

'What number do you live at?'

'That one,' David pointed.

'Go on then, get yourselves inside.'

As soon as the police car drove away, David gave her a dead arm.

'Ow man, wot woz that for?'

'Gan and ask Nelly for the key.'

Their maisonette was an upstairs downstairs one with a front door onto the street and Nelly lived on top. They went in the outside door with no glass in it and up the concrete steps. He pushed her towards Nelly's door, and as she was about to knock, Nelly opened it. She was old with rollers in her hair like Hilda Ogden.

'Wot's all the commotion?'

'Can ah have the key please?'

'Where's yer mam?'

'She's wer Billy,' said David.

'Courtin, are they?'

They looked at each other and laughed.

Nelly gave David the key, said, 'Hang on a minute,' and went inside.

David slapped her across the back of the head, so she slapped him on his red arm, and he was nearly crying when Nelly came back.

'He'yar, me little luvs.' Nelly gave her a chocolate cake on a plate. 'Bring uz the plate back will yer, there's me good lads and lasses.'

'Thank you, Nelly,' said David in his best voice, so she copied.

'Thank you very much for the cake.'

The flat was messy and hot. It was ten o'clock.

'What time's Mam gettin back?' she asked David.

'She's owt wer Billy, she'll not be back till tomorra.'

'Oh aye, ah forgot we're supposed ter be stoppin at Dad's.'

David had his serious face on. 'Yer not ter tell nee one that Dad disappeared today. Yer knar wot they'll dee if they find out?'

'We'll get sent ter the Cottage Homes.'

'Aye, so wer had a lovely day, wer stopped at his, and then wer came home, tomorra, like.'

She saluted and said, 'But where did he gan?'

David shrugged and picked Smarties off the cake, leaving holes in the thick chocolate icing. 'Should wer scoff the cake and put ower feet on the chabble?' he said.

'Aye,' she nodded. David was ellish sometimes, but he was also mostly annoying.

He shifted the overflowing ashtray from the coffee table to the shelf. Then he swiped the newspapers and pens and stuff onto the floor and pointed at the spot where she should place the cake. David sat next to her and they put their feet on the table on either side of the cake. He put his arm around her.

'Yer had a good day, ower kid?'

'Best ever, and ah'm not a kid, ah'm seven.'

Chapter 2

July 1981

Most of her friends at school had two nanas and two grandars, but she only had one of each who were still alive. Mam's dad was in the war and after he came back he was killed by a coal wagon. When Mam was seven, her mam died of cancer, so she went to live with her sister Pat. Her alive nana and grandar were from Dad's side. Grandar didn't fight in the war because he worked on the tugboats. Nana and Grandar lived at Pennywell with Gavin. Mark and Julie lived with Uncle Jimmy and Aunty Susan, who was their mam, but not Gavin's. Her own branch of the family was less complicated: she lived with Mam and stepdad Billy, full brother David, and half-brother Ian.

*

Nana had decorated the living room for the royal wedding. There was a wass flag on the wall and red, white, and blue streamers going from the corners of the ceiling to the big light in the middle. No one was to touch the nuts until the others arrived, but who eats nuts? Nana said that when she was little, she got a bag of nuts from Santie and an orange if she was lucky, or if she'd been a bad girl, a bag of cinders, which anyway sounded better than nuts.

'Why don't yers gan outside and play? Ah'll give yers a shout when it comes on,' said Nana, shooing them off her rug.

The kids from round the doors were wearing union jack hats and hods of the houses had triangle flags in the windows. She sat on the front step with David rather than go out to play; he didn't play out anymore, he was too old. She loved it at Nana's house. Everyone made jokes and told ghost stories and talked about the olden days like when Grandar got his ring caught on a machine and it ripped his finger off. She wished Dad was there, and she knew that everyone else wanted Dad to be there too, although they never said it. She'd heard that Dad was in Ryhope, although when she walked in the room, they'd shush and change the subject. 'Aye, Eddie's been in Ryhope for three month– eeee, did yer see Deirdre's weddin on Corrie?'

She wondered what Dad did in Ryhope that was such a secret. Tracy from school's dad moved away because he had another woman and a baby, and she said that all the grown-ups talked about him and went 'shush' when she came in the room. She imagined that Dad's house in Ryhope was made from red bricks with a porch and a garage and that his new girlfriend looked like Chloe, his favourite presenter from *Playschool.*

'See her?' said David, pointing to the gang of bairns in the square.

'Wee? The lanky lass wer the white top?'

'Aye, her brotha woz sent ter Borstal.'

'Neeways! Wot for?'

'Burglary and arson.'

'Shit.'

'Aye, poor bastard.'

Heads turned and people came to doors as a flash silver car came into the square. It stopped outside of Nana's and the bairns gathered to see the Hasting family get out as if the royal family had arrived. David got up from the step, 'Fuck this, ah'm off rund the shops.'

Nana gave her a pack of iced gems and while she was sitting nicely next to Julie, everyone disappeared. Over Julie's crunches she could hear whispering from the kitchen. Then Uncle Jimmy, Grandar, David, and Mark came in, and they all clapped as Nana followed with a hat in each hand.

'*In yer Easter bonnet, wer all the frills upon it, yer'll be the bonniest lasses in the Easter Parade.*' Nana had a high voice and her big boobs swung when she danced.

Nana gave her a placker bowler hat with tissue paper stuck all over it, scrunched-up like flowers. On the front, it had a picture of Charles and Lady Diana from a magazine stuck on some card and cut into an oval, framed with silver milk bottle tops folded over. She put the hat on, and so did Julie. Uncle Jimmy whistled, so they did a twirl.

'Eeee, me bonnie lasses,' said Grandar, cuddling them, one under each arm, until Julie saw his finger stump and screamed.

Nana loved the royal family. A black and white photo of Grandar meeting Prince Philip took pride of place on top of the thermostat box in the living room. Nana turned the telly up and everyone settled down: grown-ups on the settee, Gavin and Mark on the armchair, and the lasses on the floor.

The carriage arrived and there were brown horses with silver necklaces and headbands, trotting along at the sides and behind, their hard hooves clip-clopping on the red road. The horses pulling the carriage had masks over their eyes and she wondered how they could see, and she thought that when she gets married her carriage would be pulled by white horses with feathers on their heads and no masks on their eyes.

The lads started punching each other, so Nana said, 'Yers can gan outside if yers are ganner fight.'

There were two white horses behind the carriage and the brown horses pulling the carriage were skippy. This wedding was ellish so far, apart from it was boring when they showed the wheels going round and no horses. Soon there were bridesmaids in sticky-out dresses, and Nana said,

'Eeee, aren't they lovely?'

'Nor,' said Uncle Jimmy, 'they're parasites on the state.'

'They're openin the carriage,' said Nana, boobs swinging as she leaned towards the telly.

Lady Diana got out and her dress was like a git big cream cake.

'Why, man, it's all creased,' said Grandar.

'Gertcha,' said Nana, flicking her arm at him.

Lady Diana's dress and the net curtains attached to her head kept going and going and going.

'Eeee, how lang's that train?' said Nana, nearly crying. 'Beautiful, just beautiful.'

Mark and Gavin kept punching each other until Uncle Jimmy said, 'Packit in will yers, yer nana wants ter watch this.'

The bride got to the front of the church and there was a man in a funny hat, so Uncle Jimmy said, '*For mash get Smash*.'

Nana batted him with the back of her hand, 'Stop bein impitant; anyone'd think yer wer dragged up.'

It was boring when they were saying their vows apart from the posh voices were funny.

When Lady Diana said, 'I do,' Uncle Jimmy said, 'Poor cow.'

After they came out of the church and the crowds were cheering and waving flags, Nana got a tin of biscuits with Charles and Diana on the front. The lads stopped fighting and dove in. She chose a chocolate-covered digestive and Julie chose a pink wafer, the freak.

'Yer must've smelt the biscuits,' said Uncle Jimmy when David reappeared. He also took a pink wafer. Why?

Spitting pink bits, David said, 'There's a pony deein rides on the field rund the shops.'

She jumped up. 'Ha'way Julie, are yer comin?'

Nana gave them both twenty pence and she headed off with Julie to the shops to have a go on the pony.

The Walker sisters were hanging about at the end of Pickering Road; they were a family of five lasses who looked identical, and they were git canny, and on a normal day she would have played with them, but today there was a pony on the field at the shops.

She pleaded with Julie, 'Ha'way, man, let's gan on the pony.'

'Nor ah'm gannen ter play up the square,' said Julie as she slied off with the Walkers.

She could see the field and then she locked eyes on the beautiful pony and made a beeline for it – white body, white mane plaited with ribbons and white tail. She stroked the pony's nose. It wasn't wearing a blanket or bells and it had a normal brown saddle like the horses on the telly.

'She's called Jubilee,' said the lad.

'There's a queue, pet,' said someone, and she turned to see a line of people trailing down the field. She stroked Jubilee, then went and joined the end of the queue. She counted seventeen people and then stopped because everyone was moving about, and anyway, they wouldn't all be having a go, only the bairns.

She watched Jubilee trot up and down with one kid after another in her saddle, her tail flowing. It was so boring. She counted the shops that curved round the road at the top of the field, but she didn't get to the end before her mind drifted off . . . she was wearing a smart red jacket, white jodhpurs, long black boots, and a black top hat, and White Beauty had her mane plaited with bright red ribbons. People lined Hylton Road wearing union jack hats and waving flags as the parade passed by. She rose up and down in the saddle as White Beauty trotted ahead of the marching band and baton-twirling girls in short blue dresses and long white boots.

There were three kids ahead of her and guessing that the big kid was too heavy to ride the small pony, it was nearly her turn. As Nana would say, 'Patience is a virtue.' She could hear someone shouting Paula in the distance. There were hods of lasses called Paula.

'Pawla.' She heard, and again, 'Pawla,' each time getting louder until Billy pushed the buggy into her legs.

'Yer ignorin uz like?' he said.

'Nor, ah didn't hear yer.'

'Wot yer deein?'

'Nowt.'

'Doesn't look like nowt.'

She didn't talk as she didn't want to annoy him, so she waited, head down, hoping that he'd go away.

'Ha'way, wer have ter gan now,' said Billy.

She kept quiet, head down. There were two rides to go until her turn.

He pushed her shoulder. 'Eh? Eh?'

She didn't move so he prodded her again.

'Eh?'

Her heart was pounding, and her face was hot. 'Ah'm waitin for me gan on the horse.'

'Ah'll give yer *gan on a horse*,' he mocked. 'Ha'way, we're garn ter the shops.'

She closed her ears and kept looking at the pony.

'Tack yer brotha,' said Billy, jabbing the buggy at her feet.

She lifted her hands and grasped the handles of the buggy without shifting her eyes from Jubilee. Billy walked off and she breathed out.

Ian arched his back, 'Wee-wee.'

The red and white striped buggy was like a deckchair with wheels and was too small for Ian, who was nearly four. 'Alreet son, ah'll tack yer for a wee in a bit.' It was her turn on Jubilee next.

'Ow!'

She stared at the ground and her heart sank. Billy was back. As his shouts got nearer and nearer, she tensed her muscles, ready for the hit. Nothing. But she could smell him standing there, angry and sweating.

'Look at uz,' he said. 'Look at uz.'

She raised her head slowly.

'Wer garn ter the shops,' he said, pointing at the shops. Then he pointed at Ian. 'Get yer brotha.'

She didn't move. Jubilee was on the way back down the field and her heart couldn't let the hope go.

'Ow, did yer hear uz?' said Billy, 'yer not gannen on nee horse, so fucken move it.'

She stood still and gave him a blank look. His top lip was tight, and hatred flashed in his eyes as he whacked her across the face with the back of his hand to the sound of gasps and then tutting from the crowd. The clip was nothing and she'd hardly moved. It was the feeling of snakes writhing in her chest that made her want to curl up and cry; she'd *never* cry in front of Billy, no matter how hard he hit. He stuck his hands in his jeans back pockets and walked away with more edge than a broken pisspot.

As she walked away from her go on the pony, she had a melon in her throat and her cheeks were on fire. She thought about being buried deep in ice. As she pushed the buggy over the bumpy field, Ian cried, 'Wee-wee,' and she pictured the grass turning into deep white snow and as she pressed on into the blizzard, her tears turned to icicles and her soul froze so deep that no one would ever see what was burning inside. She crossed the road as Billy went into the betting shop.

'Wee-wee.'

She released Ian from his straps and he ran to the kerb and had a pittle in the gutter. When he came back, she said, 'Hold me hand or yer garn in the buggy.'

He held her hand. 'Where's Dad?'

'He'll be back soon. Why dinnet yer see how many blue cars yer can spot?'

Billy came out of the betting shop, stuffing a betting slip in his jeans pocket. He walked past her and signalled with his finger that she should follow. He stopped outside of the newsagents.

He said to Ian, 'Der yer want owt, son?'

'Curly Wurly.'

'Pawla, want owt?'

She didn't say anything because she was frozen in an ice cube that no one could get through and that would only melt the day she grew up and left home. She wasn't going to talk to the twat ever again, or as little as possible, only when absolutely necessary.

Billy came out of the newsagents and flung a packet of fags and an Aero into the buggy. 'Get yerlsel home and give them ter yer mar.' He strode off, shoulders back and swinging his arms as if he was some sort of hard case.

Hot tears welled in her eyes, and she forced them back because she didn't want them to melt the ice cube that had to stay frozen until she was old enough to leave home. While Ian stabbed himself in the face with a Curly Wurly, she grabbed hold of him, squashed him into the buggy, and then pushed off for home. She imagined Nana shaking her head and saying, 'Poor little bugger with a fatha like that.'

Ian was happy to sit cross-legged in the deckchair as long as he wasn't strapped in, and she was walking so fast the poor little bugger had to cling on. People jumped out the way as she stormed along in a fog of thoughts about Billy being hurt.

At home, Mam was in bed. Being pregnant made her bad back worse so she could hardly walk nowadays. From the bedroom doorway, she flung the fags and Aero onto Mam's bed to a grunt of, 'Thanks luv.'

She put some toast under the grill for Ian, then put the telly on for him to watch while he ate it. She ran him a bath.

'Dinnet use all the hot watter,' Mam shouted from bed.

*

She still wasn't talking to Billy, or as little as possible, only when absolutely necessary, and anyway on Saturdays, he always stayed in bed until after *Tiswas* and then he took Ian to Hetton, which meant a full day with no Billy or looking after Ian.

She felt Ian's little fingers peel her eyelids open. 'Wakey-wakey, Paula,' he said.

The living room was dark, the smell of stale smoke stung her nose. She opened the curtains, which didn't make much difference.

'Wot der yer want, son? Weetabix or Suga Puffs?'

'Tell em about the honey, Mummy.'

As soon as Ian was finished slopping cereal on Billy's racing paper, she cleared his bowl and got ready to go out. Usually on Saturdays she'd play out all day and there was always hods of kids and a game on the go. Can-on was her favourite game, which involved each team rolling a ball at an empty tin can with nails on it. She'd usually end the day by tagging along with some older kids up to Barnes Park for a game of hockles on the swings. No one ever asked where she'd been or what she'd been doing, so it was likely that today, no one would notice if she went to Ryhope to see Dad.

Gail, twelve, and Dawn, ten, sisters from the next block, were swinging on the outside door so she waved. 'Hiya.'

Gail waved and came running towards her, followed by Dawn.

'Where yer garn?' asked Gail.

'Ter see a man about a dog.'

'What kinda dog?' asked Dawn.

'A fluffy one like off the telly.'

'Can ah come wer yer?' asked Dawn.

'Aye, me anarl?' said Gail.

'Yerl have ter get some bussy.'

When Gail and Dawn went inside to ask their mam for bus fare, she pelted to the top of the road.

There were hods of people waiting for the bus into town and the first bus was full, so she got the next one and stood up downstairs in the smoke. She got off in the central bus station which was teeming with people waiting for buses and getting off buses and trying to get out of the station and into the shops and trying to get out of the shops and into the station. For a while she was carried along in the crowd with her feet off the ground and she ended up going out, along the side, and back in the other entrance.

The station had a roof made from metal beams and windows that were so small and high it was dark inside even though it was day outside. The pavements and roads were hacky-black from all the fumes. The other week when she was waiting for the bus for ages and ages and ages, she'd sussed out the stops for Ryhope were probably those that she couldn't see from the Pennywell stop. The next stop up was Silksworth, Farringdon, and Doxford Park, and the next stop down was Grangetown and Leechmere Road. The bottom stop was Seaburn via Southwick. There was an island in the middle that had the room where the bus drivers went, and she had no idea what happened on the other side, so that, she supposed, was where the Ryhope stop was.

She squashed her way into the crowd and tagged onto a group of grown-ups crossing to busman's island.

They stopped halfway to let the Downhill bus go past and then did a run–walk round the parked buses before landing. She'd never been to this part of the station before although she'd looked at it for ages and ages and ages as bus drivers went up the steps and into the room at the top while others came down the steps and got onto the bus and into the driver's seat as slowly as possible. When at last the driver starts to wind the handle, all queues look in anticipation to see if their estate comes up, like bus window bingo. 'And the lucky queue is . . . Hastings Hill via Chester Road!'

On the other side of the busman's island were three stops with queues. She went to the first stop and asked a woman, 'Excuse me, is this the stop for Ryhope?'

'Ryhope? Nor luv, yerl need Park Lane for Ryhope.'

'Der yer knar where that is?' said a gannie from the queue.

She knew where it was. 'Up past Louis,' she said.

'Eeee, Louis,' said the first woman. 'They dee smashin fish 'n' chips.'

'Aye, they dee that,' agreed the gannie as half the queue nodded.

Two buses came in the top of the station, belching fumes and making the air black, and the crowd on the island waited for a gap. After the 114 drove on, the crowd did a run–walk across the wide bus lane, dicing with death as they spilled out of the road entrance where the buses were coming in. She legged it across to the leisure centre side and walked along to Books Fashions that was over the road to the ABC pictures. It didn't open for two hours and already the queue for *Raiders of the Lost Ark* on Screen 1 was well past the Painted Wagon.

It felt like miles until she saw the blue stripes of Louis café where Nana sometimes took her and Julie for a cream cake. Next to that was Park Lane, which was an open-air station for red single-deckers and red double-deckers, whereas central station was for yellow double-deckers. Red buses went to places like Consett and South Shields, so she started to worry that Ryhope was miles away, like near Middlesbrough or Durham.

The first stop had a bus parked in it that said 'Ryhope Village' in the winding window, so she got on.

'Ryhope, please.'

'Six pence.'

She gave the driver her money. 'Is it far to Cherry Rose Street in Ryhope?'

'Yer need ter get off at the hospital. Sit at the front and ah'll tell yer when.'

People went all weird whenever she asked about Dad, which is why she didn't. Whenever she mentioned Dad to David, he got all moody and punched her, whereas Nana got all teary and said, 'He's moved away darlin,' then gave her a Wagon Wheel. Tracy from school said that that's how her family acted after her dad moved away, and when her mam called his girlfriend a slag and smashed an ornament off the wall, Tracy got to go to Lambton Lion Park. The other night, she'd heard Nana talking to Grandar, so that's how she knew the name of Dad's street, or it might be road or square, she wasn't sure, but they definitely said Cherry Rose. She wondered if Dad lived in a posh house like the ones at High Barnes. The bus was getting empty, so she leaned forward wondering if she'd missed her sign to get off.

'Next stop, luv,' said the driver.

When she got off, the only houses she could see were across the busy road and ahead of her were huts and hospital signs. She went up to the nice-looking wifey who had been on the bus. 'Excuse me.'

'Aye, pet.'

'Can yer tell uz where Cherry Rose Street is please?'

'Cherry Rose Street?'

'Aye, or it might be road or square, ah'm not sure.'

'Wot der yer wanna gan there for?'

'Ter see me dad.'

'Where's yer mam?'

'At home.'

The wifey patted her lips as she thought. 'Is that where yer mam ses he lives, Cherry Rose?'

'Aye, is it far?'

The wifey patted her lips again. 'Ah think yer should gan home and come back wer yer mam.'

'Can yer tell uz where it is? Gan on, please.'

'Sorry pet, ah've got ter dash.'

Next, she saw a man with a dog having a poo, so she walked up to him. 'Excuse me. Can yer tell uz the way to Cherry Rose Street?'

'Cherry? Why-aye, man. Yer want ter gan up here and ter the right. Yer cannet miss it.'

She did as he said and followed the path until she came to some brick posts in the road with a matching house on the side. There were more white hospital huts and a blue sign with white letters: *Cherry Knowle Hospital.* That couldn't be right? She walked up to it and read it again. *Cherry Knowle Hospital.* Her heart pounded. When Mam said, 'he's sick,' and, 'he needs lookin after,' she thought she meant Dad was a rubbish person, not that he was pooley.

She went through the open iron gates and didn't get far before a nurse came up to her. 'Can ah help yer?'

'Ah'm here ter see me dad.'

'Where's yer mam, darlin?'

'At home.'

'Does she knar yer here?'

'Nor, dinnet tell her, please.'

The nurse smiled. 'Ah won't, and ah tell yer wot, come wer me and ah'll see if ah can find yer dad.'

She took the nurse's arm and they chatted as she led her along and round to a huge red brick building that looked like the Royal Infirmary where she went to visit Grandar when he had a heart attack. Nana said it was a Victorian hospital like where Florence Nightingale worked.

'It's like the hospital where me Grandar woz.'

'The Royal Infirmary?'

'Aye, he had a heart attack. Has me dad had a heart attack?'

'Nor, he hasn't had a heart attack.'

They went up some dusty grey stone steps which had grooves worn from a million feet.

The nurse took her to a blue chair. 'Sit down.'

She did as she was told and the nurse crouched and held her hands. 'Do yer knar yer dad's name?'

'Eddie Hasting, nee *s*.'

'Ah'll see wot ah can do. Stay here.'

It smelled of school dinners and there were nurses walking about in blue uniforms with white hats and she wondered if maybe there was a Cherry Rose Street in Ryhope and that she'd got mixed up. And anyway, if Dad was pooley, why did nobody say? But that would explain why Nana cries. Maybe they don't talk about Dad because he's dying and they don't want her to be upset, like when Gavin's older brother died, and no one talked about it.

After ages the nurse appeared with a fat woman in a polo-neck jumper. The nurse put her hand on her shoulder. 'This is the social worker, she wants ter talk ter yer.'

The woman's knees clicked as she crouched and put her hand on hers. 'Hello, Paula, how old are you?'

'Ah'm nearly twelve.'

'Where's your mam today?'

'At home.'

'And where's home?'

'Pallion.'

'Does she know you're here?'

'Nor.'

The woman stood and walked away with the nurse, then the nurse came back on her own. 'We're goin ter get someone ter mack sure yer get home. Wait here, they won't be long.'

'Can ah see me dad?'

'Nor luv, mebees another day.'

'Can ah gan ter the loo please?'

'Come wer me.'

The nurse took her to the toilets, she went inside, counted to ten, and then stuck her head out. There was no sign of the nurse, so she shot out of the building and sprinted along the path. There was no way she was being taken home by a social worker because Mam would kill her. She kept running through the brick gate posts and got well down the road before she was too paggered to run any further.

A man with a sausage dog crossed over and came towards her. 'Wot's a young lass like yae deein rund here by hersel?'

She stroked his dog. 'Ah've been ter see me dad.'

'In the asylum, is he?'

'The wot?'

'Asylum. Owld-fashioned word for mental hospital.'

'Me dad's mental?'

'Where's yer mam, pet?'

She was sick of grown-ups asking where her mam was: in bed, where do you think? She smiled at the man, then ran and ran and didn't stop until she got to a bus stop. There were some lads playing footy on the grass, so she went over to them. There's no point asking grown-ups anything because they'll all liars.

'Here, laddo,' she said.

'Aye.'

'Der yer knar owt about the hospital ower there?'

He hunched his shoulders and said in a funny voice, 'The looney bin,' then danced like an idiot until an old man waved his walking stick and said, 'Knock it off, son.'

Chapter 3

July 1985

The bairns were asleep, and Mam was hiding in the kitchen while she sat on the top stair in her nightie, pulling faces at the creepy boy in the picture on the wall. Billy was shouting, 'Fucken Tory bitch,' at the telly. She wished things could go back to how they were before the miners went on strike, or as her form teacher put it, before, 'The Tory toss-pots took a steamin shite on the workin classes.'

They weren't on the nash when Billy first met Mam because he was working up Herrington Colliery, but then he got a bad back and couldn't work. Despite not working for years, when the miners went on strike, Billy stopped her ice rink money because, 'Yer cannet expect ter get pocket money when some families are strugglin ter eat.'

At least he had less of a hold over her now the ice rink money had stopped. 'Bath the lads or there's nee ice rink money,' 'Wesh the dishes or there's nee ice rink money,'

'Get a smile on yer miserable piat or there's nee ice rink money.' Billy said that cutting her ice rink money wasn't his fault and that she should, 'Blame Maggie.'

Billy kicked the kids' shoes as he snatched his leather jacket from the hook, followed by a slam. She could hear Mam tidying the shoes.

'Can ah have twenny pence for the tuck shop?' she shouted down.

'Ask uz tomorra. Now get ter bed afore he gets back,' Mam shouted.

Her bedroom might have been tiny, but it was all hers, sort of. Billy wanted her to go in with Ian and Jason so that he could keep his fishing gear in the tiny room. She got her own room on the condition that Billy could keep his fishing stuff in her wardrobe. He could barge in at any time, looking for something among the tangle of rods, and if he couldn't find it, it was because she had lost it. She'd usually put a rod across the door to slow him down when he burst in, giving her time to jump out of bed instead of being dragged out of bed to look for whatever he'd lost. The other week she was asleep when she felt crawling on her legs and when she put the light on, there were maggots all over the bed and floor. She screamed and Mam and Billy came in.

'Mam, there's maggots all ower the shop.'

'Ah mustn't have tightened the lid,' laughed Billy. He pointed under the bed at his bait box, lid off.

She ran into the bathroom, brushing maggots off her legs.

Mam followed. 'Get yersel back in there,' she thumbed with a snarl, 'and get those maggots cleaned up.'

'Nor, ah'm not garn back in there ever.'

Mam growled in her low, angry voice that sounded like the devil, 'Ah'm warnin yer, get them cleaned up or yer forrit.'

'Here-man, they're not my maggots.'

'Ah dinnet give a shite wee's maggots they are,' Mam snarled. 'Get yersel in there NOW,' she shouted in her loudest voice.

Billy did his nasty, under-breath *ha-ha-haa* as he stood over her and watched as she picked up the wriggling grubs and dropped them in his bait box. In the end, they didn't make her squirm; she had a lot in common with the maggots. She closed the lid and envied their wiggly little souls at being locked away, safe from Billy and Mam.

The tiny bedroom was better than sharing with her kid brothers, for now – only four months to go until she was sixteen and she could tell Billy to fuck off and then move in with Dad and David and change her name back to Hasting. David was long gone. He was three months off his sixteenth birthday when he chinned Billy and went. It wasn't like they'd had an argument or anything. Billy was being an arsehole like normal when David snapped, called him a 'Fucken pit-yacker,' then ploated him. She'd never forget the look on Billy's face as David's knuckle connected with his chin. Then David walked out with his Adidas bag over his shoulder and his rolled-up footy poster under his arm. David moved in with Dad at Pennywell near to Nana's and she couldn't wait to join them.

Her bed was the bottom part of the bunkbeds from when she lived at Thorney Close, which was so long ago that all she could remember was David coming down the ladder in his Hair Bear Bunch pyjamas. Dad had a photo tucked away of the three of them next to a silver Christmas tree. That's when they were all together, before Dad went to Cherry for the first time, which, like all the other times, nobody talked about – Nana, Mam, David, no one. It was as if she was expected to know everything without being told anything.

She stuck her hand between the bed and the cold wall under the window and felt about in her hidey-hole, the place where no other human hand did go – deodorant, address book, make-up bag, Milly-Molly-Monkey (missing an arm), fairy tale book from when she was little (tash and gegs drawn on Thumbelina) – until her fingertips touched her Walkman. It wasn't a proper one, it wasn't a Sony; it was red and the lid opened with a pop, not a glide like Sonya's real one. Sonya Tippexed an *a* after *Sony* so she Tippexed her name onto her nashy

Walkman and coloured it in with silver pen. The tape was already in. She had two: the charts and a mixtape. She used to have Wham! that she taped from Sonya, but Billy took it and taped Shakin' Stevens over it for Ian. When she went mad, he laughed and said, 'Look at the twist on yowr piat.' When she wasn't laughing along, he said, 'Lad alive ow, it woz arnly a tape,' then he waved his arm and told her, 'yae dinnet mind givin a tape ter yer little brotha.'

She fast-forwarded the mixtape to the end and turned it over and pressed play. She lay back and pushed the headphones closer onto her ears, listened to the whine of cogs, then the clunk of the pause button being released, and then music. She slid the volume up to max. It was taped from the telly so was fuzzy and in places you could hear Billy shouting at Ian. It was taped from the telly and had taken weeks to get a good recording without someone making a noise, and it was worth the effort because now she had the best music ever pumping directly into her brain – the theme from *Black Beauty*.

As she listened, she imagined being curled into a ball on the beach with everyone circling her: Billy, Mam, Donna Hepburn and her licky-arse mates . . . a wind blows and the sand whips up and while they are all blinking, a magnificent white stallion strides through the sandstorm and jumps high, muscles rippling, and when she sees him, she uncurls and runs and jumps on his back – there's no saddle or bridle so she squeezes her legs around his sides and grasps his flowing mane. Billy raises a fist, so she flicks him the Vs, and then turns to the horizon and rides away . . . they run after her and as they run faster and almost catch her, she tugs the stallion's mane and he runs faster and faster and then takes off and they soar up and up into the red sky, and when she looks back, her enemies are tiny specks on the sand and she turns to the sky and keeps riding and riding . . .

Wednesday
7.45 am
She stuffed her PE kit into her bag and wedged her books down both sides. She put her blazer on and was on her way out when she picked her bag up and the handle snapped, dumping her stuff on the floor. 'Shit!'

'Mind yer gob or yerl get a clip rund the lug hole,' shouted Billy from the settee.

'But Mam, it's snapped.'

'Billy, have yer got a bag the bairn can borra?'

He shuffled into the kitchen with a Benny hanging out of his gob and she could hear him open the cupboard and rustle in the ball of bags.

'Here yer gan,' he said.

'Ah'm not garn ter school with a Tesco bag, like.'

'Oooo you young-uns,' he mocked, 'yer hav ter hav the reet gear.' He thrust the placker bag at her chest and went back to watching the telly.

'Hang on, luv,' said Mam. She rummaged in her big shopping bag. 'Here,' she said, 'Clockhouse at C&A.'

'Suppose it's better than Tescos.'

'Yer break up on Friday. Ah'll get yer a new bag for September, promise.'

8:00 am

She walked to the top bus stop to avoid seeing Donna Hepburn. Donna lived in the maisonettes down by Villa and had long brown hair like rats' tails and a hacky little face that needed a good wesh. Donna reckoned she'd won a fight with a lass from Burleigh Garth, but that's crap, because like Dad said, 'Gobshites are softshites.' The other week, Donna and her mates sat downstairs on the bus and sang, 'Paula Hart stinks of fart, Paula Hart stinks of fart,' for what seemed like ages until the lad with acne got on at the Round Robin and they turned on him. 'Here, laddo, wot did yer have for yer breakfast, pizza?'

Today they were upstairs as usual, so she was safe for another twenty minutes: there were two options for getting off the bus: 1) stand up early and be at the door as it opens and jump off before the bus stops and run into school, and 2) stay on the bus and get off at the bottom stop and walk up the bank, arriving late. She was getting off at the bottom stop as there was no way she could be seen with a placker bag. Donna would crucify her. The packed bus stopped outside of the Bede, and she lowered her head and listened to feet trooping down from the top deck as the bus driver's shout of, 'Ow, layoff the bell,' was drowned out by *ting-ting-ting-ting-ting-ting-ting-ting-ting!* When the bus pulled away, she lifted her head. The coast was clear.

10:45 am

She sat on the desk with Michelle and Ally while Sonya read aloud from *Smash Hits*. Sonya's mam had a hairdresser's salon and her dad worked on the rigs. They lived in a big house on Alexander Road and Sonya always had magazines and make-up.

At the end of break, she slid off the desk. 'Ah'm not garn ter PE.'

'Yer forged a letter from Billy again?' asked Michelle. 'As if yer dad would write a letter about period cramps.'

'Here-man, he's not me dad, and anyways, he's sensitive like that.'

'Fuck off,' said Ally, 'the teachers knar yae write the notes yersel.'

'Nor they dinnet,' she said. 'Or if they dee, they dinnet care. Ah haven't done PE for three weeks.'

The classroom cleared when Richie Red Rockets came in. 'You girls got no lessons to get to?'

'Sir,' they said, filing out.

10:48 am

She decided that she'd pelt out of the back gates while everyone was changing lessons. It was the end of term so no one gave a shit, and anyway, the worst that could happen was she'd get the cane, and let's face it, being whacked with a stick by The Godfather would be fly bites compared with a clout from Billy, and worth it not to do PE.

She walked calmly down the back path and as soon as she was out of the gates, she started running and didn't stop until she got to the pregnant tree. She took her blazer off and stuffed it in her C&A bag. Her blazer was free off the nash and was made of shiny nylon with a different weave to the Trutex blazers you pay for from Caslaw's. She swapped her shoes for her nashy Hi-Tecs from Jacky White's and untucked her white/grey shirt. Looking as un-schoolie as possible, she kept going out of the top of Barnes Park and along Ettrick Grove and onto Chester Road where she got the number 15 bus to the Grindon Mill and then walked to Dad's.

Midday

'Tar for comin, ower kid,' said David, going out.

David was Dad's care person who was supposed to stay with him and stop him from being committed. She couldn't see what was wrong with Dad, he always seemed fine to her, but she knew that sometimes he turns into a different person because there was one time when she'd seen him go radgie; she was coming in Dad's side gate when David ran and nearly pushed her over with the most serious face she'd ever seen David make, as he shouted, 'Fuck off home, Paula, or yerl mack it worse.' She went away, but she'd already seen Dad running down the garden and punching the air, and then he jumped over the fence into next door's garden.

'Monopoly?' said Dad. He already had the board set out. 'Yer cannet gan out, Dave. Wot'll wer dee for a banker?'

'Ah'm garn ter see Lisa, Dar,' said David.

'Wot, Lisa the middle Walker sister?' she said.

'Aye, ah've been seein her,' said David, looking chuffed with himself, which was fair enough because Lisa was far too good for him.

Dad was counting paper money impatiently, so she signalled for David to go while she distracted him. 'Can ah be banker?'

Her strategy in Monopoly was to buy everything she landed on, whereas Dad's strategy was complicated. He always started off buying the oranges and the railways while also, usually, going for the reds. This made the free parking corner a nightmare to get round, yet he never bought any utilities. 'Utilities are nee good. Yer dinnet mack money from them, yer need property,' he'd always say.

She usually went for the water works and gas works and enjoyed adding up the rent when he landed on them, and then he'd haggle her down. Dad wouldn't move from the board until he had at least one house on each orange street and until he owned all of the reds and

Park Lane. Her and David would always rig the game so he could get what he needed quickly. His target was eighteen houses with a long-term plan to build a hotel on Mayfair. According to Dad, this was the point at which he won because from then on, the only conclusion could be the flow of all the money to him. Then he would issue other players loans so they could play on, charging them 15% interest every time they passed go.

It was best to keep Dad occupied with Monopoly to distract him from footy stats because when he started listing games and players and sketching spot-the-ball pictures, he could go for days without eating. His house wasn't like a normal person's with furniture and ornaments and pictures and curtains. Dad's living room was bare, apart from a settee and telly, and there were footy stats written all over the walls. The last time Dad ran out of exercise books, he wrote his match report and four divisions of scores on the wall at the bottom of the stairs. While sitting on the bog, she'd learned that the Magpies were in the second division and hadn't won the league since 1927 or the FA cup since 1955.

By late afternoon, Dad had three houses on each of the orange streets, and he had two reds, both browns, and Park Lane. He was chewed to bits because he only had two train stations; one was free, and she had Marylebone, which she wished she hadn't bought, but at the time, she didn't have much. He sat back from the board and rubbed his belly. 'Pop next door will yer. Maureen said she'd dee uz a pie today.'

Maureen would often cook for Dad and David. Her back door was open, the smell of mince and onions wafting out. 'Hiya Maureen.'

'Hiya, luv,' said Maureen, standing with her hands in the sink. 'Pie's just come out, yerl need ter wait til it cools down.'

'Thanks, Maureen. It smells ellish in here.'

'Have yer done yer O-levels yet?'

Maureen asked this every time she saw her. 'Nor, that's next year.' She wasn't entered for any O-levels and she probably wouldn't bother with her GCEs.

'Wot yer garn ter be?' asked Maureen, which was the second question she always asked.

'Ah'll problees gan ter Dewhirst's,' she said, wafting the pie on the bench with a Bero Man tea towel.

'Did ah tell yer about ower Deborah? She's a businesswoman yer knar, and she went ter the Bede like yae,' said Maureen, which was the third thing she always said.

It was funny how whenever she told a gannie that she went to the Bede, they said, 'Eeee, the grammar school, yae must be a clever lass.' She'd told Maureen hods of times that the Bede had been a shitty comp for yonks. Maureen's Deborah went to the Bede in the sixties and there was a picture in the living room of girls in square-necked pinafores, which had been taken in the quadrangle when it was used for netball before it was a carpark. Those 'Bedans' should see the dump now. There wasn't a chair in the school that didn't have a massive cock and balls drawn on it in marker pen.

'Can ah borra yer oven gloves ter tack the pie next door. Ah'll bring them strite back,' she said, putting them on and grasping the Pyrex dish.

She plonked the pie on Dad's kitchen table. All of the things in Dad's kitchen lived on the bench, which were three plates, four bowls, and two mugs, and two forks, a knife, a big spoon, and six little spoons, stood in an oversized SAFC mug. The kitchen cupboards and drawers were stuffed full of exercise books of footy stats, including everything that SAFC had ever done, with a whole cupboard dedicated to 1973. The exercise books used to be under the beds at Nana's house and when she asked her what they were, she said that they were ghost stories.

Dad put some plates out which caught the splatters as they forked the pie directly from dish to mouth. It was scadden, but she was clammen, and so was Dad by the looks of it. They kept shovelling pie until the dish was clean.

Dad shook the dice, kissed his hand, and said, 'Double six, please.'

The dice rolled out of sight, so she picked up his two and a five and said, 'Double six, yer spawny git.'

Dad zoomed his sports car onto Park Lane and put a hotel on it, leaving her Scottie dog in the gutter at King's Cross Station, with no houses and little more than a get-out-of-jail-free card to her name. Her watch said twenty past three and she reckoned that she could keep Dad's attention on the game until seven tonight. She rolled a double one and landed on *chance*. She read the card, 'You have won second prize in a beauty contest.'

'And the first prize went to a pig!' Dad laughed at the joke that he made about five times a game.

It was half past seven when David came in with Lisa.

'Alreet, Eddie,' said Lisa.

'Aye, canny man,' said Dad. 'Ah've got fifteen houses and a hotel on Park Lane.'

David looked at the board. 'Yer nearly livin in the station and smokin dogends, ower kid.'

'Yer not wrang,' she agreed. She had the full set of greens with one house on each, both utilities and a couple of stations, while Dad had everything else. She had two Dad loans, one at 15% and one at 5%, a rate he agreed to as long as she gave him Whitehall for half price.

'Der yer want uz to tack ower?' said David.

'He'yar,' she said, pushing the cards and money in his direction. 'Ah best get home and get ower Ian and Jason ter bed.'

Chapter 4

August 1985

'Maggie-Maggie-Maggie, out-out-out! Maggie, out! Maggie, out! Maggie-Maggie-Maggie, out-out-out!'

She opened the curtains and saw hods of gadgies coming down the road, shouting and singing and throwing bottles. Billy's life was going to Steels at dinnertime, coming home at three, swearing and going to bed, and then going back to Steels at seven, and now, at 10:09 on her digital alarm clock/tape/radio, he was stamping down the street and swearing about the Tories. The club must have run out of beer because it was early for Billy to leave.

Windows opened and voices shouted out, 'Tory bastards,' and the sound of marching got louder, and the shouts got fiercer, 'Maggie-Maggie-Maggie, out-out-out! Maggie, out! Maggie, out! Maggie-Maggie-Maggie, out-out-out!'

She hoped that Billy didn't come in her room looking for a fishing rod like he did last night, which is something he desperately needed after a night on the drink. 'Where's me good rod?' he shouted as he barged in. 'Ah'm ganner have ter sell it now the pit's shut.' She didn't dare mention that he hadn't worked for years as he dragged her out of bed.

The gadgies were standing outside for a bit and then they went down the cut, apart from Billy, who had a slash against the wall. He shook his cock and put it away and then leaned against the wall and put a Benny in his gob with his pissy-cock hand. He staggered over to the flat and when he saw her, he flung his bottle at the window, which hit and bounced off and smashed on the ground. She could hear Mam go into the kitchen like she did every night when Billy came home stotten.

He stormed upstairs and she counted – five, four, three, two, one – and he burst in as usual. She had his rods and tackle laid out on the bed, so she gave him a smug smile. He lifted and dropped his shoulders and went out. She moved the fishing stuff from her bed and got in with her clothes on; when Billy barges back in and makes her look for something he doesn't need, she would do it in a Choose Life t-shirt and jeans, not in a Choose Life t-shirt and knickers.

Billy turned the telly up to blaring and Mam went in and turned it off. 'Gan ter bed will yer.'

'By reets, she shouldn't be here,' he said, as usual. 'Ah dunnar why ah'm payin for a roof ower her heed. Wot's her fatha payin? Fucken nowt, that's wot.'

The living room door slammed as if that would stop the whole street from hearing him shouting about paying to bring up another man's child. She lay there, willing Mam to tell him to fuck off, but as usual, she didn't.

She flicked her digital clock/tape/radio to radio and listened to Night Owls. She loved Alan Robson's soothing voice and the stories of the people who rang in made her realise that she wasn't the only one with a shitty life.

'We have Helen on the line. Tell me, Helen, where are you tonight?' said Alan.

'Eeee Alun, it's amazin ter speak ter yer, like. I'm in Horden.'

'Nice to talk to you, Helen from Horden. Welcome to the show. I believe you've been havin some money worries, and I think there's a lot of people out there who are in the same boat. It started when the washin machine broke down and you had to go to a – may I say, scumbag – loan shark. You have three little ones, isn't that right?'

'Aye Alun, it was when Steve, that's me husband like, when Steve woz workin a winda round, yer knar, he was deein canny until he fell off his ladder and shattered his femur – that's a bone in yer leg like – he was on crutches from before Christmas till well after me birthder, and that's in March, and he couldn't work so wer had nee money ter pay for owt.'

'So, Helen, while he was laid up, tell the listeners what happened to you and your little darlins?'

'Eeee Alun, it's been terrible, man, ah cannet believe ah'm talkin ter yer like.'

'I believe that money was tight as you already had debts, is that right?'

'Aye, well wer already owed for the telly and the car and a few things, yer knar, oh aye, an ah owed me sister five hundred quid from wot she leant uz for Salou.'

She was biting the blankets, willing Helen to get to the part where the loan sharks shatter her husband's other leg when Mam screamed and there was the sound of splitting wood.

She went onto the landing and peered over to see Mam lying on her back in the hall on the middle part of the living room door. She came down and looked through the Mam-shaped hole in the door, which was still closed, and Billy looked back at her. There were spelks everywhere and Mam gave her the wobble-eye look, like when the Hulk gets angry, which was the signal to run: she went to the lads' room, whipped back their blankets, grabbed a small hand each, and pulled their sleepy heads out of bed. She hoisted Jason onto her shoulder and Ian onto her hip and ran out of the front door. She put them down in the street, said, 'Dinnet fucken move,' and went back in. Her heart was pounding.

Mam was on the floor and Billy was leaning on the doorway, inside the hole. 'Yer fucken stupid bitch,' he said. 'Ow much is this ganner cost uz, eh. EH?'

'Ha'way, Mam,' she said, holding out her hand.

'She'll have ter gan now ah'm skint,' he said, jabbing his finger at her.

'Fucken happy ter gan,' she said. 'Mam, ah said ah'll move in wer Dad.'

'Nor, nor, yer not movin in wer him, man,' said Billy, 'yer can gan inter care. And yae,' he turned his vicious finger to Mam, 'get this mess cleaned up.' He stepped through the hole and stood with his hands on his hips.

Mam was flat on her back with her hand over her face. She couldn't be crying because she never did, no one did, not even baby Jason would give Billy the satisfaction.

'Ah'm not surprised Eddie ended up in the nut house,' said Billy, leaning on the doorframe and taking a drag on his Benny as if he was the king or something.

She felt her face flush and she sucked her lips tight to stop them from talking.

'Eh?' he said to her.

She looked at the ground.

'Look at uz,' he ordered.

She lifted her head and stared angrily past him, so he snarled and flew at her with hands in a strangle shape, but as he straddled Mam, she sat up and headed him right in the clems. Billy's eyes bulged, and he doubled over and coughed as he scuttled into the kitchen.

'Quick,' shouted Mam, grabbing the lads' coats from the hooks, 'gan.'

She pulled her shoes from the wreckage and fled. The lads thought it was a right laugh, running up the road in bare feet while Mam tried to get coats on them to hide their pyjamas. They didn't stop running until they got to Hylton Road.

'He's a fucken bastard, Mam, wer cannet live there, man.'

'Mind yer gob in front of the bairns,' said Mam. 'He'yar, get the bus ter Nana's.'

She held the ten pence in the air as the boys jumped up, saying, 'Money, money.'

'Ah'll tack the bairns ter Aunty Pat's, just till tomorra, like. Billy's under a lot of stress. Reet then,' Mam gave her a kiss which she never did apart from when they were doing a runner from Billy. 'Ring uz at six.'

'Can yae ring me? Yer knar Nana gans mad about the phone bill.'

'Haddaway and shite,' said Mam, 'Nana's minted. Yae ring me at Aunty Pat's at six, aye?'

'Aye, gan on then.'

She was glad to be wearing clothes and shoes, rather than like last time in her winter coat over her nightie and only socks, with all the people on the bus looking at her like she was the little match girl. 'On a frozzen cold neet, in me stockin feet, wee will buy me matchsticks?'

She wasn't going to Nana's because there were already too many people staying there. Gavin and Mark in one room, Grandar in the boxroom because he snores like machine gun fire, and Gavin's two-year-old bairn Laura-Jane in with Nana. She was going to Dad's.

As she came down Dad's path, she could see the bare lightbulb through the gap in the blue sheet at the window. Dad was always up late at night and slept until late in the morning, and who wouldn't if they didn't have to go to school or work? When Dad saw her on the doorstep, he lifted her off her feet.

'Billy bein a tosser?'

'Aye. Is David in bed?'

'Nor, he's at Lisa's.'

'Can ah kip in his bed then?'

'Why-aye, man. Hot chocolate?'

Dad always had a pan of hot chocolate on the go, stirring the milk for ages to get it perfect. Sometimes he'd be normal and talk and watch telly, and other nights he'd write in his exercise books and not talk. He wasn't normal, but who is? Bastard Billy? Mam-in-bed? Even Ian was expelled from his first school because he kept punching the other kids. Everyone was fucked up in their fucked up family. She sat at the kitchen table and drank Dad's hot chocolate, which was much better than Nana's watery shit.

'Tell uz again,' said Dad. 'Billy pushed yer mam through the livin room door?'

'Aye, so she nutted him in the toons.'

David said not to tell Dad anything about Billy, so she tried not to, apart from she couldn't help it when she was angry, which was most of the time.

Dad ran his hand through his hair and his blue eyes widened. 'Did ah tell yer about when ah woz workin ower the fair and yer mam and her mates came on the waltzer?'

'Ah thought yer said yer met her on the ghost train.'

'Aye, ah met her on the ghost train, ah ran that as well as the waltzer, and yer Uncle Jimmy ran the dodgems.'

'Wot happened wer me mam on the waltzer?'

'It woz me wot introduced Big Terry ter Malcom.'

'Wee's Big Terry and Malcom?'

'Big Terry off the waltzer and Malcom from the doors. They met through me. Did ah tell yer about workin the door at the Locarno?'

'Is that where yer took me mam after she'd been on the waltzer?'

'Nor man, it's nowt ter dee wer the fair, yer not listenin ter uz.'

'Yer not mackin any sense, Dad.'

He took a drink of hot chocolate. 'It woz ah normal neet, yer knar lots a lasses tryin ter pull Jimmy, and then Viv Graham turns up with his gang in taxis, and he ses there's a raid on up the Eagle.'

'Wee's he?'

'He's from Newcastle,' he said, stopping to stare into space. He started again, 'That's it, that's why he woz pissed off, because uz beat the Mags three, nil, wer goals in the fifty-sixth minute and seventy-second minute from Bobby Kerr, and another in the eighty-eighth minute from Mulhall.' He took a breath and said, 'When the news broke, uz all piled in taxis ter gan up the Eagle.'

'Wot? A gang from Newcastle were raidin the Eagle cos the Mags lost the match?'

He looked confused, 'Nor man, ah was with the lads from the door ower the Lacorda.'

'Wot about the gang from Newcastle?'

'They wer deein the raid at the Eagle.'

'Wot, pinchin stuff and that?'

'Listen man and ah'll tell yer. So wer get outta the taxis and ah gan first and kick the door in and that, and there's Viv standin there, and ah ses ter him, fuck off yer Mag bastard, and he pulls a gun, and ah pull a knife and gans ter stab him, and Viv's like fuck, and ah'm like fuck, and yer Uncle Jimmy ses, ha'way lads, there's got ter be a better way like.' He breathed out and slumped forward. He was exhausting when he was in a talkative mood.

'Think ah'll off ter bed now,' she said.

His glassy eyes looked through her. 'Gan in David's bed. Neet luv.'

She could hear him talking to himself as she went upstairs. It was still early for him. He'd probably watch the telly or read the football *Echo* with its pink pages like candy floss for men.

In case of another night on the settee, she'd stashed a blanket in a placker bag under David's bed to keep the smell of the washing powder in and the ming of the house out. David was at Lisa's, so she wrapped herself in the clean blanket which protected her from David's smelly sheets. It was quiet without the sound of the telly and Billy and police cars and stuff.

The next morning, a lovely smell led her down the stairs like on the Bisto advert, apart from it was hot chocolate not gravy. Dad was stirring the the chocolate milk in a pan. The table was pulled away from the wall that was covered in blue pen, which was new to the kitchen. It wasn't footy stats. It was writing and arrows and sketches.

'What's that?' she said.

'It's the stratagem.' He took the pan off the heat and put it on the bench, then got a spoon from the cutlery mug and stood in front of the wall like a teacher in front of a blackboard.

'First, wer enter the buildin.' He pointed the spoon at a square. 'Then wer set the trap.'

He pointed at a jumble of lines and shapes. 'Wer gan in and wer put the rods across the hole in the door that yer mam fell through.'

'The door that Mam woz pushed through, correction.'

'Wer set a trap like this.' He pointed the spoon at a rectangle with a stick man in it.

'Wee's the stick man?'

'Billy.'

'Wot yer ganner dee ter him?'

'Ah'm ganner frighten the livin shite out of him.'

'Wot like when yer went up the Eagle?'

'Aye pet, just like that.'

'Ah yer ganner get Uncle Jimmy ter help yer?'

'Nor, this is a job for me ter sort on me own.'

He gave her a spoon and they scooped hot chocolate from the pan into their mouths and ended up passing the pan between them and drinking from it.

'Der yer want any breakfast?' he asked.

'Wot yer got?'

'Nowt, but the chippy'll be open soon, or ah could gan ter the shop, aye, the shop; wot der yer want?'

While he was gone, she set the Monopoly board up ready for another long game. She'd pop round to Nana's later and give her Mam a ring to see when she was going home. The last time they did a runner, she stayed at Dad's for two nights.

Dad came back with a twenty-pence mix-up, a Marathon, a Double Decker, a packet of salt 'n' vinegar Square Crisps, and a big bottle of Villa Sasp. All her favourites because Dad was kind and thoughtful.

He was in a thinking mood and didn't speak while they played, not even when he got his third orange street after only four goes round the board. When he went inside himself like this, he was only concerned with his game, so it was easy to engineer it in his favour, or in this case, her favour. She couldn't wait for the chippy to open because her belly was so empty even the Marathon was like throwing a stick down a well. According to her watch it was 11:39, meaning that the chippy opened in twenty-one minutes precisely. She rolled the dice off the board on purpose, chasing it across the floor to reveal a strategic 'Four.'

Dad smiled and pointed to the 'Go to jail' square and her silver Scottie dog did four jumps into the cell. She looked at her watch, 'Chippy?'

'Aye, ah'm Hank Marvin,' said Dad, collecting his cards and money and filing them away under the board.

'Ah'll gan,' she said. Based on the random stuff he'd got from the corner shop, he couldn't be trusted to go to the chippy. Everything was difficult for Dad, even standing in a queue and remembering to ask for a fish lot and a pattie lot.

'Yer got any dosh?' she asked.

He emptied his jeans pocket and his fag packet. There was one pound note and twenty-six pence in change, which was enough for the scran, and they already had a bottle of Sasp.

On the way to the chippy, she was passing the Walkers' house, so she thought she'd give them a knock to see if David was there. As Dad's care person, he was supposed to be at home with him at all times, and fair enough if he went out, but he couldn't stay out all of the time.

The youngest sister opened the door.

'Hiya, just wonderin if ower David's here?'

'Nor he went down the town wer Lisa.'

'Did he stop here last neet?'

'Aye.'

'Ta-ra then.'

'Ta-ra.'

The oldest sister had left home, leaving four Walker lasses and a mam and dad in a three-bedroom house. She wondered where they all slept and if David slept in the room with the sisters and if he went in bed with Lisa.

There was a queue outside the chippy waiting for it to open. It took twenty minutes to get served and they had to put some new chips on, which took another ten minutes.

Dad was in the kitchen when she came in with the chips. He was writing more stratagem on the wall.

'Pattie lot?'

He rubbed his hands, 'Champion, pet.'

They unwrapped their newspaper parcels and then the white sheet that was see-through with grease. Her fish and chips were lovely. Dad had a handful of chips and then went back to writing and talking. She was too busy eating to listen. She licked the last crumb of vinegar-soggy batter off the oily paper.

'Yer chips'll get cold,' she said, taking a handful of Dad's chips and ramming them into her gob. He was saying something about pressing his eye to Billy's eye to transfer thoughts and then he skipped to Sunderland's FA Cup glory and then back to Billy being trapped in the hole by his fishing rods.

'Dad,' she said. 'Eat yer chips, will yer?'

She was pleased when he sat down and had a bite of his pattie. She watched the chattie tumble in his mouth like shirts in a washing machine as he kept talking.

'Did ah tell yer about when me and yer Uncle Jimmy were workin the doors?'

'Aye, Dad, yer did. Eat yer chips and let's get back ter the game. Yer haven't got a house on Mayfair and it's after dinnertime.'

Helping herself to his chips, she wondered if he would ever stop talking and swallow.

She was pleased to get him back to Monopoly, although he was distracted and twitchy. Twice he went to roll and jerked, sending the dice in opposite directions across the floor, which made it easy for her to rig them.

When Dad saw her look at her watch, he asked, 'Wot time is it?'

'Nearly two.'

'Wot time's Billy back from the pit?'

'The pit's closed, Dad, and anyway, Billy's been on the sick for years. He'll be in Steels.' She held out the dice. 'Yower turn.'

'Shuts at three,' he said.

'Aye. He'yar.' She pushed the dice into his hand.

He flicked her away and stood up. 'Time ah paid Billy a little visit.'

David was going to kill her. He said not to mention Billy to Dad and now they were on the bus on a mission to have a word with Billy. She remembered David telling her about when he was twelve and Dad gave him some cash for some footy boots and Billy took it off him. He said you could've heard a pin drop when Dad burst into the Willow Pond and dangled Billy by his neck until he'd emptied his pockets on the floor. Dad spent ten hours in a cell because Billy rang the police. Billy was a spineless little spelk who never missed a chance to send their six-foot-four, brick-shithouse Dad to Cherry.

She'd tried and failed to persuade Dad that Billy was best left alone and that she was sixteen in December, so she could move out soon. Deep down, she wanted to see the whites of Billy's eyes flash with fear, skid-marks on his cowies, the lot.

The door was open, and inside, the place shook with the roars of Billy's snores.

'*Shhh*, dinnet wake him up,' said Dad.

'Here-man, yer could shove a rocket up his arse and he wouldn't wake up. Not after a skinful.'

Dad laughed, then looked serious. 'Aye but wer dinnet want ter arouse suspicion, man. Ah'll case the joint.' He was talking quickly. 'That's a shockin bit a plywood, a fly would've fallen through that,' he said about the door with the hole in it.

While Dad examined the hole, she had a brilliant idea. 'Billy'll be deed ter the world for hours, so ah'm garn in the bath.'

'Alreet, pet.'

She went in the bathroom and sat on the toilet. Her teeth were furry and her clothes were smelly. She ran the bath and didn't care about how much hot water she used because it was all hers. Mam wasn't back until tomorrow and Billy could fuck off.

Billy was lying face down, bare arse up, and snoring like a pig when she went into his bedroom. She pulled the basket from the back of Mam's side of the wardrobe, which was Mam's hidey-hole, the place she kept stuff that she didn't want the arm ripped off or faces scribbled on. She took the bubble bath and after a few good glugs into the bath, put it back in the basket and closed the wardrobe. Then she went to the airing cupboard and helped herself to a clean towel instead of using one that was 'Already out,' and wet, and stinking of Billy. The water was nearly up to the top when it started to run cold. It was scadden and the steam smelled like flowers. She sunk down and disappeared into thc bubbles.

School holidays were a nightmare for clothes as she only had two bottoms and a few tops. She'd already got a week out of her jeans, so her choice was a white skirt and turquoise blouse or a lacey white see-through vest top like Madonna's. Her two bras were too small, and she couldn't wear the new one that Gail from next door nicked from Littlewoods because she'd been wearing it for a week. She raided Mam's drawer. She had the same cup size but with a bigger back, so on the tightest hook, it would do. Over Mam's bra, she added the Madonna lacey vest with the turquoise blouse on top of that, open and tied in a knot above her belly button.

It would likely be a few days before they'd move back pretending like nothing had happened, so she stuck her arm down the back of her bed and grabbed her deodorant, make-up bag, and nashy Walkman, as well as some clean knickers and a nightie from the drawer. She still didn't have a new bag, so she put her stuff in the placker Benetton bag with a drawstring that she'd cadged off Sonya.

Dad was pacing the kitchen. 'Where's these fishin rods yer were tellin uz about?'

'In me room, ha'way.'

It was easy to find Billy's fishing stuff in her room because it was poking out of her wardrobe.

Dad whistled as he ran a finger down the brown rod. 'Nice piece of kit this.'

She pulled the box from under the bed and held up the vicious-looking hooks, 'Can yer dee owt wer these?'

He was occupied with the reel, then he spotted the rolls of line. 'Reet,' he said, taking a couple of spools. 'Let's spin the web.'

He took the picture of the creepy boy off the top stairs, leaving a baby-blue rectangle on the faded grey wall. He put his finger on the picture hook and gave it a tug. 'Solid as a rock.'

He moved round the corner and down the bottom stairs to the long mirror with a picture of a woman in a red dress. After he'd pulled it off the wall, she noticed how much she hadn't noticed it over the years.

'The wall looks better without the pictures,' she said.

'The squares tell a story,' Dad said. He lashed the fishing line around the top picture hook and pulled it across the stairs, wrapping it around the bannister. He went back and forth between hook and bannister until the line was tight and strong. He did the same with the bottom picture hook.

'Reet,' he said, 'have yer got a football?'

'Why-aye,' she said. She raked in the hall cupboard. 'This do?' She tossed Ian's footy to Dad.

He caught it and inspected it. 'Wer put the ball at the top of the stairs so when Billy comes outta the bedroom, he gans arse ower tit and lands in the spider's web.'

She looked at the fishing twine that was pulled tight across the stairs. 'It's not a very good web, he'll fall through the gaps. Can yer dee some criss-crosses?'

Dad pulled the spool of line in a criss-cross, making a cradle of tight wire across the top stairs. There was no way Billy was going to trip and land in it, rather he'd probably use it as an excuse not to come down and face up to Dad like a man, which, she supposed, was good. She couldn't wait to see the look on Billy's face. Dad was bending up and down and moving his hands in angles as he inspected his handiwork. She crawled on her front up the stairs and under the spider's web and when she was at the top, Dad chucked her the football.

'Put it on the landin.'

She placed the ball on the landing, then shimmied under the lines and down to the hall. 'Wot now?' she asked.

'Skippin rope?'

She laughed, 'Ah'm fifteen, Dad, ah haven't had any skippies in donkeys.'

'Weshin line? String?'

'Ah knar,' she said.

Under the sink, Billy kept a coil of fisherman's rope that he'd got off his mate from the docks. Mam always went on at him to get rid of it, and ever since Jason was born, Billy said he was going to make it into a rope ladder for the bairn, but he was too much of a useless lazy twat to ever do that.

'This any good?'

'That'll dee champion.'

Dad stuck his tongue out of the side of his mouth like he does when he's concentrating and his hands worked quickly, twisting and pulling the thick, prickly rope. He held up a hangman's loop. 'This'll put the frighteners on the bastard.'

'Shit man, are yer ganner hang him?'

'Nor luv, it's arnly people from Hartlepool that hang monkeys.'

He took the hangman's loop and looked through it. She could see his mind turning over a calculation.

'So wer just ganner frighten him?' she tried to confirm.

'Aye luv, wer ganner mack him shit himsel.'

She couldn't wait to see the look on Billy's face. 'Wot yer ganner say ter him?'

'That's for me and him. Yae stop in the kitchen and keep the door closed. Ah dinnet want yer hearin summink that might upset yer.'

'Upset uz? Reet. Like seeing Billy sufferin is ganner upset uz.'

There was a rumbling from the bedroom, so Dad dropped the rope on the bottom stair, pushed her into the kitchen, and shut the door.

'He's garn for a pittle,' she said. 'He's fast asleep. The other day, Ian and Jason were darin each other ter run in and flick his bare arse, and he kept pissin, oblivious.'

Billy started pissing, and Dad said, 'Sounds like Vaux's horse.'

They sat opposite each other at the table and clasped hands, looking at the corner of the ceiling. The sound of piss got weaker, then Billy started coughing and moving around in the bathroom. As he stepped onto the landing, they grasped hands tighter, willing him to go back to bed. There were scuffled footsteps and Billy shouted, 'SHIT!' and then there was a bang and the tap spurted as the football rolled down the stairs, ding, ding, ding-ding, ding-ding, like Professor Yaffle. They kept holding hands until all they could hear was the tap dripping. Her heart pounded and she looked at Dad.

'Der yer think he's in bed?' said Dad, eyes wide.

'Aye, that sounded like his deed-weight floppin down. He'll be flat out till he smells the doors openin ower the club.'

Dad said, 'Wait here, ah'll gan check.'

She hated her kitchen with its sloping wall cabinets with wooden doors in 1950s blue on the bottom and wobbly plastic sliding doors on the top. It was like out of the Jetsons. Even Nana had brown woody cupboards, and as for Sonya, her kitchen was pine with a wall oven and a chest freezer.

Dad came back in, closed the door, and stood in front of it with his arms out. 'Dinnet gan in there, pet.'

'Is he asleep?'

'Aye, he is that.'

'Wot next?'

Dad moved away from the door, still pointing at it with both arms. 'Dinnet gan in there.'

'Ah'm not, ah'm sittin here.'

'Have yer got a pen and paper?'

'Aye.' She stood up.

He pushed her back down. 'Dinnet gan in there,' he said, vexed.

Her heart raced and her belly knotted. 'Why not? Wot's happened?'

'Nowt, it's nowt, he's just had a bit of an accident.'

'Wot type of accident,' she said, going for the door.

He pushed her away. 'Must've tripped ower the ball, he's lyin on the landin.'

'Is he spark out?' Happy butterflies fluttered in her chest at the thought of Billy lying there, half-pissed. She hoped he'd stotted his head off something – the doorframe, the wall, or the sink would all be suitable. 'Ah'm garn ter have a squiy at him.'

'Nor, nor.' Dad waved his arms. 'Wer need ter stick ter the stratagem.'

'So wer need to wake him up and put the frighteners on him,' she said.

'Nor, wer need ter leave him out cold for a good few hours.'

'A knock on the heed winnet hurt him. If he's not awake by the time Steels opens, ah'll show me arse in Binns' winda.'

Dad ripped the cardboard lid off the box of tea. 'Pen?'

'In me bag.' She pulled her bag off the back of the chair and rummaged at the bottom, then held up a blue Bic and a nice silver pen.

Dad's eyes darted from Bic to silver to Bic to silver to Bic to silver to Bic to silver to Bic. She gave him the

Bic, which he stuck behind his ear and then he paced up and down, tongue hanging out. She counted nine walks before he gave her the pen and cardboard, and said, 'Write this down.'

'Wot for?'

'It's a note for Billy.'

She scribbled on the corner of the cardboard to get the ink flowing. 'Billy wouldn't tack notice of a note if wer nailed it ter his face.'

'Ready?' said Dad, sweat trickling from his hairline.

'Aye.'

'Ah'm leavin and nivver comin back.'

She wrote it down using Billy's handwriting. 'We'll be comin back,' she said, 'give it a couple of days.'

Dad shook his head. 'Yae won't be livin here nee more, dinnet yae worry pet, ah'll sort summink out.'

Her heart leapt with glee like she'd waited her whole life for someone to rescue her from Billy. 'Honestly, Dad, der yer mean that?'

'Why-aye, pet,' he said, putting his arm around her shoulder. 'Ah promise yer, Paula, ah'll see ter it that yer nivver have ter live wer Billy again.'

The excitement turned to fear. If she left now, that would be it. Billy was going to go off his rocker when he saw the state of his fishing stuff. She was shaking. She had to go. This was her chance.

'Any more partin words?' said Dad.

She wrote, *blame Maggie*. 'Ah'll gan stick this near his face.'

'Nor, leave it on the chabble.'

'If ah'm movin out, ah need ter get more things.'

'All part of the plan,' said Dad, tapping the side of his nose.

'Wot plan?'

'Get yer bag.'

She put the drawstrings over her shoulders like a haversack.

'Tea towel?'

'There.'

He folded it over and over. 'Turn rund.'

He put the tea towel over her eyes to make a blindfold and then backed into her. 'Piggy-back,' he said. 'Jump on.'

'Wot wer deein this for?'

'If yer don't seen nothin, yer don't seen nothin.'

She jumped on like she did when she was four years old and she felt his legs bend under her weight before he heaved her up his back and grasped her legs tight in his forearms. She held on as he lurched forward and snatched the kitchen door open. He moved quickly to the front door, and she could see the pavement fly past under the bottom of the tea towel; looked like he'd gone down the cut, not up the road. When he put her down and she took the tea towel off her eyes, they were on Pallion Road. Dad kept walking fast and he crossed over and she thought he'd stop on the other side and wait for her, but he didn't, and by the time she'd got across, he was miles away.

'Slow down will yer, ah've got a stitch,' she shouted as she ran up Fordfield Road.

When she reached him, she grabbed his hand and tried to pull him to a stop, but he kept going, pulling her arm up and down as he went as if he didn't realise that he was holding her hand. His eyes were glazed over and he kept walking fast.

'Have yer heard about the three wise monkeys of Hartlepool? See no evil, hear no evil, speak no evil,' he said, crossing the road, holding her hand and marching her arm up and down. 'Listen ter the three wise monkeys and dinnet gan back ter Peacock Street for a month, aye?'

'Aye,' she said, thinking about what to tell David when they got home. She hoped he was staying at Lisa's tonight.

Ford Estate was lined with trees that bulged from the grass verges with roots that popped pavements and made the roads go bumpy. The council had poured tarmac around the bottom of the big trees, yet they fought back as if the estate could get off their patch. She saw cars and men and then the sign for the Jovial Friar and when Dad saw the pub, he stopped, pulled her into a tree trunk, and looked from side to side as if someone was watching him. His t-shirt was drarked with sweat.

'Ah'll send a message through the Casey Man on the side of the *Echo* office.'

'Wot? The light-up football man?'

'If he's smilin and wavin is hat, the coast's clear, and if he's sad, yer need to stay away.'

Her blood drained to her feet. Dad had gone properly mental. If she could get him home, get some hot chocolate on the go, and get him chatting about the FA Cup win, then everything would be fine.

Going along with him, she said, 'How will that be different ter normal? Yer knar, like when Sunderland win, he waves is hat, and when they lose, he's gutted.'

'Aye, but there's more ter it than that, yer need to watch his eyes and mouth, he'll be wavin his hat as a distraction while he's sendin yer a message from me.'

He squeezed her hand and looked her in the eye. 'Promise uz yer'll wait for a message before yer gan back ter Peacock Street?'

'Dad, ah'm never garn back ter Peacock Street, remember, yer ganner sort somewhere else for uz ter live.'

'Nor we cannet be together, yer need ter wait for a message.' Dad's pupils were like pinheads. 'Wait for the message from the Casey Man.' He flicked her hand out of his and ran away towards the pub and then he swerved and ran onto General Havelock Road. She chased after him down the middle of the road. He was running fast, shouting and punching the air. Then he jumped someone's front fence and ran between the houses. She stopped running. He was gone. David was going to kill her.

She could've got the bus with the change from the chippy, but she decided to walk, so she could look between the houses to see if she could see Dad jumping fences. She tried to keep pace as she imagined him running down back gardens and running down passages and running across the road and into another garden. He could be halfway to Pennywell by now.

It was dusk when she got to his dark and empty house. She sat on the back step and thought about what to do. As she shivered, she realised why the general plan was always to keep Dad at home and to keep him busy with easy things.

She knocked quietly on the window at Nana's. It was late so Nana and Laura-Jane would be asleep and she could slip in unnoticed.

'Eeee, ha'way in pet,' said Grandar, giving her a cuddle.

The only light in the living room was the flickering telly. 'Where've yer been?' he said.

'Neewhere. Can ah kip here?'

'Why-aye.'

Grandar turned the big light on as she leaned over the settee to open the cupboard under the stairs.

'Yer can turn it off now,' she said, uncurling the fusty sleeping bag. She zipped herself in, then wiggled out of her clothes.

Grandar was in the chair watching telly as she stared at the ceiling, thinking about Dad running across peoples' gardens, making them shit themselves with his punchy arm, even though he was overexcited and not fighty. Grandar was watching the news and she was about to tell him about Dad when Arthur Scargill came on, and he got up and turned the telly off. The room was dark apart from the glow of Grandar's fag, until he turned the big light on, which made her retreat into the sleeping bag like a snail into a shell.

He took his ashtray into the kitchen.

'Ah'm off ter me bed.' The room went pitch-black.

She unzipped the sleeping bag and kicked her legs out. It was hot and her tummy rumbled as she thought about the smooth creamy layer and the crunchy biscuity layer of the Double Decker that she was saving for later. Dad was probably eating it. The pit of her empty stomach churned at the thought of him alone, pacing the floor, talking to himself. She was furious with David, who'd better be stopping at Dad's tonight, not playing sardines at Lisa's.

Chapter 5

August 1985

She heard the curtain open, then the insides of her eyelids went from dream to light, and then there was weight on her chest and breath on her face. She opened her eyes. 'Boo!'

Laura-Jane squealed so she cuddled her. She loved her warm, squashy body, and she pressed her nose into her ear until she wiggled free and slipped off the sleeping bag and onto the floor.

'Porridge?' said Nana.

She was so hungry that Nana's lumpy porridge was the best thing she'd ever tasted, and Nana was chuffed when she spooned it down and Laura-Jane copied.

'Can yer look after the bairn while ah gan and get ready?' said Nana.

'Aye.'

Nana kissed the top of her head. 'Luv yer.'

She was watching telly with Laura-Jane snuggled into her side when Nana came in, dressed, with wet hair. 'Ah've left the bath for yer. There's some of that Timotom shampoo.'

'Timotei.'

'Aye, that,' said Nana.

Deciding against a bath filled with two inches of lukewarm Nana water, she jammed the rubber teats of the shower onto the taps and leaned over and soaked her hair. The clear, green-tinged *Timotom* shampoo was much better than the murky pink toilet cleaner stuff that Mam got.

Nana's bedroom smelled of slept-in bedclothes and Bronnley's English Fern, which took her back to being in Nana's bed with Julie, listening to the story of the dog and the sausages, which they made Nana tell them over and over. It was the safest place in the world, lying there, drifting off to sleep, knowing that no one was going to burst in and shout, and that there'd be breakfast and a cuddle tomorrow. She was pleased that Laura-Jane was living there as it would be odd for there not to be at least one bairn in Nana's bed.

The mirror on the old-fashioned dressing table was rectangular with curved edges like a slice of Hovis, and on it was a treasure trove; a pearly brush and matching mirror lay on lace cloths either side of a black jewellery box that was painted with Japanese houses with sloping roofs and a river leading to a snowy mountain. There was a blue glass dish filled with a tangle of pearls and pretend gold necklaces and a yellow dish, or as Nana said, topaz dish, which was full of earrings. On each side were photos in wooden frames. One was of Dad and Uncle Jimmy when they were teenagers, and the other was of Nana and Grandar on their silver wedding. Nana had thick brown hair in a bun and was wearing a top with massive collars, and Grandar was wearing a suit, which made her think of the Perry Como song that Nana used to sing. '*Remember the night, yer fell in some shite, yer had yer best suit on; the one that yer got, for saving a lot, of cigarette coupons; m-a-gic, m-o-ments, memories we've been sh-a-ring.*' She couldn't do the whistling part like Nana could. Nana was a proper whistler.

The orange hairdryer was powerful and she blasted her hair until it was straight and shiny. Her clothes were creased, yet good enough for another day, so she buttoned up the turquoise shirt and tucked it into her skirt. When she came onto the landing, she found Mark and Gavin on the stairs and Nana holding the front door open. 'Tack her rund the park for an hour, there's me good lads.'

Gavin picked his daughter off the front step and headed off down the path. She knew something was up when Mark followed them, and Nana stood with her back to the closed front door.

'Wot's garn on Nana?'

Nana didn't answer, her face was grey, and she signalled for her to go in the living room.

There was a fat woman with a brown bob standing in front of the fire and she could hear Grandar coughing in the kitchen.

'This is a social worker who wants ter talk ter yer,' said Nana.

The social worker put her hand on her arm. 'I'm Carol, there's nothin ter worry about, I just want a chat.'

Her heart fell to her feet; Billy had called social services, which is exactly the type of bastard trick he would pull in revenge. The nobhead must've had a stotten headache when he woke up yesterday.

The social worker sat down and she sat next to her. As soon as this chat was over, she was going to see Dad. She hoped that he'd stopped being shouty and punchy and was back to being normal-for-him.

'Her mother should be deein this,' said Nana.

The social worker raised a hand at Nana. 'Mrs Hart is under a lot of pressure at the moment.'

'Me mam? Wot's happened?'

'Okay,' said the social worker, 'it's about your stepfather.'

'Wot about him?'

The social worker put her hand on her arm and looked down. 'I'm afraid he's had an accident and he's passed away.'

Passed away? What did that mean?

'He's died, Paula,' said Nana.

She twisted her face and looked at the social worker and then at Nana.

'Where's Mam?'

'She's at Aunty Pat's luv,' said Nana.

'It's a lot to take in,' said the social worker. 'How are yer feelin?'

'Wot?'

'Feelin, how are yer feelin, Paula?'

She felt happy and terrified. 'How did he die?'

'He had a tragic accident in the home. I don't know the details.'

She had to pretend she didn't know the details, particularly how the fishing rods and hangman's loop were all over the stairs. She could say that she'd left the note much earlier that day before he got back from Steels; anyway, she'd done it in his writing so she could deny being there.

Pretending it was a shock, she put her face in her hands and thought about the dancing bear on the news with a rope shoved up its nostril. Its eyes were so sad, shoulders slumped, like a big broken teddy bear. Then she thought about seal cubs being clubbed to death. She managed to pump out a decent flow of tears, and her nose got all bunged up, so the social worker gave her a tissue and nodded at Nana as she wiped her eyes.

'Okay then Paula, I've spoken with your mam and your nan, and we all agree that you should stay somewhere else tonight.'

'Ah'm ah bein tacken inter care?'

'No,' said the social worker, 'we've got a nice family who are going ter look after yer for a couple of days until we sort a place for yer family. How does that sound?'

'It's better than sleepin on the settee,' said Nana.

She wanted to say she'd go to Dad's. The thought of him finding out that Billy was dead made her feel sick. How would he find out? He was probably at home writing in his books. She hoped David was there and not at Lisa's.

'Okey-doke Paula, if you get your things, I'll take you to meet Mrs Shaw; she's very nice.'

She put her Benetton bag over her shoulders.

'Is that all you have?' said the social worker.

'Yip.'

'Right then, let's go.'

Nana gave her a hug. 'Ring uz when yer get there. Yer got me number?'

'Aye,' she said, tapping the side of her head. She'd never forget Nana's number.

She sat in the front of the social worker's orange Herbie car. Wham! was on the radio, but when the engine started, she couldn't hear it. As they drove off, she had butterflies, it was exciting to be going to someone's house and Billy was dead and then she remembered that she was supposed to be sad, so she did a bit of a cry.

They went towards Penshaw and from the big roundabout, they went down the cut onto the A19. On the far side she could see the red bricks of the *Echo* office tower with the Casey Man on the side. His unlit neon tubes formed an outline of a happy football man and an outline of a sad football man. She squeezed her eyes, trying to push light into his tubes, willing him to glow and give her a sign from Dad. Casey Man should be smiling and waving his hat with this result!

They crossed the river and went on for miles and she would've asked where they were going if the engine wasn't so deafening. She thought about when Billy tripped over Ian's Castle Grayskull and twatted his head off the bedside table. Knocked himself out cold. He always got up again though, so what the fuck had he done to knock himself out dead?

They turned off the road and through some brick gateposts and drove up a grey drive to a big house. When the car jerked to a stop, her bones kept shaking.

'Is this a children's home?' she asked.

'No,' said the social worker, irritated.

The door was painted glossy black and had a wass brass knocker on it like in a horror film and she expected it to creek open and for bats to come flying out.

'Hello, you must be Paula,' said a pretty woman with blonde hair in a ponytail. 'Come in.'

They went inside and into a huge living room that had velvet curtains tied back with golden ropes and tassels like at the Empire. Sonya's house was a shed compared with this mansion.

'This is Mrs Shaw,' said the social worker.

The pretty woman laughed and said, 'I'm Jenny. I'm so sorry to hear about your stepfather. Carol asked me to look after you for a couple of days until things get sorted out.'

The social worker was already out of the living room and *Jenny* looked embarrassed and dithered. 'Back in a sec,' she said, 'make yourself at home.'

She could hear them talking outside.

This place was the poshest she'd ever seen, and she couldn't wait to see her bedroom, apart from she had to act sad because a tragedy had happened. She forced out some tears, and when Jenny returned, she put her arm around her shoulder, sending a warm feeling down her back.

'Come with me.'

The kitchen was the size of about five normal kitchens and had pine cupboards and orange wall tiles and beige carpet tiles. Plonked in the middle was the biggest dinner table that she'd ever seen, and the chairs had green and white checky cushions on them.

'It's nice to have you here, Paula, but it's as strange for me as it is for you because I usually provide emergency care for children under five,' Jenny explained, her face even prettier when she smiled.

'Soz, man, that ah'm not a small bairn. Did the social dump uz on yer?'

'No, not at all,' said Jenny. 'Nobody dumps on me,' she said, giving her a strong shoulder hug. 'Have you eaten today?'

'Ah had porridge at me nana's.'

'Porridge, good stuff. I bet your grandmother makes delicious porridge.'

'Here-man, it's mingin, ah woz just starvin.'

She wondered what she'd said to make Jenny double-over laughing, but whatever it was, she was pleased because she *really* liked it here.

Jenny wafted her face. 'Why don't you sit down and I'll make you a drink.' Jenny opened a cupboard that had a full fridge inside.

'Fuck, is that a fridge, soz,' she said, covering her mouth. 'Ah swear when ah'm nervous.'

'We don't swear in this house, so if you could mind your language that would be appreciated.'

'Soz.'

'Well, it's been a bit of a day already,' said Jenny. 'I bet you didn't expect this when you went to bed last night?'

'Ah kipped on Nana's settee last neet.'

'Oh,' said Jenny with a sorry sigh. 'Well tonight you're in the guest bedroom. It should only be a night or two until they get you somewhere more permanent.'

'Where will ah be garn next?' she said, breaking into a sweat at the thought of being shipped off to a kid's home where they steal your things and flush your head down the bog.

'It depends on when they rehouse your mother.'

'Der yer knar wot happened ter me stepdar?'

'All they've told me is that he had an accident and passed away and that the police have sealed off your house.'

A jolt of fear ran down her spine. 'Wot like with yellow tape and police cars and that?'

'I'm sure it's standard procedure when there's been a fatal accident. Sprite or Coke?'

'Coke please.' She pictured the police piecing it together – the damp towel smelling of female, the mystery fingerprints on the rods, the note. She pressed the cold can on her sweaty brow as she sat on a cushiony wooden chair. She'd enjoy the Coke as it may be her last before being carted off to prison. Psycho Kim said that when she was in Durham on remand for aiding and abetting attempted murder, they were allowed two pairs of big scratchy knickers; a pair to wear and a pair they washed in the tiny hand sink at the end of each day before poking their faces through the narrow, barred, windows and singing to each other.

On the far bench next to the tall cupboard was a small cube-shaped, portable telly. 'Ah luv yer telly. Pye Redbox 9 inch. Wait till ah tell Sonya about this.'

'Would you like to watch it?'

'Aye. Your house is git posh, like.'

'Thank you, Paula.' Jenny switched the Pye Redbox telly on and after pushing all the buttons, she pulled down an invisible flap on the front which had a knob inside that she twiddled until the picture was clear. She snapped the flap shut and said, 'Would you like a cheese sandwich?'

'Aye, gan on then, thank you.'

She ate the sarnie and watched *Pebble Mill* on the tiny telly while Jenny came in and out. If she'd known that it would be this good, she would've let Billy put her into care long ago. The lass from next door to Nana's said that the children's home she was sent to was full of really hard lasses and that she had hods of fights.

'Hi,' said a teenage girl who looked like Jenny.

'Hi, ah'm Paula.'

'Charlotte,' she said. 'Mummy, who is Paula?'

'A foster child.'

'Oh,' said Charlotte, 'you don't look like one.'

'Yer mam said that ah'm older than usual.'

'I'm going into the fourth year in September,' said Charlotte. 'What about you?'

'Fifth and final year; ah cannet wait ter leave.'

Jenny came out of the washing machine room, 'Ah, you girls have met.' She hugged Charlotte and kissed her on the side of the head. 'Paula will be here for a couple of nights. Why don't you take her to your room and find her something to read?'

She followed Charlotte up the grand staircase that had bannisters made from sticks instead of planks and carpet so thick she could feel it through her shoes.

'Welcome to my humble abode,' said Charlotte as they went into her bedroom. 'Do you like horses?'

'Fuck,' she said, 'sorry, but fuck.' Her room was *amazing*.

Charlotte laughed, 'That's okay, I swear, not in front of Mummy though, she'd fucking kill me.'

Her room was wall-to-wall horses. Posters, cushions, curtains, lampshade.

'Der yer have yer own horse?'

Charlotte pointed at the pinboard full of photos. 'That's Orchid.'

Orchid was a golden horse with a white mane and tail.

'She's a Palomino,' said Charlotte.

'Yae must be stinkin rich. What does yer dad dee?'

'He owns a caravan park near Alnwick, and we're not rich. What does your dad do? I mean, that is, if you have one.'

'Aye, ah have a dad. Ah see him when he's not in Cherry like.'

'Cherry Knowle?'

'Aye.'

She got closer and looked at the photos of Orchid and of Charlotte and Orchid, and of Charlotte and Jenny smiling and stroking Orchid. Jenny was lovely and she wished she was her mam. She nodded at the wall of rosettes, and said, 'Did yer get them from ridin Orchid?'

'Some of them and some from my previous pony, Harlequinn. Do you ride?'

In her imagination she was riding all the time. 'Yeah, ah've done a bit of ridin, not properly like, nee showjumpin or owt,' she lied.

'Do you live on a council estate?'

'Ah suppose it's an estate; there's nee houses, only maisonettes.'

Charlotte gasped, her milky cheeks turning red.

'It's not that bad.'

'What school do you go to?'

'The Bede.'

Charlotte gasped louder, 'I heard they flush your head down the toilet at the Bede.'

'Wot school der yae gan tee?'

'I go to a girls' school in Newcastle.'

'Wot, there's nee lads like at St Anthony's? Ah cannet decide if that's good or bad.'

'Fucking bad,' said Charlotte.

'Yer should meet the lads from my class. Yer wouldn't touch them if they were the last lads on earth.'

'What are you girls laughing at,' said Jenny, coming in with a pile of neatly folded clothes.

'Nothing, Mummy,' said Charlotte.

'We woz talkin about Orchid.'

'Do you like horses?' said Jenny.

'Ah luv horses. When ah woz little, ah used to imagine ridin White Beauty along the beach.'

'*Black Beauty*, I love that book,' said Charlotte.

'Ah didn't knar it woz a book. Ah watched it on the telly.'

Jenny and Charlotte gave each other a telepathic look, and Charlotte went to the bookshelf and skimmed her finger along. 'Here.'

'Maybe you could take Paula for a ride tomorrow,' said Jenny. 'Paula, what do you think?'

What did she think about going horse riding? Was this what she was being asked? She was speechless.

'That's fine with me,' said Charlotte.

'Excellent,' said Jenny. 'How about I show you to your room and let you have some quiet time?'

The guest bedroom was big and decorated with blue flowery wallpaper with matching curtains and a continental quilt.

'I'll leave you to have some quiet time,' said Jenny.

Quiet time? What was that? There was no such thing as quiet time at home, only shouty time and telly blaring time and being told that you are bloody stupid time. There were so many reasons why she was over the moon to be in foster care, she punched the pillow with joy to stop herself from shouting, 'Thank you God,' and thereby blowing her cover; sad, she was very, very sad that Billy had *passed away.*

She lay on the luxurious double bed with the maroon leather book with *Black Beauty* written in gold letters down the spine. She'd never read a book before, not properly. When they read out loud in class, one painful line at a time, she never listened because it was boring, and when they were reading on their own, her mind would wander off onto horses, so she never read a single page. She was in the bottom set for English yet wasn't as thick as some people because she was in the middle set for maths. She could do numbers, although didn't understand how to use letters in calculations, so she had no chance of getting into the top set. She ruffled the pages of the book, and the dust made her sneeze. It smelled nice, like Nana's bible. She had nothing else to do, so she started reading.

The book was totally brilliant and nothing like the telly programme, which was like *Lassie* but with a horse solving the crimes instead of a dog. In the book, it was the horse telling the story and he talked with other horses about how they felt when humans were cruel. She read chapter after chapter and couldn't stop reading even when Charlotte knocked and said, 'Dinner in ten minutes.'

She heard a car pull up and two doors slam, but she was too engrossed in the fire in the stable to go to the window and see who it was.

There was another knock. 'Paula, can I come in?' said Charlotte.

'Aye, come in,' she said, wondering why she didn't just burst in and shout at her like normal people.

'Don't worry,' said Charlotte.

'Wot?'

‘The police want to speak to you.’

Her legs were properly wobbly as she followed Charlotte into the kitchen because she couldn’t stop thinking about washing her scratchy knickers with Lifebuoy soap in the tiny sink in Durham nick. The plan for now was to pretend that she knew nothing and to cry if they asked any tricky questions.

The far end of the table was set and the food in the pot on the cooker smelled like pizza and made her tummy rumble. On the near end of the table was a policeman and policewoman. Jenny turned the heat down on the cooker and handed Charlotte a spoon. ‘Keep an eye on the sauce, darling.’

She felt shaky and sick as she sat down and was glad that Jenny was next to her.

The policewoman said, ‘Ah’m very sorry to hear about your stepdad, Paula.’

‘Aye, me too,’ said the policeman. ‘Ah’m sure he’s at peace in heaven.’

This was a good moment to cry so she thought about Rob Roy and Ginger until her pain was plain to see. ‘Ah cannet believe ower Billy’s gone, wot are uz ganner dee without him? Me mam’ll be in pieces.’

‘We’ve spoken to yer mam and she’s upset at the moment. Yer might be able to see her tomorrow and maybe speak to her later,’ said the policewoman.

‘Where is he? Can ah see him ter give him ah last kiss like, yer knar, before they put him in the coffin?’

Jenny put her hand on hers, which made her feel guilty; she didn't give a shit about lying to the rozzers about being grief-stricken, but Jenny was nice.

'Now then Paula, ah'm going to ask yer a few questions, nothin to worry about,' said the policeman.

She thought about the horses in blinkers that were steered too close to the river, which made tears flow down her face.

'Can't you see the girl's upset?' said Jenny, putting her arm round her shoulder.

'We want ter know if Billy had somethin on his mind? Yer knar somethin troublin him,' said the policewoman.

'Ah dunnar.'

'When did yer last see Billy, Paula?'

'On Saturda neet.' She bit her lip; she didn't want to lie.

'Saturday, okay then, is that when you and yer mam ran away from the flat?'

'Aye.'

'Wot happened at the flat?'

'Nowt really. Me mam and Billy had a barney like normal and he pushed her through the door, but a fly would've fallen through that plywood.'

'And then wot happened?'

'Mam and the bairns went ter me Aunty Pat's, and ah went to me Nana's.'

'Is that your Nana Peggy?'

'Aye. Margaret Hasting, nee *s*.'

'Did they have a lot of barneys, yer mam and Billy?'

'Aye, but that's the stress of the strikes and stuff.'

The plods looked at each other and nodded. 'Rest in peace Billy, my good man,' said the policeman.

Her eyes were running dry and she hoped that they'd get to the part about how he died. 'Can ah ask yers a question?'

'Go on, luv,' said the policeman.

'How did Billy die? Ah mean, ah knar he woz always fallen ower mortal and that, but he always got back up. There woz this one time when he knocked himsel out on the bathroom sink and he got up after a few minutes.'

'He hasn't been so lucky this time.'

'Did he fall ower or wot?'

The plods looked at each other and back at her.

'We don't know anythin yet,' said the policewoman.

'Oh, come on, you can't expect that to wash,' said Jenny, giving the policeman a death stare. 'Tell the poor girl what happened to her stepfather.'

He held his hands up. 'He had an accident and passed away. That's all wer know.'

'Well maybe you should come back when you do know,' said Jenny. She was so gutsy.

'Okey-doke, Paula,' said the policewoman. 'Yer said that Billy liked a drink?'

'Why-aye man, he could drink through a shitty cloth.'

She was glad when the policeman laughed, apart from the policewoman wasn't laughing. 'How often would yer say he had a drink?'

'He'd be in Steels every day when it opened, home for a kip at three, then back at seven, usually until closin, unless he was skint.'

'Fall over a lot, did he?' asked the policewoman.

'Nor, not really, not considerin how shit-faced he woz most of the time.'

'Language,' said Jenny.

'Sorry,' she said.

'Did he punch yer mam often?' said the policewoman.

'The lass said he pushed her,' said the policeman, 'nothin about punchin her. That's reet, isn't it, luv, he pushed her?'

'Aye, nor, aye,' she said, bursting into tears at the thought of the little pony that wouldn't jump the high gate.

'If there's no more questions, maybe you officers should be on your way. I need to get the pasta on,' said Jenny sternly.

'When am ah garn home?' she said.

'You'll be staying here for a couple of days,' said Jenny.

'Then wot? A children's home?'

The policeman said to Jenny, 'What did social services say?' and she shooed him out of the kitchen.

She went over to join Charlotte at the pot. 'Do you like lentil and olive ragu?'

'Ah've nivver heard of it, but it smells amazin.'

When Jenny came back from chasing the police, she held up two long glass jars. 'Tubes or twists?'

'Twists,' she said.

'You girls sit down, although no, Charlotte, could you make a jug of dilutey orange please?'

She chased every garlicky, tomatoey pasta twist around her plate with her knife and fork and noticed that Jenny and Charlotte were managing with just forks. She couldn't believe that Charlotte left some, and her taste buds wept when Jenny scraped the glistening twists into a bin that popped out of a pine unit.

'Angel Delight for pud-pud?' said Jenny. 'Or maybe you should ring your mother first?'

Given the choice, she went with Angel Delight. 'Nor, ah'll speak ter her tomorra, she'll be too upset ter talk now, ah knar wot she's like.'

The digital clock on the bedside table said 6:07 and sunlight streamed through the blue flowery curtains. Her head went into overdrive and a shiver ran down her spine when she thought about Dad. She prayed that David was there with him, playing Monopoly.

She couldn't sleep so she read *Black Beauty* until Jenny knocked, came in and sat on the end of the bed.

'Oh, you're reading, how wonderful. Downstairs in five. Don't worry about getting dressed. We all wear pyjamas for brekkie in this house.'

There were three places neatly set out at the table, with matching cups, plates, and bowls. Charlotte poured cereal from a plastic container and added milk from a jug with a cow on it.

'Help yourself to cereal,' said Jenny. 'Orange or apple juice?'

'Orange please.'

'Mummy has found you some riding gear to wear,' said Charlotte.

'Some old stuff from when I was a few pounds lighter,' said Jenny, patting her tummy.

'More like a few stone lighter,' said Charlotte.

'What size shoe do you take?' said Jenny.

'Five.'

'Perfect. You can borrow Charlotte's boots.'

When Jenny mentioned going horse riding, she'd pushed it out of her mind as there's no point thinking about something that's never going to happen. When she put the jodhpurs on, she started to believe that maybe it was going to happen; however, at best, she'd get a rushed ride before being pushed off by a kid with grown-ups on their side. That was always the way – monkey bars, darts, video games – Billy would side with the other kid to make sure she didn't get a go. She wasn't going to get a ride on a horse today because something would stop it, it always did. She didn't know what, but it would be something.

In Jenny's old jodhpurs and Charlotte's spare boots, carrying Charlotte's spare hat, she felt like a proper horsewoman. Jenny dropped them at a gate, which they climbed and then headed down a dirt track lined by tall hedges that they had to squash into as cars came past, churning up dust and rocks. At the end of the track was a wide concrete yard with cars and horseboxes and people leading horses. On the far side of the yard was a huge barn made of breeze blocks with a corrugated metal roof. At the end of the barn was a wide gap with people leading horses in and out. 'Is that where the horses are kept?'

'Follow me,' said Charlotte.

Inside the barn was a central corridor and running down each side were stables that were wooden at the bottom with metal poles at the top, like prison cells for horses. The bars dipped in the middle so the horses could stick their heads out. Hanging outside the stables were saddles and blankets and all sorts of straps and buckles. Horse mixed with leather made a smell from heaven, so she took deep breaths. She couldn't believe she was here. This was brilliant.

Halfway down, Charlotte stopped and a golden horse with a white mane stuck its head over the bars. 'This is my beautiful Orchid,' said Charlotte, stroking Orchid, who stuck out her long pink tongue. Charlotte took a bridle and went into the stable.

She stayed outside and stroked Orchid's nose and said, 'Are yer ganner get yer bridle on?'

'It's a headcollar,' said Charlotte, slipping it over the horse's head. 'Pull her forelock through like this and do the clasp up.'

She stroked Orchid's forelock and mane so it wasn't caught in the headcollar.

Charlotte stepped out of the stable. 'This is a lead rope.' She attached it to a metal loop using a fancy knot, then led Orchid out and attached the rope to her headcollar. '*Et voila*, all tied up and ready to groom.'

Charlotte gave her what looked like a hairbrush but with the bristles of a shoe brush. 'You start, I'll be back in a tick.'

She brushed the horse's silky sides using her common sense rather than knowledge, or as Nana would say, 'Bullshit over brains.' At breakfast and all the way there, she'd done Charlotte's head in with a million horse questions.

'Mucking out?' said Charlotte with a pitchfork and broom in her hands and a wheelbarrow at her feet.

'Nee probs,' she said, grabbing the pitchfork.

'Straw is expensive, so just the parts with poop in it,' said Charlotte, brushing the clean straw to the side.

She jabbed the pitchfork into a pile of manure and shovelled it into the wheelbarrow. 'Me grandar would love this for his scallions.'

'Can I ask you a question?' said Charlotte.

'Aye, gan on then.'

'You don't have to answer it.'

'Wot is it?'

‘Have you ever had sex?’

‘*Err*, aye.’

Charlotte leaned on the broom. ‘What was it like, who with, are you seeing him?’

‘All the questions like.’

‘Did he finger you?’

‘Whoa,’ she said, ‘ah dunnar if ah should be tellin yer stuff like that. Jenny’ll kill uz.’

‘How many times have you had sex?’

‘Arnly twice, wer the same lad.’

Charlotte kept leaning on the brush. ‘And?’

She’d met Wayne at the ice rink and was going out with him for two weeks before he dumped her for Becky who had her own skates and her dad had a shop over Sea Road. She used to walk down to Thornhill after school and then go to his house on Otto Terrace and have sex with him in his bedroom.

Charlotte wanted more than a few titbits about Wayne, so she told her about when Ally bonked Mark Green on the steps of Barnes Juniors’ and about Sonya and Conor who hadn’t done anything.

Charlotte wasn’t so sweet and innocent, and her story about her mate’s older sister made Ally look like a nun. Rather than jumping straight into bed with a lad, there was, so Charlotte said, a polite way to go out with someone: on the first week there’s necking-on and tits inside of clothes; on the second week, front-bottom outside of clothes; on the third week, hand inside the knickers; and then after that based on her mate's sister, you fuck him and his mate, one after the other, and then give his other mate a gobble.

'Front-bottom,' she laughed. 'Is that yer minge?'

Charlotte cringed and said, 'Fairy-Anne.'

'Me nana calls it that,' she laughed.

'I'm seeing a boy from Daddy's caravan site; we'll probably have sex this weekend.'

'Wee is he? Does yer mam knar yer seein him?'

'Of course not, she'd have a hissy fit.'

'How old is he?'

'He's fifteen, he's called John, and he's *gorgeous.* Why else would I spend a week on a boring caravan park?'

'A week winnet be long enough if yer gan through the neckin-on, inside bra, outside front-bottom, carry-on.'

Charlotte laughed. 'What do you think I should do?'

'Tack yer clays off, get into bed, and fuck him.'

'Really?'

'Aye.'

With the last dollop of shitty straw deposited, Charlotte handed her the broom. 'You sweep, I'll ditch the poo, then we'll get the horse tacked up.'

Tacked up. A ride on a horse was getting closer. It hadn't happened yet.

'If you're ever confused about which way to put a bridle on, the trick is to put it on your head.' As Charlotte demonstrated her trick, laughter boomed from the man coming toward them. Charlotte turned, took the bridle off her head, and said, 'Hi there, Michael.'

'Showing your friend how to tack up?' he said.

'Yes.'

'Are you going to introduce us?'

'Michael, this is Paula,' she said. 'Paula this is Michael, who is the dad of Amanda, who has a cob mare called Whisper.'

'How do you know each other? I haven't seen Paula here before,' he said.

'She's staying with us for a couple of nights.'

'Cousins?'

'Mummy does foster care.'

'Oh, I see.'

'She usually looks after young children, so that's why I never bring them down here,' explained Charlotte.

'You don't look like a young child,' he said, 'you must be, say, fourteen?'

'Fifteen,' she said.

'Let me guess, Pisces?' he guessed.

'Nor, Sagittarius.'

'November?'

'December the fifth.'

'If you're a Sagittarius, you must be good at horse riding?'

'Ah've had a few goes like, but ah wouldn't say ah'm good.'

Charlotte laughed, and said, 'I think he's referring to Sagittarius being half man, half horse.'

'Oh aye, ah nivver thought of that,' she said, wondering what they were talking about.

He smiled, showing his perfect teeth. 'Is Dorothy in the office today?'

Charlotte shrugged. 'Orchid hadn't been mucked out.'

He pursed his lips, 'Whisper neither.' As he walked away, he gave them a back-wave and a waft of spicy aftershave.

She did her best to listen to everything Charlotte said as she added items to the horse, bridle, saddle pad, saddle. Feed the girth through the saddle pad and attach it to the billet.

Charlotte fastened the lead rope to the bridle and said, 'Approach the horse from the side, nudge her with your shoulder and walk.'

Charlotte gave her the lead rope and she walked the horse out onto the yard. Charlotte put her hat on. 'Where's yours?'

'On the floor outside of the stable door.'

'I'll get it,' said Charlotte.

As she waited anxiously, she pressed her face into Orchid's cheek – any moment now, a posh girl was going to push her out of the way and go off with Charlotte, leaving her for dust, or frogs would rain from the skies, or something would stop this dream from coming true, it was inevitable.

Charlotte plonked the hat on her head, checked that the strap was tight enough, and then took the rope and led the horse to some red plastic steps. 'On you get.'

Cowboys and jockeys never used plastic steps. She usually mounted her imaginary winged stallion by taking a short run-up, one foot in the stirrup and flinging the other leg over. The plastic steps made it easier and as she sat in the saddle, not a million Billys nor a pack of rabid dogs were going to stop her from riding this horse. She wiggled her feet into the stirrups properly.

'How do they feel?' said Charlotte.

'A bit long,' she said, lifting her feet to where the stirrups should be.

'That's too short, what are you, a jockey?' Charlotte grabbed her leg and put it in the right place. Then she lifted the stirrup and fiddled with the strap.

Orchid nuzzled Charlotte as she took the lead rope and walked. As hooves clip-clopped on the concrete, her stomach did somersaults. This was happening. They clop-clopped onto a dirt track with a forest on one side and a field of horses on the other. Orchid snorted and Charlotte replied, 'Yes, good idea,' and stopped. 'Press your ankles down and your knees in.'

She did as she was told, and it wasn't easy to hold the position.

'Shorten your reins.'

When Charlotte saw her fumbling like a fool, she came to her rescue. 'Between your fingers, now take more of the slack, that's it. Tuck your elbows in.'

As the tension on the rein increased, Orchid nodded her head. Charlotte took the lead rope and began to walk down the track, and glancing up, said, 'Ready?'

'Yep,' she said, properly ready.

Charlotte said, 'Trot-on,' and upped her pace, making Orchid trot.

It was amazing to be trotting on a horse! She'd never felt so free! No one could take this feeling from her, no one!

They slowed to a walk beyond the horse field and over the high hedge she could see an arena with a sandy-coloured floor. Charlotte opened the gate and took the rope off. 'Give her a heel and walk over to the far side.'

She gave Orchid a tap on both sides and did her best to sit tall, press her heels down, and tuck her knees and elbows in. When the horse didn't move, Charlotte said, 'Give her a proper dig. She's waiting for your instructions.'

As they clopped back into the yard, she wondered if there was a word for when the best thing that has ever happened to you comes to an end.

'Jump down,' said Charlotte.

She stretched her aching legs. As they took the saddle off and filled the hay bag, Charlotte gave her feedback about her riding and said that she wasn't bad for a beginner.

Jenny made them kick the kerb to get rid of the straw and horseshit before they could get in the car.

'Did you girls have fun?'

'Aye, man, it woz brilliant, but me arse is killin uz.'

'Language.'

'Soz.'

They took their boots off at the mansion door and followed Jenny to the washing machine room, where they took their riding gear off and put it in the washing machine. She went up and changed back into her white skirt and shirt and when she came down, Jenny led her into the washing machine room and said, 'Why don't you pop those clothes in the wash, and I'll find you something clean to wear.'

In her pants and Mam's bra, she followed Jenny, and instead of going along to the guest bedroom, they went the other way and into Jenny's bedroom. It had a bed that was the size of two double beds.

'Have you ever been in a shower?'

'Aye, at the leisure centre.'

'The swimming baths?'

'Yer press the rubber bleb wer yer foot and it macks the watter come out.'

Jenny opened a door in the bedroom which led into a tiny bathroom with a shower box instead of a bath.

'This shower has a dial on the wall, not a *bleb* on the floor.' Jenny leaned in and turned the dial. 'You can adjust the temperature here. Towel is on the rack. I'll put some clothes in your room.'

This was miles better than the showers at the leisure centre and she stayed under the hot water for ages, thinking about telling Dad about riding Orchid. Who'd have thought that she'd be taken to a lovely foster home and get to ride a horse all because Billy died?

She wandered back to her room wrapped in a fluffy towel and was glad to find some brand-new knickers and a bra laid out on the bed. She wasn't so pleased with the flowery dress with lacey collars and buttons down the front from Laura Ashley. But she had nothing else, so she put it on and then stood in front of the mirror with the theme from *Little House on the Prairie* playing in her head. 'Gee Papa, I can't wait to show everyone the priddy dress that Mama made for me.'

Jenny and Charlotte were in the kitchen looking at takeaway menus. 'Chinese?'

'Aye.' She loved Chinese. Sometimes on a Saturday when Billy had had a win, he'd send her down to the Happy Valley takeaway.

'What do you usually have?' asked Jenny.

'Special fried rice and gravy, ah pick the prawns out though, and Billy has them.'

'Is Billy your stepfather?'

They were both looking at her with sad faces, so she breathed out and slumped. 'Poor Billy. Ah had such a good time today, ah almost forgot he's deed.'

'How about I telephone the order and you girls go and collect it?'

Charlotte linked her arm. 'Yes, we'll go.'

Riding boots completed the Laura Ingalls look and she hoped she wouldn't see anyone she knew, which was unlikely in Boldon. Charlotte's mind continued down the single track of John from the caravan, who, it turned out, she'd pecked on the lips twice, although she wasn't really seeing him yet.

'Wee does he gan ter the caravan with?'

'With his grandmar and younger sister. They have a static.'

'A wot?'

'A caravan that's parked permanently.'

'Does he live there?'

'Practically, during the summer. And guess what?'

'Wot?'

'Van twenty-three is empty for all next week. I checked Daddy's booking book.'

The Chinese was on the counter when they got there, and Charlotte took the bags and handed over a twenty. As they headed down the road, Charlotte swung the bags of takeaway and looked sheepish. 'I have something I need your help with.'

'Wot?'

'Follow me.'

She followed Charlotte into the newsagents and to the shelves of magazines.

'Don't tell Mummy,' said Charlotte.

'Tell her wot?'

Charlotte reached up and pulled a magazine from the top shelf, which she handed to her along with the change from the twenty. 'I'll wait outside while you pay, and don't tell Mummy.'

Charlotte swanned off, swinging the bags of food, leaving her to pay for *Playgirl.* On the cover was a bloke with a tash and she flicked through the pages looking for some cock, but no luck. All she got was bare chests and cleverly positioned pot plants. A bloke with tattoos and big muscles standing next to a bookshelf gave her tingles, but he was holding a book in front of his dick.

She took the dirty mag to the counter where there was a pile of *Echos*. She read the headline: REDUNDANT MINER IN FATAL ACCIDENT. Hands shaking, she picked it up and read. *William 'Billy' Hart was found dead at his home in Peacock Street West, Pallion, yesterday. The alarm was raised by friends after he failed to attend a darts and dominoes meeting at Steels Social Club. Shortly after midnight, police confirmed that Billy had passed away. Chief Inspector Mark Clifford stated that Billy had fallen foul of a tragic accident and that a post-mortem was ongoing as to the cause of death. Family man Billy was father to seven-year-old Ian and four-year-old Jason––*

'I heard he was decapitated,' said the man behind the counter.

'Wot?' she said, tearing her eyes away from the newspaper.

'His head came off,' said the shop man.

'Wee's heed?'

He nodded at the *Echo* she was holding.

Frozen to the spot, she dropped it and handed over the money for the porn mag.

'You okay, pet?'

'Aye, thanks, ta-ra.'

Charlotte was waiting at a safe distance and when she gave her the mag, she untucked her blouse and stuffed it down the front of her jeans. 'Don't tell Mummy.' She swung the bags of takeaway at her. 'You carry these and I'll run to the loo as if I'm bursting. Are you okay? You look like you've seen a ghost.'

'The gadgie in the shop ses Billy's heed came off.'

'Fuck.'

'It's on the front of the *Echo*. Ah'm ganner ask yer mam if she knars owt.'

'No, don't do that!'

'Why not?'

'Because she'll ask why you were in the newsagents. Mummy knows everyone around here. If she knows you went in there, she'll go in and speak to him.' Charlotte lifted her blouse and flashed *Playgirl*. 'She *cannot* find out about this. Promise you won't say anything?'

'But ha'way man, me stepdar's deed and ah wanna knar wot happened ter him.'

'How did his head come off exactly?'

'The newsagent man ses he woz decapritated.'

'You *cannot* tell Mummy you were in the newsagents. Promise?'

She was too busy thinking about Billy to haggle, yet by the time they got to the mansion, she'd agreed not to say anything in return for five rides on Orchid and she keeps the riding boots.

The table was laid out as if it was Sunday dinner which seemed odd as the best thing about a Chinese is that you get to kneel at the coffee table and eat from the carton like a gissy at the trough. Jenny unloaded the bags into the middle of the table and Charlotte sat down, having got rid of the mag from down her trousers.

'Special fried rice, that'll be yours, Paula.'

She emptied her scran onto her plate and flattened the rice pyramid with her fork before howking out the prawns. Jenny and Charlotte filled their plates with stuff that looked like Grandar's compost heap. She put the prawns round the side of her plate, and after she was sure that they were all out, she poured the gravy on and mixed it in. She could see Jenny and Charlotte smiling at each other.

'Are yers laughin at me prawns?'

'Here.' Jenny handed her a small plate.

As she flicked the prawns one by one onto the plate, she felt sorry for them with their shells ripped off and their soft pink bodies fried in oil. She didn't like them because Skips were minging and because the prawns were her favourites in *Fingerbobs*. Seemed so long ago, sitting with Nana watching *Fingerbobs*, and then they'd laugh at the 'trump' in *Trumpton*, back when life was fun before Mam met Billy, and everything went shite. Her heart fluttered at the thought of Billy lying on the bathroom floor with no head. The bathroom mirror had been hanging by a thread since Ian flung Jason into it, and when Billy hit his head on the sink, it probably fell off and shattered on his neck.

'Ah saw a sandwich board outside the newsy that said summink about Billy,' she said to Jenny, making Charlotte choke on her spring roll.

'Really, what did it say?' said Jenny.

'Ah'm not sure cos uz woz on the other side of the road.'

'Oh well, Colin will bring the paper home, so we can see if there's any news then.'

'Can wer put the telly on?'

'I'd rather we didn't while we are eating.'

'Gan on, please, it's deein me heed-in; a need ter knar wot happened to me stepdar like.'

'Go on, Mummy, just this once.'

'Wot's the point of havin a telly in the kitchen if yers dinnet watch it while yers are eatin?' she asked.

Jenny took the serviette off her knee and put it on the table. 'Fine.'

As Jenny twiddled the knob, the theme tune to *Look North* played. The picture was wobbly, but you could make out Mike Neville. He started talking about unemployment and went on for ages as they scoffed their food. Then he said, 'And also in the news today.' They lifted their heads and looked at Mike in anticipation.

'Tributes have been paid to miner Billy Hart, who passed away in an accident at his home in Pallion, Sunderland, on Sunday night. He leaves a wife, two young children, and two stepchildren. Members of the local community and his colleagues at Herrington Colliery have spoken of how he was a kind-hearted family man who will be sadly missed.'

It cut to a policeman standing outside of Gillbridge. 'I can confirm that our officers were called to the scene at 11 pm on Sunday night and found that Mr Hart had passed away in a tragic accident. His death is not being treated as suspicious at this time, and we are waiting for the pathologist's report.'

Mike Neville went to the next story, and she was gutted that there was no info on the 'accident.' And anyway, 'kind-hearted family man'? They'd obviously never met him. 'Not suspicious at this time.' What did that mean?

'Billy had another stepchild?' said Jenny.

'Me older brotha. Him and Billy hated each other.'

'I had no idea that you had an older brother. How old is he?'

'Twenty.'

'Where does he live?'

She couldn't be bothered to explain about David, and the first thing she could think of was, 'He lives down Middlesbrough with his wife.'

'Charlotte told me that your father is unwell.'

'Aye, he's been in Cherry, that's why ah dinnet live wer him.'

She was saved from all the questions by the weather on the Redbox. 'The outlook for the next few days is more warm and sunny weather with continued areas of high pressure all over the county.'

'Looks like you're in for a great week at the park,' said Jenny to Charlotte.

'Yer cannet trust the weather report. Have yer got any good magazines in case it's hoyin it down?' she said.

Charlotte shot her a death stare.

Jenny took her empty plate and she wanted to tug it back and lick it clean like at home when she'd stick her face into the silver carton and lick the juice and get the last few bits of sticky rice with her tongue.

'Are you all packed for the off?' said Jenny to Charlotte.

'Yes, Mummy.'

'Right then, pudding. Trifle?'

Jenny placed down two mini trifles that were nothing like Nana's massive one with hundreds and thousands that bled colour into the whipped cream.

They finished their *pudding*, and she was helping to tidy away when Jenny said to Charlotte, 'Sounds like Daddy's home.'

From the photos all over the house, she'd already decided that Jenny's husband was not good enough looking for her, and when he came in, he was much older and fatter than in the photos.

'Who's she?' he said.

'She's staying for a couple of nights,' said Jenny.

'Hello, ah'm Paula,' she said, holding out a hand.

He recoiled at her hand like she was a leper and blanked her. 'Are you ready, Lottie? We're leaving in five.'

If she'd known *Daddy* was such a twat, she'd have told *Lottie* to get stuck right into John. She hoped that he gives her a good seeing to in daddy's caravan.

When *Daddy* and *Lottie* left, Jenny turned the telly off, and the house was quiet.

'Can ah ring me Nana?'

'Of course you can. Do you know her number?'

'Aye.'

She sat on the velvet chair next to the phone table in the echoey hallway. 'Hello?' It was Gavin, which was good as she might get some information out of him.

'Gav, it's Paula.'

'Alreet Paula, did yer hear about Billy?'

'Aye, well sort of, man, wot the fuck happened, ah heard his heed came off.'

'Wee telt yer that?'

'Doesn't matter wee telt uz, wot the fuck happened?'

'Ah dinnar the details like, but the rumour is that for some bizarre reason, he put a fishin line across the stairs, and he slipped, and it sliced his heed off.'

She did a full-body shiver.

'Paula, yer still there?'

'Aye, gan on. Tell uz again wot happened, slowly like.'

'Supposed ter have been proper gory like, blood all ower.'

She could hear Nana in the background saying, 'Knock it off, Gavin, the lass dissent want ter hear all of that.'

'Have yer seen David?' she asked before scuffles and then Nana.

'Hello pet, wot's the foster home like?' said Nana, trying to act like Billy hadn't been in a 'tragic accident', just like when she tried to act like Dad hadn't been sent to Cherry.

'It's brilliant here, ah've been horse ridin today.'

'Eeee, have yer, wee with?'

'A lass called Charlotte.'

She was on the phone for twenty minutes, which was much longer than she was allowed when Nana was paying for it. She said bye to Nana and then to Gavin, Laura-Jane, and Mark before Nana took the receiver, said bye again, and hung up. When she wandered into the kitchen, Jenny said that she should go to bed and read her book, and she was happy to go so she could be on her own and think about everything.

She lay on the bed and all was quiet, so she opened *Black Beauty*. '*To my mind, fashion is one of the wickedest things in the world.*' After reading the same line ten times, she gave up. Is setting a trap that *accidentally* kills someone murder? It's not like they planned to kill him; he fell down the stairs when he was palatic. The policeman on the news said that it wasn't suspicious, i.e. no murderer. Nana said that when Billy didn't turn up at the club all night, a couple of his mates called by the flat. The door was open, and when they went inside, the walls and ceilings where dripping with blood, and Billy's body was dangling above the top stairs, while his head was in the hall with its tongue hanging out. Both of his mates were prescribed pills for the shock, and the police said it was the most gruesome thing they'd ever seen. She wished that Dad had let her see the bloodbath and she wondered what he was doing now. Hopefully writing in his books and sending a sign to Casey Man that the coast was not clear. Sounded like the police were crawling all over the flat and that everything was well fucked up.

The light woke her up at 5:43 am. Her heart was racing and her hair was drarked with sweat. Felt like she'd been running all night away from all different things that she couldn't remember. She drifted off to sleep and then the slam of a car door made her jump a foot off the bed. It was 7:14 am.

She looked through the curtain, peering down to see a police car parked outside. The whole world fell out of her arse. They'd come for her. They'd figured it out, or they'd spoken to Dad who'd spilled the lot. Shaking and sweating, she hid under the covers and closed her eyes and thought about what she was going to say: she went to Peacock Street in the morning to have a bath and get some things and then she went to Nana's. She wouldn't mention Dad unless they mentioned him.

She listened hard to the men's voices below and couldn't make out what they were saying. They talked for ages and then she heard footsteps on the gravel and more talking. A car door slammed, and then another slammed, and the engine started, and the car drove away.

It was silent, apart from the hammering of her heart as she waited for the bedroom door to fly open and the police to drag her out of bed like Billy used to. He might be dead, but he wasn't gone, not until he was in the ground, or better still, in the incinerator, all evidence burning to a crisp. She thought about the arresting officers downstairs, sweating cobs at the fear of being thrown in the van and carted off to Durham prison.

There were footsteps on the landing. She closed her eyes and put her hands on her face. The footsteps faded, then more footsteps, then nothing. Time stood still, then,

'HOLY MOTHER OF FUCKING JESUS!'

She jumped up and snatched the door open to find Jenny, tears streaming down her face.

'Sorry,' said Jenny, 'I forgot you were in there.'

'Here-man, there's nee need ter apologise ter me. Wot's garn on?'

Jenny scurried off to the end of the landing and she followed her into a room painted yellow with a jungle scene covering a full wall. On the rug was a small lad playing with a wooden train.

'Choo-choo,' he said, pushing the train along.

'His arm,' said Jenny. Her face was bright red.

She bent down and said to him, 'Ah wer ganner have hods of fun at Jenny's house?'

His blue eyes lit up. 'Aye.'

'Ah'm Paula and wot's yowr name?'

'Danny.'

Then she saw what Jenny was talking about on his arm. Looked like a couple of ciggie burns.

'He'll be alreet, trust uz.' She held an arm out. 'Ah had one much worse than that, and look now, yer can hardly see it.'

Jenny's tears kept coming, 'Did Billy do that to you?'

'When ah woz eight. He arnly did it once, ah nivver give him the chance ter dee it again.'

'What kind of a shithouse does that to a child?' Jenny covered her mouth. 'I really mustn't swear.'

'Ah wouldn't worry, Danny boy'll have heard worse than that.' She picked the little lad up. 'Ha'way then rotten bottom, let's get yer changed.'

Jenny opened drawers and pulled out nappies. 'Will this fit?'

'How old are yer, Danny?'

'Free.'

'Eeee, there's a big lad for a nap-nap.'

Jenny waved a nappy in each hand, jaw flapping.

'Ah'll get this off him and stick him in the bath. Wer should put big boy pants on after that. Have yer gor a placker bag? Feels like there's a couple of chods in here.'

'You have experience with children, do you?'

'Why-aye man, ah've got two younger brothas.'

'How old were they when your mother potty trained them?'

'Here-man,' she laughed, 'if ah hadn't potty trained ower Ian, he'd still be in nappies now, and ah had ower Jason outta nappies as quick as cos there woz nee way ah woz wipin his shitty little arse if ah could help it.'

Jenny started crying again, so with stinky Danny on her hip, she left her to it and went to the bathroom and ran the bath. Danny reached for the bottle of blue bubble bath, 'Bubbas,' and despite the, at a guess, two-day-old nappy and seeping burns, he seemed like a happy enough kid. He'd fallen on his feet at Jenny's house.

Jenny appeared with a bag and a face that looked like it had had cold water splashed on it. 'Stick his trousers in there with the nappy.'

She took off his trousers and nappy all in one go and plopped them into the bag, then sat him on the netty. 'Danny dee a kacky?'

'You're a natural with children. Your mother must be proud of you. You must be a big help.'

Help, she wanted to say, I do *everything*, but she didn't because she didn't want Jenny to ask what Mam did most of the time.

'Yae gan and mack breakfast and ah'll sort Danny out. Der yer have any clays for him?'

'Are you sure? I shouldn't really leave a child with you.'

'Am ah sure?' she snorted. 'Why-aye.'

'Right then. I'll put some clothes out for him.'

She shooed Jenny out. 'Gan and mack breakfast.'

The table was laid with matching crockery and there was a cushion on a chair for Danny. He smelled of soap and looked like a little old man with his wet hair combed into a parting.

Jenny said, 'Orange or apple juice?'

'Orange please,' she said.

Danny reached out his hands, 'Oran jus.'

Jenny poured milk onto his cornflakes and then into his cup. 'Drink your milk first and then you can have some orange juice.'

When Jenny turned away, Danny poured his milk onto his cornflakes, and when she turned back and saw his empty cup, she said, 'Good boy,' and gave him some orange juice.

He didn't drink much before his head drooped forward.

'Ah'll tack him for a lie down, shall ah?'

'Would you? The bed is ready.'

On her way up, the phone rang, and she knew it was about her because Jenny said, 'Wait a second, could you?' Once she was upstairs, Jenny talked quietly.

Danny went out like a light, the poor little bugger. She stroked his face. 'Ah wish ah could kill the rotten essence wee did this ter yer son, but yer ah clever little lad, so ah reckon yer'll dee canny for yersel. Sleep tight, mind the bedbugs dinnet bite.' She kissed her fingers and pressed them on his forehead.

Jenny crept across the room like a burglar and whispered, 'Is he asleep?'

'Yer didn't need ter whisper, he's well gone.'

'That was the social worker on the phone, she'll be here for you in an hour.'

Her heart sank. 'Am ah gannen in a children's home?'

'No, good news, the council have found your family a house.' Jenny hugged her and she hugged her back because she loved her, not because of the *good news*. She hoped it wasn't a house in Marley Pots like where her mate had to move after her dad battered her mam.

She didn't think that saying goodbye to Jenny would be a moment of excruciating pain, but it was. She forced back tears with a melon in her throat like she used to when Billy was being a twat, only this felt good/bad, not bad/bad. As the growling Herbie car moved, she was too gutted to speak. She had no choice but to go wherever she was taken. It was going to be fine because she'd spent so much time standing in bus queues that she knew the routes; wherever she was dumped, she'd get the bus into town and up to Dad's.

She was pleased when they headed south over the river past the two faces of Casey Man on the *Echo* tower, still silent with no message to give. She prepared herself for a maisonette down the Villa pop factory end of Pallion, near to Donna Hepburn and her licky-arse mates. Things started looking up when they turned off along Springwell Road and went past Broadway School. They went across the lights at the Prospect and then turned off Premier Road. They stopped in Powis Road. She had mates on this road who she envied because it was walking distance to school. 'Is this it?' she said, excited.

The social worker pointed to a lovely house. Since Billy had died, things kept getting better and better, so she made an effort to act sad. Mam answered the door, white with red eyes, her cheeks blue and hollow as she tugged on a fag. The social worker let her go first into a nice living room that smelled of paint.

Mam sat on a brand-spanking-new settee with her head in one hand and a fag in the other while David gave her a shoulder hug, head down, face in hand. When he looked up, he had tears in his eyes, which made her panic because David *never* cries, so something bad must've happened.

'How are you, Mrs Hart?' said the social worker.

'Copin,' said Mam who looked ten years older than when she was running up the street three days ago.

David sniffed and hugged Mam. 'Yer can gan now,' he said to the social worker.

'Right,' said the social worker. 'If yer need anythin, yer have the number of the person to call?'

'Aye,' said David.

'Ah'll let myself out.'

When the Herbie engine rumbled, David dropped his arm from Mam's shoulder and said, 'Ahhh! Did me crocodile tears have yer garn?'

'Nor,' she said, batting his slappy hand from her cheek.

'And nivver mind me Oscar performance,' said David, 'wot the fuck's that dress? Yer look like summink outta the Little House on the Prairie.'

'And nivver mind everythin, wot the fuck happened ter Billy?' she replied.

'Mind yer gob,' said Mam. 'Ah'm a widow now and ah deserve some respect.'

David's eyes twinkled with delight. 'Wot have yer heard?'

'That his heed came off.'

'Oh, here-man,' said David, 'he'd done this fishin line thing and made a noose and wrote a suicide note.'

'He wozn't tryin ter kill himsel,' Mam snorted. 'Ah knar wot he's like, he'll of been tryin ter mack out he was depressed ter get more benefits. Dickie's wife from the club gets thirty pund a month for bein depressed.'

'Does she?' said David in amazement.

'Wot did the notesay?' she asked as if she didn't know.

'Dunnar,' said Mam, 'ah'm waitin for his stuff ter be released.'

'From where?' she said.

'There has to be an autopsy,' said David.

'Wot like on *Quincy*?' she said.

'Aye, like that.'

She hoped it wasn't Dr R Quincy doing the autopsy as he'd easily figure out what had happened.

'Wer cannet bury him till they release his body,' said Mam.

'Wot about his heed?' she said.

Mam and David creased with laughter. 'Shhh,' said Mam, waving her arm, 'stop laughin will yers, the bairns have lost their dad.'

'Here-man, Paula, did yer hear how they found him?' said David.

'Nor, nee one's telt uz owt.'

'Macca and Den went lookin for him and when he didn't answer, they pushed the door open and the whole fucken place woz red wer blood and Billy's heed woz on the deck.'

'It rolled down the stairs,' said Mam, 'after it woz sliced off.'

'How the fuck did the daft bastard manage ter dee that ter himsel?' she asked.

David and Mam shook their heads.

'Dunnar,' said David. 'They reckon he woz tryin ter hang himsel.'

'Mack it look like he woz tryin ter hang himsel,' said Mam.

'Aye, Mam, but your tack on it dissn't mack any sense. He could've pretended ter hang himsel without the fishin lines.'

'Mebees he woz ganner use the fishin lines, then he realised it woz a shite idea, so then he got the rope. He woz a sackless twat,' said Mam.

This was topper. She hoped the police were having the same debate rather than looking for a murderer. 'Have yers spoken ter the police?' she asked.

'Aye pet, ah telt them everythin ah knar,' said Mam. 'Ah said he wozn't the sort ter kill himsel and the police said it didn't look like he wanted tee. They ses it woz a cry for help.'

'A cry ter scam the nash outta thirty quid a month more like,' said David.

'Aye,' said Mam, 'ah telt the police that he woz a reet scrounger.'

David raised his brow. 'Have yae spoken ter the pigs yet, sis?'

'They came to the foster home. Ah telt them that Billy was a reet piss artist.'

Mam and David nodded.

'Honestly David, yer should've seen the house they sent uz tee. There was a Pye Redbox in the kitchen.'

'Nor,' he said, 'they must be loaded.'

'Well, this house'll be a come down for yer now yerv seen how the other half live,' said Mam.

'Is this ower house?' she said. 'Or are wer just here till they clean up the blood down Pallion?'

'Three bairns and a husband wer nee heed,' said Mam, 'strite ter the top of the housin list.'

'Ah live here now?'

'Why-aye yer live here. Der yer wanna see yer bedroom? It's done out all modern.'

It was a nice normal house and not a horrible maisonette. The living room, stairs, and bedroom had a plain carpet that looked like biscuit. There wasn't a swirly pattern or faded shade of gold to be seen. Her bedroom was tiny with grey and pink striped wallpaper and a continental quilt on the bed. She lay face down and stretched her arms and legs out like a starfish. She couldn't believe what Dad had done. For the unseeing eye, he was a madman writing on the wall, but look how the stratagem had worked out. She wondered if Dad had planned to kill Billy. Was madness and brilliance the same thing?

Mam barged in, and with the usual reflex reaction, she jumped to her feet.

'He'yar,' said Mam, dumping some C&A bags on the bed. 'Yer Aunty Pat got yer these.'

Aunty Pat worked at C&A and gave her all of the clothes she had. 'Will ah be gettin me jeans back from the washin basket at Peacock Street?'

Mam laughed and said, 'Nor, they're problees covered in blood.'

'Ah thought he died on the stairs?'

'Aye but the blood from his neck was like a volcano eruptin – hit the ceilin and everythin. Police said every room woz covered,' said Mam.

She laughed. 'How did the daft twat manage that?'

'Dinnet speak ill of the deed. Ah knar *we* winnet miss him, but the bairns will; he woz their dad.'

'Where are they?' she asked, emptying the goodies from Aunty Pat onto the bed.

'Through Hetton.'

'Nana Hart must be gutted that her son die– oooo, that's nice,' she said at the cerise pink batwing jumper, 'Sonya's got one of these.'

'She's lost her son so she's proper gutted like. Ian and Jason are tackin her mind off it.'

'How long are they stayin?'

'Till yae gan ter Hetton and pick them up. Yer can get the Easington Lane bus from Durham Road.'

'Nor, ah'm not garn, ah dinnet knar Billy's family.'

'Yer dinnet think of nee one else but yersel, der yer? Have a squiy at all of this,' said Mam, opening her arms to take in the room and the new clothes. 'Ah give yer *everythin* and yer cannet even dee me one little favour.'

David was lying, feet up, on the new settee, watching the telly. 'It's got a remote control,' he said. 'Look.' He pointed the remote control at the telly and pressed the button, making it change channel. 'Billy should fucken cark it more often. This is ellish.'

'Wot yer deein here?' she said.

'Wot d'yer mean, am ah not welcome?'

'Nor, ah mean where's Dad, and wot about Lisa? Are yers still together?'

'Ah came here ter look after Mam till yer got back.'

'Where's Dad? Shouldn't yer be at his?'

'Oh aye, ah thought it'd be all be my fault,' he said, sitting up and turning the telly off with the remote control.

'Wot's your fault?'

David had his serious face on. 'Dinnet gan off on one.'

'Wot's garn on David?'

'Dad's back in Cherry.'

'Fuck.'

'And his house burnt down.'

'WOT?'

David gave her yesterday's *Echo* with Billy splashed all over the front page. 'Page three,' he said.

Chapter 6

September 1985

On the first day back of her fifth and final year of the seniors, she walked to school with kids from her new road. They all knew about Billy and after a few hushes and nudges, she turned to the group behind. 'Are yers whisperin about me stepdar like?'

'Uz heard his heed was chopped off,' said Lee from her class. 'Yer dinnet have ter talk about it, if it's too upsettin like.'

'Nar, it's fine. He woz me stepdar and ah didn't like him,' she said. 'The rozzers haven't telt uz much, der yers knar owt?'

'Me mam's mate said that the blood spurted so hard that it made a hole in the wall,' said Melanie with the lazy eye.

'They reckon his heed woz still alive for eight minutes after it came off his body,' said Lee.

'Wee telt yer that?' said lanky Trevor from the sixth form. 'A couple of seconds mebees, but not minutes like.'

'Der yer reckon his body ran about like a heedless chicken?' said Melanie with the lazy eye.

'Nor,' said Lee, 'his body woz hangin from the fishin lines.'

'Ah bet it woz twitchin like fuck,' said lanky Trevor, so Lee did an impression of a twitching corpse.

This was ellish, not only because she wanted to hear more gossip about Billy, but also because it overshadowed Dad being picked up by the police for running down the Broadway in his bare feet while his house was on fire. There was a picture of his burnt-out house on page three of the *Echo*, yet no one said a thing. MAN ESCAPES BLAZE. The *Echo* said that the neighbours smelled smoke and the occupant managed to escape before the blaze took hold. Nothing about the occupant legging it in a psychotic stupor. It was mostly about how the firemen fought the fire and how nothing was left and how it was started by a ciggie.

As they walked down Bede bank the chat moved on to Jackie from Fawcett, who was up the duff to a lad from Seaham who was a total headcase, which was a shame because Jackie was a canny lass. As they got closer to school, the yellow double-deckers spilled swarms of schoolies at the top gate and she could tell the first years from the others because their Adidas bags were the same size as them and weren't covered in graffiti. They were also smiling, which wouldn't last long at this hellhole.

She hadn't even got as far as her form room when Andrea, head of the Ettrick mafia and hardest lass in the school, stopped her. She had five lasses walking behind her. You don't mess with Andrea, not after she kicked the shit out of a seventeen-year-old lad in the bus station.

'Dinnet look so worried,' said Andrea. 'Ah like yer.'

She didn't speak and Andrea's gang made a circle around her.

'Ah heard about yer stepdar like, and uz have agreed if anyone ses owt ter yer, yae tell me, and ah'll fucken bray them.' Andrea was smiling instead of snarling like a Doberman.

'Ta,' she said, expecting Andrea to laugh, say only kidding, and punch her.

'Ah heard his heed came off,' said Andrea.

The deal was Andrea wanted gory details in exchange for protection, so she told her gang about how Billy's head lived for eight minutes and that his body ran about like a headless chicken. By the end, Andrea was her best mate because she hated her own stepdad and would love the same thing to happen to him.

*

On the third day back, she had double PE before dinner. She didn't have a gym skirt, her PE top was titty-tight, and she hated PE, so she'd decided not to do it at all this year. It would take the school a few weeks to realise that she'd been dollen, and by then she'd be sixteen so she could tell them to fuck off, and leave.

After break, she headed off, and as she passed the hall, the top door of the upper school was blocked with kids trying to come in and kids trying to get out, and the stairs were so packed nothing was moving. When radgie Brian from the fourth year saw the crowd, he ran and jumped on it, crushing the kids on the stairs and sending books and calculators flying as he punched and kicked, body-surfing his way down. A tiny ginger lass emerged from the crush, crawling on her knees and searching for her gegs. When she put them on, the lass looked at her as if to say, 'Is this what it's always like?' She looked back as if to say, 'Only another five years of horror to go.'

She walked swiftly out of the back gate into Barnes Park and out of the bottom gate of the park onto Colchester Terrace. She walked along to St Gabriel's and then along Kayle Road. She couldn't resist going back to have a look at the maisonette and she wanted to have a look at Dad's burnt-out house. She had an eery feeling that Dad might have left a sign, a note, or something to tell her what was going on. She was glad that he was in Cherry as he'd be safe there and she agreed with David not to go and see him, not because she couldn't, but because she didn't want to jog his mind of the stratagem – who knows what he saw that day and what state of mind he was in now? He could tell them everything. She'd wait before going to visit. Like David said, he'll be so full of drugs that he'll not know what planet he's on.

As she walked down Peacock Street West, she stayed on the Steels side of the road and kept her head down, avoiding eye contact with anyone, until Dawn and Gail's Mam, Margaret, pulled the net curtain back and waved. She'd been rumbled so she thought there was no harm in getting a closer look at the maisonette. The windows and doors were boarded-up with metal and there were no splats of flesh and no police notices. It looked like any other boarded-up flat. Margaret was outside and waving to her to come over.

'Eee luv, how are yer? Ha'way inside.'

Margaret's flat smelled of fish.

'Ah've got some fish fingers under the grill. Owr Dawn'll be home soon. Der yer want some? Ah can hoy another couple under?'

'Aye, gan on then, ta.'

Margaret put two more fish fingers under the old-fashioned grill that was at the perfect height to see your food and get hot fat spat in your eye. 'Can yer put some bread on the chabble?' said Margaret.

She emptied the end of the sliced loaf onto the top plate from the pile and put it on the table. 'Did yer hear wot happened ter ower Billy?' she said, setting out the other plates.

The fish fingers spat as Margaret poked them with a fork. 'Yer arnly need ter set two plates, ower Gail's at Dewhirst's now.'

'Is she?'

There was a clatter of door and feet as Dawn, who was in the fourth year at Pennywell, got home for dinner.

'Hiya, Paula. Wot yer deein here? Eeeeee, wot about yowr Billy?'

'Aye, ah knar. Did yer see owt?'

Margaret yanked the grill pan out and wafted it at head level, causing them both to duck as she launched fish fingers onto the plates. 'Dawn, can yer get the marge out?'

While Dawn went to the fridge, Margaret said, 'Ah'm watchin yer knar, for the murderer.'

'Mam, shurrup, soz but she's got it in her heed that Billy woz murdered. Ah telt her it woz an accident,' said Dawn, putting the marge and ketchup on the table.

'Wot ah dinnet understand,' said Margaret, 'is why he would kill himsel? Ah mean, he wozn't the type. Ah reckon it woz a clivver hoax and he woz actually murdered.'

Her blood ran cold. 'Dinnet talk daft man, it woz an accident.'

'Mam, dinnet,' said Dawn. 'She's been at the winda since it happened, she's convinced the murderer's ganner show up.'

'Murderers always return to the scene of the crime,' said Margaret. 'Der yer knar when the funeral is? Yer need to be lookin for anyone suspicious, someone shifty like.'

She was glad to get out of there even if it was interesting hearing about Gail who was a machinist at Dewhirst's. Dawn said that Gail finished school before starting in the factory, but that there were hods of lasses who left school early. Margaret had peeled herself away from the window long enough to show her the brochures of the hotel in Benidorm where Gail was going on holiday now that she was earning a few bob.

As she turned the corner into Pickering Square, she could smell burn. David was spot-on when he said that the house was destroyed and the picture in the paper didn't do it justice. All the windows were charred holes with nothing beyond but darkness, and the roof was naked timbers that were charred and black. The door was boarded up with metal and police tape like something you see on the news.

She ventured down the path when Maureen came out. 'Hiya, luv. Shockin isn't it?'

Maureen stepped back inside and fully opened her door, so she hopped over the wall and went in. Maureen hugged her. 'Ah'm sorry, pet. Nee one woz hurt though, that's the main thing.'

'Did yer see wot happened?' she said.

Maureen filled the kettle and then lit the cooker with a long match. She blew out the match and shook her head. 'The neet it happened, me and Jack watched the news and went ter bed at half-ten, and wer weren't asleep long when wer heard sirens like getting louder and then deafenin, and then the bedroom's flashin wer blue lights. Outside wer can see smoke, and then there's a bang on the door.'

'Shit, then wot?'

'A fireman telt uz ter get out, so ah ran out in me nighty, and Jack put his big coat on, and wer stood on the other side of the square and a policeman put a blanket rund us. There were three fire engines.'

'Shit.'

'All of the windas were gone by that point, and there woz flames comin out and the heat made everythin look wobbly,' reported Maureen.

'Like standin next ter a bonfire?'

'Nor luv, much hotter than a bonfire and ah've nivver smelt owt like it in me life.'

'Then wot happened?'

'The police got everyone outta their houses and made us all get outta the square.'

'Shit. Must've been terrifyin man. Woz everyone in their nighties?'

The kettle whistled and Maureen poured the water into a blue teapot and coughed. 'Air still tastes smoky in here, gets on yer chest.'

'Are they ganner rehouse you and Jack?'

'If arnly. Wouldn't mind being nearer ter ower Deborah.'

'Wot through Chester-le-Street? Won't Jack miss the club?'

'Oh luv, me and Jack are shufflin along the perch. Mebees the fire woz a blessin. Brought up two bairns in this house but ah'm ready for a bungalow.' Maureen gave her a mug. 'The neet of the fire, the police evacuated us. Should ah seen the look on Deborah's face when me and Jack turned up smelling of smoke.'

'Ah can imagine. Wot's Deborah deein now? Is she still workin for Rumbelows?'

'Aye, she's a manager.'

'Eee well that's canny.'

'She's a clivver lass ower Deborah.

Unlike her unmentionable son, who was doing a stretch for aggravated burglary, Maureen was never happier than when talking about Deborah. She was keen to ask more about the night of the fire and whether she'd seen Dad jumping fences, but there was no stopping Maureen when she was talking about Deborah. Sounded like she had a mint job and a lovely house and she had a timeshare, whatever that was.

After drinking the last drip and last last drip, she put her cup on the bench. 'Ah best be off, nice speakin ter yer though, Maureen.'

'Eee luv, yer welcome here anytime.'

As she opened the back door to let herself out, Maureen shuffled off and came back with a black bin bag. 'Jack found this in the hedge. Looks like a few things that Eddie grabbed as he ran.'

She glanced inside and knew that it wasn't a bag of stuff that he'd grabbed as he fled. It was his sacred belongings to be spared the flames.

'They say the fire woz started by a ciggie that got ower close ter some newspaper,' said Maureen.

'Here-man, ah woz always warnin him about fallin asleep with a fag.'

'He's deein canny now, though? They lookin after him in Cherry?'

'Aye, he's deein canny,' she said because it was easiest.

'Give him me luv will yer, pet?'

'Aye, see yer then.'

She made it out of the square before sitting on a wall and delving into the bin bag: 1937 FA Cup Final Football Echo, 1973 FA Cup Final Football Echo, 1973 FA Cup Final Wembley programme, 1967 Football Echo, 'Bobby Kerr's goals shoots down the Magpies.' TDK C90 with the best of The Beach Boys taped on it, a photograph of Dad, David, and her in front of the silver Christmas Tree in Thorney Close in 1974, and a tin of Ambrosia creamed rice.

*

When the postie knocked and gave her a brown parcel with her name and address on the front, she didn't know what it was. She'd never got a parcel before, or a letter. She ripped it open to find brand new jodhpurs and a red polo-neck jumper, a Body Shop bath set, and a book. She loved Jenny. There was a letter sealed with Sellotape and marked as highly confidential.

Dear Paula,
I hope that your new house is great and that your mam and brothers are doing fine. I don't know why I am writing this letter as there is nothing going on here to tell you about. I didn't tell you about what happened with John from the caravan park – not that there is anything much to tell you. On the first night at the disco in the clubhouse (would not be seen dead there, only I went to see him), he kept following a girl who looked about seventeen – as if she would go out with him! I decided that I didn't fancy him, so I stayed in the caravan all week and read both Adrian Mole books (v. good).

School is v. boring, how about you? When do you break up for half-term? Can you come to the stables? You could get the Newcastle train. Write back and send your phone number. Mine is at the top of this letter.

I have to go now and revise for a history exam (yawn, yawn).

TTFN, Charlotte. xx

Mam was in bed and the boys were at Nana Hart's in Hetton, so she took the chance to give Charlotte a call. Her heart raced as she dialled her number.

'Hello?'

She was pleased it was Charlotte.

'Hiya Charlotte, it's Paula. Ah got yer letter and can yer thank yer mam for the gorgeous clays.'

'Nice to speak to you Paula, only I'm on my way out to school.'

'Ah'll not keep yer, but ah woz wonderin wot time ah should come ter the stables at half-term?'

'Oh, yes, come on the first Monday at about ten. Will be great to see you, lots to tell, must dash, Mummy's waiting in the car.'

'See yer at half-term, bye.'

'Can't wait, bye, bye, bye.'

She couldn't wait to horse ride again and she didn't know what she was going to do with herself between now and Monday 21st October.

*

It was ellish to have two choices of outfit for Billy's funeral: riding boots, jodhpurs, and red polo neck with Aunty Pat's black suit jacket over the top, or black patent leather kitten heels, black skirt and cerise batwing jumper with Aunty Pat's black suit jacket over the top. She couldn't wait for his coffin to roll into the fire – she'd been shitting herself for weeks, expecting the police to take her to prison. Only Dad knew the truth, and he was in Cherry, so if he spills the beans, they'd probably think he was being mental.

The funeral cars were leaving from Nana Hart's house and she'd taken the boys there on the bus last night. Nana Hart's house was nice and Billy's family were canny, but his brother looked the double of him, which made her shudder. She was still in bed when Uncle Bobby came to pick Mam up and drop off Aunty Pat's black suit jacket.

Mam shouted, 'Ger owt of yer pit and get ready. David will be here in half an hour,' then slammed the front door.

The bath, sink, and loo in the maisonette were the same shade of pink as the lumps in sick and were made from plastic, whereas in the new house, they were white and made from pottery, and there was a shower on the wall in the bath. Mam banned toys from the bathroom and put a basket of shampoo and soap on the windowsill and a pile of fresh towels on the shelf. It was brilliant that Billy was dead and soon buried. Horse riding at half-term: bonus. And no one could stop her because no one knew about it.

David arrived with Lisa in her dad's shitty Yugo.

Lisa gave her a hug and a kiss. 'Yae ready?'

Lisa was lovely and she was glad that she loved David, although God knows why.

'Where's the stuff from the pigs?' said David, striding into the living room.

She pointed at the bag on the floor.

'It's lovely in here,' said Lisa, flopping in the armchair. 'Smells all new.'

David read from Billy's death certificate, 'Cause of death, misadventure.'

'Wot does that mean?' said Lisa.

'It means that he was too much of a sackless twat ter kill himsel proper like.'

'Eee, dinnet speak ill of the deed,' said Lisa, 'not on the day of his funeral.'

'Wot the fuck's this?' said David, holding the clear bag with the suicide note in it. 'I am leavin and never comin back.' David read from the tea-box lid. 'Fucken stupid twat.'

The part about *blame Maggie* had been ripped off and she wondered who'd done it, probably the police. When she thought about Billy being denied his final words that weren't even his own, she burst out laughing.

'It's not that funny like,' said David.

'Oh, it is.' This would be her private joke forever.

'Yer ready then, sis?'

David floored the Yugo down Houghton cut. The traffic was slow past the Burn pub and crawled all the way to Hetton-le-Hole before it stopped. David wound down his window.

'Here-man, can yer hear that?'

'Brass band,' said Lisa.

'That'll be why wer stopped. Colliery band procession. Aye-up, here's the flatties,' said David.

When a police motorbike pulled on each side of the car, she shit a brick, thinking they'd come for her because like Margaret said, they knew the murderer would be at the funeral. It said on the news and in the paper that the police weren't treating his death as suspicious and maybe this was part of the ploy to smoke the murderer out. There might be an undercover team looking out for anyone shifty in the church.

As they sat in the traffic with the sound of a brass band getting nearer, she asked. 'Wot's happenin with Dad? When did yer last see him?'

'The other day,' said David, giving nothing away.

'Is he still drugged up ter the eyeballs?'

'Yer haven't telt her, have yer?' said Lisa.

'Telt uz wot?'

'Dad's outta Cherry,' said David.

'Eh? But he burned his house down. Doesn't that get yer life?'

'Wot macks yer think he burned the house down?' said David, whipping his head round and looking her in the eye.

'Nowt, he's just mental, that's all.'

'Aye, but he would nivver torch his memorabilia,' said David.

'The firemen said it woz a fag,' said Lisa.

'How come he's outta Cherry?' she asked David.

He punched the steering wheel, and Lisa said, 'Dinnet, just dinnet. Remember wot ah telt yer about punchin stuff.'

'Is he alreet?' she asked Lisa.

'Nor,' said David. 'Ah'm not.'

Lisa leaned through the gap in the front seats, 'There's a new care in the community thing where they look after yer in a house instead of in hospital.'

David punched the steering wheel again, and Lisa said, 'Wot have a telt yer about punchin stuff?'

The drumming and trumpeting got louder and cars on both sides of the road pulled up on the kerb to let the marching band pass by. They were dressed in black suits with red trims and their cheeks went in and out as they puffed into shiny twisted tubes, fingers pushing pistons, legs marching in time. It kept coming for ages, and as the drum thumped off down the road, it all went quiet and a long black car with the coffin floated past followed by six black cars of weeping people dressed in black. Lisa put her head down and did the cross thing, and David said,

'Wot yer fucken deein? The bloke woz a twat.'

'Eeee, dinnet speak ill of the deed,' said Lisa, crossing herself a few more times.

'Should wer park down that street and walk?' she said, keen to get to the church and mingle like a non-murderer with the other non-murders.

'Yous can,' said David, 'Ah'll pick yers up after.'

'Are yer not comin like?'

'Haddaway and shite,' he laughed, 'Mam said yer needed a lift, nowt about me garn in the church. Ah'm glad the cunt's deed.'

Lisa punched him in the arm and crossed herself a few more times.

It hadn't occurred to her that she didn't have to go to the funeral and that no one would notice if she wasn't there.

'If you're not garn,' she said, 'then ah'm not garn.'

'Ah'm not bothered,' said Lisa.

'For fuck's sake,' said David, pulling a U-turn in the standstill traffic. The atmosphere was tense as he ragged the Yugo until he hit Houghton cut and they nearly had to get out and push it up the hill.

When they stopped at the Board Inn roundabout, she dared speak. 'Ah yer ganner tell uz wot's garn on wer Dad or wot?'

Lisa grabbed his arm, 'Dinnet punch owt.'

'Yer said he's in a house?'

As they crossed the roundabout, David put his foot down, sending her flying backwards followed by tapes, fags, and a tube of eczema cream that hit her in the face. He drove like a tit up Durham Road, stopped only by a red light at the Prospect. Lisa turned around and put her finger on her lip, so she clung on and kept quiet as David drove like a twat, screeching to a stop outside her house.

She was out of the car quickly, and Lisa came to the kerb and gave her a hug, which was lovely, apart from it was only to distract her from David, who was punching the steering wheel and sounding the horn, which made people come to their windows.

'Wot's garn on?' she asked Lisa.

Lisa shrugged. 'Dinnar exactly, but they've moved yer dad down Hendon. Ah said ter Dave that that's a good thing, aye?'

'Whereabouts down Hendon?' she said. 'Is he there now?' Before Lisa could answer, she was back in the car. 'Where's Dad?'

'Amberley Street,' said David.

'Why didn't yer tell uz, yer fucken twat.'

'He's arnly just moved there.'

'Ha'way then, foot on the pedal, let's gan,' she said.

Amberley Street had Victorian red-brick terraced houses on both sides. David stopped the car.

'Looks nice,' she said.

David and Lisa's faces appeared in the gap between the front seats.

'It's not nice rund here,' said David.

'Keep yer heed down,' said Lisa.

For someone from Pennywell to call an area rough was a worry.

David locked the car, then she followed him to the front door, which was opened by an old bloke in a white trilby hat and red cravat. It was much bigger inside than what it looked on the outside. It was slummy and smelled like a five-day-old grill pan. They covered their noses as they made their way along the corridor and up the stairs. The landing was dark and smelled of piss. David knocked on a door and they could hear movement inside. Lisa hugged her. After there was no answer to his second knock, David booted the door open, sending spelks flying. 'Ah telt them not ter put a lock on it,' he said, stepping inside.

The high ceiling and bay window made it feel huge, although it was small and seedy with a nasty patterned carpet and walls that hadn't been painted for decades. There was a single bed pushed against one wall and a kitchen unit in the corner with a kettle on the bench and a sink full of dishes.

David stuck his head under the bed. 'Dad, ower Paula's here ter see yer.' There was shuffling, then nothing. David stepped away from the bed and said to her, 'Ah telt yer wot it would be like.'

Lisa was bright red and quivering like a pan of milk on the hob.

'Wot?' said David.

'So wer supposed ter come down here every day?' said Lisa.

'Yae dinnet have ter come down here, ah've telt yer that a million times,' David replied.

'So wot like, ah'm sat at home while yae here bein Eddie's minder?'

'Carer.'

'It's not yower job.' said Lisa.

'It shouldn't be,' said David, 'but wot can ah dee?'

Lisa glanced at the bed. 'Wot the fuck der wer dee now?'

'There's nee point coaxin him out,' said David. 'Wer might as well get off home.'

She looked at the peeling paint and rancid carpet. 'And leave him in this shit pit?'

'Got any better ideas?'

'Ah could stay with him for a bit,' she said.

'Be my guest,' said David.

'Nor nah,' said Lisa. 'Paula's nivver seen him like this before.'

'Der yer want her ter help or not?' said David.

'Aye.'

'Reet then sis, he's all yowers. There's a phone box at the end of the road if yer need owt. We'll be down tomorra.'

'Ah'm gannen home later,' she said, 'Mam thinks ah've been at the funeral.'

'Oh aye, forgot about that. Well, if yer can stay as long as yer can, that'd be topper.' David gave her a hug, which was weird. If he'd given her a dead arm of approval, that would've been normal.

'Are yer sure yerl be alreet?' said Lisa.

'Nor,' she shrugged. 'Why have they tossed him outta Cherry again?'

'Ask the fucken Tory bastards,' said David, swinging an arm that Lisa tried to grab too late to stop him punching the wall.

'Why dinnet yers gan?' she said.

'Thanks, Paula, yer knar for stayin,' said Lisa, giving her a hug and a kiss.

Lisa was lovely and David had done well to go out with her for over a year. It was like having a big sister, but she supposed that Lisa had so many sisters it was natural for her to act that way.

When they'd gone, she took off her kitten heels, kneeled down, and looked under the bed. 'Dad, it's me, wot yer deein under there?'

She could see him curled up like a cat and she would've crawled under and snuggled up to him if it hadn't been so thick of dust. She didn't know what to do, so she sang:

'Whisht! lads haad yer gobs, an ah'll tell
yer awl an awful story,
whisht! lads haad yer gobs, an ah'll tell
yer abowt the worm.
One Sunda morn young Lambton went
a-fishin in the Wear,
an catched a fish upon is hewk, e thowt
looked vary queer.
But wot kind a fish it woz, young
Lambton cudn't tell,

he waddn't fash ter carry it hyem, so he
hoyed it doon a well.
Whisht! lads haad yer gobs, an ah'll tell
yer awl an awful story,
whisht! lads haad yer gobs, an ah'll tell
yer abowt the worm.'

She only knew one verse and the chorus and she sang them until she couldn't bear it anymore and then sang 'Wake Me Up Before You Go-Go', which she knew all the words to.

Dad showed no signs of shifting from under the bed, so she made herself useful by picking up the shit from the floor – clothes, ashtrays, newspapers, food wrappers. She did the washing up without hot water, washing-up liquid, or a dishclout. There wasn't a radio, never mind a telly. The bare lightbulb was dim and flickered.

She kneeled down and peered under the bed. 'Ah'm off now. Ah'll be back tomorra wer Monopoly and some pens.'

Dad didn't move, but she could hear him breathing. She'd rather him under the bed than pacing the floor and talking to the man in the moon. The purple Venetian blind hung at an angle halfway up the window and the cords were so tangled that after jiggling them she ended up pulling them tighter. She turned the light off and left.

It was dark and spitting-on outside and if she'd known this morning that she'd be pelting along a road in Hendon, she'd have worn the riding outfit. She decided that she wasn't going to school tomorrow because she was going to look after Dad.

Chapter 7

October 1985

She perched on the windowsill in the corridor with Sonya and Michelle while the form teacher walked up and down looking for faces to mark in the register. In the second week of term, he gave up trying to get a class of thirty-seven to sit quietly while he called out names. He realised that he got much less jip by letting everyone do what they liked. As soon as he'd seen her face and ticked his list, she ran out of the building and out of the bottom front gate, along with at least ten others, all of them in younger years, so as a fifth year who was about to leave, she was low priority. Anyway, fuck school, she had to look after Dad.

She'd heard about Hendon but hadn't been there before Dad moved to Amberley Street. Nana and Grandar talked a lot about growing up in the East End, which was the main place to live in the olden days when estates like Plains Farm and Town End Farm were actual farms. Hendon was now the roughest part of Sunderland, which made her mate from school laugh because she was born in Hendon in London, which she said was really posh.

She came out of the bus station and headed to the big WHSmiths on High Street, not the small one next to the train station. She didn't know how much Monopoly cost, but probably more than 30p. She loved WHSmiths. Downstairs first, starting with pencil cases, pencils, pens, and rubbers in the shape of Swiss rolls that smelled like Swiss rolls. She held a cherry-shaped rubber to her nose and the smell took her back to the juniors and Rochelle White's collection of smelly rubbers and sparkly pencils.

Upstairs, past the globes, and the textbooks, there was a wall of games, including all the ones she wished she had when she was a kid, especially Mousetrap, which Sonya said took forever to set-up. On a separate display was a stack of long red boxes with one propped up showing MONOPOLY across the front and the top-hat man poking through the O. The box was bright red and dazzling white, not like the one from Dad's, which was battered and covered in tea stains and fag burns. She took a box of Monopoly downstairs and queued at the till at the front of the shop. It was busy and people were coming in and out and a girl with a pushchair and screaming baby was struggling with the door, so she stepped forward and helped her inside. In the commotion, she slipped out of the shop and along

High Street, her heart pounding, expecting a heavy hand to grab her shoulder and drag her to the ground. She passed Littlewoods with the game under her arm as if she'd bought it and forgot to put it in a bag. As she passed Joplings, still no hand on her shoulder, and by the time she'd crossed the busy junction at the Mowbray, she knew she'd got away with it.

She passed the house with the YMCA letters vertically down the front and carried on for ages down Toward Road. She imagined what the grand, four-storey town houses looked like eighty years ago when rich Edwardian families lived there. They probably didn't think that their grand drawing rooms overlooking Mowbray Park would become run-down bedsits for poor people.

Standing in the road outside of Dad's was a skinny woman with long bleached hair and three-inch black roots. She nipped inside. Dad's room door was as she'd left it last night; jammed and twisted from where David had kicked it in. Nothing inside had changed apart from Dad had come out from under the bed. He was wearing cut-off denim shorts and he was gurning and sweating. He had a full beard and tash and his hair was wild. She'd never seen him this bad before.

'Monopoly?' she said hopefully. She held up the gleaming red and white box. 'Brand new.' She opened it. 'Look, the money's nivver been touched and the car is all shiny.'

'They're comin yer knar,' he said.

'Wee's comin?'

'There it is,' he said, listening. His eyes were closed and he swayed gently, smiling, floating on a peaceful journey, until a furrow gripped his brow. He crouched and put his ear to the bunged-up-with-dust air vent under the window.

There was a loud sniff and she turned to see a gadgie standing in the half-open door. He was thin with shaggy hair and buck teeth.

'Jeff,' he announced.

'Nice ter meet yer, Jeff.'

Q: What do you do if you are in a room with two loonies?

A: Sing George Michael's 'Careless Whisper'.

She knew all of the words from *Smash Hits*. As she sang, Dad grimaced and gazed, every so often bending down to receive messages through the clogged air-vent, while Jeff lingered and shuffled from foot-to-foot. She knew most of the words to 'Hopelessly Devoted to You' from *Grease*, so she sang that and then she did 'Maggon the Dragon', and then the first verse and chorus of 'Oh Little Town of Bethlehem'. By now she was lying on the bed looking at the high yellow ceiling, and she wished Jeff would bugger off because he smelled of pittle.

After half an hour, she couldn't sing anymore, and she was starving. She had 30p, which wouldn't get her much at the shop, and there was nothing to eat at Dad's, not even a tin of beans. She searched the likely places he might have put some dosh and found 5p in an empty fag packet and 2p in his jeans. She could get two packets of crisps for 37p.

'Ha'way, Jeff,' she said, 'are yer comin with uz?'

She stepped out of Dad's room and jammed the door shut.

Jeff said, 'Jeff,' and started following her until she bolted as fast as she could down the stairs and out of the front door. The skinny woman with the black roots was still in the road and a group of bairns were biting off bits of ice pop and flinging them at her.

As she made her way up to the main road in search of a corner shop, she spotted a phone box. She was going to ring David to ask when he was going to get here, but the phone box was smashed up and stunk of shit, and anyway, she was too hungry to spend 10p on the phone.

When she got back from the shop, the skinny woman was gone, and the bairns were playing footy with a hacky tennis ball. Dad was at the window peering down, eyes darting from side to side like an Eagle Eye Action Man. She crept up the stairs, eager not to alert Jeff.

'Ah got yer this,' she said to Dad, waving the Football *Echo* that she'd half-inched from the shop. The headline was 2-2 and Casey Man was neither happy nor sad.

'Look, it's a sign from Casey Man. He ses that Billy's been cremated and nee one knars owt about how he died,' she said.

Dad moved cautiously away from the window, grabbed the paper, stuck it under his armpit, then went back to the window.

'Lion Bar?'

He screwed his face.

'Ah knar wot yer mean, ah wanted a Double Decker but they wer ower close to the counter.'

He was muttering and she couldn't understand what he was saying. She lay on the bed and opened a bag of Monster Munch. She offered him one now and again, although he didn't look like he'd be eating anytime soon. He was sweaty and jumpy and constantly looking from side to side as if the walls were out to get him.

She picked pickled onion goo out of her teeth. 'Monopoly?'

'Can yer hear him?'

'Wot, the bairns outside or the bangin downstairs?'

'Nor, it's Bob.'

She knew this. She could talk him into a better place. 'Eeee, is it Bob Stokoe?'

'Shhh,' he said, irritated, 'ah cannet hear the instructions.' He concentrated as if trying to listen to a song on a crackly radio, turning his hand on his ear to tune it in. 'Two-four, two-four, over.'

'Does he want the team list?' she said.

Dad dropped his hand from his ear and smiled. 'Why-aye man, of course he does.'

She wished she'd nicked some pens and jotters rather than Monopoly. 'Yae say it out loud and ah'll send the message in Morse code ter Bob,' she said.

'Will yer?'

'Aye,' she said, pleased that he was going for it. 'Start wer number one.'

'Jimmy Montgomery, Dick Malone, Ron Guthrie, Micky Horswill, David Watson, Richie Pitt, Bobby Kerr, Billy Hughes, Vic Halom—'

'Slow down will yer, ah cannet keep up wer the Morse code.'

'Ian Porterfield, Dennis Tueart, David Young, yer got all that,' he said, pointing at the table she was tapping her finger on, sending a message about the team to the manager.

'Wot positions shall ah tell him ter play them in?' she said.

She tried her best to keep him on footy, but it was hard as he became agitated by the sound of the kids on the street. She wanted to lean out of the window and tell them to shut the fuck up.

'Where am ah?' he asked in a robot voice.

'Hendon.'

'That macks sense.'

'Wot does?'

'The KGB telt uz ter gan ter a safe house; this must be it,' he said. 'Ah cannet hear nowt ower the noise, can yer turn the telly down?'

She hugged him and tried to crush the demons in his soul, and he twitched like he was about to explode like dynamite, so she hugged him tighter. It reminded her of when Ian was a baby and she'd curl her body around his and hope that he'd stay still and quiet, but it would never last long enough. She steered Dad toward the bed and got him to sit down. He was mumbling and sweat poured down his beety face.

'Is that a helicopter?' he said.

'Nor Dad, there's nee helicopters.'

The windows rattled as a noisy car stopped outside and the kids cheered. The slam of the car door made Dad jump to his feet. He ran to the window and looked down, shouted, 'Keegan!' then pelted out of the room.

She legged it after him along the dingy landing. He got to the end door and hammered on it. He turned to face her then Jeff opened the door, he stepped in, and the door slammed shut. She knocked on it a few times, then something slammed downstairs and there was the sound of breaking glass.

As she went down to see what was happening, yellow light spilled from the front room into the dark hall. She edged cautiously inside. It had a high ceiling, peeling wallpaper, a grimy swirly carpet, and a bed with a stained velvet headboard. The old man with the white trilby hat and red cravat was shaking his knee and singing like an alcoholic doing Elvis, while the skinny woman with black roots was lying on the bed with her arms above her head, screeching, 'Eeeeeee.' In the bay window was a normal-looking man in an anorak, pulling papers from a briefcase. He had a massive perm and that's when she clicked why Dad had shouted Keegan.

'Excuse me,' she said.

The man in the anorak looked up. 'Hello. Client or visitor?'

'Visitor. Me dad's upstairs.'

'Good. Can yer get a glass of water?'

'Where from?'

'Anywhere,' he said as if she'd asked a dumb question.

She went upstairs to fill a mug in Dad's sink. She was glad that the man in the anorak was there, hopefully to give Dad his medicine. He didn't look like a doctor, so he was probably one of the mental health workers that David said were 'Next ter useless.'

She put her ear against Jeff's door, and everything was quiet. Then, she went back to the front room. 'He'yar,' she said.

'Can yer give it ter Mrs Warren?'

'Who? Her?'

'A-ha,' he said as if she was thick to doubt Mrs Warren's ability to hold a mug of water while rocking and screaming.

'I gave a letter to the postman, he put it in his sack,' sang the old bloke, with a hand on his wobbly knee. *'Bright early next morning, he brought my letter back.'*

As Mrs Warren rocked forward, the man in the anorak lobbed a handful of pills into her mouth. She passed him the mug, and he grabbed the woman's chin and sloshed the water in her mouth and all over her face, making her blink and swallow. 'That's one done,' he said. 'Ha'way then, Bill, get ter yer own room, give Mrs Warren some peace.'

They all looked at Mrs Warren who had no chance of getting some peace any time ever. Bill shuffled over to the bed and pulled a quart bottle of rum from his baggy pocket. 'He'yar pet, get some of this down yer.'

'Nor Bill, dinnet give her that,' said the man in the anorak. 'Yer shouldn't be drinkin anyway. They'll kick yer out of here—'

There was a loud bang and shouting and as she got to the bottom of the stairs, Dad was hurtling down, two at a time. She spread her body, making a web to catch him, but he sprung over the bannister, ran along the corridor, and out of the wide-open front door. Bill dithered in the hall, blocking her path, so by the time she got outside, Dad was so far away there was no point chasing him. She watched him get smaller, her heart in her mouth, wondering what to do. There was a rustle of anorak and a tickle of hair on her face as an arm went round her waist. 'Let's go inside.'

As the saying goes, there's no point locking the door after the mad man has bolted, yet anorak man locked it, put the latch across, and closed the bolt at the top. 'That should stop them from escapin,' he laughed.

'Or stop me dad from comin back in.'

'He can knock. Ha'way.'

She followed him to the dark back of the house. His keys jangled as he unlocked a door.

'Quick,' he said, pushing her into a dark room. A strip light fizzled and flickered for ages and then came on and blinded them. The tiny room had white kitchen units down one side and a strip light that was full of dead flies. It had probably been a cupboard in Victorian days.

'Keith,' he said, shaking her hand. 'And you are?'

'Paula, Eddie Hasting's daughter.'

He rummaged in his briefcase and pulled out a yellow folder.

'Shouldn't wer ring the police?' she said.

'And say wot? A man's ran away from home? They winnet dee anythin. Ah, here, Edward Hasting.'

'He's got nee clays on.'

'Wot, he's starkers?' he said in a serious voice.

'Well, nor, he's wearin his shorts and socks, like.'

'Any idea of where he's off too?'

'Wot's the KGB?'

He put his head to one side and sighed.

'Well, wot is it?'

'The Russian secret army.'

She nodded. 'Ah see why yer sighed.'

'He'll come back, or the police'll bring him in.' He put the folder on the bench. 'You stay here while ah dee me rounds. If yer dad's not back in ten minutes, we'll have a think about wot ter dee, okay?'

She leaned on the bench. 'Okay.'

As soon as he was gone, she read the single sheet of paper in the yellow folder.

Name: Edward John Hasting. DOB: 25/4/1944
Next of kin: David Hasting
25/6/1960. Schizophrenia, chronic

Presentation. psychosis, severe. MHA psyc admission/discharge: July/Oct 66; March 68; Jan/July 74; April 81/Feb 82. 23/8/1984. Apprehend police 7.30pm. Confused state. Emergency Dept. S/land General. Agitated. Delusions. Mood: aggressive required restraint. Suspected alcoholism. 23/8 10.20pm diazepam 10 IV. 11.30pm. General admission. 24/8 7.30am diazepam 10 IV. 2.30pm Hostile. diazepam 10 IM 25/8/85: Transferred psyc CKH.

25/8 diazepam 10 IV; repeat BID. 26/8 diazepam 10 IV; repeat BID. 27/8 diazepam 10 IV; repeat BID. 28/8 ambulant, TPN withdrawn. Lithium 1200 PO, diazepam 10 IM. 29/8 Lithium 1200 PO, diazepam 10 IM. 30/8 Lithium 1200 PO, diazepam 10 IM. 31/8 Lithium 1200 PO, diazepam 10 IM, metoprolol 50mg po. 31/8: diazepam 10 IV repeat bid. zuclopenthixol 25mg po. Metoprolol 100mg po. 1/9: diazepam 10 IV repeat bid. zuclopenthixol 25mg po. Metoprolol 50mg po. 5/9 Perform basic AL w/o assistance, mild psychosis, mild agitation. Lithium 1200 po, diazepam 10 IM, metoprolol 50mg po.

25/8 admitted Elms Ward ; auditory hallucinations ; paranoid delusions ; sedated. 26–27/8 ambulatory ; dressing with assistance ; feed unaided ; joined television room. 28 Aug hearing voices ; agitated. 29/8 full pysc assess: partial remission.

10/9: Discharged Elm's ward. Care in the community. Lithium 1200 po; metoprolol 50mg po. Assess in 1 month.

It was like reading Greek, yet she understood schizophrenia. When she was twelve, she went to the big library in town and looked-up 'schizo' in a medical dictionary. That's when she discovered the full word: schizophrenia, translates roughly as splitting of the mind and causes delusions, hallucinations, disorganized speech, trouble with thinking, and lack of motivation. She'd even copied it down in her address book before going to the library museum to see Wallace and the other stuffed animals, particularly the mole and the eagle, which were better than the bog-eyed lion. Sonya and her family said Dad had a split personality, which was wrong because his personality always stayed the same. They were kind though; the only people who talked about him, asked how he was doing, if he was out of Cherry and stuff.

There were bangs and shouts and Bill belting out, *'You're the devil in disguise, yes yer are, the devil in disguise.'*

When anorak man came back, he pulled the light cord, and it went dark, he said, 'Shit,' then pulled the cord again. When the light fizzled on, he looked flustered. 'Time wer left.' He stuffed the papers into his briefcase. 'Ah've left yer dad's tablets in his room.'

'Are wer ganner gan lookin for him?'

'No point. He'll either come home, or he'll be in a police cell. Shall wer go?' His perm shimmied. 'Where der yer live?'

'Plainsy,' she said, nearly saying Pallion.

'Ah'm off ter Azalea Terrace, so how about ah drop yer at the infirmary? Can yer catch a bus from there?'

'Aye, that'd be ellish, man. Are yer sure yer dinnet mind?'

His car was a worse banger than Lisa's dad's and the racket it made had people twitching their curtains.

'Keep yer eyes peeled, ah'll drive slowly,' he said, giving her a cloth to wipe the side window.

He put the blowers on full blast and put the radio on, which made it impossible to hear as she said, 'That could be him,' about every bloke they passed, even though they were all wearing clothes.

He pulled into the bus stop next to the Royal Infirmary. 'Dinnet worry about yer dad, ah'll keep an eye on him. Ah'll look in on him tomorra.'

She got out of the car. 'Thanks, Kevin, that's kind of yer.'

'It's Keith!'

*

David went mad when he found out she'd rang Nana and told her about Dad being down Hendon. She didn't know that by the time Nana and Jimmy got down Amberley Street, Dad would have returned from his wander and be in his room. David was mostly radgie at everything as usual and now he was furious at Nana for interfering, although Lisa was over the moon with the sharing of duties. Now they had a rota for looking after Dad, and Nana fetched some stuff for his room. The tangled blind, or as Nana called it, 'the strangulation hazard', was gone and replaced by the yellow curtains that used to be in Nana's living room. There were tins in the cupboard, milk in the fridge, and a toasted sandwich maker. Nana even accosted Keith and got a key to the front door and to the cupboard room, and she took control of Dad's tablets.

*

The train pulled out of Seaburn station, and her eyes flickered as the tall houses flashed past and were replaced by an estate of posh houses, with what must have been, she reckoned, Monkey House on the far edge. Then green fields with a scattering of tumbled-down farmhouses and yards with knackered-out vans, and caravan camps with washing lines and dogs and ponies. It looked the same as it did six years ago when Nana took her and Julie to see Fenwick's window. They'd got off the train at Heworth so they could ride the Metro, which was a yellow train that Nana said was special, although a disgrace that it didn't come to Sunderland as she'd paid for it with her taxes.

They'd got off the Metro at Monument and held Nana's hand tight as they fought their way through the crowds. It was teeming with people, and as the Fenwick's sign and green canopies came into sight, the crowd was so thick, Nana swapped both of them into one tight hand grasp and pushed her way nearly to the front. She stood on her tiptoes and all she could see was an elf's long pointy shoe moving up and down and she was so cold and hungry that all she could think of was the Wimpy at the station. After seeing the windows, they pushed and elbowed their way inside and into a packed lift. The doors opened on the fourth floor: toy department. They tugged to be released from Nana's grip as she dragged them over to a chair opposite the lift. 'Ah'll wait here. Come back when yers are bored. Got it?'

'Aye, yer'll be waitin here, near the lift,' she said.

Julie wasn't listening.

'Julie,' said Nana, 'yer knar where ah'll be?'

'Near the lift.'

Nana let go of their hands and they ran in different directions. It was exactly like what she imagined paradise to be like – a room so big you couldn't see to the end that was full of toys, and not the shit toys that she had, proper toys like the ones in the Janet Fraser

Catalogue that they played bagsy on. She jumped into the soft toy pit and cuddled an enormous King Louis and then a life-size tiger before moving on to a shelf with about a hundred more Snoopys than in Binns. She loved Snoopy and she loved Spike more because he was skinny and had knotted-rope whiskers and circle eyes. Next, she climbed into the pit filled with too many green hippos to count. In the middle was a hippo the size of a dinner table, and piled on its back were hippos from huge to medium to small. She felt sorry for the children with mams who stopped them from climbing in and cuddling them all. She played for ages until Nana appeared, swinging her red rectangle shopping bag and waving for her to get out. She chose one small hippo to take home, which she would've gotten away with if Julie hadn't appeared with Mr Frosty, Etch a Sketch, Ballerina Sindy, and Stretch Armstrong; Nana took one look at Julie and declared that all toys were too expensive and they had to drop everything. Nana let them choose a one-pound-fifty animal in a matchbox.

On the train home, some shitty kids snatched her hippo-in-a-matchbox, then Julie swapped her panda-in-a-matchbox for a yo-yo and slied-off and sat with them. When the shitty kids got off at Boldon Colliery, Julie came licking back, offering the *Penguin* she'd pocketed at Nana's that morning. It was lucky for Julie that she was starving.

As she made her way out of Boldon Colliery station, she half expected to be chased down the street by a gang of animal-in-a-matchbox thieves. Instead, she found a normal estate. She weaved her way to the main road, which was lined with trees and massive houses, and she wondered what it would be like to be stinking rich. She'd have a horse for a start.

People were coming and going as she proudly strode across the concrete yard in her riding boots, jodhpurs, and red polo-neck jumper. She was shivering but didn't want to spoil the outfit with her donkey jacket, which was like the ones that binmen wore apart from it didn't have plastic on the back.

A car that was the size and colour of a tank kicked up dust as it parked in the yard. Charlotte and another girl got out and went into the portacabin. She wandered into the barn and headed for Orchid, who was popping her head out of the stall. Orchid pressed her nose into her chest and she stroked her neck and smelled her horsey-ness.

'Hello, lovely girl.' She wanted to go in and start brushing but thought it best to wait for Charlotte. When they didn't appear for ages, she wandered out to the yard. Charlotte and the girl were outside of the portacabin, so she wandered over as if she'd just arrived and hadn't been standing in the barn for half an hour.

Charlotte waved and skipped over. 'You made it.'

'Aye.'

'Come, meet Maddy,' said Charlotte, taking her hand. *Maddy* looked the same age as Charlotte and was wearing a smart navy jacket that people wear for showjumping.

'Paula, Maddy, Maddy, Paula,' said Charlotte.

'Hiya,' she said to the girl who smiled. 'Der yer have a horse?' she said, trying to make conversation.

'Yah,' said Maddy, 'I'm waiting for Daddy to bring him now.'

'Wot type of horse is he?'

'Arabian. Ex-racehorse,' said Maddy. 'Look, there he is, come on.'

Maddy waved to the man driving the car pulling a trailer, then ran off to greet him.

'I'm going to tack up Orchid. Why don't you go with Maddy? Wait till you see her horse,' said Charlotte.

She reluctantly sidled her way over to join Maddy, who ignored her as she opened the trailer. She stood awkwardly as Maddy led out a huge bay horse with a black mane and continued to take off the horse's legwarmers, with her back turned like she wasn't there.

'Wot's his name?' she said, hopefully.

Keeping her back to her, Maddy replied, 'William Shakespeare, or Billy for short.'

'Me stepdad woz called Billy.'

Maddy spun on her heel to face her. 'The one who had his head sliced off with the fishing line?'

'Aye that's him, stupid twat.'

Maddy gasped, then laughed through her nose.

'Ah hated him,' she said.

'It must've been ever so gory.'

'Didn't see the corpse. The pigs sealed the flat off. Ah heard that the blood came out wer such force that it splattered into every nook and cranny.'

Maddy wrinkled her nose. 'You live in a flat?'

'Ah did before the bloodbath. Ah live in a house now.'

Maddy turned her back and took off the horse's headcollar.

'Woz Billy a proper racehorse, in races like?'

'Oh yes, he ran on the flat a few times.' Maddy patted Billy who clomped a hoof.

'Did he win owt?'

'No, sadly not. But that was lucky for me because Daddy bought him.'

Billy nuzzled Maddy's face. She wished she was rich. Imagine your dad buying you a racehorse. Lucky git.

When Maddy led Billy across the yard it was obvious that he was the biggest horse she'd ever seen and she couldn't believe that a tiny thing like Maddy was going to ride him. Charlotte was in the stable getting Orchid ready, so she made herself useful by sweeping although it didn't need sweeping.

'How's yer mam?' she asked Charlotte.

'Good, thanks. She sends her best wishes.'

'Tell her thanks for the book.'

'Jodhpurs fit you then?'

She stretched out a leg. 'Aye man, they're amazin. Ah'll problees gan ter bed in them.'

'How is your poor mother coping with being a widow?'

'Oh yer knar, she's lovin it.'

Charlotte laughed.

'Yer ganner tell uz the gossip on the lad from the caravan?'

Charlotte snorted, then said, 'Nothing to tell. I fancy someone else now.'

'Who?'

'Ben.'

'And? Details?'

'He plays on the St Roberts' badminton team. He's drop-dead gorgeous.'

'Yer met him playin badminton?'

'It was a tournament. I was playing doubles with Maddy.'

'And yer eyes met over a crowded net?'

'Not exactly.'

'Wot der yer mean, *not exactly*; yers are together?'

'No not yet, but Maddy has invited him to a party on Saturday and he said he's going to come.'

'Der yer knar anythin else about Ben wee plays badminton?'

'He won the fourth-year boys' singles.'

'Have yer spoken ter him?'

'No not yet, I will at the party.'

The stall went dark and they looked up to see the door blocked by Billy and Maddy. 'Have you asked her?'

'No, I was going to.'

'Asked uz wot?' she said, suspecting that she was going to be sent to buy *Playgirl.*

Charlotte plucked a tenner from her pocket. 'Could you buy me some voddy for the party?'

'Wot's voddy?'

'Vodka,' said Charlotte blushing. 'Or anything really.'

'Yer want uz ter get yer some booze ter tack ter the party? Why-aye, nee probs.'

Maddy pulled out a twenty, 'Could you get me some too?'

'Voddy?'

'Yah and some Jack,' said Maddy. 'When can you get it by?'

'Dunno, Wednesda or Thursda, mebees.'

'I'm not here after tomorrow,' said Charlotte.

'I could come down,' said Maddy. 'Let's say Thursday?'

'Aye, ah'll dee me best.'

As Charlotte and Maddy led their horses out to the yard, Orchid looked small next to Billy. Charlotte and Maddy chatted about school and she tried to join in but soon decided not to speak as she tagged along behind. She could see them give each other sideways glances of *what the fuck is she doing here?*

They each led their horse in a circle to the plastic steps, put a foot in their stirrups, and swung a leg over. Maddy looked so elegant sitting on Billy as they clip-clopped off. She walked behind, imagining what it would be like to be Maddy. When they got to the gate, Maddy gave Charlotte a look of *if you don't tell her to fuck off, I will.*

'I'm sorry Paula,' said Charlotte, 'we're off on a hack. You'll have to go back to the yard. Michael will be down soon looking for someone to groom Whisper.'

Her heart sank and as she turned to walk away, Maddy said, 'Gate,' sounding the T as if she was telling a dog to sit.

As she attended to the gate, Charlotte said, 'Thanks Paula. Are you coming tomorrow?'

Her heart leapt. 'Tomorra,' she repeated, 'aye, ah'll be here, about ten?' She lifted the latch and lingered, waiting for Charlotte to agree before letting them pass.

'I'll be here all morning.'

She opened the gate and magnificent Billy clopped through as Maddy stuck her snotty nose in the air.

It was spitting-on, and she was nithered, so she went into the barn to wait for Michael. She hoped he remembered her. It seemed like a lifetime ago when she was the foster kid. Whisper wasn't sticking her head over the bars and she wondered if it was okay to go and bother her. There were a few horses popping their heads out, so she chose a pony called Apple to stroke and cuddle up to for warmth.

After ages, she wandered in search of Michael, and finding the yard empty, she went into the portacabin in search of life. There was a desk covered in papers, a small sink with a kettle next to it, and a table with school chairs. It was nice to be in the warm, so she sat down and waited for someone to come in who she could ask about Michael. With nothing else to do, she got the book out that Jenny had sent her. She hadn't read much because it wasn't as easy to read as *Black Beauty*.

Miles away, reading about Velvet's family eating dinner in a dingy room, she heard, 'Ahem!'

She looked up to see the woman with the weathered face and tweed jacket who she'd seen earlier shouting at children and cars. Charlotte said she was called Dorothy and that she was the livery manager.

'What are you doing hare?'

She held up her book. 'Readin.'

'*National Velvet*, what a joy. I always dreamed of winning the Grand National.'

'Is that wot happens? Velvet wins the National like?'

'Oh my poor child, I've gone and totally ruined it for you.'

'Dinnet worry, ah should've guessed.'

Dorothy laughed like a horse. 'Very nice but we're not open to waifs and strays, so orf you go.'

She felt her face go beety. Her head said sprint to the train station while her arse was rooted to the chair. 'Ah'm waitin for Michael, der yer knar when he'll be here?'

'Michael?' said Dorothy with horror.

'Aye, ah'm ganner groom Whisper.'

Opening the door and extending an arm outward, Dorothy said, 'You'll need to wait somewhere else.'

She folded over the corner of her page and as she put the book in her bag, she asked, 'Wot's a piebald?'

Dorothy's forehead wrinkled as she raised her eyebrows. 'See Alice, stall three,' she said, doing that clicking noise like trying to chivvy a horse.

Alice had black and white patches like a cow and she mooched over and stuck her nose out to say hello. She put her arms around Alice and pressed her cheek into her face. She stood there until she heard Dorothy shout, 'Michael!'

As she came out of the barn, Michael was walking across the yard with Dorothy making a beeline for him at a fast pace with the odd skip. He was wearing a green Barbour over a powder blue shirt that was open at the neck, and his kecks were chinos with a sharp crease, tucked into green wellies. He stood with his shoulders back as Dorothy talked at him and rubbed her hip. When he spotted her lingering in the barn entrance, he patted Dorothy on the shoulder and walked away, and as he came towards her, the look on Dorothy's face was classic.

He smelled of expensive aftershave and cheap hair gel. 'How are you on this fine October day, Miss Paula?' His accent was posh with a hint of North.

'Good ta.'

'Did you come on the train?'

'Aye.'

'Are you here with Charlotte?'

'Ah woz until she went on a hack. She ses yer might need a hand wer Whisper.'

Michael opened Whisper's stall and they went inside. 'Ah excellent, all ready.'

Whisper had her mane plaited with blue and white ribbons. She looked stunning.

'My sister's showjumping this afternoon.'

'On Whisper?'

'Yes, hence the ribbons.'

'Ah thought she woz yer daughter's horse.'

'She is, aren't you,' he said, patting Whisper's neck. 'Amanda is sunning it up on the Costa del Sol with Mummy.'

'Where's that?'

'Spain.'

'The furthest ah've been on holiday is Haggerston Castle.'

'Beautiful part of the world. Did you get over to Holy Island?'

'Nor, it woz stotten it down, so uz spent the week playin cards in the caravan.'

He stroked Whisper's sleek back. 'Do you want to help me get the nag in the trailer?'

'Aye, that'd be mint. Wot do ah need ter dee?'

'Get the headcollar.'

She got the headcollar from the hook and slid it gently over the horse's nose. As she threaded the strap under the horse's neck, Michael leaned in and grasped it, holding it taught as she fastened the buckle. He stepped out of the stall and returned dragging a bag of horse stuff with his foot. He delved inside and pulled out a brush made from wood with a hand strap across the top. 'How are you at grooming?'

'Aye, canny,' she said. She set about brushing even though Whisper was as already as smart as a carrot and ready for the show ring. Michael held Whisper by the headcollar and chatted about his villa in Spain with its hand-fired terracotta tiles and rustic charm and the terrace and pool that made up for being a mile from the beach. He said that his wife and daughter enjoy the villa, yet he never has time to go. She pictured his wife as Olivia Newton-John lounging in a gold lama bikini, sipping a pink cocktail. 'Someone has to feed the cat and look after the horse,' he joked.

'Yae must have a good job ter afford a villa in Spain and a horse.'

He chuckled. 'I'm a good accountant that's all.' He looked at his watch. 'Better get this nag in the trailer. Need to get to Ponteland by one.'

He shook her hand and said, 'See you next time.'

She wanted to ask when next time was, but she knew he didn't mean it. He was being polite. As he led

Whisper to the trailer, she headed down the track to the gate, and when he pulled up in his big car, she opened it like the gate monitor. He hooted his horn.

She had one foot in the house when Mam shouted from the living room, 'Where did yae slope off tee at the crack of dawn like?'

'Nee where.'

'Dissn't smell like nee where,' said Mam, now standing half out of the living room. 'Ah had ter look after them bairns all day. Yerv got nee consideration.'

She ignored the usual background noise of Mam moaning on and undressed directly into the washing machine like she did at Jenny's.

Mam came into the kitchen, pulling her angry pout. 'Yer cannet put the machine on just for that, der yer think ah'm made of money or wot?'

She pushed past Mam and went upstairs and emptied the overflowing laundry basket onto the bathroom floor. Then she came back down with an armful of colours, which she stuffed into the machine. 'Happy now?'

The radio came on quietly at 5:00 am and she went to the hall and flicked the switch on the heating. She'd get up at 7:00 and flick it off so no one would be any the wiser that the radiator had been on full blast. When she came down at 7:00, the heating had managed to turn itself off. Luckily, it had stayed on long enough to dry her jodhpurs and the polo-neck jumper, which had shrunk. She was glad it was damp as she wriggled into it, stretching its squeaky fibres into shape.

There was a note on the kitchen table. *Dinner money. Back this afternoon, Mam.* She knocked on Mam's bedroom and when there were no grunts, she went in. Mam's bed was empty. Sly bitch. Jason and Ian came out of their rooms.

'If yers are good lads and eat yer breakfast and get ready, ah'll tack yer ter see some horses.'

They jumped with happiness, then hugged her legs.

At the Prospect bus stop, Ian and Jason got hods of bairns to join a game of all-pile-on, and as a bus got near, she dragged them into the queue.

'Get yer bussy ready,' she said to Ian, who had insisted on holding it himself.

Ian shook his head and shrugged.

'Where've yer put it?'

'Up me arse and two doors on the left,' said Ian, making the bairns laugh and the grown-ups tut.

This was going to be a long day. At least Mam had left two quid, *i.e. I've shafted you, but buy some crisps and pop.* She was probably at home, lying on the settee, watching telly. Lisa said she was a sloth bitch who should look after her own bairns.

They had barely made it over the bridge when Ian finished his crisps and pop, slipped off the seat, and ran along the train, followed by Jason, who shed Wotsits as he ran. She buried her head in *National Velvet* and blanked out the shouts and screams until someone poked her in the arm.

'Are yer ganner get yer bairns under control or wot?'

'They're not mine,' she snapped, putting her book away as she headed off along the carriage.

Jason was on the floor in the door area pinned down by Ian who had a knee on each arm, while he did the typewriter on his chest.

'Get up *now*,' she shouted, hooking her arm around Ian's neck and dragging him off Jason who picked crisps off the floor, which she knocked out of his tiny hand. 'Hacky! Leave them.'

She was glad when they got off the train and they ran away and climbed on the station railings. They hung upside down like bats and she wondered if she should leave them to play; they'd be happy on the railings for a few hours.

'Get down, or there's nee gan on the horse,' she said.

She didn't expect them to drop off the railings and stand still like normal kids.

'Wot type of horse is it?' said Ian, a face like Christmas.

'Are uz really gettin a gan on a horse?' said Jason.

'Mebees, but arnly if yers are really good lads. The posh people at the stables dinnet like kids wee break the rules.' It was a promise she couldn't keep, but if it meant they would behave themselves, then what else could she do?

Apart from the odd, 'Look at that wass house!' from Ian, and 'Are wer nearly there yet?' from Jason, they walked sensibly and quietly like she imagined they did on a school trip.

At the stables, Dorothy was shouting and directing tank cars and there were so many horses, the lads didn't know which way to look.

'Black one!'

'Brown one!'

They held her hand as they crossed the yard and they both squeezed it when she said, 'Ha'way, let's meet the horses.' There were a few horses with their heads over the stalls and the lads were too awestruck to speak, let alone make a dash for trouble. Orchid was hiding at the back of her stall, so she lifted Jason up to see in. 'That's the horse ah woz ridin.'

'Strites?'

'Aye, ah woz trottin and everythin.'

Whisper's stall was open with a wheelbarrow parked outside. As she made her way to see if the horse was in there, Michael led her out.

'Mornin,' said Michael when he saw her.

She let go of the lads' hands and they did a best behaviour walk toward Whisper and gave her a stroke.

'Who are these two fellas?' he said.

'Me brothas, Ian and Jason.'

The lads kept stroking, hypnotised by the horse.

'They've nivver touched a horse before,' she said, 'they're not usually this quiet.'

'Right then fellas, get a broom in your hands.' He pointed at the brushes.

They weren't so quick to help with anything at home, or do anything that wasn't punching and screaming, yet there wasn't a murmur from either of them as they brushed the stable with smiles on their grubby faces.

As Michael put Whisper's blanket on, Charlotte and Maddy came in, soggy from the rain.

'Doesn't look like anyone will be getting out today,' Michael said.

The lads raised their heads from their work with pained faces, and she looked back with equal guttedness.

'It's only a shower,' said Charlotte. 'Are these boys your brothers, Paula?'

'Aye, the biggun's Ian and the littlun's Jason.'

The lads stopped brushing and stood to attention. They knew how to be angels when they wanted something, and she hoped that they didn't speak as that could blow the act.

'Can I ask you something in private?' said Charlotte, taking her hand. 'Back in a tick,' said Charlotte to

Michael, dragging her off and leaving him with the lads. She suspected that this was going to be about porn mags or booze.

Once they were in Orchid's stable, Maddy pulled out a wad of notes. 'Can you add some more to the order?'

'Ah dinnar man, yer already want more than ah can get in one gan.'

'Have you ever been on a hack?' said Maddy.

She took the cash. 'Wot der yer want?'

'Voddy and Jack,' said Maddy.

'Wot horse will ah be ridin on the hack?'

'I don't know yet,' said Maddy, wafting her hand the same way that Mam did when she didn't give a shit about what she'd just said.

'No hack, no Jack,' she said, waving the notes. 'Saturda? Ah'll bring the booze.'

Charlotte shrugged. 'Orchid does lessons on Saturdays.'

Maddy exhaled and dropped her shoulders as if going on a hack was a chore. 'What about wonky Alice?'

'Doing lessons,' said Charlotte. 'What about Isambard?'

'Good idea!' said Maddy.

'Wot colour is she?' she said, wishing she hadn't. What an idiot. As if the colour matters.

'*He's* dapple grey.'

'Should wer meet here on Saturda at two?'

'God, you're keen,' said Maddy.

'If yer want the booze, ah'll need ter ride Isibird. And ah'll need ter borra a ridin hat.'

'Fine. I've got loads.'

'Have yer? How many like?'

'Err, eight *like*.'

She went to rescue Michael from the lads and found them stroking Whisper and behaving themselves. Michael attached the lead rope and gave it to her. 'Can you walk Whisper to the trailer?'

'Why-aye,' she said with Ian and Jason at her side, as good as gold.

'I'm going to talk to Dorothy about the boys having a ride. I'll meet you at the trailer in five minutes.'

The wet ground sparkled in the sunshine as they walked with Whisper. 'Did yers ask Michael for a ride on a horse?'

'Aye,' said Ian. 'Ah ses, would it be possible for uz ter have a quick gan on a horse, please sir.'

'Wot did he say?'

'He ses he'd have a word wer Dorothy.'

She put a hand on Ian's shoulder and gave it a squeeze. 'Well done son, that's why he's talkin ter Dorothy.'

'Are uz gannen on the horse?' asked Jason.

'Mebees,' she said, 'mebees.'

They stood to attention, including Whisper, as Michael came striding towards them, his checky shirttails flapping from under his green padded body warmer.

'Righty, get yourselves in the office and wait for Dorothy,' Michael said, brushing her boob slightly as he took the lead rope from her hand.

'Can ah see how yer put the horse in the trailer, please?' said Jason, clinging to Whisper's side.

Michael tussled Jason's hair. 'Hold this while I open up.'

'Have yer sorted out a ride for the lads?' she asked.

He dropped the ramp and signalled for Jason to walk the horse inside. Jason turned his shocked little face from side-to-side looking for any known impediment. She nodded him on and with shoulders back, he walked Whisper into the trailer.

'Alice is a horse who knows how to deal with excited children,' said Michael. 'You must do what Dorothy tells you.'

With the horse locked in, Michael patted the top and bottom pockets of his body warmer and finally found his keys in the trouser pocket of his brown cords. He twirled the keys into his hand. 'Nice to meet you, boys. Look after your sister.'

Ian and Jason bowed. 'Nice ter meet yer, sir.'

In the portacabin the lads sat quietly as if they were different bairns to those she'd left the house with earlier. She gave them the cheese pasties she'd got from town, which they clasped in their grimy hands as they tucked in.

Without warning, Dorothy was in the portacabin. 'What's that narsty smell?'

She braced herself for Ian to say his usual answer to this question, 'Yer nose is too close ter yer arse,' but instead, he stuffed the last chunk of cold pasty into his mouth and stood up. Jason copied and they did their best to smile sweetly while chewing and pinging pastry flakes off their jumpers. Dorothy flinched as if realising the full nashyness of the Hart family, but she was holding a small riding hat in each hand and only a total shithead would've whipped that away from Ian and Jason.

They went outside to find Charlotte with Alice the piebald. The boys gasped and staggered towards the horse until Dorothy commanded, 'Hats on!'

Ian and Jason stood politely while Dorothy checked their hats. 'Right, you, small one, here.' Jason stepped forward and Dorothy grabbed him around the middle and hoisted him up, dispatching him into the saddle. Dorothy cupped her hands into a stirrup for Ian's foot and hitched him up and over in one movement. There was nothing wizened about this old bird, she'd probably wrestled plenty of stallions in her time. The saddle was big enough for two little bums, Jason at the front and Ian at the back. Dorothy took the lead rope from Charlotte and Alice tossed her mane and clopped a hoof.

Charlotte gave her a hug and said, 'Sorry I couldn't sort out a ride on Orchid today. You'll have fun on Saturday though.'

'Aye, nee probs. Tell Maddy two o'clock.'

As they made their way down the track, Alice snorted steam from her nostrils and the more the lads giggled, the more she bobbed up and down, eyes twinkling and ears waggling. Dorothy was walking fast and every so often she did a skip making Alice sway her bottom and making them squeal with laughter as they clung on.

As she sat on the fence and watched the bairns having the time of their lives, she wondered how the heck Michael got Dorothy to run round the arena with two scruffy little urchins. Accountants have loads of money and he was good-looking for an older bloke, so Dorothy was probably living in hope of some hot sex in the portacabin.

Dorothy gave them a good half-hour and although they were gutted as they headed back to the yard, they didn't say a word or punch each other. They jumped down from Alice with a look of that thing that there is no word for. Jason managed to fight his tears despite a major lip wobble.

'Thank you so much,' she said to Dorothy. 'That's the kindest thing anyone has ever done for us.'

She expected Dorothy to say 'Gertcha' like what Nana does when you tell her you love her. Instead she said sternly, 'Right you are.'

'Thank you for the ride,' said Ian, 'it woz ellish.'

'Ellish?' said Dorothy.

'Mint,' she clarified.

'I'm glad you boys had fun. Now it's time you went home,' she said, doing that clicking noise like trying to chivvy a horse.

On the train, Ian stared out of the window in a daze and Jason bounced up and down making clip-clop noises. She wanted to tell the woman giving her daggers that she understood her irritation with Jason's clip-clops, yet this was him being well-behaved.

Mam opened the door as they came down the path, her mouth open, ready to shout at Ian and Jason as they kicked and punched their way into the hall. Her mouth closed as the lads knocked clarts from their shoes against the step. They took them off and placed them neatly down and then hung their coats on the hook rather than the floor.

'Bath?' she said.

Mam's mouth hung open as they ran up without the usual barney.

She pulled her riding boots off. 'Ah'll bath them, shall ah?'

*

Friday was her day on the rota to look after Dad. He was dressed and shaven and had the Monopoly board set up on the foldaway table from Nana's. She made him a baked bean toasted sandwich and while he was concentrating on his game play, she got him to take his tablets.

By early afternoon Dad had houses on orange and red and he was getting agitated as he tried to get a full set of blues. It was impossible to rig the dice because whenever they rolled off the table and out of sight on the floor, he decided it was a foul and that the player had to roll again. The dice had to be visible on the table. New rule.

'Der yer fancy a wander ter the shops?' she asked. 'Get some fresh air.'

'Nor,' he said, sweating and kissing his clasped hands as he shook the dice, blowing between his thumbs before releasing them.

She was pleased when he landed on the last blue and bought it. He was less sweaty and shaky once he had three sets. He didn't have Park Lane or Mayfair, yet he seemed happy, so she mentioned it again. 'Ha'way Dad, let's gan ter the shop. Yer haven't been out for ages.'

She ushered him along the street, hoping he wouldn't spot the KGB helicopter firing guns at the SAFC FA cup final squad.

The corner shop was long and dark and stuffed full of everything. She'd been in a few times so knew where the exercise books and pens were and now with the cash from Maddy, she could buy Dad whatever he wanted. He was acting like a normal person, or normal for him, as he chose a five-pack of exercise books, two red marker pens, and two black marker pens. The booze was next to the counter, so as Dad gave his items to the shopman, she said casually. 'Oh, nearly forgot, Nana said yer were ter get some vodka.'

'Did she?'

'Aye, for ower Gavin's twenty-first.' She picked up a couple of bottles of vodka and put them on the counter. 'Can yer see any Jack?'

'Got any Jack Daniel's, mate?' Dad asked the shopman.

The shopman unlocked the reinforced glass cabinet that had a punch-shaped crack in it, mended with gaffer tape. He took out a square bottle of black stuff. 'Fifteen quid, mate.'

'Ow much?' said Dad. 'Throw in a small bottle for half-price, and yerv got yersel a deal.'

'Aye, gan on then,' said the shopman, putting a smaller square bottle of black stuff on the counter. 'Have yer tried that Pernod?'

'Nor,' said Dad, 'wot is it?'

'Ah dunnar,' said the shopman, 'yer mix it wer blackcurrant, it's all the rage down the town.'

They needed four placker bags to carry the booze and they made a right racket as they clinked down the street.

It was good that Dad had negotiated a top deal, but as she dropped the bags on the bedroom floor, she wondered how she was going to get this lot to the stables on her own. Dad was thinking ahead of her. From the wardrobe he pulled out Grandar's old brown sports bag that Nana must have used to bring the bedding. She remembered how she used to fight with David over not being the one to carry it because it was old-fashioned and looked like a hot-dog crossed with a turd. Dad carefully arranged all ten bottles inside the turd bag and zipped it up.

'There'yar. Job's a good un.'

*

On Saturday morning, Dad was curled up under the bedcovers and the sun streamed through the yellow curtains, making the room glow. Her jaw flapped when she saw the wall next to the bed – a row of eleven shirts with stripes coloured red with the marker pen, and across the top, so high that she wondered how he'd got up there, was an SAFC banner with red stripes and red tassels. Every inch between the shirts and the banner was covered in dates and scores, and down each side, there were team lists for the 1937 and 1973 cup finals. She wished she had a camera to take a photo of his amazing creation.

She opened a tin of corned beef and made him a sandwich, which she put on his side table next to a glass of water with his tablets. He didn't stir as she whacked the side of the portable telly that Nana had brought. She twiddled the knob and moved the arial and the best she could manage was a wobbly programme about fishing. Dad was still under the covers when she heaved the strap of the turd bag across her body and left to get the train to Boldon.

The key to making it in and out of Amberley Street without being ambushed by rough kids was to keep your head down and walk quickly but not run. The lippy kid with dirty hair was on the opposite kerb with his gang.

'Here lasso, wot's in yer bag?' said lippy kid, walking into the road. She kept her eyes down and walked at a regular pace, ignoring the gang that were tagging along. They followed her to the main road, then got distracted by a fat bloke. She was sweating like a pig and the strap of the turd bag was cutting into her shoulder. She took it off and put it on the pavement while she had a rest.

Switching the strap to the other shoulder got her as far as the YMCA before that side was also in searing pain. She took a deep breath as she hoisted the small handles into the crook of her elbow. She did a burst of running, put the bag down, burst of running, put it down, running, put it down, all the way to the station. She was glad to get on the train and she blew on the deep, purple, strap marks across each palm that stung to buggery.

Before she got off the train, she'd already decided to take the turd bag as far as the gate and no further. She dragged it off the train and dumped it on the platform. Her shoulders had recovered so she used them first, making it to the big houses before both shoulders were in agony. Next was an elbow carry, and then hand-grab and run, drop, hand-grab and run, drop, most of the way down the main road. She spat on her hands and rubbed them on her jodhpurs before picking the turd bag up and running across the road into the long grass where she dumped the fucking bastard thing for the last time. If Maddy wanted it, she'd have to come and get it.

She leaned on the gate and shook her burning palms in the cold, soothing air. The first thing along the lane was a horsebox the size of an actual lorry and she wondered how it was going to get down the track. It stopped, Maddy jumped out, opened the gate as the horsebox drove in, and then closed the gate.

'Have you got the alcohol?' Maddy said.

'Aye, ha'way, it's in the grass down the lane.' She led Maddy into the long grass and unzipped the turd bag.

Maddy bent down and looked inside. 'Gosh!'

'Me dad negotiated a good deal on the Jack Daniel's wer the man in the shop.'

Maddy was well-pleased. She'd definitely get a ride on Isibird. Maddy took out a bottle. 'Grand Marnier, you absolute scoundrel.'

'Here-man, me dad haggled the bloke down from fifteen quid to eight.'

'I thought he was dead.'

'Nor, that's me stepdad. There's some Pernod in there. Have yer tried it?'

'No, what is it?'

'Ah dinnar but yer mix it wer blackcurrant. They're drinkin it in all the pubs, apparently.'

They took a brown handle each and carried the off-licence-in-a-bag from the long grass and down the lane. By the time they reached the gate, Maddy was blowing on her hands. 'Fack that's heavy.'

'Ah knar, ah heaved it all the way from Sunderland,' she said, holding up both palms, showing the throbbing welts.

The yard was busy with cars and horses and lucky little gits who were having riding lessons. They made it to the portacabin before they had to put the bag down. Maddy wiped her brow and raised her eyebrows. 'One last push should do it,' she said, nodding into the barn. 'Orchid's stall.'

'The ride on Isibird better be worth the massacre,' she said, blowing on her hands before taking the strain.

With the booze stashed in the hay, they crossed the yard towards the lorry-sized horsebox.

'That's the biggest horsebox ah've ever seen.'

'Horse transporter,' said Maddy.

A bloke was in the driver's seat reading a newspaper. 'Is that yer dad?'

'Yah, that's Daddy.' Maddy said, unlocking the side door and dropping the ramp. Inside were two huge horses. 'Meet Isambard. Seventeen hands high, Irish Draught gelding.'

The huge horse was iron grey with a white stripe down his nose and a white tail. She couldn't believe she was going to ride him, although she wasn't on him yet, so she took a deep breath and got a grip.

Maddy chucked her some keys. 'Fetch the saddle from the tack locker, will you?'

On the other side of the 'horse transporter' was a panel with a lock which opened like a door to reveal a tack locker that was bigger than her bedroom.

She watched Maddy tack up Isibird in the front stall while Billy poked his nose out of the other stall. When she was done, Maddy attached the lead rope, walked him down the ramp, and gave her the rope. As Maddy talked to her dad, a green Capri drove across the yard and parked next to the horse transporter. A girl got out. She was wearing expensive-looking riding gear and was about the same age as Maddy.

The girl came over and stroked the horse. 'How are you today, Mr Brunel?'

'Hi, ah'm Paula.'

The girl replied, 'Minty,' without looking at her.

'Did she bring the liquor?' said Minty to Maddy as if she wasn't there.

'Yah. So now I have to take her for a ride out.'

'I'll tack up Billy,' said Minty.

'Meet you at the top of the field at three,' said Maddy.

She glanced at her watch. Ten past two. Fifty minutes of riding would do.

Maddy's dad got in the Capri and shouted, 'Be back by four.'

'Okay, Daddy,' said Maddy, waving him off.

She kept hold of the lead rope while Maddy and Minty went into the horse transporter. She sunk her face into Isibird's mane, taking a deep breath of his grassy, sweaty, earthy smell.

When Maddy returned with a plastic step, she clenched her muscles to contain the excitement. 'Here,' said Maddy, giving her a riding hat. 'Put this on. You can keep it.'

As she put it on, her tummy did flips. This was actually happening.

'Climb up. Take the reins in one hand, leg over.'

She did as she was told and there she was, sitting on the beautiful horse with a choir of angels singing in her head. Maddy led them across the yard, past the training arena, and along a woodland path. They didn't speak and she listened to the clop and crunch of the hooves as she gazed over the foggy countryside. This horse was proper high. It was funny how he kept reaching for a nibble on a tree.

She listened to his tail swishes and his snorts, drinking in every last drop as they made their way to Minty who was at the top of the field with Billy. Maddy was pleased to see her mate as if the nightmare had ended.

'You can jump down now,' said Maddy.

She took her time getting off, then gave him a stroke. 'One last stroke before ah nash.'

Minty pulled a horrified face and said to Maddy, 'Whare is she from?'

'A council estate,' said Maddy, also pulling a face.

She hoped that the turd bag ripped Maddy's hands to shreds.

'Is that a dustbin man's coat?' said Minty.

'Aye, but without the plastic on the back,' she said, turning to show the piss-taking posh cow the back of her donkey jacket.

'Can I have a go?' said Minty.

'Wot?'

'Can I try on the dustbin man's coat?'

'Are yer tackin the piss or wot?'

'No, genuinely, I need a new coat and I didn't think you could get dustbin coats for garls.'

She took off her 'dustbin man's coat' and said, 'Ah'll have ter dee a swap like cos it's fucken brass today.'

Minty took off her padded jacket that was the colour of diarrhoea with a brown checky collar and lining. It was warm and had a deep inside pocket. Maddy snorted with laughter at Minty in the donkey jacket and even Billy curled his lip and whinnied.

'Wonder if it rides well?' said Minty.

'Ah had nee probs wearin it today. In fact, it's toasty,' she said.

Maddy mounted Billy and tugged his rein, making him walk in a circle.

She took a grudging step away from Isibird. Horse riding is the closest thing to dreaming while still being awake. There isn't a word for when it comes to an end.

Minty put her boot in the stirrup and swung a leg over Isibird. Even wearing a donkey jacket, she looked stinking rich. The *garls* smirked at each other, then heeled their horses and set off at a canter down the field. She tightened her chinstrap, put her purse in the inside pocket of the diarrhoea coat, and zipped it up. When the horses were dots in the distance she pelted along the path and, without looking back, kept going as fast as she could all the way to the train station. She now had a riding hat and a riding coat to add to her equestrian wardrobe. Minty could keep the donkey jacket.

The train took yonks to come and then it stopped for about twenty minutes in the middle of nowhere and then it was chaos at Seaburn with all the footy fans. It was dark when she emerged from central station and the town smelled of hops and chips. As she passed the taxi rank, a pissed bloke knocked on her riding hat, so she took it off. When some lads tried to grab the hat off her, she took her new jacket off and wrapped the hat in it.

The cold wind felt lovely on her sweaty head as she made her way along Fawcett Street towards Dad's. She had twelve quid left from the money she got from

Maddy, so she decided to see if Dad wanted a Chinese. There must be a takeaway in Hendon and she was clammen for some special fried rice and gravy.

Amberley Street was dark and quiet except for light flooding from the top and bottom windows of one house, and as she got closer, she could see it was Dad's house. His bedroom window was open and the yellow curtains were flapping in the wind. The front door was wide open and Jeff was standing in the corridor. As she tried to pass, he put his arm out and stopped her.

'Wot yer deein, Jeff, it's me, Paula, come ter look after Eddie.'

He kept blocking her path, so she darted under his arm making him squeal like a boiling kettle. Trilby Bill appeared from the shadows and the sober look in his eye told her that something was wrong. She took the stairs two at a time, chased by Bill and Jeff. She looked under the bed and in the wardrobe, and then she shook the bed sheets in the hope of shaking Dad out of them.

'He's gone, pet,' said Bill, 'took off an hour agan. Bit of an artist yer fatha?'

She looked at the wall next to the bed and nodded, 'Aye he is.'

'Nor luv,' said Bill, pointing at the opposite wall.

From the kitchen unit and all the way to the ceiling was a picture of a weird Lambton worm with pointy teeth, black stripes and *fuck the magpies* scrawled over and over. There were brown blobs everywhere, which was odd as he didn't have a brown pen. She got closer and when the whiff hit her nose, she stepped backwards. 'Is that wot ah think it is?

Bill put his crusty claw on her arm. 'Aye, it is.'

She looked at the Sunderland wall that was full of pride and glory and then at the Newcastle wall splattered with shit.

'Fuck,' she said, 'he's gone proper schizo.'

'Why nor, pet,' said Bill, 'that's not bein a proper schizo, that's bein a proper Mackem.'

She took the key to the cupboard room from the drawer and moved so fast that Bill couldn't follow. She locked herself in the cupboard room and waited for the strip light to fizzle on. Nana said only to use the phone in emergencies, i.e., the phone that was in the drawer that Keith kept quiet about and they only found out it was there because it started ringing when Nana was sorting out Dad's haloperidol. She opened the drawer and dialled Nana's number.

It rang twice. 'Hello, Hylton 5346279.'

'Nana, it's Paula.'

'Wot's wrong, luv?'

'It's Dad,' she said, her voice all croaky.

'Paula, are yer there?'

'He's written fuck the magpies all ower the wall and there's shit everywhere.'

'Reet,' said Nana calmy, 'the wall needs paintin anyway and the room can't be worse than it was last week.'

'Nor Nana, there's actual kacky everywhere.'

'For cryin out loud,' said Nana. 'Wot's he deein now?'

'Dunnar, he's gone. Took off about an hour agan.'

When the troops arrived, Mark and Gavin were with Nana in Uncle Jimmy's car. They followed her to Dad's room and she let them go in first. They covered their noses and gagged as they inspected the walls.

'Nice work on the Sun'lun side,' said Mark.

'Here-man, squiy the detail on that banner,' said Uncle Jimmy.

'Ha'way, out, the lot a yer,' said Nana.

'Aye, ha'way,' said Gavin, 'it's fucken ripe in here.'

Nana hit Gavin across the back of the head, 'Less of the language.'

The woman next door and two little heads peered around the curtain as they stood in the street and waited for Nana who was on the phone in the drawer to the police even though they all agreed that phoning the police was a waste of time.

'Nice coat,' said Uncle Jimmy, 'how'd yer come by that?'

'A mate give uz it.'

Gavin raised his eyebrows.

'Wot?' she said. 'Ah knar it's a shitty colour like, but it's warm.'

Gavin said, 'Tack it off a minute, will yer.'

'Why?'

'Just gis it here.'

She gave Gavin the coat and Uncle Jimmy inspected the label, then whistled. 'It's the real McCoy.'

'Wot is?' she said, grabbing it back and putting it on.

'Wee give yer that?' asked Gavin.

'A lass from the stables, why?'

'It's a Burberry,' said Uncle Jimmy.

'Is that good?'

'Good?' said Gavin. 'That's a five hundred pund coat.'

'Neeways!'

'Aye.'

'Yer knar wot,' she said, zipping it up, 'Ah've got a new favourite colour.'

Chapter 8

November 1985

Nana promised to tell her if there was any news about Dad and threatened to call the school to make sure that she was there. He hadn't been seen for five days, which was a record for him.

Thursdays weren't bad because it was cookery all afternoon. Today they were making rabbit stew with suet dumplings, or in her case, chatties, onions, and narkie stew with suet dumplings, with no meat. Only Trish and Sarah had rabbit. Most of the other girls had a chop or a tin of corned beef. Once the pots were in the oven, they stood about and chatted while the teacher went for a fag with the geography teacher.

'Wot yae deein here?' Sarah asked her.

'Wot der yer mean like?'

'Dinnet bite me heed off man, ah woz arnly askin cos yerv hardly been in this term.'

Sarah was a canny lass and she felt bad that she'd bitten her head off. 'Aye, ah knar, ah've been lookin after me dad, he's bad like.'

'Is he in Cherry-knocker?' asked Tracey.

'He woz until the Tories turfed him out.'

'Ah fucken hate the Tories,' said Sarah.

There was a general murmur of, 'Aye, me anarl.'

She poured the vegetable and dumpling stew into the Pyrex bowl she'd took from the new house. It was brimming and all she had was some tin foil, which stopped the steam, but would no way stop the slop. Keen to get home before it went cold, she didn't wait for anybody and walked as quickly and steadily as she could, cookery basket over her arm. She crossed Durham Road and was on the last leg home when she heard screams and looked behind to see radgie Brian. He should've been at a special school with the other dodgepots, but the council people thought it best for poor little Brian to go to a normal school. *Nice sentiment if you aren't the one being punched in the face*, she thought, as he came running towards her, all feet and fists. She held her cookery basket above her head to stop it from being booted.

'Gis a cake,' he said.

'Stew and dumplins,' she said, arms aching.

'Ugh.' He swung a foot, which landed right in her minge, and then ran off.

She put the basket on the ground and clutched her crotch. What a total twat. She couldn't wait to leave school.

The lads were disappointed that she hadn't baked cakes, yet they didn't kick her in the fanny over it. She forked the narkie into Ian's bowl because Jason hated any vegetable except chatties, and even though she sawed the dumplings into two equal rock-hard lumps, they argued over who had the most. The stew was lukewarm, not that they minded, and they didn't care if the dumplings broke their teeth. The cookery teacher said, 'If yer can't cook a suet dumplin, yer'll struggle ter pass CSE home economics.'

They poured red sauce over the dumplings, mixed it together, and then shovelled the mash-up into their gobs like they'd never been fed.

She was cleaning the slops in her cookery basket when Mam shouted, 'Wot's the witch deein here?'

Her blood drained to her feet and she felt sick. Something must be wrong for Nana to arrive unannounced. She ran down the path to Nana, who was getting out of Uncle Jimmy's car.

'Have they found him?'

Nana shook her head. Her face was red and her eyes were teary. 'He's died, luv.'

As Nana hugged her against her huge boobs, she closed her eyes and prayed there had been a mistake;

he couldn't have died because he was alive and he went for a roam like usual and he always comes back. Uncle Jimmy pulled her off Nana and bundled her in his car. She sat in the back seat, the same place she'd sat six nights ago when they were driving around the East End in the dark, slowing down whenever they spotted a figure in the shadows. She watched Nana go inside. He couldn't have died. Uncle Jimmy got in the driver's seat and rubbed his hands around the steering wheel.

'Wot happened?' she said. 'He can't be deed.'

Jimmy reached over and squeezed her thigh. He drowned in the sea. His body was washed up on Redcar beach this mornin. Police ses he problees went in the river on Saturda neet.'

'Are they sure it's him? Have yer seen him? Can ah see him?'

'Nor, neebody can see him. He'd been in the watter a lang time, decomposed like.'

Her heart burst, leaking acid in her chest. Her nose stung as her eyes pumped out hot tears that made the world go blurry. Next thing she knew, the car was moving, and she could hear crying outside of her head, and then she was tumbling, falling, and Nana was holding her head on her chest and all was good and then fear sprang like an evil Jack-in-the-box, and all was bad, forever. The car stopped and she could see her feet walking on pavement and then on steps. A body blocked her path; it was warm and smelled nice, and it was hugging her, and a hand was stroking her hair.

'Eeee, dinnet yae worry about nowt, it's all ganner be alreet,' said Lisa. 'Yer hear uz? Me and Dave are ganner look after yer.'

Her knees gave way and she didn't know who scooped her off the floor or who was carrying her up the stairs or who was screaming. Then she was lying on Nana's bed and the screams were louder and coming from her mouth, so to make them stop, she held her breath. The smell of Bronnley's English Fern took her to a happy place of eating scrambled eggs from a tray, and she clung to the past and prayed it was real before today kicked in again, and so did the screaming.

She could hear David and Nana's voices and then the light went on.

'Eee pet, come here.' Arms wrapped around her and Nana's boobs filled her face. 'He's at peace now,' she said, rocking gently, 'up in heaven with me mam and dad, and his Uncle Joe, and his dog Rex. Broke his heart when Rex died, used to say he couldn't wait to get to heaven to throw him a stick.'

She laughed and a snot bubble came out of her nose as she remembered Rex. Dad had a photo of him and the black and white mongrel that was taken on his nana's front step down Noble Street. It was weird to think they were all in heaven now.

'He'yar pet,' said Nana, ripping a fistful of tissues from the crocheted tissue box and mopping the tears flowing down her face.

She couldn't stop thinking about Dad floating all cold and alone in the vast sea. 'Uncle Jimmy said he went in the river,' she croaked.

'Police reckon he problees fell in near Hendon dock.' Nana blew her nose. 'The current woz strong and the watter woz cold, so he problees went strite under and that was that. They say that when yer drown, oxygen bubbles gan ter yer brain that mack yer feel happy. One of the nicest ways ter gan, apparently.'

It had been years since she'd slept in Nana's bed, and she knew that Nana was glad to have her there now that Gavin and Laura-Jane had moved out. She didn't expect to sleep anytime ever, yet she closed her eyes and thought of Dad, putting each thought into a compartment, which she filed as things to think of now, later, and never.

The sun pierced her eyelids and as her eyes opened, her chest was skewered by a stabbing pain, which she tried to make stop by jumping out of bed and flinging the curtains open. The woman across the square was in her dressing gown getting the milk in, and next door's ginger cat was asleep on the wall in the weak morning sun. It was as if nothing had changed and she kidded herself that nothing had, but the truth kept poking her in the heart, sending steely shocks down her arms and legs. Dad was gone. No matter where she looked, all over this earth, in every place, she wouldn't find him. How could a person be here and then not be here?

*

It had been six days since Dad died. Six days of keeping busy, of not thinking or feeling. Six days of everyone that Nana knows coming to the house, six days of Grandar being mostly down the club, and six days of not going home, apart from twice. It was quiet at Mam's. She couldn't stand to be there. She had to be at Nana's, close to Dad. Mam was probably going mad that she'd been left to look after the lads and Lisa said it would be good for her, and anyway, Dad was dead, so fuck her.

Nine days from being washed up on the beach to having a funeral was quick compared with Billy. It took over a month before the police were done with Billy's body and she was glad they burned him instead of burying him, yet she kept wondering if they'd found any clues. They probably had a file of corpse photos waiting for some clever detective to piece it all together. The police weren't so interested in Dad's rotting body. Cause of death: accidental drowning.

Lisa's youngest sister sent a black dress round to Nana's for her to wear to the funeral. It was from Etam and knee-length, made from velvet, with a low neck that was shaped over the boobs and lace sleeves with puffy shoulders. She put on the black tights Nana had bought her and then she slipped the dress over her head and bent her knees so she could see what she looked like in Nana's dressing table mirror. The pearly brush and hand mirror on the lace cloths were in the same place they'd been all of her life, and the Japanese jewellery box was like a castle, defending the dressing table from time. Nana used to tell stories about the people who lived in the houses with sloping roofs and the monster who lived on the snowy mountain. She picked up the photo of Dad and Uncle Jimmy, and kissed it.

Downstairs, they were all waiting, dressed in black with red eyes. Uncle Jimmy looked terrible. Nana gave the nod that it was time to go, so they buried their faces in their black scarves and filed down the path to the funeral cars that looked like a line of black beetles. The family next door was standing in their garden, heads bowed, and the people across the road came out.

Dad was, as Grandar said, 'Ridin up front,' in a coffin covered in red and white flowers. She was in the car with Nana, Grandar, Uncle Jimmy and Aunty Susan, and in the car behind was David, Lisa, Mark, Gavin, and Julie.

The funeral man in the long black coat with a top hat under his arm leaned into the car and said softly, 'We're garn ter set off now, okay?' He stepped back, put the top hat on, and knocked his black walking cane on the pavement. Another funeral man closed the car doors. The man with the top hat and cane walked in the middle of the road in front of the cars, and all the neighbours lined the pavement and bowed their heads as the black beetles glided quietly out of the square.

Nana and Grandar stared out of the window with glassy eyes full of sorrow.

When they stopped outside of St Luke's church, the man with the top hat opened the door, leaned in, and said softly, 'Okay, we're takin the coffin into the church now. Do wer have the pall-bearers?'

'That's me husband and son,' said Nana, 'and David, Gavin, and Mark, in the car behind.'

The church was huge and echoey. She expected it to be packed like it was at Great Aunt Beryl's funeral. She counted roughly thirty people and wondered how many people would come to her funeral if she died tomorrow as it was good to keep the mind occupied with trivia; all the kids in her class would be there, so that'd be thirty-six for a start, and with Dad's side of the family, she counted sixty people.

The vicar sprinkled holy water on Dad's coffin and she felt terrible that he was lying there, all cold and nailed in. Nana said he'd been embalmed with fluid and was wearing a suit and an SAFC scarf. She looked at the coffin and pictured a zombie from the Thriller video, oozing and green, with an eye dangling out, an arm missing, and bones piercing rotting flesh.

Nana, Lisa, and all the Walker sisters were crying when the vicar started talking, and Uncle Jimmy's shoulders were shaking to buggery. David wasn't crying. Years of showing Billy no pain had turned him to rock. She remembered how she used to imagine that her heart was frozen to keep the pain out. As 'The Lord is my Shepherd' started, she imagined an iceberg the size of the church, which got her through the first verse, but at 'death's dark veil,' her soul exploded, melting the ice, leaving her in a pool of tears. David put his arm around her and like a lighthouse in stormy seas, guided her to the familiar bedrock of feeling nothing. She wiped her eyes and pushed back her shoulders. David gave her the same look of pride he'd given her when Billy lashed them with his belt and she stood firm, showing nothing on the outside when she was screaming on the inside. Take a breath and force the air down the throat into the chest to dilute the pain, and then gently blow it out through the mouth with pursed lips to dry the tears before they fall.

Dad's cousin Philip gave a speech about the olden days that made the end of her nose tingle, which felt horrible, but she managed not to cry. She wasn't listening because she was distracting herself with thoughts of riding a dapple-grey horse. People were laughing at Philip in between sniffles and men blew their noses into handkerchiefs, probably trying to stop their nose tingles.

The beetle cars rolled along St Luke's Terrace and people stopped and took their hats off. It was a cold day, and she was shivering, having left Aunty Pat's black jacket at Nana's, so as not to spoil a lovely dress. She reckoned it would be warm in the crematorium and she thought about what it would be like to lie on a conveyor belt and go through a curtain into a furnace. She'd never been to the crematorium before.

Soon the black railings of Bishopwearmouth cemetery were running beside them, leading the way to the incineration of the last physical trace of Dad. They went through the cemetery gates and as they slipped quietly past the misty headstones, grave-tenders lowered their heads. Deep inside the graveyard, they turned down a road with tall trees looming on each side, making it go dark. They rolled in eery quiet towards a chapel that concealed an oven. Nana said that in India, they throw the wife on the fire with her dead husband, which seems harsh but solves the problem of how to carry on without him – she hadn't figured this out yet as she was leaving it until after Dad was totally gone; while he was in the coffin, he was still on the earth.

The funeral man slid the coffin out on a tray and Grandar signalled for the men to step forward. The only sound was footsteps as everyone followed the coffin inside.

It hurt like hell to drive away from the crem, Dad no more than ashes, but she was pleased to get back to Nana's.

The nice funeral man shook Nana and Grandar's hands and gave the signal for the black beetles to glide quietly out of the square.

The smoky living room was full of people and all the lights were on and all the windows were open. Her tummy rumbled as she inspected the table that was spread with triangle sarnies and slices of Gala pie on plates covered in cling film. In the middle was a chocolate gateau with glacier cherries on top. She hadn't eaten much since Dad died and even now didn't feel like eating. She hoped that Nana hadn't put Pease pudding in all the ham sarnies. '*Pease pudding hot, Pease pudding cold, Pease pudding in the bin, fuck off Pease pudding.*'

Lisa directed folks to the kitchen where Jimmy was on drinks duty. She pulled a Babycham from the pack and then went outside to find David.

The red sun was setting behind the houses at the end of the garden and David and his mates were drinking cans behind the greenhouse.

'Can yer open this?' she said, giving David the Babycham.

He flipped the lid off the bottle with his lighter and she took a swig. It was sweet like pop but with a kick of heat that went up the back of her nose with an aftertaste of flowers. She was cold, and David and his mates were talking about football, so she wandered off. The shed door was open, and feeling tipsy and brave, she let herself in even though you never let yourself into

Grandar's shed because it's full of goblins and things that are bad for little girls who go poking their shnecks where they don't belong.

'Dinnet touch me tools,' said Grandar from the shadows, making her jump.

There was so much stuff in the shed that it was difficult not to touch things, and apart from a shaft of sunset that made an orange circle on a car battery, everything was dark and oily and sinister.

'Yer gannie will have me guts for garters if she knew about this,' he said, handing her a rusty biscuit tin.

'Wot is it?'

He nodded for her to open it. It was full of cut-out newspaper articles.

'Clippins from the *Echo* about yer dad,' said Grandar.

'Why does Nana not want uz ter see it?'

His shoulders dropped. 'It's been hard for her, yer knar, wer owr Eddie and that.'

'The schizophrenia?'

'Aye, why, it woz a lang time before anyone said he was pooley. Everyone thought he was a wrang'un.'

'Wot did he dee?'

'Oh pet, wot didn't he dee? He was always in trouble. There woz this one time when he painted graffiti on the side of the chippy down Thorney Close shops.'

'Words or a picture?'

'Words, a jumble though, like the inside of his heed, didn't mack much sense.'

'Footy?'

'Nor, if arnly. It woz summink about the communist dictators.'

'Wot happened?'

'He got away wer a caution, but yer nana woz mortified. Wozn't lang after that someone smashed the winda on the front door. It was understandable like, wot wer Eddie causin havoc on the estate. Yer Nana woz at her wit's end so wer moved here.'

'Ah thought yer moved ter Pennywell cos Dad and Uncle Jimmy grew up and moved out.'

'Yer Uncle Jimmy was married ter his first missus, but Eddie woz still at home.'

'Yer fled ter Pennywell because of Dad?'

'Aye pet, suppose wer did,' said Grandar, laughing. 'It wozn't lang after wer moved that Eddie got some young lass in the club.'

'Me mam?'

'Aye.'

'Der yer knar where they met? Me dad said it woz when he woz workin down the fair, but she ses it woz at school.'

'Ah dunnar pet, but wot ah dee knar is that he nivver worked down the fair, or anywhere. He couldn't stick at anythin. The first ah knew of yer mam was when he brought her here wer a babbie in her arms.'

'David?'

'Eddie moved in wer yer mar up Thorndale Road and then yae came along. Happiest yer nana had been in years. She thought Eddie had grown up, yer knar, nee more gettin inter trouble.'

'And then he was committed, and we moved ter Pallion?'

'Aye.'

'Is that when he first went ter Cherry?'

'Oh, ah dunnar.'

'Yer dee knar,' she said. 'Wot happened, ah mean, the final straw like?'

'Yer'll have ter read the clippins. That's why ah kept them, in case yer wanted ter knar about Eddie like.'

He rummaged in the tin. 'Here yer gan,' he said, 'that's Eddie on top of the Prospect in 1973.' It was a picture of crowds of people all over the road at the Prospect junction. 'Taken from the open-top bus with the FA cup team as they came down Durham Road. That's Eddie on the roof of the pub.' Grandar pointed to Dad among the people waving scarves on the roof of the Prospect.

'How did he get up there?' she said, marvelling at the grainy black and white photo. At a quick count, there were seventeen other people on the roof. 'It wozn't just me dad.'

'Nor luv, but it woz arnly Eddie wee shinned up the Chimley.'

'Oh, reet.' She put the clipping back in the tin. 'Is that why he woz sectioned?'

'If arnly,' said Grandar.

She rifled through the clippings and Grandar touched her hand. 'It's not in there.'

'Are yer ganner tell uz how he first ended up in Cherry?'

'Nowt unusual for him like. He was picked up by police on North Moor roundabout.'

'Wot, actually on it?'

'Aye,' said Grandar with a sigh. 'Anyhow, he was rantin like a madman, so they took him strite ter Cherry. Simple as that. After all the years of rantin like a madman, someone finally thought ter tack him ter hospital rather than bangin him in a cell.'

'How long woz he in Cherry for?'

'Ah dinnar luv, but it woz a weight off yer Nana's mind that he woz bein looked after and he woz a looney not a wrang'un.'

'After he woz committed, Mam slagged him off all the time. She used to go on and on about how he was useless.'

'Aye well, she woz always quick ter put him down, but after yer dad went ter Cherry if it wozn't for yer Nana, you and David would've starved.'

She laughed as she remembered sitting with David at the kitchen table while Dad made them skinheads on a raft. If it wasn't for baked beans and bread, she wouldn't have made it to her fifth birthday. She could see that Grandar was holding back, and she was going to hassle him for more info when the shed door crashed open. 'Wot yer deein in here?' said David.

'Nowt,' she said, stashing the tin under her arm.

'Ha'way, out of me shed,' said Grandar, glad to see David and to end the awkward chat.

There were all sorts trodden into Nana's carpet. She wanted to chat to Great Uncle George who she hadn't seen since she was ten and probably would never see again, and she wanted to hug Fiona Walker for letting her borrow the dress. However, with the tin under her wing, she advanced directly to Nana's bedroom and tipped the clippings onto the bed. There were so many, including four front pages! Dad was such a legend.

POLICE END SCHOOL SEIGE. Police were called to Thorney Close School on Thursday afternoon when a fifteen-year-old boy armed with a replica gun climbed onto the roof and forced the evacuation of three hundred of his fellow pupils.

MAN RESCUED AFTER FA CUP GLORY HIGH JINKS. Rescue services were called to the Prospect Hotel, Durham Road, yesterday to aid a man who had climbed to the top of a chimney to see the FA Cup victory procession.

MAN ESCAPES BLAZE. Fire services were called to a house in Pickering Square, Pennywell, yesterday. It took firefighters four hours to get the blaze under control and to secure the property. The single occupant escaped unharmed and neighbouring residents were evacuated.

BODY FOUND ON REDCAR BEACH. The body found by a dog walker on Redcar beach on Thursday morning has been identified as that of missing local man Edward Hastings of no fixed abode.

She spread out his lesser escapades on the bed: Graffiti scum caught red-handed. Garden intruder falls foul of rake. Bridge closed for three hours. Busker gets violent. Shoplifter claims socks are Raich's.

Chapter 9

December 1985

The first thing she thought of before and after opening her eyes was Dad. Today, as usual, she swallowed the pain and prepared for life going on without him, gone forever, not coming back, never to be seen or heard ever again. She'd think about the man in the Fella's ice cream van who used to look down and sing as he handed her a cone, '*Smile though your heart is aching, smile even though it's breaking,* that's ten pence, sweetheart.'

The letterbox squeaked as the postie dropped today's letters. Most likely, a gas bill that was high because she'd spent too long in the shower, an electricity bill that was high because she'd spent too long listening to her tapes, a telephone bill that was high because she was always on the phone, etc. She wondered if there was a letter for her: 1) From Dewhirst's to say she could start as soon as she left school; 2) From the BBC to say that they were going to fix it for her and her brothers to eat a pink slice while going upside-down on the corkscrew at Spanish City in Whitley Bay; 3) From school, apart from they could fuck off because she'd been to most lessons since Dad died.

It was cold and she was glad of the towelling dressing gown that she'd cadged from Nana. She collected the post on the way to the kitchen and her heart leapt to see her name on an envelope and cringed that it was Miss Paula *Hart*. She tore it open, hoping for good news and unfolded the letter. It had a blue and red card glued to it. Like a credit card or something. She peeled it off and read it: National Insurance Number card. She knew what it was. She was sixteen. NY 66 42 81 C was the tax number she needed to give to Dewhirst's when she started work. Ally was the oldest in the year and had already got her National Insurance card. 'Owld enough ter pay tax, not owld enough not ter vote,' was what Ally said. 'Taxation without representation.' Ally knew about stuff like that because her dad was a politics lecturer at the polytechnic, and she lived in a big house on Ewesely Road that was rammed full of books. She hated being called Hart. Now she was sixteen she didn't need anyone's permission to change her name back to Hasting.

She tucked her tax card into the Sunderland and South Shields building society book that she'd kept in the back of her address book since she was in the juniors. There was one quid in the account that she'd won in an easter egg decorating competition. Her entry was a hedgehog made from a hard-boiled egg, coloured brown with felt-tip pen and with thorns from a rose bush stuck on as spines, using nail varnish as glue. Everyone who entered won a bank account with one pound in it, even the kids that had really shit eggs. Ginger Steven won ten quid for his egg in a racing car made from a bog roll middle, which they put in the window down Chester Road.

*

For her birthday, Nana got her a cookery basket cover with pictures of strawberries on it and Delia Smith's Cookery Course book with a picture of Delia holding an egg on it. Mam got her some plastic dangly triangle earrings that matched the turquoise blouse Aunty Pat got her from Clockhouse. The lads gave her a part-used bottle of bubble bath that they'd lifted from Nana Hart's house, and they sang, '*Happy birthder to you, squashed tomatoes and stew, bread and butter, in the gutter, happy birthder to you.*'

She couldn't believe it when the postie delivered a brown paper parcel with her name on it. She unwrapped a lovely lacey bra and pants set from Marksy's, a Body Shop basket with fifteen things in it, and a polo-neck jumper! Also, a 'top secret' letter from Charlotte that was sealed with a lump of wax.

Dear Paula,
Happy birthday! Sixteen at last! I have really good news – for a birthday present do you want to have a ride on Orchid with me on Whisper? Michael said it was fine for 3 o'clock on Sat 7 December. We need to work on your trot. See you at the stables at 3 pm. Ring if you can't make it.
TTFN,
Charlotte xxxx
p.s. The party was mental – I'm never drinking again – tell you about it when I see you.

*

Her nice dream was destroyed by the rattle of Ian flinging back both curtains with both arms. 'Wakey, wakey,' he said in a lost little voice. They'd talked before about how he missed his dad worst when he first woke up, and she said that she was the same. He pulled the covers off her face.

'Here-man,' she said, 'ah woz havin a nice dream there.'

'About yer dad?' he said, jumping in beside her.

'Aye,' she said, 'when ah dream about him, he's alive, and then ah wake up and he's gone, so ah sleepwalk through another day.'

He buried his face in the crook of her neck, 'Ah, miss me dad too, Paula.'

'Smile though your heart is aching, smile even though it's breaking.' She didn't know any more of the words and it didn't matter because Ian got up and pulled the bravest face in the world.

When she got back from footy with Ian, Mam was lying on the settee watching telly, and Jason was lost in a game of cars involving ramps made from placemats propped up by tins. She needed to be on the 2.45 train to Newcastle.

Her Burberry coat was far too good to be worn, yet she hated Mam's long maroon padded coat and her black leather jacket. She didn't mind the Fila ski jacket she'd got from David, but it was obviously a bloke's size.

In Jenny's castoff jodhpurs, Charlotte's riding boots, and the birthday polo-neck, carrying the long maroon padded coat, she felt proud to be at the place where all the horse things happen.

It was mayhem in the yard as Dorothy held the cars with a palm as a line of little girls on ponies trooped across. In the barn, the sight of Orchid being tacked up made her belly do skips and hops. The horse riding dream was about to come true for the third time.

'Hiya,' she said to Charlotte, who hugged her.

'How are you?'

'Good, aye, better ter see yae and this lovely horse.'

'Dorothy is giving us a lesson in the training arena,' said Charlotte, raising her eyebrows. 'For free.'

'How come like?'

Charlotte giggled and put a hand over her mouth. 'Michael has a soft spot for Mummy.'

'He fixed it for me?'

'Dorothy adores Michael,' said Charlotte, 'would do anything for him.' They looked at each other and burst out laughing.

'As if he'd touch her with a bargepole,' she noted.

'She's an amazing teacher,' said Charlotte, detaching Orchid's rope. 'Here, take her to the yard while I fetch Whisper.'

She watched the smug little girls get off their ponies, and when Dorothy saw her hanging about like a spare part with a Palomino horse, she was straight over, waving a finger. 'Coat on, girl, can't have it flapping around spooking the horses.'

She did as she was told while Dorothy stood over her like a headmistress. 'Button it up. Hat on.'

She put the horrible maroon coat on and zipped it up as instructed.

'Take your horse to the block.'

She took that to mean *take Orchid to the red plastic steps and get on*, so she did.

Sitting on top of the world she took a moment to take it all in, blinking her eyelids like a camera shutter, then holding the image in her head long enough for it to become a mental photo: never forget this.

Charlotte led Whisper to the block and got on. When Charlotte kicked Whisper's sides, she copied, and Orchid started walking. Clip-clopping hooves on concrete is the best sound.

Dorothy headed off down the track and they followed, horses walking side by side.

'Gan on then, tell uz about the party. Wot's with nivver drinkin again?'

'I was throwing up from about eleven and had to go home. Didn't feel too bad the next day, but when I got a whiff of fennel in Mummy's pasta, it made me gag.'

'Wot's fennel?'

'A vegetable that tastes of aniseed, the same as Pernod.'

'Wot like aniseed balls?'

'Yes, aniseed.'

'Neeways! Ah thought Pernod was fruity.'

'Nope, defo not fruity.'

'Ah'm guessin there woz nee leftover booze?'

'Oh my goodness, Paula, it was a brilliant night before I started throwing up.'

'Did yer get off wer badminton Ben?'

'Did I heckers like.'

'Shit, wot happened?'

'He turned up with a girl.'

'Oh, man, yer must've been gutted.'

'I was until I started talking to Josh. He's in the sixth form at Whitburn, he's *really* good-looking and he plays in a band called the Synth Panthers.'

'Wot instrument?'

'The synthesizer. He's got a big one, state of the art.'

'He's got a big one, has he?'

Charlotte laughed. 'Go away, I didn't mean that.'

'Have yer shagged him?'

'Not yet.'

'Ooooo, *not yet*. It's on the cards then?'

'We're going out,' said Charlotte, putting her head down.

'And? Spit it out.'

'We've done everything apart from sex.'

'Whoa,' she said, 'nice one, ah mean if yer like him like.'

Charlotte sat upright and gasped like she'd remembered something terrible. 'Don't tell Mummy.'

She zipped her mouth closed with her finger and thumb. 'Me lips are sealed. So ha'way then, are yers in love?'

'Yes, but don't tell Mummy.'

'Ooo, yer love him. Wot's that like? Ah mean, ah've nivver loved nee one before, not properly like.'

'When I think about Josh, I feel happy, as if nothing else matters.'

'And it macks yer Fairy-Anne gan all tingly?'

Charlotte went beety. 'Yes, I suppose so. Will having sex with him make that stop?'

'Nor, it'll problees mack it worse.'

'What, like being stuck between a cock and a hard place?'

She burst out laughing, which made Orchid judder, and Dorothy, who was miles ahead, turned around and scowled. Steadying herself, she decided to use the moment of mirth to face the coat music. 'Did Maddy have a nice time at the party?'

Charlotte pursed her lips. 'She's furious that you stole Minty's coat.'

'Here-man, she's the one wee nicked-off in me donkey jacket. Ah woz stood there for ages and ah didn't knar if she woz comin back, so ah went home.'

'You're lucky she didn't ring the police.'

She smirked at the thought of ringing the police about a coat – as if the police would give a diarrhoea.

'You shouldn't laugh. Madeleine's dad was furious.'

'Wee's dad?'

'Madeleine, Maddy.'

'Wot like the ragdoll off *Bagpuss*?'

'Yes, I suppose so.'

'Maddy's short for Madeleine. Yer learn summink new every day.'

'While we're learning new things,' said Charlotte, 'it's not *Isibird*, it's Isambard, as in Kingdom Brunel, the engineer.'

Her cheeks went hot. 'Ah've nivver heard of him.'

'Built bridges and railways, and ships, I think.'

She'd said *Isibird* all afternoon and Maddy never corrected her. She was glad that she'd nicked her mate's coat. 'Were they tackin the piss out of uz at school?'

'Minty was.'

'Minty. Wot kind of name's that?'

'Short for Araminta.'

'Nor, nah, yer havin uz on now!'

'No, honestly, there's a couple of Minty's at school.'

On that bombshell, she tugged down with the left rein, and as she steered Orchid off the track and into the arena, Dorothy gave her a despairing look.

She was buzzing after her first proper riding lesson, which, as she got down from Orchid, made the feeling with no name sting more. It was getting dark and cold, and the cars were gone except for Michael's silver tank without the horse trailer. She walked Orchid and Charlotte walked Whisper into the barn, and once inside, they swapped horses. Charlotte quickly got Orchid's saddle off and led her into the stable, and then Charlotte untacked Whisper while she lingered, trying to make the day last longer.

As she made her way across the yard, she knew it was over. She wanted to ask if Charlotte would be down during the Christmas holidays, or the holidays after that, or any Saturday, Sunday, or school day; she could make any time on any day. Instead, she just said, 'Say thanks to yer mam for sortin this for uz.'

Charlotte looked puzzled. 'It wasn't Mummy; it was Michael who suggested it.'

'Ah thought yer said yer mam asked if ah could borrow Whisper? That he has a soft spot for her.'

'Shush,' said Charlotte, 'don't let him hear you say that.'

'He's not here,' she said as he came out of the portacabin with his Barbour slung over one shoulder. He waved and walked towards them. 'How did it go?' he said in his calm voice.

'Amazin,' she said, 'thanks for sortin it out.'

'You're welcome,' he said, squeezing her shoulder. 'How are you ladies getting home?'

'I'm going to walk,' said Charlotte, 'meeting a friend in ten minutes.'

'A synth panther?'

Charlotte went beety and batted her arm.

'Are you sure I can't give you a lift, at least up to the main road?'

'No, but thanks. Nice to see you, Paula,' said Charlotte, stepping backwards, away from a hug and questions about riding next time. 'Best be off.' And she was, at a jog.

'Can I offer you a lift home?' said Michael.

'Are yer sure yer dinnet mind? Yer can drop uz at the station if yer like, that would be canny.'

She had to climb up into his car. It had leather seats and smelled of luxury. He put the radio on as they drove off, not speaking until they got to the main road.

'Did you work on your trot?'

'Not as easy as it looks, man.'

'Remind me, where are we going?'

'Plains Farm, other side of the river.'

Even the indicator sounded expensive, with its plonk-pause-plonk, not like the ticky-ticky-ticky of Lisa's Dad's Yugo. As they passed the shops and the big houses with Christmas trees filling the bay windows, 'Do They Know it's Christmas?' came on, and they drove for ages, not speaking. When the song stopped, Michael said, 'I didn't want to say earlier and make you feel sad when you were having so much fun, but I'm sorry about your father.'

'Which one?'

'How many have you got?'

'Stepdad, deed, real Dad, deed.'

'Oh,' he said. 'Your real Dad.'

She wrinkled her nose. 'My real Dad?'

'Of course.'

'Most people are arnly interested in me stepdad wee had his heed sliced off.'

'Yes, I heard about that, poor chap.'

She swallowed her bile. 'Ower Ian and Jason miss him.'

'Your real dad. How are you coping?'

The occurrence of someone giving a shit about her feelings made her laugh out loud.

'Why is that funny?'

'Nee reason,' she said, shaking her head. 'Ah'm okay, yer knar, ploddin on canny.'

As they went along Boldon Lane, 'Together in Electric Dreams' came on the radio. 'Love this song,' said Michael turning it up, 'let's dedicate it to your father.'

The road narrowed and he put his foot down. As they dropped the dips and rounded the curves, the speed and the music made her feel alive, like she was here, she was now, she was Paula Hasting, someone, not no one. Old grey stone houses appeared on both sides and when they stopped at the crossroads with the pretty café on the other side, she knew she was in Whitburn. He sped out of the village and when they passed Souter Lighthouse, the road was dark with shadowy hills on one side and ink-blue sea stretching to a lilac horizon on the other.

'Wot's that for?' she asked, pointing to the vast brick building built into the hillside. She'd seen it before on the bus with Nana and imagined it was an abandoned troglodyte village.

'It's a lime kiln. Huge quarry behind it.'

'Reet.' She didn't know what a lime kiln was and she couldn't be bothered to ask. She was about to say that they were going the wrong way when the car slowed with a plonk-pause-plonk. Michael pulled onto a track the size of a footpath, which turned into grass with the sea beyond.

'Where're wer garn?'

'There's a place I want to show you.' When he turned the car lights off, it was completely dark. 'Come on,' he said, getting out.

He stopped close to the cliff edge which plunged down to the waters that raged and crashed. She stood next to him and he put his arm around her. It was blarn a hoolie and her hair whipped against his waxy Barbour.

'Beautiful spot. I come here to think.'

'Ah knar wot yer mean. The sea reminds uz of how insignificant we are.'

His arm felt nice and she leaned into him as they watched the indigo sky turn black. She wanted to stay on the cliff edge all night with the twinkling stars and the endless sea.

'Should we go back to the Rangey?' he said.

'The wot?'

'The car.'

As she waited next to the passenger side door, expecting him to open the car, he put his arms around her and hugged her to his chest. Then he pressed his lips on hers, closed at first, then he opened them, so she did the same, and then they were kissing, not washing machine necking-on like the lads down the ice rink, proper, passionate, movie kissing. Holding her tightly with one arm, he popped her top popper, then the next, and the next until her coat was open. He ran his hand up her side, then cupped her boob, so she grabbed his bum, pulling him close to signal that she was up for what she hoped was going to be more than a kiss. As he moved his hand down her belly, she breathed-in to make a gap in her waistband and he slid his cold hand directly into her hot throbbing knickers. There was no fumbling, he knew what he was doing. She was pinned to the car with tingles spreading in all directions, every part of her craving him. He broke the kiss. 'Let's get in the car.'

She climbed in the back, arse first, kicking her muddy riding boots off before sliding along the leather seat. He got in and lay half beside, half on top, and pressed his mouth on hers. As they kissed, he unzipped his fly, then took her hand and moulded her fingers around his hard cock.

'Have you ever had sex?'

'Nor, am a virgin.'

Outside of her house in the Rangey, she saw the curtains twitch. Mam was halfway up the path before she got out of the car.

'Wee's car woz that?' Mam asked as Michael pulled away.

'A bloke from the stables.'

'Bloody stables? Ah've been waitin on yer for an hour. Get in that house,' she snarled. 'Ah'll be back at ten.'

The boys clung to a leg each.

'Yer smell of horse,' said Ian.

'Can yer tack uz ridin again?' said Jason.

'Mebees if yers are good lads.'

Jason knocked her boots on the front step while Ian helped her undress into the washing machine. They watched the telly while she ran a bath and spoilt for choice with her Body Shop set, she selected pomegranate bubble bath, apple bodywash, and coconut shampoo. She could smell Michael all over her skin, and the thought of his cock made her feel horny. He said that they could do it again if she wanted, and she didn't know if he meant horse riding, sex, or both, so she said yes. She sunk into the bath. Best birthday ever.

Chapter 10

December 1985

For her birthday Sonya gave her Madonna's *Like a Virgin* album, copied in high-quality from her tape-to-tape hi-fi, and Ally gave her a mascara she'd nicked from Boots. She turned the volume high and danced while she tonged her hair, blasting each twirl with hairspray. In the end, she tied it up to show off her earrings better. She tucked in her turquoise blouse and bagged it over the elastic waistband of the black skirt from Aunty Pat that she didn't wear to Dad's funeral. The tatty black kitten heels would have to do, and she wished she had some tights.

She'd expected to have to work hard to persuade Mam to let her go out round the town, yet all she said was, 'Dinnet come in this house fallin about palatic.' Earlier tonight, Mam had even given her a fiver to say thanks for taking the lads to Hetton, which was too good to be true, so she wondered what task she was agreeing to by taking it. She added the fiver to the three quid that she already had, making plenty for a night out. She could pay five pence on the bus as a child and Sonya said it's 47p for half a cider and they were going in six pubs.

The bus was packed with people who were all dressed up and it smelled of perfume, aftershave, and smoke. She was meeting the others at the pressy buttons in the central bus station at half-seven.

When she got off the bus, Sonya was already there wearing her black Miss Selfridge dress and high heels.

'Yae look nice,' she said, hugging her.

'Ah'm fucken frozzen,' said Sonya, rubbing her bare arms, 'the others berra hurry up.'

'Wee's comin?'

'Ally and Michelle. Alex can't mack it cos her dar's a nob.'

They heard someone shout, 'Lasses,' and turned to see Michelle waving and running from the bottom stop. She was wearing a blue lacey dress that you could see her bra through, and it was a relief to see that she wasn't wearing tights even though her legs were like slabs of corned beef.

'Yae lasses look nice, are yers ready ter party?' said Michelle, wiggling her hips.

'Too reet,' said Sonya.

'Where are uz garn first?' said Michelle to Sonya who was the only one who'd been round the town before.

'Ah think wer should start in Victoria's, then Digby's, Central, the Continental, and lasts in Fifth.'

Ally appeared behind them. 'Evenin ladies.' Ally was tall and would have no problem getting past the doormen.

It felt weird to be going up the leisure centre steps for a grown-up night out. The queue for the ice rink went down the ramp and around the corner, and the queue for the splash-in went out of the door, over the bridge, and down the stairs next to Parker's chippy.

They cut through the tunnel with the pool on one side and the ice rink on the other. As they walked, they peered through the twenty-foot-high glass panel into the huge leisure pool and dry beach that was already full of teenagers. The view from the tunnel was a paedos' paradise.

'Oh here-man, there woz this one time when ah was swimmin,' said Michelle. 'See the side ower there in the deep end?'

'Aye.'

'Ah sees this flowery ball in the watter, and ah didn't have me gegs on or owt, so ah jumped off and landed on it, and it woz arnly some wifey's heed – she was wearin a swimmin cap.'

After they stopped decking it, Sonya said, 'Yer look nice without yer glasses on.' She pointed at Michelle's eyes that had blue eyeshadow and clumpy blue mascara on her ginger eyelashes.

'Wot about yae, Paula? Swimmin or ice rink?' said Ally.

'Ice rink,' she said, running up the ramp to the point where you could see into the ice rink. There was a girl in the small rink having a lesson with the awful skate coach woman in the green woolly hat, and she thought about how she would've loved to have had lessons. The ice rink was mint, and she missed sailing round, with the music playing, and the disco lights flashing. Ally and Sonya joined her at the window.

'Ah remember that coach wifey with the woolly hat,' said Sonya. 'Me and ower Simone used ter come for lessons on a Saturda and if yer dared skate too close ter her little princess, she'd give yer reet daggers. Ah wouldn't mind, but the lass she woz coachin woz always on her arse.'

The top end of town was teeming with Dewhirst lasses in their yellow overalls, long white socks, and Kicker boots. Friday is payday, which was why they were stotten, falling all over, and singing. She couldn't wait to leave school and go to Dewhirst's. They don't take you until you officially leave, as she'd been recently informed by the truanting officer, so that would be Easter. Not long to go.

They all stood tall and acted over eighteen as they waltzed past the doormen of Victoria's. She had her fake date of birth ready if asked, i.e., David's birthday, an easy lie.

It was a squash at the bar and she was glad to get warm. 'Half a cider, please.'

'Dry or sweet?'

'Sweet.' She didn't understand how a drink could be dry.

They found a space and stood in a circle and Ally lit a fag and they all wafted her smoke away.

'Yae shagged gorgeous Conor yet?' asked Michelle.

'Fuck off,' said Sonya, 'Ah'll let yer knar when ah have.'

Conor was from a stinking rich family that Sonya's dad knew from the golf club. Conor was eighteen, lived in Durham, and looked like Emilio Estevez according to Sonya, although no one had seen him to confirm it.

'Ah've yer done owt at all?' needled Michelle.

Sonya was good at changing the subject. 'Wot about yae, Paula? Yer shagged that bloke at the stables yet?'

'Nor,' she said, pulling a disgusted face. 'It's not like that, he's someone's dad.'

'Yer rode his horse though?' said Ally, straddling her legs as if riding a horse and then bouncing up and down as if riding a bloke.

'Ha ha,' she said. She'd already vowed never to tell anyone about shagging Michael in his car. Not one single person, ever. The cider was sweet and was going down like pop.

'Is that Leanne Cooper's sister ower there?' said Ally.

'Aye, fuck,' said Sonya, putting her head down.

'Wot?'

'Here-man,' said Sonya, 'she's a right officious bitch and she knars wer underage.'

'A wot bitch?' they all said.

'Sup up, lasses. Let's get out of here.' Sonya put her head back and tipped her cider and black down her throat.

They linked arms in a wall of bare flesh as they headed past the funeral place and the Empire. There was a group of lasses up ahead shouting, so they broke the link and ran to see what was going on. Outside of the fire station, there were fireman doing stuff to a fire engine while the lasses were shouting, 'Get yer kit off,' and, 'Get yer cock out!' Then a gaggle of lasses came running over the road, screaming, 'Eeeeeee!' and lifting their tops up, flashing their tits.

'Ha'way,' said Sonya, dragging Ally away from the firemen.

She'd never noticed there was a pub between the gas shop and the Early Learning Centre, which was probably because, by day, it was a closed door, whereas tonight, the door was open and surrounded by bouncers.

'Welcome ladies, in yer gan,' said the doorman as they piled inside and down the steep stairs into a totally underground pub with a low ceiling. The bar end was chocka and it took yonks to fight their way to the front.

'Half a cider please.'

'Dry or sweet?'

'Dry,' she said, hoping to solve the mystery of how a drink that is wet, can be dry.

They found a table made from a barrel to stand around. It was squashy and smoky, and they were all coughing, including Ally who lit a fag. After two gulps of dry cider, she clicked how a drink could be dry and couldn't decide if dry was better than sweet. They were both wet in different ways.

'Der yaes keep gettin yer arses nipped?' said Ally.

'Aye,' said Sonya.

'Me anarl. It happened a couple a times in Victoria's, but in here, it's all the time,' said Ally. She turned to the lads behind her, 'Here-man! Fuck off will yers!'

Sonya said to Ally, 'Ha'way then, spit it out.'

'Aye, ha'way,' said Michelle.

Ally went beety. She'd been seeing Kev for six weeks. Kev was gorgeous, so if she was in Ally's shoes, she'd have jumped his bones by now.

'We did it,' said Ally, breathing out with relief.

'And?'

'And wot?'

'Owt else?'

'Like wot?'

'Like woz it nice?'

Ally went beety again. 'Aye, it wer canny like.'

'Did yer use owt?'

'Wot like a blob?'

'Aye, yer dinnet want ter get preggers.'

'Can yers remember when uz did sex education at school?' said Ally, changing the subject.

Michelle and Sonya snorted, which was the usual reaction whenever anyone mentioned the legendary day she'd missed because she was dollen off PE. She'd heard about how they all got dressed in their blue tops, navy gym skirts, and red sport socks, despite not doing PE that day. After the usual half an hour sat in a line on the gym floor, they were marched over to the dusty, creepy, ES room in the upper school.

'Can yer remember the chabble at the front?' said Sonya.

'Aye, it woz full of fanny pads like pillows and git thick rubber johnnies,' said Ally.

'For fuck's sake Paula, yer should've been there,' said Sonya.

'Oh, man, remember the fanny pad with the loops on?' said Michelle. 'There woz this fucken belt that yer were supposed ter put on and attach the loops.'

'Fucken'ell, ah'll nivver forget when hump-back Watson put the *sheath* on her hand,' said Ally.

'*Sheath*,' they all snorted.

'That's wot she called it,' said Michelle. 'Remember how much uz were fucken deckin-it?'

It was spitting on when they came out of Digby's, so they huddled together for warmth as they made their way along High Street.

'Are yers lookin forward ter Chrimble or wot?' said Ally.

'Aye. Cannet wait to eat a wass plate of turkey and roasties,' said Sonya.

'Aye, me anarl,' said Michelle.

'Wot yer gettin?' said Sonya, 'Ah'm gettin a portable telly for me room.'

'Yer lucky bitch,' said Ally. 'Ah'll problees get some smellies and pyjamas.'

'Me anarl,' said Michelle.

'Are uz comin ter yowrs ter watch telly?' she said, linking Sonya's arm tighter. 'Ah bet there's some good James Bond on ower the holidays.'

'Yers can come if yers bring yer selection boxes,' said Sonya.

'Haddaway,' said Ally, 'ah'll have mine eaten by Boxin Day.'

'Oh, here-man, ah usually get a wass Toblerone,' said Michelle. 'Yer can help yer sels ter it, ah dinnet like nugget.'

It started to pelt-it down, so they legged it into Miss Selfridge's doorway.

'Eeee, wad yer dare?' said Ally, pointing at the dress on the dummy.

'Did yer see the lass in Victoria's wearin it?' said Michelle, 'Looked canny on like.'

'Nah, wouldn't be seen deed in it,' said Ally.

'Aye, me anarl,' said Sonya.

When the lashing rain died down, they followed Sonya down the side of British Home Stores and along a back alley and into the Central. It was a long pub with a white tiled floor and a handful of people.

'Ah didn't knar this woz here,' she said.

'It's fucken deed,' said Sonya.

'Aye, but we'll get served,' said Ally.

It was weird to sit down in a pub and there was plenty of room in the booth.

'Ha'way drink up, let's gan rund the Continental,' said Sonya.

'Shall uz gan ter the bog in here first?' said Michelle.

The bogs were busier than the pub and the floor was swimming. There was a group of trollied Dewhirst lasses in front of them in the queue. One of them said, 'Alreet lasses, yer havin a good neet on the hoy?'

'Aye canny,' said Sonya. 'It's me mate's sixteenth, she's ganner work at Dewhirst's soon.'

There was a chorus of 'Happy birthder' from the Dewhirst lasses.

'Yer dinnet want ter work on the press, yer want ter be a machinist,' said the one with Christmas baubles dangling from her earrings. 'Ah'll tell yer wot, today ah woz sweatin me tits off on the press and there's this lass, Linsey, the fucken line checker, waltzin up and down, deein nowt. Ah'm like, ah'll dee her job.'

'Finish yer sewin exams,' said the one with the spiral perm. 'Have yer made a pair of trousers yet?'

'Aye wer did that last year,' she said, 'mine were fucken crap. Ah'm shite at sewin.'

'Nee bother so am ah, yerl fit reet in,' said the lass. Then she banged her fist on the cubicle door, and shouted, 'Ha'way lasses, stamp yer feet!'

The cubicle opened, five lasses came out and four Dewhirst lasses went in.

The Continental had a pink carpet and mirrored pillars. Everyone was wearing trendy clothes, and she imagined that when she was older she'd come in here wearing the latest thing from the window at Miss Selfridge. She also imagined how the fit man in the grey flecky suit and red skinny tie would dump the bitch with the electric pink lips and stilettoes and come and chat her up.

It was busy outside of the Continental. There were groups of lasses and lads and everyone was mortal. They linked arms, Sonya on her left and Ally on her right, and they huddled in close as they made their way along Thomas Street. The cider was heating her insides, but the bits that dangled or poked out were ravaged by the biting wind.

Halfway down Fawcett Street, Sonya did a swingy sideways step, and sang, '*Here we come, walkin down the street*.' They joined in with the steps and the song, '*we get the funniest looks from everyone we meet*,' then their Monkees steppy-walk got fast, '*hey hey, we're the Monkees and people think we monkey around*,' Ally's legs got tangled, and she tripped, pulling the rest of them crashing into Gowan's window, as the doormen on Fifth Avenue decked it.

'In yer gan lasses, strite down the stairs.'

It was another underground pub but this time with flashing lights and a silver light-up dancefloor like on the Billy Jean video. The music was loud, and Sonya shouted, 'Ah telt yer it woz more like a neetclub than a pub.'

They got a half a cider and stood against the wall. It was a cool place despite the low ceiling and sticky carpet and smell of toilet. There were hods of lasses dressed in nice gear and on the dancefloor was Lorna Beeks who had been a few years above her at school. Lorna was wearing a neon blue off-the-shoulder top and skin-tight neon blue satin trousers, her eyes and cheeks were shimmery pink, and she danced to Whitney exactly the same way as Whitney dances.

It was filling up and they were being pushed and jostled from their quiet corner. 'Are wer stayin here? Should uz get another drink?' said Michelle.

It took ages to get served and once she had her second drink, half of it got spilled as she pushed her way out from the bar. They regrouped in a circle among the elbowy, drink-sloshy carnage, and when Michelle downed hers, they all copied. It was better than spilling it.

'Dancefloor?' said Ally.

They pushed their way towards the dancefloor that was too packed to get on to. Michelle put her hand out for their empty glasses, stacked them neatly, then turned to the bloke who had his arms around her middle, kissed him a bit, handed him the glasses, and then turned back and danced.

It was topper in here and she was leathered and when 'Girls Just Wanna Have Fun' came on, they joined hands and Sonya led the snake between the bodies to the middle of the dancefloor. The bloke that Michelle had dumped the glasses on was having a good go on her boobs while they kissed, and while most of his spotty mates tried to pull Ally, the tall one in the green Lacoste top danced with her and Sonya. It was pushy and squashy and the flashing tiled dancefloor was swilling and full of broken glass.

'And after one for the girls, here's Denise Williams, 'Let's Hear it For the Boy',' said the DJ. They got moshed, and when the chorus came on, the blokes shouted, 'Get yer tits oot for the boys!' while all the lasses batted off an ambush of hands. She was glad when it stopped, a fleeting calm, then Slade descended and everybody swayed with their hands above their heads, '*So here it is Merry Christmas, everybody's having fun*,' they joined hands above their heads, '*Look to the future, it's only just be–gun*.' It felt brilliant and the bloke in the Lacoste top had his arms around her waist, so she turned and he pulled her close and kissed her. He tasted of fags and smelled of Kouros and she had to cling on to him to stop herself from slipping over. She wiggled from his arms and joined Sonya and Ally. 'Where's Michelle?'

'She gone off wer that lad,' said Ally.

The music stopped abruptly, an ear-splitting bell rang, and a doorman shouted, 'Last orders at the bar, last orders at the bar!'

'Eeee, ha'way, it's five ter eleven,' said Sonya, 'let's gan.'

They joined the crush off the dancefloor, and after climbing the steep stairs with a big sweaty anus pushed in her face, she took a lung full of fresh air. Outside a thick sea mist had blown in, and she had to feel around for her mates. Sonya made contact and locked arms. 'Where's Michelle?' asked Sonya.

'She's wer that lad,' said Ally.

They held hands, minus Michelle, and crossed the road, dropping hands at the other side so they could switch to a jog.

'Where's yer bus stop?' said Ally, her breath turning to icicles in the night air.

'Holmeside,' said Sonya. 'All the buses from central station stop there.'

'Aye, but they'll be stowed-off by the time they get ter Holmeside, best off garn rund the station,' said Ally.

At the thought of not getting on the last bus which left central station at eleven, the jog turned into a run. The cider sloshed in her belly, and she imagined that she was a racehorse with hot breath puffing from her nose, her neck and body lathered with sweat. She was keeping up with Sonya and Ally until one foot felt wet and cold making her slow to a stop as the others disappeared into the fog. Barefooted, she backtracked, bending down to see which pavement had stolen her shoe, and she'd been going so fast, it was bloody miles away. As she yanked at the shoe to try and dislodge the kitten heel that was stuck firmly between some wonky slabs, a tall figure appeared from the mist.

'Need a hand?' He bent down and pulled the shoe free. 'He'yar,' he said, handing it to her. It was the bloke with the Lacoste top from Fifth Avenue.

'Ta,' she said, putting it on. She would've hugged him to say thanks but then they'd probably start necking and she needed to catch the last bus. She had no chance of making it to the station, but if she ran, she'd make it to Holmeside. 'Ah've gotta run or else ah'll miss the last bus.'

'Me anarl,' he said. 'Holmeside?'

'Aye.'

She jogged along and she could tell he was trying to run slowly even though she was going as fast as she could. They stopped at the end of Fawcett Street and the sea fret was so thick that you couldn't see the museum across the road.

'Foggy the neet,' he said, waving his arms as if swimming towards her. He grabbed her hand and they jogged holding hands until the bright lights of the bars and burger joints on Holmeside shone through the fog, guiding the pissheads safely to the bus stop, halfway up, where all the buses stopped.

The queue filled the pavement and spilled onto the road, and as a Pennywell bus turned Carrick's corner, the crowd surged forward. When the bus pulled short of the stop, the people down the queue bulged into the open doors, and then a Holborn Road bus turned the corner, and the people at the front ran backwards and then forwards as it pulled round the first bus and stopped further up. Then two beams shone through the fog and all heads turned and squinted at the rectangle, Farrington . . . people ran in all directions like on Mike Reid's 'Runaround' . . . the 126, the 114, or the 102 . . . *G-g-g-go!*

She had to elbow a group of lasses to avoid being pushed onto the road, and as she teetered on the kerb, the bus slowed, and the doors *shhh*-ed open right in front of her. The crowd pushed her aboard.

'Five please,' she said to the driver.

'How owld are yer?'

'Sixteen. Ah'm still at school.'

'She's wer me,' said Lacoste top lad, looping an arm over her shoulder and dropping a pound coin into the money tray.

She followed him, squashing her way upstairs. The windows of the top deck were steamed-up and the bus was packed with wankered people. There were no double seats left. Near the back he found a single seat, and he sat and patted his knee. He was okay looking, a big forehead maybe. She sat on his knee and jiggled from side-to-side as he checked his pockets, pulling out some fags, 'Snout?'

'No ta.'

He put a fag in his mouth. 'Me name's Marcel by the way.'

'Marcel, that's fancy. Ah'm Paula.'

He lit up, put his lighter away, and then threaded his arm around her waist.

There was a group of lasses at the front singing 'Last Christmas', and on the back seat, there were people having it off. Marcel's fag was halfway down when he flicked it onto the floor. Then they started kissing. It was awkward until he pulled her close and felt her bum. After yonks, her jaw was aching, and the bus jolted, and everyone went flying forward. Loads of people got off and the bus moved again so they started kissing again. At the next stop, he leaned over the man sitting next to them and wiped the window. They were at the Barnes.

As the half-empty bus pulled away, her head said go downstairs and wait for her stop because her heart said that she didn't fancy Marcel, but her arse was glued to his knee and an invisible force drew her mouth to his. She imagined she was kissing Michael.

She could feel the bus chugging up Bede bank. 'It's nearly me stop.'

'Come ter mine.'

'Where der yer live?'

'Middle Herrin'ton.'

'Wot, on yer arn like?'

'Nor, wer me parents. They're away so ah have the place ter mysel.'

'If yer sure it's alreet?'

He put a hand up her blouse and said, 'Great tits.'

They kissed for ages until there was hardly anyone on the bus.

As they walked in the freezing fog, she didn't have a clue where she was, and she couldn't see a hand in front of her.

'Where does yer name come from, ah mean, is it foreign?' she asked.

'It's French.'

'You're not French though.'

'Nor, me Gran's French Canadian. That's where me parents are.'

'In French Canada?'

'In Quebec.'

'Like in the song?'

'Aye, that's the one.'

His sitting room was big with a stone fireplace and a bay window with velvet curtains and a Christmas tree. It wasn't a normal Christmas tree with a jumble of baubles and tinsel, and multi-coloured flower-shaped lights that short circuit the house on Christmas Eve. This tree was like the show-tree at Binns. It was a perfect green triangle with one type of silver bauble scattered evenly, one piece of silver tinsel twisted from top to bottom, and a string of silver carriages that twinkled with white light. It was ruined by the homemade, primary school-looking angel on top.

'Cute angel,' she said, as Marcel kneeled and fiddled with the gas fire that looked like a real one. 'Did yer make it?'

'When ah woz ten.' The glow of the fire made his shiny forehead turn orange. She fancied him a bit, sort of. He said nice things and kissing him was nice, so she decided that she'd have sex if he wanted to.

He took his jeans off and lay on the grey furry rug next to the fire. He had spindly white legs and black boxer shorts with stars on them. Her eyes said no, yet her body said go.

'Yer can tack yer clays off if yer want,' he said, sticking his hand down his boxers.

She was glad to lie next to him to make the room stop spinning. She slipped her skirt down and pulled her blouse off over her head, and lay there, legs mottled purple from the cold, yet feeling sexy in her lacey bra and pants from Jenny. The flames were dancing between the pretend coals and the carriages were twinkling on the tree and she felt warm and chemist and horny. And then they were fucking and it felt brilliant.

She was asleep on the rug and Marcel was gone and she didn't know what time it was. She turned over to swap her fire-facing side with her chilly wall-facing side when Marcel woke her up, standing over her wearing a footy kit.

'Sleep well?' he said.

He was less attractive now than last night in the glow of the gas fire. On the bus he had said he was twenty-one, and now in the sober light of day that was coming through the vertical blinds and splitting her head, she could see he was about seventeen.

'Aye, not bad,' she said, feeling around for her knickers. As she untwisted them, she could see that he had a stiffy, so she lay back on the rug, she may as well, as she was here, and then they were fucking again.

She counted four bedrooms on her way to the bathroom, which had a pink corner bath and a sink that was scalloped like a shell. Her face was pale and her eyes were black and splashing water on her face made her black eyes worse. She couldn't believe that she'd had sex with a strange lad and that she was in his house. She wiped her eye make-up off on the soft pink towel and pulled her hair around her face. It was a shame she didn't fancy Marcel because his parents' house was lovely and he was good at sex. Just because they'd shagged, didn't mean they were together, and it's not like he said he wanted to see her again, so it was fine to split without leaving her number.

As she came down the stairs, the front door was open and there was a car full of lads outside beeping the horn. She felt rare when Marcel started kissing her on the doorstep.

'Yer ganner get home alreet?' he said.

'Aye, ah'll be champion. See yer then.'

'Aye, see yer.'

She walked up the road, and as they drove past, they shouted, 'Whey-hey,' out of the windows.

Last night she had no idea what lay behind the fog, and now on this crisp December morning, it was all new. The wide road was lined with fancy walls and hedges, behind which lay stunning gardens, stretching back to big semi-detached houses with expensive cars in the long-driveways. Every so often there was a detached house with high iron railings and gates. When she got to the junction, she found out that she was on Summerhill, leading to Hillview, leading to more big houses, some of which were proper mansions, until she popped out next to the garage on Durham Road. Glad to stumble, shivering to the bus stop at the Board Inn, she knew she was almost home.

'Five please,' she said, giving the driver her child's fare, enjoying the warm air of the bus.

'Good neet, pet?'

'Aye,' she said, ripping the purple ticket from the machine.

Mam was in bed when she got home, and she hoped she would stay there while she had some Shredded Wheat with hot milk and watched *Saturday Superstore*. She couldn't be doing with a million questions about where she'd been, how everything she did was shit, and how the only way to stop it from being shit was to go and get the lads. If Mam asked, she'd say she stayed at

Sonya's. Mam liked anything to do with Sonya and her loaded family.

She washed Marcel off with Body Shop pomegranate sensation and pondered which of her clothes were least bad; jeans too tight, white skirt not warm enough, black skirt from last night covered in booze and reeking of smoke. The black cords that Aunty Pat gave her were proper whip-lashes, but as they were the only bottoms that were clean, she put them on, solving the flares by stuffing the legs inside her riding boots. She headed out to Hetton.

Chapter 11

December 1985

Mam deserved an Oscar for playing the grieving widow, and Ian and Jason did well for presents, bless them. The Hetton Lodge Durham Miners' Association had raised money to get the boys with the tragic dead dad some presents. Ian squealed when he opened his Masters of the Universe Castle Grayskull that replaced the one that got splattered with gore. Jason was gobsmacked at the Tonka dump truck that was big enough for him to sit in. She got the usual stuff, pyjamas, lipstick, bubble bath, bra, pack of knickers, pack of pens, as well as, she couldn't believe it, a *real* Nike sports bag! It was red and square with a white Nike mark on the front. As she held it in the air in amazement, Mam said, 'Ah spoil yae rotten.'

Today was topper. Whenever she got something she treasured, Billy would enjoy taking it away so much, that she soon learned never to reveal what she valued, so Billy didn't know to destroy it. He couldn't smash and stamp on this Christmas because he was ash blowing in the graveyard.

They rustled as they squashed into the Yugo. She wanted to ask David where her pink and green Kappa shell suit had come from, but she didn't want to sound ungrateful, and whatever wagon it had fallen off, she loved David. The lads' shell suits were from Geordie Jeans and David told them that it was cool gear that all the sports stars in America were wearing.

As they set off to Aunty Pat's, David started the sing-along, '*Jingle bells, Batman smells, Robin is a twit, The Batmobile, lost a wheel, and skidded in some shit.*' The lads giggled and rustled, and David sang it again getting them to join in, correcting their mistakes, and making them start over. By Hylton bank, Ian could sing it on his own and David nodded with pride.

'*While Shepherds washed their socks by night, all watching BBC, the angel of the lord came down, and switched to ITV.*'

As was tradition, now passed down to Ian and Jason, when Aunty Pat opened the door, they kneeled, and said, 'We bring yer gold, Frankenstein, and mercury.'

*

Boxing Day

The arguments at Nana's house over where to spread Dad's ashes came to a head on Christmas Day when

Uncle Jimmy stormed out with a cup of ashes to spread down the Cat and Dog Steps, leaving the rest in the urn for Nana to take to Penshaw. Penshaw wasn't a place Dad had cared about, and Jimmy's argument against it was the shit-splatted Lambton worm that Dad drew on the wall. Nana was having none of it, and said that Penshaw Monument was so high, Dad could look out across all of Sunderland. It didn't matter where the ashes were spread because they were ashes from Ally's fire. Dad's real ashes were in a Tupperware container under her bed, which was clever thinking of Ally who'd seen it in a film. The real ashes were going to Roker Park. That's what Dad would have wanted.

She'd never been to Roker Park and only vaguely knew where it was. Sunderland were playing Sheffield United today and she didn't have a ticket for the match because she wasn't going to stay. She'd go in, sprinkle the real Dad, and then get out before all the footballers got on the pitch. The lads at school said she should go to the main entrance at the Roker end and ask for the groundsman.

Town smelled of hops from Vaux and was teeming with people and footy fans. She followed a group of blokes with cans of lager and got on a packed bus that went over the bridge in a line of other packed buses that moved slower than the crowds that were walking. She had no idea where she was, and when she got off, she was swept along a street of old terraced houses. Dad's ashes were deep inside the pocket of her Burberry coat. A special coat for a special occasion.

She turned the corner and came face-to-face with Roker Park. The stands had corrugated roofs and towered so big the houses looked like matchboxes. In front of her was a ten-foot brick wall with railings painted red and a sign that said Fulwell End. There was no main entrance, only turnstiles in the bricks with long queues streaming from them. The entrance could be down either side, so she picked right. As she made her way through the crowds of men and boys and a few women, the smell of fried onions got stronger. Down the long side of the ground, there were more queues coming from the turnstiles in the wall that had another sign on it that said Fulwell End. She was on the wrong side, shit. Rather than backtrack, she continued forward, past a group of grown men, stripped of their footy shirts, singing their bare-chested, fat guts out in the bracing wind that whipped off the North Sea. The smell of fried onions got stronger, peaking at the burger van that had a queue of lucky bastards with enough money for a long sausage in a long bun with fried onions and salad cream.

Further along from the burger van she could see a man in a bright yellow top, like what an official person would wear, someone who could guide a lost girl to the main entrance. She made her way among the sea of red and white towards the yellow top that bobbed in and out of view. She followed him round the corner, and there, towering above the crowd, were policemen in bright yellow bibs, one on a huge brown horse and one on a huge grey horse. She picked her way towards the beautiful creatures, then gave the grey horse a stroke and a sniff, *ahh*, the smell of horses. The man in the yellow top waved a carrot at the mounted policemen who nodded. The grey horse rolled its lips back and grabbed the carrot with its teeth. The man smiled and took another carrot from his pocket. He held it out, 'Der yer want ter feed her?'

Her heart leapt. She took it, and said, 'Carrots are like chocolate for horses.' The grey horse slobbered on her hand as it wrapped its lips around the carrot.

'Wee yer here with?' said the man, stroking the horse.

'Ah'm on me arn.'

'A Sunderland fan are yer?'

'Ah've come ter scatter me dad's ashes.' She patted the Tupperware container in her pocket. 'He was a fan.'

He looked up at the policeman and then back at her. 'Yer problees best ter come on a non-match day, when the ground is empty.'

Her heart sank and she felt like an idiot. 'Wot day der yer think?'

The man smiled and touched her arm. 'Hang on pet, ah'll gan ask.'

She stroked the horse and waited for him to come back. He wasn't gone long.

'Ah've had a word, and yer need ter come back on Monda at ten.'

'This Monda?'

'Aye. Gan ter the entrance in the Roker End and ask for Ronnie. He's the groundsman.'

It dawned on her how stupid it was to think she could scatter Dad's ashes on the pitch at Roker Park on a match day, and the look on the man's face hinted that she wasn't the first to make this mistake. She hit herself on the side of her head, muttered, 'Match Day,' and thrust her tongue into her bottom lip, '*drrrrr*.'

The man smiled. 'Dinnet worry luv, come back on Monda at ten.'

'And ask for Ronnie,' she said, hugging Dad.

'That's reet, now get yersel home and look after them ashes.'

*

On Monday at ten she found the Roker End which was an entire side of the ground with a main entrance. There were windows like a school but with red panels instead of blue and a porch on pillars with Sunderland AFC on it. There were cars parked outside and people coming and going from the main entrance under the porch.

There was a man in the foyer who came over to her as she came in. 'Wot brings a bonnie lass like yae here?' he said. He was short and stocky and totally bald like Kojak.

'Can yer tell uz if Ronnie is about?'

The man looked confused. 'Ah'm Ronnie. How can ah help yer?'

'It's about me dad's ashes.' She patted her pocket. 'Ah want ter scatter them on the pitch.'

'Oh,' he said, rubbing his chin. 'Ah dinnar about puttin them on the pitch, it's not usually allowed, like.'

'Gan on, ah'll arly be five minutes, me dad loved Sunderland.'

'Wait there a minute,' he said, 'ah'll gan ask them.'

If they said no, she would tell him about how Dad's body was washed up on the beach, and if that didn't make him take pity, she would cry.

He returned smiling and rubbing his hands. 'Reet then pet, ah've cleared it. Ah telt them that yerv come all this way on yer arn, so they said, just this once.'

She followed him through a warren of dark corridors and then a light corridor, at the end of which she could see green. Then they emerged into a huge wooden stadium that was empty and silent apart from the seagulls. The pitch was green and perfect and vast.

Ronnie pointed. 'In the goal at the Roker End.' He winked. 'That's where the Roker royalty are scattered.'

The pitch was much bigger than it looked on the telly and much more eerily quiet than she expected. As she jogged toward the goal she imagined the stand crowded with men in overcoats and flat caps, chanting abuse at the referee. She stood in the goal, got Dad out of her pocket, and wondered whether to run and streak him behind her, or whether to sprinkle him like seeds. She held up the box and said, 'Reet then Dad, let's put yer ter rest.'

She decided on the penalty spot, which was much further away from the goal than it looked on the telly. She kneeled on the springy grass and turned Dad out like turning out a cake. 'Yer'll get the best view from here.'

She patted the pile of ashes into the penalty spot while singing the first verse of the Lord is My Shepherd, then she stood, took a solemn step back, and hung her head. This wasn't the place for tears. She said the Lord's Prayer under her breath, ignoring Ronnie in the corner of her eye, who was waving from the side of the pitch. She could've stayed there forever. She turned and walked away from the spot as if walking from his grave. He was at rest now, at peace.

Ronnie hustled her along the tunnel, and she followed him along a light corridor and then a dark corridor, and when they came to the end, he held a door open. She expected it to lead to the main entrance, not a small room that smelled like a PE cupboard. There were all sorts of sports stuff stacked neatly on a row of wire shelves, it was amazing. The door swung shut and he turned to face her.

'Now it's yowr turn ter dee somethin for me,' he said, reaching out and grabbing her boobs with both hands. She was frozen to the spot. She didn't realise that there was a deal. He got his dick out. It was the size of a thumb and the colour of a saveloy. She stepped toward the door, and he lunged and pushed her face against the white brick wall. 'A favour for a favour like, it's arnly fair,' he said, lifting her skirt up and pulling her knickers down. She didn't know what he was doing so she stayed still and then he clamped his arms around her from behind and started thrusting, pushing her face into the wall. She couldn't feel much, but she knew he was having sex with her, so she tried to wriggle free, and as she moved, he grabbed her tighter, then he jerked and went still. He let go and she stayed against the wall until she heard the door swing shut. She took a clean white towel from the wire shelf, wiped his spunk off her fanny and legs, then dumped it on the floor. What a disgusting fucking bastard. She found her way back to the main entrance and slipped out.

On the bus, she felt like crawling under the seat and licking the dirty floor. She couldn't stop thinking, *A favour for a favour, it's arnly fair.* She was such an idiot. Then she thought about Dad at rest on the penalty spot. That's all that mattered.

At home, she ran the bath, and thought about putting bleach in it. His nob was so small that she couldn't feel it, so it didn't count as sex. It didn't happen, not properly.

Chapter 12

January 1986

When she gave Michael her number, she didn't think he'd phone. It was a quick call and he said that he'd pick her up at the Seaburn Camp bus terminus and not to bother bringing her riding hat because the plan was to get Whisper ready for showjumping. She didn't ask if they'd be having sex even though she'd been thinking about having sex with him almost every minute since it happened. The tingling, throbbing feelings of Michael cancelled out the creeping, curdling feelings of rape-man. It's like Nana said, 'The Lord giveth with one hand, and taketh away with the other.'

She sunk into the leather seat of his Rangey. 'Is yower Amanda in Spain with yer wife?'

'Does a bear shit in the woods?'

It was weird hearing his gentle voice swear.

'Do they ever come home?'

'They're hacking in Andalucía.'

He was fine to talk about his family if they were in Spain, yet any talk of their lives in Tynemouth was off limits by the way he changed the subject. Before, when she asked him about his job, he said he comes to the stables to forget about work and then he changed the subject. He liked cricket and she pretended to be interested in off spin and leg spin, and in return, he pretended to be interested in her mates.

'Me best mate Sonya's seein this stinkin rich lad.'

'How rich are we talking?'

'His dad has factories that mack summink ter dee wer telephones.'

'Absolutely stinking then.'

'Here-man, Sonya reckons Conor looks like Emilio Estevez, from *Breakfast Club* and *St Elmo's Fire*.'

'And does he?'

'Dunnar, nee ones seen him.'

'Maybe she's worried you'll steal him.'

'If he looks like Emilio Estevez, ah might.'

When Michael turned off the road for Boldon and onto the road for Cleadon, it didn't look like they were going to the stables. There was a big bungalow, a two-storey oblong house, a two-storey house with a church window, and a bungalow with a front like a church. Each one was different and made from the same sandy stone. They went through some fancy gates, then he turned the engine off. 'Here we are.'

He got out, took his Barbour off and threw it on the front seat. When her boots hit the gravel, she knew she was somewhere special, and she enjoyed the feel and sound underfoot as she strode up the driveway of the expensive house with Michael in his stone-coloured chinos and blue shirt.

He unlocked the house. 'In you go.'

It was like a cathedral. The hallway went all the way up to the roof and the stairs were made from wood and were floating. The bannister was a steel pole propped up with a sheet of glass like in a spaceship.

'Is this where yer live?'

'No,' he said, 'I'm house sitting for a buddy.'

'Ah yer ganner show uz the garden?' she smirked.

'Thought we'd start with the bedroom.'

The bedroom had a wall of mirrors that were wardrobes and black wallpaper with a red stripe. It had the biggest bed she'd ever seen with red silky covers and a black leather headboard. Michael sat on the bed and unbuttoned his shirt.

'Stand there,' he said, pointing to the centre front of the wall of mirrors.

'Der yer want uz ter suck yer nob?'

'Have you done it before?'

'Nor.'

He lounged on an elbow and stuck a hand down his chinos. 'Take your clothes off.'

'Wot, like ah'm a stripper?'

'Yeah if you like,' he said, unzipping his fly.

She felt like an idiot as she tried to act sexy while tugging her jodhpurs off and she was glad she was wearing her lacey knicker and bra set. By the time she got her jumper off, he had his shirt and kecks off, and his full cock and balls were dangling over the top of his tight underpants. She'd never given a gobble before because it sounded minging, but there was nothing she didn't like about naked Michael with a hard-on. She closed her eyes as she plunged her open mouth down and sucked his soapy cock, and as she sucked, he groaned, so she sucked harder. Her mouth was dry and her knees were hurting when he hauled her onto the bed.

As they drove out of the luxury gates, she felt warm and hazy as she wondered if this is what they meant by having your brains fucked out. She didn't want to ask if he was going to drop her off at home, she'd wait and see, and she wasn't taking much notice of where they were going until they went past the lime kilns, which was the wrong direction for home.

'Where wer garn?'

'Marsden Grotto,' he said, driving into a busy carpark with a white hut at the end.

She'd been to Marsden Rock before with Nana and Julie when they'd climbed down the millions of steps to the beach and played in the rock pools. They had crisps and stottie sarnies, apart from Nana tried to be posh by saying balm cake instead of stottie.

Today was the first time she'd been along the tunnel and down in the lift to the pub carved from under the cliffs. 'It's mad in here,' she said, following him into the cave pub.

'What would you like to drink?'

'Half a cider please.'

She sat on a stool at table that was a barrel which was next to an actual cliff face covered in netting with entangled plastic starfish and crabs. In a peaceful daze, she gazed out over the golden beach and the sparkling sea and up the craggy rock that was covered in squawking seabirds.

Michael sat down and undid a couple of buttons on his shirt which was uncreased despite being thrown on the floor and kneeled on.

'How are you?' he said, plonking a glass of cider on the wobbly barrel.

She took a swig, and it made her shiver. 'Good ta.'

'Have you been here before?'

'Not in here, but Nana used ter bring uz ter the beach.'

'Do you get on well with your nana? Tell her things?'

'Wot like am ah ganner tell her about wot we've just done?'

'You're a clever girl. You can see right through me.'

'Nor ah'm not ganner tell Nana owt, or anyone, not even Sonya.'

'You're an attractive girl, you know, special, you need a boy of your own age. I'm not the one, you know that?'

'Aye, ah knar that.'

'Come on, let's go for a walk, bring your drink.'

They went out onto the patio and down the steps and onto the beach. He walked quickly, his shirt billowing in the wind as he strode off along the sand, and she did her best to keep up. He stopped at the opening to a cave in the cliffs, and she hoped he was going to drag her in and fuck her again. He leaned against a crag, and she stood next to him, too windswept to speak. He moved in and kissed her and she tried not to spill her cider as he slipped a hand up the front of her jumper. She heard zipping and then he guided her free hand to his stiffy, clamping his hand on top, showing her a wanking motion, before letting go. They were kissing, and she was wanking him, and then he pulled away suddenly. He turned his back and zipped up his trousers. She went up behind him and wrapped an arm around him, pressed her sideways cheek into his broad back, and said, 'Wot's the matter?' He shrugged her off and walked away, so she tottered behind him sloshing cider everywhere.

He was at the steps up the cliff when she caught up with him. 'Ah dinnet understand wot's garn on,' she said.

Leaning on the rail, he sighed, and rubbed his chin. 'The thing is Paula, I'm a married man. It would be a problem if I fell in love with you.'

She swallowed the last of her cider.

'Do you know what I'm trying to say?'

'Not really.'

'I don't think we should see each other anymore.'

There was a sharp pain in her chest, like an elastic band pinging. She was being blown out, not that they were ever together. 'Oh, okay then.'

His soft eyes narrowed and hardened. 'You do understand?'

'Aye, ah understand,' she said, a bit scared. 'Can ah have a lift home?'

'How about I drop you at the bus stop? We don't want your mother asking questions.' He grasped her forearm roughly and dragged her towards him. 'If anyone finds out about us, there will be consequences. Understand?' He switched his clenched fist from her forearm to a friendly shoulder squeeze, and joked, 'Steps up the cliff or take the lift?'

Chapter 13

March 1986

'Ah still reckon yer should report Saveloy Dick. Wot he did woz proper shan, like,' said Sonya.

'And say wot?'

'Tell them wot happened.'

'Aye, but ah didn't exactly tell him not to, and anyways, it's not like ah felt owt.'

'How big did yer say it woz?'

'Fucken tiny,' she said, showing Sonya the size of his dick with her thumb.

'You girl!' said Mrs Speed, coming towards her, pointing her twisted finger. She pulled at her fabric. 'Is that all that you've done?'

When Mrs Speed walked away Sonya stuck her two fingers up behind her back.

She wasn't going to tell anyone about what had happened and it was only because she was pissed last Friday that she'd told Sonya. She'd stayed at hers when her folks were away and her older sister Simone gave them a bottle of Merrydown. When they were palatic, Sonya told her that she'd lost her virginity to Micky Morris in his car and that Conor must never find out.

'Why did yer dee that Sonya?'

'Dunnar, ah felt like it.'

'Yer knar, when yae first said that Conor looks like Emilio Estevez uz all thought yer were bullshittin, but he actually does. And he's rich, so why fuck Micky Morris?'

'Dunnar, ah felt like it.'

In return she told Sonya about the man from Dad's ashes and was pleased that she didn't think that she was an idiot. Sonya called him Saveloy Dick and said that he was a sex offender. Sonya promised not to say anything about it, but then she told Simone who said she was the victim of a sex attack and that she should go to the police. She wished she'd never told Sonya, and she'd better not tell Michelle. Simone reckoned the police could find him. She was glad that she'd told Sonya it was a random bloke and not Ronnie the groundsman. If she went to the police, they'd probably ask loads of questions about who she'd had sex with and think she was a slapper. Saveloy Dick would deny everything anyway. Her word against his.

'Yae comin out on the lash on Frida?' said Michelle, turning round.

'That's it!' said Mrs Speed, standing up, flapping her arms, and striding down the classroom in her Scholl sandals. 'All of you, stop what you are doing and stand up!'

There was a collective groan as the sewing machines stopped and chairs scraped. Mrs Speed walked between the desks, pulling at fabric and tutting. While they were standing in silence there was a class change and a swarm of kids banged on the window and stuck their two fingers up. One kid shouted, 'Speedy, yer frigid bitch!'

She put her head down and tried not to laugh and she could sense Sonya shaking with laughter next to her. They were made to stand until the kids had cleared and all was quiet.

'Okay, ladies,' said Speedy, doddering back to the olden days, 'you may sit and continue sewing.'

The machines hummed. She was making a beanbag, or rather a beanbag cover that would never be full of polystyrene balls. Mam said that she wasn't made of money and that she was lucky to get the scratchy fabric for the bag without the extra expense of the beans to fill it. She guided a row of flowers under the needle as she stitched another hexagon-shaped patch to another hexagon-shaped patch to form a big floppy football shaped thing. Every time she moved her arm forward, she got a whiff of sweat.

*

She'd heard that if you piss in a clean plastic pop bottle and take it to Fairview chemist next to Books Fashions, it costs six quid for a pregnancy test and you get the result in three days. She didn't need to do this because her school skirt didn't fasten, her tits were like melons, and the smell of the bin/cold grill pan/inside of the fridge made her gag. She didn't keep track of her periods and they were all over the place anyway. When she thought back, her last period was in December before Marcel and before the second fuck with Michael, and it was nothing to do with Saveloy Dick because they were standing up so the spunk dripped straight out. She was probably too far gone for an abortion, and anyway, she didn't want to get rid of it, she wanted to have it and look after it and live in a house of their own. Loads of lasses she knew had bairns and all of them had a nice house and enough benefits to live on. She'd practiced it in the mirror. 'Ah think ah'm pregnant.' 'Ah'm pregnant.' 'Eeeee, yerl nivver guess wot?'

Whichever way she said it, it sounded scary. Telling Sonya was nothing compared with what was to come. She'd have to tell Mam and Nana and the doctor and then she'd have to go to hospital and have a baby come out of her fanny. If she felt too shan to tell Sonya, how the heck was she going to have a baby? She had to tell someone, Sonya first.

She sat at the back next to Sonya in maths. They opened their textbooks and then the teacher talked really quickly and scribbled a calculation on the board. She had no idea what he was talking about.

'You get on,' he said, then left.

They both rocked back on their chairs against the wall, and she took her chance. 'Ah'm pregnant.'

Sonya rocked forward with a crash. 'Neeways! Wee's is it?'

She rocked forward and didn't answer, she hadn't figured this out, but Sonya's mind was skipping fast, 'How pregnant are yer? Have yer been ter the doctors?'

'Ah dinnar. Yae the first person ah've telt.'

'Am ah? Eeee thanks,' said Sonya, giving her a hug. 'Ah cannet believe ah'm ganner be an aunty, can ah be an aunty? Wot der yer want a boy or a girl?'

She told Sonya about when she had her last period and Sonya concluded that it must be Marcel's, so she went along with it. Michelle was seeing his mate for a couple of weeks after getting-off with him in Fifth Avenue, so she knew that Marcel was seventeen and in the sixth form at St Aiden's, and not a twenty-one-year-old graphic designer like he said he was. It didn't matter who he was because she wasn't going to tell him that he was going to be a dad.

Chapter 14

April 1986

Despite Mam being fine with having a pregnant teenage daughter, mostly because she was sixteen when she had David, her punishment was to look after the lads more than usual. At the meeting at school, Mam sided with the deputy head, agreeing that her daughter should be ashamed of herself because she was an all-round disappointment. The deputy head talked about her sitting her GCEs and Mam pretended to know what subjects she was doing. They were allowed to leave by the main entrance and as she went down the grand stone steps, she did a wet fart. She wouldn't be back for her exams or anything ever.

Since leaving school she'd spent hours with Mam watching telly and eating salt and vinegar crisps, which was the only thing that stopped her from feeling sick. It was nice to be mother and daughter, laughing at people on gameshows.

'Name an animal with a name from the Latin for a hundred legs.'

'Spider.'

'For fuck's sake,' said Mam, 'even a thick heed like me knars that's a centipede.'

She'd tried talking to Mam about giving birth, which always diverted into a conversation about how lucky she was not to be flung out of the house and how lucky she was to have a mam who defended her against the social worker, even though the social worker had defended her against her mam. 'Ah see your point Mrs Hart in respect of your own relationships, but I don't think it's helpful to say that it's a good job there's no dad on the scene.' The social worker had looked at her as if to say, this baby is your ticket out of here. In Mam's defence, she lied to the social worker about making sure she goes to her exams.

*

When she walked the lads to school, it was mint being among the mams. They all asked her how far gone she was and if she had any names picked out. One of them offered her a cot and a highchair. She'd made mates with a lass called Gillian who had a kid in Jason's class and she'd usually go to her house in Perth Road for a cup of tea after they'd dropped the bairns off. Gillian said that she was going to make a brilliant mam.

'That's not what the woman at the hospital said.'

'A midwife?' said Gillian.

'Nor, ah dinnet think so. Ah dinnar wee she woz apart from a sour-faced bitch.'

Gillian laughed. 'Did she say yer'd ruined yer life?'

'Aye, and that ah woz settin a bad example ter other lasses.'

'Here-man,' said Gillian, 'dinnet listen ter nee one up that hospital. Wot did they say down the DSS?'

'They woz canny like, yer knar, nice ter uz.'

'Wot about the housin office? Ah had ter wait hours in that place,' said Gillian. 'Did yer put down for a house at Plainsy?'

'Aye, or Springwell.'

'Ah put Farra first, then Silky, and got this place,' said Gillian. 'Ah love it here mind.'

'Here-man, ah gave the wifey in the housin office a reet sob story about how me stepdar committed suicide by slicin his heed off and how ah need ter live near me widowed Mam.'

'Billy Hart woz yer stepdar!'

'He woz a reet bastard. Dinnet believe wot it said in the paper.'

'Ah heard that both eyeballs popped out and he crapped himself.'

Crapping himself was a new one. 'Pissed himself anarl,' she said.

'Ah dinnet mean ter be nebby like,' said Gillian, 'and just tell uz ter shurrup if yer want, but woz he havin a strangely wank?'

Another new one. 'Wot der yer mean?'

'Like when yer strangle yersel, yer get a reet stiffy?'

'Der yer?'

'So ah've heard like.'

She pictured Billy's headless corpse dangling in the fishing lines with its nob hanging out. 'It ses death by misadventure on the death certificate. Nowt about his eyeballs or a strangely wank.'

'Ah'm sorry, yer knar, about everythin.'

'Nee worries, ah hated the man. All the arse-holey things he did ter uz when ah woz a bairn, when ah woz too young ter fight back.'

'Eeee, that's proper shan that is.'

'Aye, why, it's like me nana says, everythin yer dee catches up wer yer in the end.'

*

Ally hung out of her bedroom window with a fag while Sonya lay on the bed next to her with a hand on her bump. They were both in their uniforms and had walked out of school after the register, although you couldn't tell that Sonya was wearing a uniform because her grey skirt was from Sgt Peppers and her white shirt was from Chelsea Girl. Michelle was at school because she was doing O-levels in English, English lit, history, and geography, and had a chance of at least Cs. Ally was entered for O-level English and history, and CSE everything else and could do well if she could be arsed.

Ally flicked her fag onto next door's garden, 'Me dad wants uz ter stay on and dee A-levels.'

'Wot *are* yer ganner dee?' said Sonya, like she was the one to judge.

'Dunnar. Get a job.'

'Gan on a govie more like,' said Sonya.

'At least ah'm not garn ter wax fannies in South Shields,' bit Ally.

Sonya moved closer and put her head against her bump.

'So yerv decided then, ter dee beauty therapy?' she said.

'Ah'm not hairdressin, that's for certain,' said Sonya. 'And beauty therapy isn't just hair removal, it's make-up and nails and facials and all that. It's two days at college in South Shields and the rest is on-the-job trainin.'

'Where at?'

'A beauty clinic in Durham,' said Sonya.

'Conor's dad's clinic,' added Ally.

'His mam's clinic,' snapped Sonya. 'His dad has factories that mack fibre-optic cables.'

'Have yer shagged him yet?' said Ally.

'Nor, wer tackin it slow.'

'How fucken slow? Yerv been seein him for five months, yer must be gaggin for it,' said Ally.

'And when are uz ganner meet him?' she asked.

'Fuck off with all the questions,' said Sonya.

Chapter 15

June 1986

In the kitchen cupboard: two large tins of baked beans, a tin of corned beef, a tin of vegetable soup, a tin of pineapple rings, and a tin of sardines. In the red plastic veg basket: two sprouting chatties. In the bread bin: half a sliced white loaf. In the fridge: a tub of margarine with a scraping left in it, an empty pot of jam, two eggs, a piece of going-green cheddar, two Ski yogurts, and half a pint of milk. In the freezer: two fish fingers and three peas. It was always slim pickings, and now it was worse because Aunty Pat had stopped giving Mam a lift to Savacentre every Wednesday. Sliced corned beef and chatties had to go in the deep flat pan, not the pot, and she covered that with vegetable soup, put the lid on and let it boil down, adding water now and again and a couple of sachets of pepper. She'd finely sliced a few sardines and added them as well as a bit of fish-juice to the corned beef and chattie casserole to give it a kick, and she toasted some bread, cut it into squares, and made a dipping toast stack, leaving enough bread for breakfast tomorrow as there was no cereal left.

At the kitchen table, all you could hear was slurping, including Mam who lifted her plate to drink the juice. 'That was nice, pet. Is there any left?'

'Aye,' she said, fetching the pan and slapping the last slice of corned beef onto Mam's plate.

'Pass uz the rest of that loaf, will yer?' said Mam.

Mam mopped her plate with tomorrow's breakfast as the lads looked on with sad faces because their plates were empty.

'Yoghurt?'

'Aye.'

'Aye.'

'There's strawberry and there's cherry.'

'Strawberry,' they both said, then Ian punched Jason in the arm and said, 'yer havin cherry.'

She put the pots on the table and let them scramble, Ian winning strawberry.

'Are there any yogurts left?' said Mam, with a bit of corned beef on her chin.

'There's pineapple rings.'

'Ah'll be in the livin room, put them in a bowl and bring them in will yer, luv.'

*

Mam gave her twenty quid to go into town and get some shopping and she was glad to have a reason to leave the house. The biddies at the bus stop tutted because she was pregnant but none of them dared say anything to her.

There were work people going into Phoenix House and the pavements were wet from the squirty-sweepy-beeping wagons that fanned out the litter for the men in orange trousers to sweep up. On a tip-off from Nana, she was banging down the door of Ibbetson's and was the first customer. White tiles, white coats, and slabs of chops and chunks and ribs and mince and rings of sausages with green flecks and with red flecks. She had happy memories of queuing in the smelly market for a saveloy dip with Nana on a Saturday afternoon. She always had her saveloy with stuffing and no pease pudding, and Julie had hers with pease pudding and no stuffing.

'Can ah help yer?' said the man with the white hat and white smile.

'Ah woz lookin at yer mince, 39 pence a pound, is it?'

'Aye, quality beef, cut by myself not less than an hour ago.'

'Ah'll have two pounds then, ta.'

He covered his hand in a bag, scooped up the mince, and slapped it on the scales. 'Two pounds, that's 78 pence,' he said, twisting the bag of mince and writing 78p on the side. 'Anything else for the young lady?'

'Have yer got a bone for me dog?' she asked. First come, first served was the tip-off from Nana.

'Hang on,' he said, disappearing through the blue and white ribbon curtain.

He returned with a cow's thigh bone. 'This do yer?' he said, holding it up.

'Aye, ower Rex will luv it.'

'Rex, that yer dog is it?' he said, wrapping the bone in newspaper.

'He's a Via Mirana,' she said, based on Sonya's dog.

'Is he really? Well,' he said, leaning over the counter and winking, 'ah think Rex will love this bone, boiled down with some carrots, onions, and celery.'

'Nana nivver said owt about celery, der the sell it in Prestos?'

'They do aye, and chuck a clove of garlic in. Tasty, git continental.'

Prestos was full of more biddies who tutted and gave her a glance of 'silly girl' and 'total slag'. She needed suet and chatties so the bags were going to be heavy, and now she could see the point of old lady wheelie trolleys, yet she'd never stoop that low. She'd rather heave bags. She got carrots and onions, and garlic was expensive, so she didn't bother with celery. The sausages were much cheaper than at Ibbetsons, and at 22p for six, she doubted they were pork. She could carry one more bag, so she had to make brutal decisions. She could manage to carry a tin of corned beef, which would do for when the three packs of sausages were gone. She'd seen Nana feed the five thousand with a tin of corned beef and a carrot.

The cow's thigh bone was too big for the big pan, so she took it outside and whacked the ball socket off the back step, shattering it on the second go. It exploded further down the bone than she wanted, but at least she could get the lid on the pan. She filled it with water, added chopped vegetables, and didn't know what to do with the garlic, so she peeled the papery outer skin, sliced off the stalks, then bunged the lot in. Four hours, low heat.

When Ian came in from playing out, the confusion on his little face was a scream. 'Wot's that weird smell?'

'Garlic, git continental. Der yer like it?'

He went into the kitchen in a cloud of boy dust, lifted the pan lid, and stuck his nose in.

She took the lid from him. 'Bugger off and talk ter Mam.'

Jason also wanted a look at the big bone in the pan, egged on by Ian, so she shooed them both away. 'Get outta me kitchen, the pair of yers. Gan watch the telly till ah call yers.'

She stood on a chair as she poured the contents of the pan into a sieve on the top of the brown oven pot from Nana's. It was bloody heavy and she was glad to toss the pan and bone into the sink. She squashed the vegetable soupy mush into the sieve with a wooden spoon until she couldn't get another drip out, then heaved the contents of the sieve into the bin. The garlic hadn't changed at all.

The soup in the brown pot was green with shiny circles of oil on the top. She chopped more onions and carrots and plopped them in, then in the yellow mixing bowl that Nana gave her, she mixed up some cheap Prestos flour and added a third of a packet of Atora Suet, the proper stuff, you can't scrimp on suet. After adding a cup of water, she shaped the suet into eight rounds and plopped them in the pot, and opened a 22p six-pack of piss-tube and arse-flap sausages, chopped them into pieces, and put them in. The bay leaves were an investment at 63p for a nice full bunch. She pushed the pot into the hot oven. The key to fluffy dumplings, according to Nana, is not to open the oven at all. If the cookery teacher had told her this when she made fluffy dumplings at school, then she wouldn't have opened the oven and prodded the 'Marsden Rocks' with a fork every ten minutes.

With the casserole under control, she ran the bath for the lads, adding a good slug of the Fenjal bubble bath that they'd nicked from Nana Hart's house. They were watching the news with Mam.

'Ha'way, bath before tea. Up the apples and pears.'

She didn't expect them to do as they were told without making her tell a rude joke in trade, and another one for getting their clothes off, and another for getting in the bath.

As they wriggled out of their baggy underpants, she did their favourite poem, *'Arty-Clarty had a party, everyone was there; Tooty-Frooty let off a beauty, and everyone gasped for air.'*

Then Jason sang, *'Ower Paula is a funny-un, Got a face like a pickled oni-on, Got a nose like a squashed tomato, And legs like pit-props; One pink one, one white one, and one with a bit of shite on–'*

She chased them, giggling and screaming into the bathroom and they climbed into the bubbly bath, keen to avoid having their bums slapped by the big-fat-hairy-hand.

Margarine was healthy, it stopped you having heart attacks and was 34p, whereas a slab of death butter was 17p. So what if it was like concrete? She flamed a knife and sliced a knob from the slab, and it sizzled and hissed as it hit the warm frying pan. She arranged slices of chattie in the bubbling butter and watched like a hawk, prodding and lifting with the plastic fish slice, making sure they didn't burn and that the butter didn't smoke. When they were done, she howked the golden, crispy circles out of the pan and onto a plate, turned the heat off, and went to get the little urchins into their pyjamas.

Ian picked plain blue pyjamas and Jason went for the Transformers, Robots in Disguise pyjamas that he was gutted to get for Christmas from Nana Hart because clothes aren't presents. They stood nicely while she combed their hair and then hugged her from both sides.

'Luv yer, ower Paula,' said Ian.

'Aye, me anarl,' said Jason.

She shook them off. 'Ha'way, let's gan get some scran. Are yers clammen?'

'Aye.'

'Aye.'

Mam's eyes popped out of her head when she came in to find the lads scrubbed with hair combed in ironed pyjamas and sitting side-by-side without fighting as they waited to be served their tea.

'It's liften in here,' said Mam, sitting at the table and flinging a fag end into the sink.

She dragged the bin outside, which made the kitchen smell more of garlicky niceness and less of eye-watering harshness. She put the golden, buttery, fried chatties on the table, slapping the lads' hands as they reached for a sneaky bite. 'Wait until ah bring the casserole,' she said.

The lads did as they were told while Mam broke off a piece with her nicotine fingers, shovelled it into her gob, and licked the grease from her wrist.

The heat blasted from the oven as she reached in and pulled out the pot, which she put on the hob without opening the lid.

'Drink?' she said.

'Dilutey orange please,' said Ian.

'Me anarl please,' said Jason.

'Me anarl, ta,' said Mam.

She put the drinks down and shifted the pot from the hob to the warped bread board in the middle of the table. She was about to lift the lid and reveal the amazing fluffy dumplings when a knock on the front door made everyone jump and look at her as if she should know who it was.

She opened it to find a tall man standing there. 'Hello,' she said. He was wearing glasses and a hat identical to the man in Hammer House of Horror.

'Paula?' he said softly.

She pondered whether to go and save the lads from the pipe that was about to spurt blood onto the table. 'Yes, why?'

'Ah'm Ken Wilkinson, Marcel's father. Can ah come in?'

Slightly better than being a grisly psycho, yet less easy to explain to Mam. The only person she'd mentioned Marcel to was Sonya, who, by the looks of things, and as expected, had mentioned it to Michelle, who mentioned it to Marcel's mate. She took a deep breath and let him inside.

Mam shouted, 'Wee ist?'

'Der yer want ter wait in the sittin room?' she said to him.

She casually put her head around the kitchen door, and said to Mam, 'The babbie's dad is a lad from Herrin'ton and his dad's in the livin room.'

Mam was off her arse so fast, she thought she was going to throttle her. Instead she checked her hair in the hall mirror, smiled at her, and mouthed, *'Herrin'ton?'*

She followed Mam into the living room and wanted the earth to swallow her and then for the universe to swallow the earth and then for the universe to get sucked into a black hole.

Without his hat on, the man looked like an older version of Marcel. 'Ah'm Ken, nice ter meet yer both.'

'Welcome, Ken,' said Mam. 'Marie.'

'Sorry for not callin sooner, Marie. My son Marcel only found out he's to be a dad last week.'

Mam shook her head and shot her weird daggers, 'Ah telt yer to ring him, didn't ah?'

'Paula has told you about Marcel?' he said.

'Of course she has,' said Mam. 'Tells me everythin. Says he's a lovely lad.'

Mam was siding with her, and she couldn't believe it, so she joined in before she changed her mind. 'Ah meant ter ring him a few times like, but ah didn't knar wot ter say.'

Ian shouted from the kitchen, 'Mam, wee ist?'

'Have ah come at a bad time?' he said.

'Nor,' said Mam, 'come and meet me lads.'

The boys had eaten some chatties but hadn't opened the pot.

Mam sat down. 'This is Ian and Jason. Boys, this is ower Paula's babbie's grandar.'

'Welcome to my humble abode,' said Jason politely.

Ken Marcel's dad slotted himself between the end of the table and the oven and she was worried that he was going to burn his kecks.

'Der yer want ter join us for a bit of tea?' said Mam without asking the person who had cooked it if there was enough.

'No thanks, ah must get off, just wanted to call by and say that we're lookin forward to the new member of the family. Wot do you lads reckon, boy or girl?'

'Boy,' said Ian, 'called Gary Lineker.'

Ken Marcel's Dad laughed. 'But what if it's a girl?'

'Mary Donna!' said Jason, chuffed with his joke.

'Who's going ter win on Sunday?'

'England!' they chimed, and she willed Jason not to stand on the chair and do his World Cup willy-wiggle dance. She distracted him by lifting the lid on the pot, and as the steam cleared, they all leaned in and gazed as if she'd opened a pot of gold. The dumplings were as white as clouds. Ian and Jason each stabbed a dumpling with their forks and, bypassing their plates, went straight to mouth, nibbling like eating hot toffee apples. As they wafted their open mouths, she could see that the dumplings were *very* fluffy.

'Graisse de rognon dumplings?' said Ken Marcel's dad.

Mam gave her an approving look of well done on getting pregnant to someone from Herrington whose dad speaks all foreign.

'The fat from a cow's kidney,' he explained, 'there's no literal French translation for suet.'

'Eeee, are yer French?' said Mam.

She held her breath and hoped she didn't say anything stupid, like asking him if he had a video.

'No, ah'm from Castletown. Me missus is French Canadian.'

'Eeee, she's from Canadia,' said Mam.

'Ah'll let yer get back to yer tea,' he said, 'let's catch up through the week.'

'Nice ter meet yer,' said Mam. 'Paula, see Ken out will yer?'

She led him out and once he was on the step, she said, 'Soz like for gettin pregnant. Ah dinnet want owt from yer family, if that's wot yer wonderin.'

He put his hat on. 'That's a shame because ah want to welcome you and the baby to the family.'

'Really, yer not just sayin that, ah mean, why?'

'Well Paula, ah'll tell yer this, but yer not ter say anythin ter anyone.'

'Gan on.'

'Ah've always quite fancied mysel as a grandad and now's me chance.'

He was joking, obviously, in a nice way that was so nice she couldn't believe it.

'Are yer free on Tuesday mornin?'

'Aye, ah'm always free nowadays.'

'Ah'll pick you up at ten. We can go get some things for the baby, what der yer say?'

'That'd be mint, thanks.'

*

She stood sideways in front of the mirror, pulled her pyjama bottoms over her bump, and sang 'Humpty Dumpty Sat on the Wall'. Her belly had overtaken her boobs which was mad because she'd had to borrow a bra from Nana which had cups you could fit your head into. The lacey bra and knicker set from Jenny looked like Sindy clothes. The only things that fit were some tracksuit bottoms and the dungarees she'd bought with the pittance the nash had given her for maternity clothes. The shell suit that David got her still fit. If the baby was a boy, she was going to call him David, and if the baby was a girl, she told everyone she was going to call her Fern because that was Nana's favourite name, even though there was no way she was calling her baby Fern. If she had a girl, she was calling her Chloe after Dad's favourite *Playschool* presenter.

Ken was ten minutes late and she had already slapped herself in the face twice for being so stupid to think that he would turn up. He did turn up, in a long white car that looked expensive.

'Your carriage awaits,' he said.

She turned her bump toward him and nodded for him to touch. The baby had been playing football all morning so now was a good time for a kick.

He was chatty all the way into town, talking about how his wife was a retired French teacher called Coralie and about how Marcel was going to Leeds to do teacher training if he got his finger out with his exams. He said that he had worked as an engineer at Grundfos Pumps for over twenty years, and he was chuffed when she asked if he was an engineer like Isambard.

He stopped outside of the train station. 'Get yersel into Binns. Ah'll park and meet yer in the baby department.'

There was a department for everything in Binns. She knew the make-up counters, the Snoopy stuff corner of the haberdashery department, and 'Lifestyle' the trendy furniture shop on the fourth floor, where everything was white, black, or red, and there were posters of women with blue eyeshadow talking on melting telephones. She'd hung around in Binns plenty, never with anything to spend but time, and never in the part of Binns on the other side of Fawcett Street.

She went down the steps into the men's clothes department that went under the road and went on for ages. She came up the steps on the other side into the green chair department. A woman in a uniform came up to her, looked at her belly, and said with a smile, 'Third floor, pet.' She got out of the lift on the third floor. Prams, pushchairs, rocking cribs, Moses baskets, a cot with tall sides and white covers with yellow elephants, and a cot with open sides and a patchwork blanket with frogs and hedgehogs and moles.

She was raking in the maternity dress sales rack when a store detective caught her scent and stood, as if she hadn't seen him, casually next to the cow jumping over the moon. From the corner of her eye, she could see that he was watching her from the corner of his eye, and he probably thought that her bump was a stash of stolen jumpers, which is what shoplifters want store detectives to think, while their unsuspicious accomplice cleans up. She'd never stolen from Binns, not even a smelly rubber.

It all changed when Ken came striding between the cots and the prams. The store detective fucked off and two women in uniforms came over and asked when the baby was due. She couldn't believe that the baby was going to have a nursery at Marcel's house and that Ken said she could pick whatever she wanted. She didn't want to take the piss, so she went for the cheapest cot, which was gorgeous, with a yellow blanket with a teddy bear on it, yellow gingham sheet, cushion, and nappy sack. Ken picked up a matching lamp and a mobile that had yellow teddy bears and bunnies dangling from it. She enjoyed the look on the shop woman's face when he ordered the cot, the blanket set, and the curtains, and then he made the woman go find a lamp that wasn't chipped.

'Go grab yersel some maternity clothes while ah sort this lot out,' he said.

In the café in Binns, she ate cake while he talked about how Coralie had three sisters in Canada. Ken asked her about school and her family and when she didn't have much to say she ended up telling him that REDUNDANT MINER IN FATAL ACCIDENT was her stepdad. Ken pretended like he didn't know and asked how Mam and the boys were coping, which made a weird change from being asked about the head rolling down the stairs. She explained that they were coping fine, and that it was better now that there was no Billy making their lives a misery.

'Every cloud,' he laughed.

She didn't tell him that MAN ESCAPES BLAZE was also a family headline, although she knew Michelle enough to know that in the same breath as betraying her pregnancy secret to Marcel's mate, she'd have let slip about the heed-off stepdad and washed-up-on-beach Dad.

'Ah dinnet want the babbie ter have his name,' she said. 'It was horrible puttin Hart on the DSS forms and when the nurse said, *how is baby Hart?*, ah thought neeways.'

'Wot's yer dad's surname?'

'Hasting, nee s.'

Ken insisted she went directly to the Post Office to change her name by deed poll. He gave her twenty pounds, and said, 'Go.'

She took her bags of new maternity clothes out of Binns and headed up to Market Square. The queue at the Post Office was out of the door, the wait, however, would be short compared with the years she'd waited to change her name to her own name. She remembered queuing in this very spot with Mam to get the deed poll form to change her name to Hart – as they moved forward, one step every ten minutes, her boredom turned to anger and she vowed that for as long as she shall live, she'd never accept Hart. After that, her records at school were changed so she had to answer to it. Not anymore. Goodbye, Paula Hart smells of fart; hello, Paula Hasting needs a pasting.

The Post Office smelled of piss and was full of old people.

'She problees thinks she's gettin a doll ter dress up,' said one biddy.

'Aye, why, wait till the babbie's here, she winnet knar wot's hit her,' said another.

She looked at the floor and tried not to scream, 'Ah'm pregnant, not deaf.' And anyway, she knew one thing that hadn't hit her, a netball, that's what. She vowed that for as long as she shall live, she'd never behave like that towards a stranger in a queue whose life she knew nothing about.

It took an hour to get to the counter. 'Sorry about the wait. How can ah help yer?'

'Ah'd like ter change me name by deed poll please.'

'Ah'll get yer the form.'

The woman must've gone to another country to get the form. She was pleased when she pushed it under the glass screen.

'Yer need to fill this in, then bring it back with the items on this list,' said the woman, pulling it back under the screen and then circling the list with red pen. 'There's an eight-pound charge, so bring cash or a cheque.'

'Then wot?'

'We send it off and they send yer a certificate to confirm the change.'

The woman was smiling and apart from having to come back and stand for another hour, it seemed too easy. 'Is that all ah have ter dee?'

'It's git straightforward. Wer dee hods of these.'

'Der yer?'

'Stepdad, is it?'

'Aye.'

'Get the form filled in and we'll get it sent off.'

Chapter 16

June 1986

Ken picked her up from home and dropped her at his house in Herrington. He had to go to work and Marcel was at school. He said that Coralie was looking forward to meeting her.

The only thing she remembered about the outside of Marcel's house was a bright light cutting through the thick fog above a door with a Christmas wreath on it. When she'd left the morning after, she didn't look back. Now in the summer sun, Marcel's house wasn't flash, rather a lovely, red-bricked semi with a tidy garden and a long driveway leading to a glossy red garage door. She remembered coming out onto the street with Marcel's mates in the car, not coming down a drive, and she was sure that the house had a bay window, which it didn't. A thin woman opened the front door and waved. She was wearing a long flowy gold skirt and a black fluffy jumper with gold beads on the shoulders. 'Coralie?' she said.

'Bonjour Paula, come in,' said Coralie, hugging her and tickling her nose with fluff, making her sneeze. 'Bless you.'

Coralie ushered her into the living room. The window looked bigger without the Christmas tree, and the rug was more of a beige than the grey she remembered. Sunbeams from the wide front window cast a moving picture of clouds on the polished table in the open-plan dining room.

Coralie stared at her with a faraway gaze and she waited awkwardly for her to speak, then like a jump-up toy that had out-sucked its spittle, Coralie jolted her head back and burst into a big smile, '*Est-ce ma petite fille*?' she said, pointing at her bump.

She lifted her t-shirt and Coralie put a hand on her skin, closed her eyes, and turned her face to the chandelier. In her head she said to the baby, 'Meet your nana, this would be a good time to kick.'

They sat together and picked baby things out of the catalogue and then Coralie made tea and cake. Coralie told her about her sisters in Canada and how Marcel could speak French. She said she worked at a school in Seaham and now she's retired and does charity work for the church. They talked loads about being pregnant and having a baby which was topper because no one else wanted to talk about it. Mam had no useful advice to give, and remembered nothing but the pain of having a 'spoilt rotten baby that wouldn't stop cryin'. Nana had Dad and Uncle Jimmy at home, and she said that she just had to get on with it. Coralie described everything about when she had Marcel, and she could tell that she'd been a teacher by the way she explained the baby being fed by the placenta.

The cake was lovely and she would've had more if she didn't feel like she'd swallowed a bottle of acid. Her heartburn was now entire-inside-of-the-chest-burn. When Coralie took the cups to the kitchen, she lay sideways, with her head propped-up on two cushions to keep the acid down. She closed her eyes. It was so quiet and peaceful. Coralie eased her feet out of her jellybean shoes, lifted her legs onto the settee, and put a blanket over her. Her body quivered as if being stroked by a feather, and she curled around her baby imagining their hearts beating together as she drifted off to sleep.

Another vivid, twisted, sweaty-titty dream of her being on *Crackerjack* and the Buckaroo slipped from her grip and they gave her a cabbage, and she was pretending like she was fine with the cabbage, and they gave her another cabbage and it was Billy's head, and then, *bang!* She woke with a jolt.

'*Arrete le vicarme*!' hissed Coralie in the hall. Heavy feet went up the stairs. She loved that her baby's family spoke French. 'Bonjour David or Chloe,' she whispered.

Coralie crept in. 'Oh, you're awake.'

She pushed herself upright, 'Woz that Marcel comin in?'

Coralie nodded. The plan she'd talked about with Coralie earlier was that Marcel would show her the nursery, as a way to break the ice. She hadn't seen him or spoken to him since riding him on the rug, and she couldn't wait to see the nursery.

Marcel was facing out of the nursery window and when she came in, he turned round. He was wearing jeans and a white school shirt, untucked and open at the neck, and his face was like she remembered. A big forehead, okay looking, and sexy brown eyes.

'Hi,' he said, awkwardly, 'do yer like the room?'

It was yellow with a line of elephants marching along the wall behind the most expensive cot and not the cheapest one that she'd chosen.

'Yae alreet?' he said. 'It's full-on in here.'

'Wot der yer mean?'

'All this.' He raised his hands and swivelled his head.

'It's beautiful, ah cannet believe it. Soz like, about Sonya openin her big gob. Ah wozn't bothered if yer didn't want ter be involved like. Yer knar, nee pressure. Ah'm not one of those lasses wee got pregnant ter keep a lad, like.'

He smiled and shook his head. 'If yer were ganner trap a lad, yer wouldn't have chosen an ugly bastard like me.'

She laughed. 'Yerv got a nice house though,' and raised her shoulders, 'so yer knar, yer a catch like.'

He decked it and put his arms around her. As he hugged, she felt warm and welcome, and the baby tumbled its creams as if it knew that Daddy was close. 'Ah thought yer were on the pill.'

'How come?'

'Because yer had sex with uz.'

She screwed her face up, searching for the logic.

'Me last girlfriend wouldn't let uz fuck her until she went on the pill,' he clarified.

She wanted to ask him more about his last girlfriend and about everything about him: what's your favourite band? What's your favourite food? How many people have you had sex with? Do you prefer cats or dogs? Instead, she asked, 'Wot did yer dad say when yer telt him yer'd got a lass pregnant?'

'Oh, man, it was weird,' he said, shaking his head.

'He didn't chin yer then?'

'Nor, but ah know wot yer mean, that's what me mate's owld man did ter him.'

'He must've been pissed off, ah mean, ah cannet believe how happy yer mam is, considerin yer've got a stupid slapper up the duff.'

His eyes flashed with anger, and she thought he was going to hit her as he grabbed her shoulders. 'You're not a stupid slapper, reet?' His eyes were vexed with kind.

'Aye,' she said.

'Don't ever say that again, or think it, got it?'

'Suppose so.'

He took his hands off her shoulders and dropped his head. 'Yer bonnie like and ah dinnet say that ter many lasses.'

'Ta, but ha'way, neebody wants this for their son, a pregnant lass from a council estate. And ah'm from a mental family.' The baby kicked, so she lifted her top. 'Put yer hand here.' He put his hand on her stretched flesh. 'Can yer feel it kickin?'

She wondered what he was touching, probably the baby's head as the feet were booting the opposite side. His eyes were welling up and his chin trembled.

'Ah'm sorry ah got pregnant, yer can still gan ter college, yer dinnet need to help or owt.'

He took his hand from the baby and crossed himself. 'There's somethin yer need ter knar. They said not ter say owt in case it upsets yer.'

'Ha'way then, spit it out.'

'Me mam had a baby called Jodie who died.'

She gasped and put her hand over her mouth.

'Now yer see why they don't want yer ter knar.'

'Is that why yer mam's so happy about the babbie?'

'Here-man, ah could've killed me mate when he let it slip ter Kev about me gettin a lass up the duff; Kev's seein me half-cousin, and she told me dad.'

'Wer yer loggin-it?'

'Loggin-it, aye. When ah got home and saw the big light was on in the sittin room, me cowies were like the startin grid at Brans Hatch.'

'Wot happened?'

'Me mam was cryin, which isn't unusual for her, and me dad was hoverin in and out of the kitchen like he does when she's cryin, only she was smilin, like properly smilin, like she did when ah was a kid.'

'Before Jodie died?'

He kissed her cheek. 'Thanks for sayin her name.'

'Nee bother,' she said. 'It's weird isn't it when someone dies and no one ever mentions them, like they think if they say their name, yer'll burst inter tears.'

'Jodie was their prayers answered, they'd tried for years for another baby. She was born with a heart problem and lived for four days.'

She put her arm around his middle and put her head on his arm. 'How owld were yer?'

'Twelve.'

'Is that when yer mam stopped bein a teacher?'

'That's when she stopped eatin, sleepin, smilin, everythin.'

'She's been smilin today.'

He pushed her away and shook his head and she thought he was going to tell her to stop shoving the baby under his mam's nose.

'Look at me,' he said, holding his arms out to the side. 'Ah've spent six years prayin for a miracle like a good Catholic boy, and ah never thought it would happen.'

'Are yer sayin the babbie's a miracle?'

'Ah've never seen me mam so happy, and as for a clip rund the ear, me dad shook me hand. If that's not a miracle, ah dinnar wot is.'

She was as hard as nails yet being pregnant had changed that; the other night she broke her heart at some Ethiopians on the news, and yesterday, she had to force back tears when she saw a little girl with an eye patch. She couldn't cope with kindness from Marcel and tears rolled down her face, dripped off her chin, and plopped like raindrops into her cleavage.

'Don't cry, for fuck's sake,' he said, 'me mam'll gan mad that ah telt yer about Jodie.'

She fanned her face.

'Have yer got any names in mind?' he said, wiping her tears with his thumb.

'If it's a boy, ah woz thinkin David after me brotha.'

'Oui, Daveed, ce'st bon name.'

'Eh?'

'David is pronounced Daveed in French.'

'Ah knar wot yer mean. There woz a lass at Bede called Annick, which is Anneek in French.'

'Anneek,' he laughed, 'owld wifey name in France. Yer not thinkin of callin the baby that, are yer?'

'Am ah fuck! Chloe for a girl.'

His eyes lit up, 'With an acute accent on the e?'

'Wot?'

'A sloped line over the e,' he said, holding up a hand and slanting it. 'Chloe's a French name. Mam'll be ower the knot, but don't tell her, wait until it's born.'

'Ah'm not tellin nee one, so yae better not, promise?'

'Ah promise. And ah know it sounds soppy, but ah promise to be there for you and the babbie.'

*

When Mam came into the kitchen, they stared at her in amazement and a fish finger dropped out of Ian's sarnie. She was hardly recognisable under the red lipstick and black eye liner, and backcombed and tonged hair that was solid with lacquer and probably a fire hazard.

'Wot?' said Mam. Her shoulder pads touched her ears as she put a fag in her mouth and lit it. Her power jacket was black with neon blue lapels, and she teamed it with a neon blue pencil skirt and black high heels, which made her stand like a statue.

'Yer look like Alexis off *Dynasty*,' she said, making the lads laugh.

'Don't be so stupid,' rasped Mam, blowing smoke all over their tea.

'Yer cannet smoke up Herrin'ton,' she said. 'Coralie doesn't let anyone light up in the house.'

When Ken beeped outside, the woman from over the road came across with her two bairns who aeroplaned down the path. 'Ah yer sure yer dinnet mind?' said Mam. 'Ah'll arnly be gone a couple of hours.'

'Nee bother,' said the woman. 'Go on, gan have yer important dinner.'

Ken had to open the car window because he could hardly breathe over the smog of Dior's Poison and Silvikrin. Mam was in the front seat and she imagined her glee as they turned off onto a road lined with trees and big houses. Coralie was waiting on the drive.

'Get yersel in,' said Ken to Mam.

As Mam tottered down the drive in her stilettos, Ken helped haul her huge pregnant body out of the car. She cringed when Coralie welcomed Mam with a double cheek kiss.

The living room smelled of garlic and her mouth watered. Mam was nervous on new territory, so she reached for the familiar. 'Do let me apologise for my daughter.' Mam's posh voice was mortifying.

'Apologise,' Coralie frowned, 'whatever for?'

'For gettin pregnant. Yer poor son didn't ask for this,' said Mam.

'We're delighted with the news,' said Coralie, patting her bump.

Mam's red lips opened and closed.

'A baby is a gift from God,' said Coralie sternly. 'God makes no apologies.'

She winced and waited for Mam to pull her wounded face and say, 'Well that's me telt.' With no comeback for the word of God, Mam said, 'Wot a lovely house yer have, is that Lladro?'

'Royal Doulton,' said Coralie.

Mam's least embarrassing subject was ornaments. She liked women in blue dresses and white aprons carrying small animals, whereas Aunty Pat liked ballerinas staring wistfully into space with their blue-grey hair and matching ballet shoes. 'Eeee, yer should see me sister's house. Top ter bottom Lladro; she likes ballet dancers.'

Ken came in and said, 'Marie, this is Marcel.' Then he turned to see that his son wasn't there, went into the kitchen, and dragged him into the living room.

'Nice ter meet yer,' said Marcel, shaking Mam's hand.

Mam gave him a full up and down, then nodded with approval.

'Can ah have a word wer Paula,' said Marcel.

They went into the back garden. 'Full-on that,' said Marcel, getting his ciggies out.

'Soz, for me mam like.'

He shook his head. 'Here-man, yerv got ter stop apologisin.'

'Aye, but have yer seen her? The look on her face when she saw yer house. She thinks she's arrived.'

'Me dad invited her here so he can talk about money.'

'Wot der yer mean?'

'He's goin ter give yer an allowance only it has ter be off the record.'

'As long as nee one talks about the birth plan, ah'm good,' she said. 'Me mam thinks she's garn ter be there – can yer imagine it, *yae keep pushin while ah nip for a fag.*'

'She's not that bad.'

'She is. At least yowr mam would be useful. Mortifyin though, her seein me Fan-Anne-Tut.'

'She'd be too busy deein hail Marys ter bother wer the original sin comin out of yer Fan-Anne-Tut.'

'Ah've nee idea wot that means,' she said.

'It means she'll be prayin that God forgives us for the sin of creatin a baby.'

'Earlier the babbie was a gift, and now it's a sin?'

'Aye Paula, yer catchin on canny.'

'Yer mam is lovely though. Ah'd rather have her at the birth than me own, but ah'm plannin on just a midwife.'

The lasagne steamed and the garlic bread made her mouth water as she hung her head and thanked the Lord for the food that they were about to receive. When Mam asked how to make lasagne, Coralie managed to prolong the conversation for ages. When Coralie had finished explaining, most of the food had been eaten, which was consistent with Mam setting the pace: the rules at home were the faster you can fork the grub into your gob, the nicer it is. That wasn't the way they usually did it at the Wilkinsons, rather a meal could last an hour, and at intervals they put their knives and forks down, took a drink, or chatted. Marcel and Ken were happy to eat like gissies on this occasion.

'What's your go-to dish on a weekday?' asked Coralie, her efforts to connect with Mam unwavering.

'When yer a widow wer three kids ter feed, bread and butter is yer go-to dish,' said Mam wobbling her head when she said *go-to dish*.

'And chippie tea,' she noted, making Ken and Marcel laugh.

'And graisse de rognon dumplins,' said Ken.

'Me dumplins wer as fluffy as clouds,' she said, the half-chewed lasagne burning her insides. The baby tumbled and a hot meaty burp came out.

'Excuse you!' said Mam. 'Ah dee apologise Coralie, ah didn't bring her up like that.'

'The babbie kicked me stomach,' she explained, 'ah didn't knar ah woz ganner burp.'

'No need to apologise,' said Coralie. 'How's your heartburn?'

'Here-man, nivver mind *her* heartburn, wot about *my* nerves, it's hard enough wer three, without a babbie anarl. Ah'd dee owt for me bairns though, mack the sacrifices,' said Mam, jumping from cross to pedestal, as she does.

'Vanilla ice cream with maple syrup?' said Coralie.

'Yes please,' she said, rubbing her bump.

Telling Mam how to claim benefits was like telling a gannie how to suck eggs. Five hundred now, five hundred after providing a *father unknown* birth certificate, then two hundred a month, cash-in-hand. Ian and Jason played who can jump off the highest stair while Mam smoked in the front garden, holding the cheque, that was, 'Nee good ter me, if it's made out ter yae.'

Chapter 17

July 1986

Being seven months pregnant was mint because the baby was fully formed and she could feel him/her moving and she absolutely loved the baby more than anything she'd ever loved before, ever. The picture in the leaflet from the hospital of a baby in the womb made her think of the stuff in jars that lined the laboratory at school: a scorpion, a tapeworm, a toad, all pickled long ago, suspended in time, cold and lonely, while life went on. The pickled creature she most felt sorry for was the lizard that was all curled up with sad eyes and tiny teeth. When she tapped the jar with her ruler to try and cheer it up, Mrs Chen tossed the blackboard rubber at her. It wasn't easy getting comfortable in bed with a great big baby moving about and when she did get to sleep, her dreams were freaky.

'Who is the father, Paula?' said the woman. Timothy Claypole appeared, and then the doorman from Fifth Avenue, and she's going along the line of potential fathers, looking for Marcel – Noseybonk, Sonya's dad, the postman, Ian from *EastEnders*, Big Daddy, Herman from Guess Who, and then a Dalek is chasing her down the school corridor. She's running in block-a-boots, and she tries to get down the narrow stairway, but it's piled high with squashed children. She climbs over their heads and gets out, and she's in Mowbray Park and she picks up a baby octopus and she wades across the lake to the telephone box on the island and on the floor in the telephone box is her baby wrapped in a blanket. She picks it out of the piss and broken glass and unwraps the blanket and it's Billy's rotten head. She reasons, it's fine, I can look after this rotten-head baby, no one need know that Billy was murdered, then Jason said, 'Paula, yae awake?'

*

It was the last week of school before the six weeks holiday and Ian ran off as soon as he saw Nigel. She wasn't going to Gillian's today because she needed to go into town to pay the gas and do a shop, and she'd promised to get Ian some footy stickers. She walked slowly along to the Prospect, hoping to miss the buses packed with people smoking on the way to work or school, and instead catch the first off-peak bus that was packed with biddies who shook their heads and tutted at the teenager who couldn't keep her legs together.

It was a lovely day, and the sun was splitting the pavements everywhere apart from Walworth Way, which was a dark, concrete, wind tunnel. She was glad to be in the cool as her tits, which bulged over the top and out of the sides of her bra, were properly lathered. She wasn't far from the gas shop when she saw Michael heading towards her in jeans and a short sleeved demin shirt. Her heart skipped, and she was going to put her head down and walk past until he looked at her and then looked away like she was nothing. Her chest filled with rage and her mouth shouted, 'Hello Michael,' without her brain telling it to.

He stopped. 'Hello, Paula. How are you doing?' he said, pretending like he'd just seen her.

The smell of his aftershave took her back to him fucking her doggy-style. She didn't answer. The bump told him how she was doing.

'Who's the lucky man?' he asked, smiling and walking sideways, trying to get away from her.

'Can't yer remember? Seven months ago, in yer mate's house?'

The colour drained from his face.

'Yae alreet?'

'I thought you were on the pill.'

'Nor, why would ah be? Ah woz a virgin before ah met yae.'

'You sure it's mine?'

'Ah've had nee visit from Angel Gabriel, but yer nivver knar.'

'Fack,' he said, pale faced.

She'd decided that the baby was Marcel's, so even if it was Michael's, it wasn't. She felt bad about stringing him along until she thought about him clinging to her and shouting, 'Jesus!' as he shot his load.

He looked torn between a hug and a punch. 'Let's get a drink,' he said, marching off.

Her sweaty side-tits chafed against her oxters as she waddled after him, and by the time she got to Burton's corner, he was miles along High Street. He stopped outside of Notrianni's and she could see him looking about to see if anyone had seen him.

She liked Notrianni's because it was dark and old-fashioned and sold cakes and chips, but it mostly sold ice cream, which was why it was cold.

She followed him to the counter. 'What would you like?' he said.

'A lemonade and vanilla float wer monkey's blood, nee wafer.' Well, it was Notrianni's.

'Go and sit over there.' He pointed to the shady back corner.

She shimmied into the sticky booth, its 1950s ice cream parlour glory well-faded. She emptied the sachets of sugar, salt, and pepper into her bag, and was about to raid the next booth when Michael headed towards her with a tray of drinks. He was manly and handsome and the thought of his cock pounding into her, made her tingle.

She prodded the ice cream with the small plastic spoon.

'It can't be mine,' he said, with urgency in his voice. 'When's your due date?'

'September fifth.'

He sat back and she got a waft of spice and pine as he worked out which shag had done it. 'Have you told anybody it's mine?'

She swallowed a lump of ice cream and got head freeze. 'Nor, nee one knars about me and yae, not even Sonya.'

'Who do they think it is?'

'Wot der yer mean?'

'What do you say when people ask who the father of your baby is? You must've told someone, a doctor, a teacher, someone?'

'Ah just ses it was some lad ah shagged and ah dinnar his name.'

'And they believed you?'

'Wee believed uz?'

'Your mother, teachers, Sonya, they all think you *shagged some lad*?'

'Why-aye, they believe uz.'

His shoulders dropped as if the weight of the world had been lifted from them.

'The nash are keen for a name. Man, they dee gan on, who is the father, Paula? You must have some idea, Paula? It's enough ter mack uz wanna say Michael

Smith, an accountant from Tynemouth, wer a daughter called Amanda and a villa on the Costa del Sol.'

His face went white and he mopped his brow with a serviette.

'They're all gaggin for a name, anyone will dee, a man ter pin it on wee they can mack pay for sixteen years.'

He drum-rolled his fingers on the claggy table, then held a finger in the air. 'If it's money you need, I can arrange that; what do you say? Nobody needs to know, I'll deny it anyway, say you're making it up – you've had a hard time with your stepfather and father, enough to drive a young girl to make up all sorts.'

'Ah dinnet want yer involved. Ah knar yer've got a family and that, but bairns are pricey, and ah want this one ter have the best of everythin.'

'Okay, so I give you enough so that you can take care of the baby and then you never mention my name, or come near me or my family again?' He looked at her with disgust unlike when she was licking his bellend.

'Ah'm not after money, ah just want me child ter have the best in life.'

'How does three thousand sound?'

Based on the five hundred quid from Ken, she didn't expect him to go in at three thousand. She rubbed her belly. 'Three thousand! That's peanuts.'

He raised his eyebrows. 'How much were you thinking?'

She stirred the monkey's blood into the ice cream and scooped a pink dollop into her mouth. She held the end of the spoon and sucked it like Dad used to suck his pen while thinking of what offer to make on Mayfair.

'Four thousand, final offer,' he said.

She could see he was desperate to get out of there.

'Ten.'

'I can write a cheque now for four. I can't give you any more.'

She rubbed her bump. 'Ah can feel the babbie kickin, go on, touch here.'

He reached into his trouser pocket. 'Five,' he said, pulling out a cheque book.

'Ten.'

'Seven.'

'Ten.'

'Seven.'

'Eight.'

'Eight, done.'

She scooped ice cream into her mouth as he wrote the cheque. 'Mack it out ter Paula Hasting, ah changed me name by deed poll.'

He ripped the cheque off the pad and gave it to her, and as she went to take it, he whipped it away and leaned in. His face was mean like he would've slipped his hands around her neck if he could've. With a whiff of stale garlic and fresh Polos, he rasped, 'Keep away from me and my family; or I'm warning you, got it?' He held the cheque back until she said, 'Got it,' then he dropped it on the table and left.

She looked at the cheque as she prodded the last island of ice cream floating in the mush; lemonade and cream aren't a good combination. She couldn't believe he'd written a cheque for eight thousand pounds only. No man in their right mind would trust the word of a slag like her. She picked it up. Midland Bank. Mr MJ Smith FRCS. She didn't know what the letters meant, probably something to do with his work. She was so excited about having so much money that some piss came out, so she stuffed the cheque in her bag and went to the loo.

She sat on the bog and wafted her arms like chicken wings, trying to dry the sweat. 'Hey little one, just wait and see the brilliant life yer ganner have, ah totally promise,' she said rubbing her bump.

With toilet paper stuffed under each oxter, she headed for the bus station and got the first bus that went up Chester Road.

Unlike the long queue when she came to pay in Ken's cheque, the Sunderland and Shields Building Society was empty, so she waddled to the counter and pushed the latest cheque under the screen.

As the woman read it, her eyes popped out of her head. 'Okay then, ah need ter speak ter me manager, back in a minute.'

She wondered if the cheque was a dud and whether she should run for it.

'Miss Hart?' said an older woman who was wearing a white shirt with navy rectangles and red triangles all over it. She looked important.

'Miss Hasting, nee s, ah changed it by deed poll,' she said.

'Do come through.'

She hovered and thought about running, but they had the cheque.

'Nothin ter worry about, just want ter have a chat about some options for yer money.'

They went into a small room that had a carpet which matched the woman's blouse but with a navy background with white rectangles and red triangles.

'Okay then Paula, ah see yer have a cheque for a substantial amount of money, may ah ask who it's from?'

'It's off me babbie's dad. He's married and wants nowt ter dee with uz, so he paid uz off.'

The woman leaned forward and put her hand to her mouth like telling a secret. 'Off the record, may ah say, what a bastard.' She sat back and straightened her blouse. 'Ah'll get yer some leaflets about the accounts wer have because the junior starter isn't going ter work hard for yer money.'

'Der yer knar wot those letters stand for?' she asked, pointing to the name on the cheque.

The woman frowned. 'Not sure, somethin ter do with being a certified accountant, mebees. Back in a tick.'

When the woman returned with the leaflets, she gasped and climbed on a chair to open the window. 'It's hot in here today.'

'Imagine wot it's like carryin a babbie.'

The woman wafted her face with a leaflet as she spread the others out. 'Here we are, Paula. Ah recommend that yer invest yer money in a medium-term bond. An advantage of a bond is that yer money won't affect yer welfare payments.' The woman put her hand out, palm down, 'Not that ah'm assumin yer claimin at the moment?'

'When the babbie's born, ah'll be garn on benefits. The woman at the DSS asked uz if ah had any savins and when a telt her about the five hundred quid, she said it didn't matter but not to write it down on any forms.'

'Eight thousand pounds is more significant, so that's why we recommend a bond.'

'Hide it like?'

'Well, not really,' the woman frowned.

'It's alreet, ah knar how it works. It's like when me mam put me stepdar's money from the pit in me brotha's name, so the dole didn't find out about it.'

'Did she really?' said the woman, picking a purple leaflet from the table. 'You'll find our family bond is the same as puttin yer money in yer brother's bank account, only it's legal.'

She took the leaflet and read the big orange writing. *12% on savings**

'Yes, so if yer invested the full amount, without doing a thing, that would earn yer—'

'Wot does the star thing mean?'

The woman took the leaflet. 'The star thing means that yer only get the twelve percent rate if yer leave your money in for three years.'

The woman couldn't have known the hours she'd spent haggling over percentages with Dad. 'Is it twelve percent interest over three years, or each year?'

'Give me a minute,' said the woman, looking pleased to flee.

She used the family bond leaflet to fan her face and lifted an arm to fan an oxter. A youngish man with a tie that matched the carpet came in. He took a leaflet, folded it in half, and used it to wedge the door open.

'Hot in here today,' he said, pulling the chair away and sitting down almost touching the wall as if she had the plague.

'Ah'm Paul, Manager of Sunderland and Shields Building Society, and ah'm happy that yer brought the cheque ter uz.'

'Are yer?'

'Of course. Ower job is ter help yer build equity.'

'Wot does that mean?'

'Get rich.'

'Oh, reet. That's canny like.'

'Linda said that yer've got eight thousand pounds ter invest, and yer need help calculatin the interest on the family bond?'

'Ah can calculate it if ah knar if it's interest ower three years or each year?'

'Each year,' he said, pulling a calculator out of his inside jacket pocket. He jabbed away at it. 'So that's—'

'Have yer got a pen?' she asked.

He gave her a Bic from his inside pocket.

'Yer dinnet want ter keep a shit pen like that in yer pocket, leaky as fuck.'

'You're not wrang,' he said. 'Last one ruined me Pierre Cardin jumper.'

She jotted down the figures on the purple leaflet. 'After three years, ah'll have about eleven and a half thousand.'

He looked at her in amazement. 'Not far off.' He held the calculator up to face her. 'Eleven thousand, two hundred, and thirty-nine.'

'Can ah borrow yer calculator a minute?' she said.

She calculated out loud as she tapped. 'There's fifty-two weeks in a year, mackin one hundred and fifty-six weeks ower three years, which equals nearly twenty quid a week in interest.'

'It's the highest rate we have,' he said. 'Great deal.'

'*Great deal*,' she said. 'It's a spectacular fucken deal! Soz for swearin man, but that's more than yer get on the dole.'

Mam was talking crap when she said that if she didn't pay the gas bill today, they'd be cut off. It was dinnertime before she got to the gas shop, so the queue was long. As she waited, she let it sink in that she was rich beyond her wildest dreams, unless the cheque bounced, like when Michael gets home, changes his mind, and stops it. He was shit at negotiating; you'd think he'd be good with money. She got to the counter, paid the bill, and as she was on her way out, she passed a bald, stocky bloke in a blue trackie top and when he caught her eye, she froze.

'You alright there?' he said in a nice voice.

'Aye,' she said, 'yer remind uz of someone that's all.'

'Someone bad I hope,' he laughed, so she laughed too.

Outside, she leaned against the gas shop window in the glaring sun. She closed her eyes and as the darkness quenched the sunspots, Saveloy Dick's face formed on the back of her lids. What a fucking dirty cunt. She opened her eyes and let the rays blind her. It wasn't 'a favour for a favour.' He'd raped her. The word made her shudder. And then a sea of anger raged inside, sweeping her to Fawcett Street and onto the first bus over the river. She couldn't wait to see the look of terror on Saveloy Dick's face when he sees her big baby belly. Eight thousand quid to sod off forever was a lot, so she was willing to go lower.

At Roker Park, there were cars parked outside of the main entrance and people were coming and going so she waited until it was quiet before slipping into the foyer.

There was a woman behind the desk, so she asked her politely, 'Could ah speak ter Ronnie please?'

'Wee?'

'Ronnie, tell him it's the lass wer the ashes.'

'Oh reet, yer'll need to speak ter John. Hang on.'

She could hear her in the backroom saying that there was a young lass wanting to see about spreading ashes.

A tall bloke came out, 'How can ah help yer, luv?'

'Ah'm here ter see the groundsman.'

'Ah'm the groundsman.'

'Nor, is yer mate here? The other groundsman.'

'Wot's this about, luv?'

'Ah need ter speak ter the groundsman wee let uz scatter me dad's ashes on the pitch,' she said, knowing this would get Ronnie into trouble and she didn't give a fuck.

'Nee one scatters owt round here,' he laughed. 'Can yer imagine if every deed Sunderland fan ended up on me pitch? The lads would be knee-deep in ash. Yer'll need ter fill out a form if yer want the club to consider it, and it won't be on the pitch.'

'That's not wot Ronnie said.'

'Ah think yer Uncle Ronnie was tellin porky pies.'

'He's not me uncle, he works here, he's a groundsman.'

The man raised his eyebrows and shook his head. 'Ah've never known anyone called Ronnie that works here and ah've been head groundsman for ower ten years.'

'He's short, bald,' she said, expecting him to realise who she meant.

'Nor pet, doesn't ring a bell.'

She pivoted on one foot, one leg wanting to run, the other wanting to show the rapist her bump. 'Ah yer sure?'

He said, 'Wait here,' and went into the backroom.

She suspected that the tall man was currently telling Ronnie to show his face. A woman came out.

'How can ah help yer, pet?'

'Ah'm here ter see Ronnie, the groundsman.'

The woman was as baffled as the tall bloke. 'There's nee Ronnie here, can yer describe him?'

'Short, bald, blue tracksuit.'

'Ah'm sorry luv, nee one like that works here.'

'He does, he works on a Monda at ten, can yer check?'

The woman took a step backwards as if edging away from a rabid dog. 'John,' she shouted.

The tall man came out and the woman said to him, 'The lass said the man she's lookin for works here on a Monda at ten.'

John smiled, 'We have a staff meetin on a Monda mornin and there's never been a bloke called Ronnie on the staff, not in my time anyway.'

The pit of her stomach churned. Cold milk poured down her back as the horrible realisation dawned – who the fuck was Saveloy Dick? If the staff were in a meeting, it figures why the place was deserted. She shouldn't have been anywhere near the pitch. She pulled the corners of her mouth into a smile, said, 'Okay then, sorry ter have bothered yers,' then fled.

She ran as far as she could, boobs swinging. She sat on a garden wall halfway down the street of terraced houses.

A woman came out. 'Are you okay there?'

She stood, 'Aye, needed a sit-down, hot day.'

'Can I get you a drink?'

'No, ta.'

'How far gone are you?'

'Seven months.'

'Have you got any names picked out?'

'David for a boy and Chloé for a girl, with an accent on the e.'

'That's lovely. Are you sure you don't want a drink?'

'Aye, ta. Bye.'

She kept walking, her head was a mess: who was Saveloy Dick if he didn't work at Roker Park? She was such an idiot. Was the bloke with the yellow top and the carrot for the horses in on it? There were other young lasses stroking the horses that day. Her gut clenched with guilt. What if Carrot Man and Saveloy Dick made a habit of it? What if they'd done this to other girls? She should go to the police, yet she couldn't go to the police as it would make things worse. For a start, when they see a pregnant slapper, they're bound to ask about the baby's dad, and she didn't want to tell them about

Marcel because his family could *never* find out about Saveloy Dick. And then there was the money she'd got from Michael. She couldn't tell *anyone* about him, so when it comes to 'possible fathers', she'd have to lie. And it's like Nana says, 'A tangled web that we weave, when we seek to deceive.' She was still in a tangle of lies about accidentally murdering Billy without more lies to contend with.

On her way down Roker Baths Road a car of lads slowed down next to her and wound down the window. She thought they were asking for directions, and she was about to say that she didn't live here, when one of them leaned out, and shouted, 'FUCKEN CHARVER!'

Chapter 18

August 1986

As she waited at the Prospect, the sky was blue with white aeroplane trails and there was a cool salty breeze. She could tell it was going to be a scorcher because the lads' teeth had chattered all the way from the house, and now they shivered and ran onto a patch of sun on the grass. They pretended to fight each other with sticks, like on *Monkey*. She looked across the busy road at the Prospect Hotel and imagined what it would've been like when the road was a dirt track with horses and carts going past. The roof of the pub was high. Dad must have been amazing at climbing to get up there.

They got off the bus in Hetton, crossed the busy road, then she watched them run up to Nana Hart's house before waiting for the same bus to come in the other direction. She couldn't stop singing, '*Born from an egg on a mountain top … monkey magic, monkey magic.*' She wished she could summon a cloud rather than get the bus.

Lisa said to come over any time after ten. She couldn't wait to see her and David's new house. They'd done loads of work on it. She got on the Presbury Road bus and got off on Presbury Road at the top of Pennywell.

David answered the door. 'Aye-up, sis.'

The house was lovely. The red carpet was plain, and they had a brown leather settee, a brick fireplace, and taking up most of the room was a Moses basket. Lisa had her legs curled up, so she bent down and gave her a hug and Lisa pulled her down on top of her.

'Get the kettle on, Dave, while ah give yer sister a cuddle.'

She pushed herself off Lisa. 'Can ah give the bairn a cuddle or is she sound?'

'Yer can pick her up, she's due for a feed.'

She looked in the Moses basket at baby Brooke. She was perfect. She stroked her silky head and whispered, 'Bless you, gorgeous girl.'

'Dave, yer got the bottle ready?' Lisa shouted at David in the kitchen.

Brooke Elizabeth Hasting waggled her fingers and scrunched up her tiny pink face. She picked her up, and held her to her chest, resting her head on her shoulder. When she went to see Lisa and Brooke in hospital, the look on David's face was choss. It was like he couldn't believe he'd created a little person.

She was going into the kitchen with baby Brooke on her shoulder when she noticed a hole in the door.

'Fucken-ell man, yer weren't wrang when yer said he'd punched a hole in the door. From the hand of God to the hand of David,' she said.

'Here-man,' said Lisa, 'he's arnly just calmed down, wotever yer dee, dinnet mention the football.'

The kitchen was small and the units were old but the tiles were modern.

David shook a bottle. 'Wot's that fucken dress? Are yer a sailor or summink?'

'Fuck off. It's maternity wear from Binns. Sixteen quid this cost.'

'Mam telt uz that the bairn's dad's rich like, nice one ower kid.'

Brooke chirped and she rubbed her back the same way she did with Jason when he was hungry and she hadn't got the bottle ready – a nursery rhyme and a backrub could buy time while she warmed it up. Brooke's chirps turned to clicks, like when Jason first started to wake up, which was usually followed by squeaks, which was a three-minute warning before a house-shaking, Billy-waking, 'Shut that thing up!' big hungry cry.

The happiness in David's eyes hadn't worn off and he peeled Brooke off her. Brooke was wearing a spotty babygrow and when she rested her sleepy head on his shoulder, her cheeks were even chubbier.

She left them to it and sat on the settee in a position she'd never get out of. The baby was busy today, kicking and moving about.

'Two weeks ter gan,' said Lisa. 'Have yer heard owt about yer house?'

'Nowt yet. Ah put down for Plainsy or Springwell.'

Lisa pointed at the videos that filled the shelves in the alcoves. 'Der yer want ter watch a fillem? Tack yer mind off yer piles.'

'Nee piles thank God, but fuck me, heart on fire.'

David came in with Brooke on his shoulder and as he rubbed her back she burped, sending a milky slick down his bare arm.

'Give her here,' said Lisa, 'Close the blinds and put a fillem on, will yer, Dave?'

David closed the blinds and put the big light on.

'Wot's wer the bricks?' she said, about the small gas fire that was surrounded by bricks with matching bricks in both alcoves. On one side, the bricks continued out of the alcove, forming a curved wall under the window into which the video was slotted.

'Ah built it,' said David, hands on hips admiring the brickwork. 'Nice innet?'

'Nor yer didn't,' said Lisa as Brooke did a wet burp.

'Aye ah did, not on me own like, wer Scott and his brotha.'

'Me mate Sonya's fireplace is made of sandy bricks, all different sizes and that. Those bricks look like the ones yer build houses from.'

'That's because Scott lifted them from a school he woz buildin through Washerton.'

'Nice arch across the top of the fireplace. How come it doesn't fall down?'

'Scott's magic wer bricks,' he said, running his finger along the shelves of videos. 'Here wer gan. *Gremlins*. Have yer seen it?'

'Nor. Ah didn't think it woz out on video.'

'It's not,' he said, getting to his knees and putting it in the machine.

A blue line ran down the blank telly and buzzed each time it reached the bottom. Lisa said, 'Adjust the trackin, Dave.'

'Ah knar wot ah'm deein thanks,' he hissed.

When the video came on, he turned the big light off and it was dark like in a cinema.

Gremlins with popcorn cartons on their ears, singing *Hi-ho* to Snow White! *Gremlins* was officially the best film she'd ever seen. As the words came up, she was gutted. The words finished and as the video clunked to a stop, the screen turned to square snow with that annoying noise. Brooke was sleeping on David's shoulder and Lisa was snoozing with her mouth open. David rubbed Brooke's back and with an annoyed face, edged over to the telly, reached a foot out, and kicked the off button. The room went dark with sun leaking through the dots in the blinds.

'Ah'm ganner put her down upstairs,' said David, making Lisa wake with a jump.

'Is the fillem finished?' said Lisa.

'Aye.'

'Did yer like it?'

'Ah want a pet Gizmo.'

'Gizmo's topper, and Spike.'

'Stripe,' she said, gripping the cushion as a million period pains rippled from the top of her head to the tip of her toes.

'Yae alreet?'

'Aye, nor, ah dinnar,' she said, gripping tight.

'Yer look pale,' said Lisa. 'Yer might be havin contractions.'

'Nor, ah'm not due for ages.'

'So why are yer diggin yer nails inter me good cushion?'

'Heartburn.'

'When did it start?'

'About the same time that Stripe jumped in the swimmin pool.'

'Any more after that?'

'When the Gremlin went in the nuke, and when Gizmo was dressed as Rambo.'

'Fucken-ell, sis, yer in labour.' Lisa looked at her watch. 'Ah'm puttin the kettle on, and if yer get another bout of heartburn before it boils, were garn ter the hospital.'

She could hear the kettle and Lisa crashing about and if she could've got off the settee, she would've punched another hole in the door. She couldn't shout the pain away because that would wake Brooke and David would kill her. When Lisa returned and saw that she was biting the cushion, she didn't care about waking Brooke.

Lisa shouted up to David, 'Paula's in labour, yer'll have ter tack uz ter the hospital. Ah'll ring me mam, see if she'll come and look after Brooke, yer'll have ter gan and pick her up.'

David came down without the baby. 'Keep yer voice down, she's asleep.'

'Paula needs ter gan ter the hospital.'

She linked arms with Lisa as they made their way among the warren of buildings and huts. When they got to the reception of maternity, Lisa heaved her from her side and placed her hands on the front desk. 'Pant if yer need tee.'

Eyes peeped through the tilted blinds in the backroom, yet it was ages before a nurse came out.

'Can I help you?'

'Aye, me sister-in-law's in labour,' said Lisa.

'Is she now? What's your name?'

She looked up and said, 'Paula Hasting, nee s,' then a pain like all the period pains ever all at the same time made her grasp the desk and moo.

'Are you sure?' said the nurse. 'I can't find any notes.'

'Ah'm sure she's in labour, man, so can wer get her ter a delivery room?' said Lisa.

'Nobody's in labour until I say they are,' said the nurse.

As the pain eased, she panted like Lisa said.

'Paula Hart,' said Lisa, 'look for that in yer box of cards.'

'A-ha,' said the nurse, 'Here we are, Paula Hart. Due date, September fifth. You're not in labour, I suggest you go home and have a bath.'

'Ah'm tellin yer, she's in labour and wer need ter get ter delivery,' said Lisa without losing her rag. She loved Lisa and was glad she was here and not Mam or Coralie.

'Are you a midwife?' said the nurse.

'Nor, but me mam had both of me younger sisters at home, and ah helped ter deliver me owlder sister's second'un, and ah've had one of me arn, so ah'd say Paula's havin contractions.'

'We'll be the judge of that,' said the nurse, going off into the backroom.

'Pant if yer need tee,' said Lisa, rubbing her back.

She dug her nails into the counter, dreading the next wave of pain.

A different nurse came out and hissed, 'Where's your mother?'

She was going to say, 'Watching the telly, where do you think she is?' but another contraction made her double up and she mooed with pain.

'Breathe through the pain,' said Lisa. 'Can wer get her ter delivery?'

'Nobody's going to delivery,' said the nurse. 'She's not due for another two weeks, now take your sister home.' The nurse went into the backroom, which was for the best because Lisa looked like she was going to slap her.

'Are yer good standin here?' said Lisa.

'Aye,' she said, glad the pain had eased. She wondered how she was going to get home and whether Lisa had a hot water bottle she could borrow.

The nurse put her head around the door. 'What are you girls still doing here? Take your sister home and come back in two weeks with your mother.'

'She's in labour, wer need ter get her ter delivery,' said Lisa.

She couldn't lift her head and she gripped the counter, focussing on the green lino as the flickering of pain got bigger and bigger until it rippled down her body making her howl like a wolf. She would have felt shan if she wasn't in agony. She gripped harder and prayed for the pain to stop, then something popped.

'Have yer got a mop?' shouted Lisa.

*

Since leaving Lisa and David's yesterday, everything had been a blur. She remembered Lisa saying that two hours was a quick labour, and telling her to ring Ken, before clapping out and waking up on a ward of screaming babies. Her fanny knacked as she sat on the side of the bed and picked Chloé from the rectangular cot. She was five pounds, four ounces. She was perfect and she'd never loved anyone or anything anywhere near as much as this ever before and if anyone did anything to harm her, she would kill them. The baby's face was tiny and chubby, and she didn't look like anyone, which was good because it ruled out the worst-case scenario, i.e. the baby was identical to Michael or worse. Ian and Jason came out looking like Billy so Chloé's resemblance to a sleeping marshmallow was a blessing.

The plastic label around her ankle said Baby Hart and she wanted to cut it off. This was Baby Hasting. She held her tiny hand and stroked her silky head and wondered how it was possible to be a miniature human being.

The lass from Redhouse with the twins hissed, 'Shhh,' at the visitors clodhopping down the ward. As it filled up with people, balloons, and flowers, she hoisted herself up and reached for a hair brush. The first baby to break rank and scream was big twin, followed by all of the babies except for Chloé who was beautiful and she couldn't help but stare at her and love her. Heads turned as a Pooh the size of a real bear came through the swing doors. Ken gave her flowers and Marcel plonked Pooh on the bed.

'Here she is,' said Ken, admiring Chloé while Marcel fiddled with Pooh's ears.

'Yer can pick her up if yer want,' she said.

Ken gently pulled the blanket from Chloé's face and when her eyes popped open, he stepped back, startled. 'She's got my mam's mouth,' said Ken, shaking.

The flood of relief was so intense that some piss came out and stung her stitches like vinegar.

Ken picked Chloé from the tray and held her to his chest. 'Thank you, Paula,' he said with so much honesty that more piss came out, making her wince. 'Do you have a name?'

Marcel said, 'Chloé,' then looked at her to confirm that she hadn't changed her mind. She nodded.

Ken was never letting Chloé go, so Marcel stood close, face-to-face, with Chloé between them, making a baby sandwich.

'There's an accent grave on the e,' she said.

'A middle name?' said Ken.

She wasn't going to give her a middle name, but as Ken stroked Chloé's irresistible head, she felt grateful to him for loving her. He was another person who would look out for her forever, no matter what.

'Wot's yer mam's name?' she asked.

'Anne, she was called Anne.'

More vinegar piss stung her stitches at the relief of Anne and not Elsie. 'How about wer call her Chloé Anne?'

She'd never seen two grown men cry before.

On the second day in hospital Mam came to visit with David, Lisa, and the lads. Ian and Jason couldn't believe they were real uncles, and they stared, doting, at Chloé, Ian stroking her head, Jason marvelling at her tiny fingernails. Mam busied herself with the flowers and the big Pooh, making sure all the other families knew that Chloé's dad had a few bob.

On the third day in hospital her boobs felt like sponges that had been dunked in water. It was a strange sensation feeling them fill up. Like the other lasses, over the past three days, her boobs had been mostly out. She felt sorry for the young lad with the meals trolley who got an eyeful. Eventually, her boobs were huge and swollen and on fire and Chloé was screaming like a banshee. She'd seen the woman in the next bed lob a boob out and she watched how her baby felt around for her nipple then sucked, his little cheeks going in and out while his tiny hand touched his ear. She tried the same, but Chloé was screaming and not interested in the nipple that was dribbling milk. She was desperate for Chloé to suck and release the boiling milk, yet feared that if she hit the right spot, the force of the jet would choke her. All afternoon she tried to decant the saturated sponges into Chloé's tummy, yet the little cherub was having none of it, and the hungrier she got, the more she screamed until someone dragged a reluctant midwife over. The midwife's cold hand felt lovely on her hot boob, then she squeezed it and milk squirted out in a fountain of relief.

'I'll get a breast pump.'

She sat on the edge of the bed as the midwife stuck a plunger on her boob and got her to pump the handle. As fresh white milk like from a cow flowed from her body, she'd never felt so proud.

After four days of non-stop screaming and no sleep, Ken arrived with the pram she'd chosen from the catalogue, which lifted off into a carry cot. It wasn't like the old-fashioned bouncy prams with big wheels like what they had in the 60s and 70s. How did Mam get that pram up the steps at Thorney Close?

Coralie was waiting to see her new *petite-fille*. When she imagined how she'd feel if her beautiful baby died, it caused a pang of agony, and then a scene in which she was diving in front of a truck and pushing Chloé's pram out of the way. Since giving birth she couldn't stop thinking about baby Jodie, her tiny little body lying all lonely in the morgue. Now she understood, like *really* understood, how losing baby Jodie had destroyed Coralie's life.

First stop, the registrar. 'Ah'll wait here,' said Ken.

She pushed the pram across the carpark and to the front of hexagon city as she considered her best approach. The civic centre welcomed people with a pyramid of small steps or, on this occasion, a ramp that cut a zigzag through the steps. She pushed the pram for ages before popping up in another space and time. Walled by the hexagonal building from outer space was a piazza with so many steps and walkways it was confusing. It was made worse by the hexagon patterns everywhere and the same shade of red for everything. As she pushed on and hoped for the best, she spotted a blue sign, and as she got closer, she saw a blue door. Inside were more blue signs, including an arrow to the registrar's office. The woman at the desk said to go down the corridor and wait.

No one else was waiting, and as she wheeled Chloé up and down, she thought about what she would say to the registrar. When she was pregnant and sitting in the orange plastic chairs at the hospital, she heard two lasses talking about birth certificates. One of them said that if you say you don't know the dad, they take you to court, and you have to prove you don't know who he is. When the social worker asked her about 'the father', she told her about the shady man in the football cupboard, which made the social worker totally back off. So, although she didn't want to think about him, yuk, it was the most convincing half-lie she could think of. It could've been him. Who's to say, apart from now, when Chloé was sleeping, she looked so much like Marcel that anyone would wonder if anyone else took part in her creation.

The door opened. 'Register a birth?'

'Aye,' she said, going in. She'd pictured the registrar as an old man in a suit with a hammer for a head like in that music video, not a woman from the seventies in a flowery blouse and brown flares.

'Sit,' she said while standing and looking into the pram. 'She's a doll. I see a lot of babies, but not many are as pretty as—?'

'Chloé, with an accent on the e.'

'Chloé with an accent. What a lovely name. Let's get her registered, shall we?'

The woman tested her fountain pen on a pad before lining up a certificate on her desk.

'The baby's full name?'

'Chloé Anne Hasting, nee s.'

'Date of birth?'

'16th of August 1986.'

'How was the birth?' said the registrar, lowering her pen.

'Canny, two hours labour, short so ah'm telt.'

'Two hours? You lucky thing. What did baby Chloé weigh?'

'Five pounds, four ounces.'

'Oh bless, a tiddler. Place of birth, Sunderland General Hospital?'

'Aye.'

The registrar did a fancy swirly signature, swizzled the certificate round, and pushed it towards her. 'Here's your certificate.'

Pleased not to have been asked any tricky questions, she took the certificate and was about to stand up, when the registrar said, 'The long form and then we're finished,' placing another certificate squarely on her desk.

'Your name?'

'Paula Hasting.'

'No s?'

'That's it.'

'Occupation?'

'Er, none.'

'We can leave it blank.'

She could see by the look on the registrar's face, what was coming.

'Is the baby's father here with you today?'

'Ah dinnar wee he is,' she said in a panic. 'Ah went ter Roker Park ter scatter me dad's ashes, then this gadgie wee said he woz the groundsman, but he wasn't, tacks uz in a back room and then he raped uz.'

The registrar listened and didn't tut and say, 'Best one I've heard all day,' like the doctor did. The registrar took a deep breath, stretched her arms out, put down her pen and picked it up again. 'If you want to enter a father's name, he'll need to be here, or you'll need to provide documentation of his name and address.'

'The dad needs to be here ter gan on the birth certificate?'

'Yes.'

'Nee one telt uz that.'

In the car, she gave the birth certificate to Ken. 'Yer not allowed ter put the dad's name on it unless he's there.'

'Ah didn't knar that,' admitted Ken.

'Did yae register Marcel's birth?'

'Aye, I registered his birth and Jodie's.'

She could hear his heart breaking and she had to fight back tears.

As they pulled onto the drive, she could see balloons in the living room. Ken took Chloé in the carry cot and she wondered how Coralie was going to cope. She got out, took a deep breath, and danced about to check that everything was working. Her stitches had stopped stinging, and her bump felt smaller. She couldn't wait to look in the mirror with no clothes on as it was difficult to see what was going on because her boobs were a double-G cup. The midwife gave her a bra from the jumble box to contain them.

Inside, as well as the balloons, large bunny, and pile of presents, there was a Moses basket, towels, a baby bath, and a pile of disposable nappies, even though she'd said she was going to use terry nappies because they were cheaper. It already smelled of baby. Coralie cuddled Chloé while Ken hung around in and out of the kitchen. He needn't have been nervous because Chloé had her eyes open and was blinking at Coralie who was melting. It didn't look like Coralie was about to break down in grief or that she'd be handing her *petite-fille* back anytime soon.

Coralie stroked Chloé's head. 'What time is she due her next feed?'

'Anytime now, ah better mack a bottle.'

'Has your milk come in?'

'Aye but ah need ter pump it inter a bottle,' she said, opening her cardigan to show two wet patches on her sailor suit maternity dress. 'Mebees best ter give her formula for now.'

'Let's get her on your breast,' said Coralie, signalling like a teacher for her to sit in the chair.

She dropped the dress to her waist and was down to her bra when Ken came in and said, 'Crikey,' and walked out, shutting the hall and kitchen doors.

'Did yer breastfeed yowrs?' she said because it was the obvious question to ask and she had to include Jodie even though thinking about Jodie made her teary.

'Marcel, yes, Jodie, no. She was too pooley.'

'Ah dunnar how anyone copes with losing a babbie,' she said, as a tear dripped into her cleavage.

Coralie looked at Chloé with a faraway gaze. '*I will walk with frost and fire and death and snow, and my feet will want to find you wherever you lie sleeping, but I will stay alive.*'

More tears splashed on her boobs and soaked into her bra along with the leaky milk.

'I'm sorry, Paula. Didn't mean to reduce you to a blubbering wreck.' Coralie smiled and whipped the muslin cloth off her shoulder and gave her it. 'That was from a poem by Pablo Neruda. It's about how life goes on after someone dies.' She kissed Chloé's head. 'Did you do poetry at school?'

'Wer did Wilfred Owens.'

Coralie shook her head. 'Why are the British so obsessed with the war? Did you read any Yeats or Kipling?'

'Kiplin wee macks exceedingly good cakes?'

Coralie burst out laughing and Chloé clicked as if to join in the joke. 'Sounds like she's hungry,' said Coralie. 'Here, let's see if she'll latch on.'

She took her bra off, lay back on the chair and wrapped her arms around her precious bundle. Coralie held her boob still as she guided Chloé's head to it. Coralie had talked a lot about breastfeeding when she was pregnant and she was happy to try it to keep her happy. There was no way she was getting a boob out in public. She was going to mostly bottle feed.

*

The health worker was sweet and helpful and assumed that Coralie was her mam. Anyway, she didn't ask. The social worker was another matter. People from the council couldn't see her being showered with love by Marcel's family as they'd ask too many questions. As far as the social worker needed to know, she was a single mother living with her widowed mam and two brothers in a house that was too small.

Ken took her and Chloé to Mam's and helped carry all the loads of baby things into the living room. It seemed even smaller now that she'd been living in a big house, and it was so smoky that Ken opened a window. When the lads came in to see their niece, Ken backed out, mouthing,

'See yer at four.'

The social worker who visited when she was pregnant said, 'No one is here to take your baby away.' She said that because she was 'a minor with a care record, they had a responsibility to support the family.' She wasn't worried they'd take the baby away as she'd heard the women talking in the orange chairs down the hospital, and not the ones talking about birth certificates, say that they never take your baby away, well not at first, anyway. As soon as she could feel her baby kick, she decided that no meddling do-gooder would ever part them, fact. And what the heck did the *care record* say about her? She wondered if the truanting officer had got her two penneth in. She was a right bitch with her clipboard and green cagoule, always saying that 'all absences would be recorded on file', as if the SAS were watching her. Apart from accidentally murdering Billy, it's not like she'd done anything wrong, so it was unfair that she'd ended up with a record. On the bright side, being the teenage mam from the gruesome curiosity family helped smooth the way with the council. She wondered if social workers preferred the decapitated dad family to the alcoholic dad family.

Mam made herself look presentable by changing from her dressing gown into a short black skirt and yellow blouse, her top and tails letting her down – fag in mouth, big toe poking out of the hole in her slipper. As the social worker came in the gate, Mam flicked her butt into the bushes then came inside, leaving the door open.

'Gan sit ower there,' said Mam, shooing her from the window so she could stand there, dabbing her eyes like a grieving widow.

'Hello. Can I come in?' shouted the social worker.

They both said, 'Shhh!'

'Sorry,' whispered the woman, creeping into the room. 'I'm Doreen. How are you all getting on?'

Mam turned the tears on and off as she told Doreen about her tragic loss and how hard her sons had taken it. When Doreen got a word in edgeways, she waffled about making sure that she was ready to care for Chloé on her own and whether it would be better for her to stay with her mam who could provide additional support.

'Look, Doreen,' said Mam, 'the arnly additional support ower Paula needs is a roof ower her heed.'

Chloé's clicks and chirps escalated into a squeal, which caused eight thousand tiny maids to start a-milking. 'Ah better give her a feed.'

It was cool and calm in the kitchen. Chloé latched on and sucked as if she'd never been fed, and she watched her little cheeks go in and out. She couldn't believe how minuscule her fingernails were, how cute her face was, or how warm her tiny hug was.

There were footsteps, and she looked up to see Doreen, who said, 'Wow,' as if stumbling across a wolf feeding a feral child in the forest. She'd never had so much praise. Breastfeeding was a freaky mother-and-daughter sideshow.

'You really are a wonderful mam,' said the social worker.

'Dinnet forget ter write that on me care record.'

Chapter 19

September 1986

Two-bedroom house, Somerset Square, Springwell. The Wilkinsons had treated her like a princess and she had no idea how she would have coped with a new baby without them. Despite everything, after a week, she was saying her own version of grace in her head 'For what we are about to receive, may the Lord make us truly thankful, and if you can receive me a house, soon, that would be ellish, thanks.' It was mad how much they prayed. Before each meal, before bed, before checking the pools coupon. The council came up trumps with a house after two weeks, and although she'd miss being looked after, you can get too much kindness, and garlic.

She went in first, carrying Chloé in her bunny babygrow and knitted hat, followed by Marcel and Ken. The room was small with three big people in it. It had wall-to-wall woodchip painted white and a scratchy carpet that was going to be covered with a rug.

'It's okay in here,' said Marcel.

Ken pulled the net curtain and looked out of the window.

'Give uz a cuddle before we go,' said Marcel, taking Chloé.

'Ah'll be down on Tuesday,' said Ken. 'Could have a run over the sea front if yer fancy it?'

'That'll be good.'

'Ah can stay if yer want,' said Marcel.

'Nor, we'll be fine. Go home and get some sleep while yer can.'

'Ring if you need anythin.'

'We'll be fine,' she said, taking Chloé, 'won't we?'

'Ha'way then son,' said Ken, 'let's get off.'

A cool breeze came wafted in the open window, yet the room was quiet. Not like down Pallion when a breeze came with car doors slamming and back-firing exhausts. She released her bra and flopped her big milky wabs out. On the phone last night Mam said, 'Has yer milk dried up yet?' as if this was a good thing to happen. She didn't tell her that the free supply of milk that didn't need a sterilized bottle or any warming-up was still flowing. Mam would always say, 'Peace at last,' whenever her children took themselves out of her sight. She stroked Chloé's cheek and thought, this is peace at last. Peaceful in a way she didn't know existed.

After another night of feeds, she couldn't believe that it was possible to be this tired and be awake. She tilted the blinds and put the telly on, then lay Chloé down on her sheepskin rug on the floor. She stepped over a pile of baby clothes and towels that were covered in poo and opened the kitchen blinds. There was a mound waiting to go in the washing machine that was still full of yesterday's load. She put the kettle on and then ran back to make sure Chloé hadn't rolled over, knocked into the table, and was lying squashed under the telly. She was lying on her back gurgling into space waving her arms and legs in her pink babygrow and white cardigan with pearl buttons that Ken's sister had knitted.

The place was in a right state. It was amazing how something so small could cause so much mess. She made some tea which went cold while she fed Chloé and made another one that went cold while she changed her nappy. The uncomfortable position she was in when Chloé dozed off on her shoulder didn't matter because she was so tired, she could sleep on hot pokers. While they were snoozing, there was a gentle knock on the window and the sound of men talking. With Chloé on her shoulder, she opened the front door. It was Marcel with some tall dude with a skinny face and beard.

'Hello, sorry, ah would've rung but ah didn't want the phone ter wake the baby up,' whispered Marcel. 'Ah thought ah'd have a wander down, see if yer needed anythin.'

'Yer dinnet need ter whisper, she's awake.' She rubbed Chloé's tummy. 'Aren't yer?'

'This is William, me mate who ah was tellin yer about.'

'Ha'way in.'

Marcel and William stepped over the shitty babygrow and the sicky muslin and moved blankets and stuffed lions and elephants from the settee as they sat down. 'Looks like you've got everythin under control,' said Marcel.

She was too tired to figure out if he was being sarcastic. 'Yerv nee idea how much mess a baby macks.'

'Ah can see,' he said, holding his arms out to welcome his daughter. He folded her to his chest and stroked her cheek gently. With tears forming, he said, 'William meet me precious Chloé.'

William wangled out of his coat as he stood up, then rummaged in the inside pocket. 'Photo.' He produced a camera and took a picture of Marcel and Chloé. As Marcel lay Chloé on the sheepskin, she kicked the baby junk across the floor so William could get a good shot.

'Did yer have a good time at the beach yesterday?' asked Marcel.

'Aye it woz canny. She woz mostly asleep but when she opened her eyes, ah held her up to squiy the sea and the lighthouse.'

'Let's have one of Paula and Chloé,' said William.

'Not lookin like this,' she said.

'Why don't yer go and have a lie down? Ah'll look after Chloé,' said Marcel.

'Ah'll give her a feed first,' she said, holding her arms out for Marcel to pass her his precious girl.

She went to go upstairs when Marcel said, 'Don't go in the other room on our account. I've seen your tits hods of times and William will look the other way.'

Marcel watched her feed Chloé with what he'd previously described as 'breastfeeding envy' and then he whisked his baby away to be burped. Her face was squashed and cute when he propped her chin between his thumb and forefinger and rubbed her tiny back.

As her head touched the pillow, and her eyes drifted shut, she thought about how lucky she was that she'd shagged Marcel and not some other random dumbfuck. She didn't think lads cared about bairns; most of the lasses she knew had to take the lad to court to get them to take responsibility. Not Marcel. He loved his baby so much, he was on the verge of tears most of the time.

It was mid-afternoon when she woke up and she felt so much better that she didn't care if Marcel was having a nightmare downstairs, although she doubted there was a poo, a puke, or a sleepless night that could deter him. She was looking forward to him going down Leeds to college.

Apart from the wobbly skin on her belly and her double-G cup, her body was back to normal, so the sailor dress hung on her like a tent. The maternity dungarees weren't too bad when they were cinched at the waist with a thick turquoise leather belt, the spare denim bagged over the top. It looked fine, like she was in Bananarama, so she wrapped some black tights around her head, tying them in a bow at the front, and then did the dance from 'I Heard a Rumour' in front of the mirror until she could feel her boobs leaking.

Marcel and William had excelled themselves. The place was spotless, and Chloé was in a fresh babygrow, sleeping on Marcel's chest.

She picked her off him. 'She needs a feed, then we're garn ter see me Mam.'

'Like the look,' said William.

She smoothed her maternity-come-cool dungarees, and bagged the top over her belt more.

'Very Dexys Midnight Runners,' said Marcel.

'Dexys! Yer cheeky bastard.'

At least Mam put her fag out before picking Chloé from the pram. 'How's me bairn?' Mam said, taking the baby and leaving her to wrestle the pram into the house.

She went to see if the lads were about and was surprised to find that Ian had moved into her bedroom. As the oldest, she thought he'd boot Jason out and claim the big room. The Wham! poster was replaced by a footy poster. 'Howard Gayle,' she said when she saw his face among the disinterested rows of players.

'Wot about him?' said Ian, wrinkling his nose, 'Wot about Gordon Armstrong or Eric Gates?'

'Dad said Gayle was a great player, yer knar, tough, got stuck in like.'

'Is it true that yer dad knew all the footy stats for the Mackems and Mags garn back centuries?'

She loved how Ian remembered the stuff that she'd told him about Dad and how he was in awe of a man who used to write match reports on the walls. By being in Dad's house, she'd absorbed a lot of footy information, and the only person who had ever been impressed was Ian. 'The footy league started in 1887, Sunderland joined in 1890,' she said.

'Yae should gan on *Mastermind*. Paula Hart, specialist subject, SAFC players and goals from owlden times till now.'

'Ah couldn't dee that. Me dad could though. Fuck, could he.'

'He sounds better than my dad, he was a reet bastard.'

She couldn't agree more yet tried never to say that to the poor bairn. Now that he was dead, she made out to Ian that Billy was an okay bloke in an attempt to tape over his memories of being treated like dirt. 'Yowr Dad was good at pickin horses, studied their form and everythin,' she said, 'and we all knar that horses are better than footballs.' She dug Ian in the ribs and he threw himself sideways onto the bed.

'Have yer missed uz?' she said, pinching his toe.

He flicked her hand away. 'Nor.' His face was white and his eyes dark and sunken like he'd missed a week of meals.

'Is she feedin yer?'

'Aye, wer had chippy tea last neet.'

'The neet before?'

He rolled on his back. 'It's not the same when you're not here. Wer dinnet have a laugh nee more. It's like, borin.'

As he stared wistfully into space, she jumped on stop of him, straddled his belly and held his wrists down with her knees. 'Attack of the chest typewriter!' She poked on his chest with her Peter-pointers while he cried with laughter and squirmed in pain.

Mam's fridge was empty and the cupboard was down to two tins of beans, a tin of peas, and a tinned mince and onion pie. Ian was good at fending for himself if he had some basic rations to fend with.

She'd rather not leave Chloé with Mam and she made her promise that she'd go in the garden to smoke.

'Ah yer tryin ter tell uz how ter look after a bairn?' said Mam.

'Nor, just that—'

'Here-man, ah've had fowr of me arn.'

She had an hour to get into town, do the shopping, then get back for Chloé's feed. Mam gave her a tenner and moaned because it was only two minutes since she'd done a shop. As she walked along, swinging her arms and looking at the sky, it felt ellish to be free, like visiting a past life, yet by the time she got to the bus stop, it felt like something was missing and she couldn't wait to get back to Chloé.

As she waited for the bus, she could hear the biddies chatting. 'Look at her, out galivantin already. It'll be her mother wee brings that bairn up, mark my words.'

Chapter 20

September 1988

Coralie always bought Chloé expensive clothes, most recently, the gorgeous pink coat from Michael de Leon that she was wearing on top of her nightie. She was a funny thing. It was mad to think of how miserable her life was before she had her.

'Toast?' she said, putting the plate down. 'Tack yer posh coat off first, yer dinnet want ter get jam on it.'

Chloé did her glum face as she took the coat off and cheered up when the telly went on.

'Eat yer brekkie and watch the telly.'

Chloé nodded as she stuffed toast in her mouth.

'And nee deein wot yer did yesterday, yer little tinker. Slices of bread aren't letters and the video isn't a postbox.'

She could hear Chloé giggling as she went to get ready.

Tracksuit on Monday and Tuesday. Jeans or black skirt or black jeans with a tracksuit top or one of two horrible jumpers on Wednesday, Thursday, Friday, and Saturday. Pyjamas on Sunday. Coat: denim jacket. Unlike Chloé's extensive collection, her own wardrobe was depressing. She ran her hand along the hanging clothes. At the end of the rail was her Burberry riding coat, still in perfect condition. She hadn't worn it since last summer at Sonya's BBQ. Next to the coat was Jenny's Laura Ashley dress. It was a shame that she didn't keep mates with Charlotte. When she was pregnant, she rang her a couple of times and nobody picked up, so that was that. And it's not like she could go anywhere near the stables because of Michael.

She put the Laura Ashley dress on, which was too big, but less too big than when she'd worn it at Brandon's christening. She'd only worn it then because Lisa said wear a dress, so it was either her short, red going-out dress or the Laura flora. It felt the same as it did before, i.e. like the dress of a murderous stepdaughter. At the christening, David laughed at her, but she could see in his face that he was thinking about when the social worker brought her home and they pretended to cry over Billy.

She put Chloé in her pushchair, and they walked through the park with its winding path and bridges over the dry stream, up past the old dairy and along past the building in the woods that was mostly red roof. Chloé was happy being pushed along as they took in the sights of Grindon and Pennywell.

Nana's house was quiet now that only her and Grandar lived there, yet never very quiet. Chloé was delighted to find that Julie had left two-year-old Ellie-May at Nana's while she went down the hairdressers. Nana sat her new crop of bonnie lasses at the table and fed them cheese sandwiches cut into triangles.

'Ah've got a dress like that upstairs, yer can have it if yer want,' said Nana.

'Nor thanks, Nana, ah dinnet actually like dresses, it woz clean that's all.' She tugged the lacey waistband. 'Ah got this from Jenny, the foster woman.'

'Der yer still hear from her?'

'Nor.'

Nana gave her the dress anyway, which was more Danny La Rue than Laura Ashley.

'Thanks, Nana, it's lovely. Have yer got a bag?'

When Julie walked in with a massive perm, Ellie-May burst into tears.

'Nee need ter cry,' Nana laughed, 'it's not that bad.'

Julie let Ellie-May touch her poodle hair, which was so stiff with hair lacquer it didn't move when the bairn pulled it.

'Where did yer get that done?' she asked. 'It's nice, suits yer.'

'Ta, got it done down Chester Road.'

Julie was living in Grangetown with Douglas who was twenty years older than her and who worked at

MFI. He was boring and had pockmarks all over his face and if you watched Uncle Jimmy carefully, you could see him cringe when Douglas spoke. David said that Uncle Jimmy wanted to ploat him when he found out that he'd got Julie up the duff and only didn't because he got him an ex-display kitchen for well cheap.

'Yer comin up ower David and Lisa's?' she asked Julie.

'Nor,' said Julie. 'Ah'm garn inter town ter pick Doug's Calvin Klein coat up from the cleaners, then ah'll problees gan rund ter Marksy's for a chicken curry wer rice, Doug's favourite.'

She was glad to get out of Nana's. She pushed Chloé up to David and Lisa's. When she released her from the pushchair, she darted inside.

'David out wer the videos?' she asked Lisa.

'Aye, he's deein Town End today.'

'Have that many people got video players? They must be wot, three hundred quid for a cheap one?'

'Hods of people have them and they'll pay three pund ter rent a fillem.'

'And the vids under the seats?'

'Aye, why, it's fifteen for a porno, that's where he macks his money.'

'Ow much?!'

'Fifteen, ah knar, fucken perverts,' said Lisa. 'Ha'way in.'

Brooke was in vest and pants, bouncing on the settee, and baby Brandon was pulling himself up, and slavering everywhere. Between Brooke and Brandon there was always lots going on all over the living room and up the stairs and under the kitchen table, yet there was never any mess. She didn't know how Lisa did it. It was like all the toys and half-eaten bananas evaporated.

'How's yer nana?' asked Lisa.

'She's canny. Lovin the bairns. Eeee, ower Julie got a perm, it's nice like, ah'd get one, but ah haven't got the reet type of hair.'

'Ower Fiona got a perm, cost her eighteen quid and it dropped out after a week. Tea?'

'Aye, gan on then.'

Next to the microwave were two glass jars with 'In' and 'Out' labels sellotaped on. They were both full of coins and notes, and the 'In' jar was fuller than the 'Out' jar.

Lisa opened the back door and the bairns went into the garden, squabbling over who carries Brandon, while Brandon struggled to breathe under Brooke's arm as Chloé tugged his legs.

'Have yer seen the sloth bitch recently?' said Lisa.

'Who, Mam? She comes ower on a Sunda.'

Lisa snorted and shook her head. 'Yer still feedin Ian and Jason?'

'Nor, not every neet,' which was true, just about. Mam was good at making egg and chips and fish fingers and beans, and at buttering bread, and the lads' clothes were clean, even if they were nashy.

'Those poor bairns would be starved wer nee shoes on their feet if it wozn't for yae,' said Lisa. 'It's not fair yer knar.'

'Aye, why, life isn't fair, and ah dinnet mind. Mam usually manages ter iron the school shirts in between *Neighbours* and *Home and Away*,' she laughed.

Lisa wasn't laughing. She'd heard too much from David about what Mam was like.

'Ah'm garn in the garden ter check that Brooke and Chloé haven't killed Brandon,' she said, escaping the lecture.

The bairns were playing in the rhubarb and there were a couple of gadgies in next door's garden. The one in jeans and a Fred Perry top came to the wire fence, and said, 'Alreet?'

'Aye, canny,' she replied.

'Mike,' he said, sticking his hand out.

'Paula,' she said, shaking it.

'Yae David's sister?'

'Aye. Der yer live here?' she said.

'Nor, this is me mam's,' he said. 'Grew up here. Moved in in 1951, when the estate woz first built.'

'How owld were yer?'

'Ah'll ah been eight.'

'So that mack's yer forty-five, born in 1943?'

'Aye,' he said, stepping back in amazement. 'Wer used ter live down Millfield, after the war. It woz brilliant when wer moved here, it woz posh as owt ter have an inside bathroom. Down Millfield ower netty woz outside. Imagine that now?'

'Nor ah cannet. Must've been frozzen in the winter.'

'Aye it woz. The houses were frozzen anarl, nee radiators. Coal fire in ivry room.'

'Yer mam's house's got central heatin now though?'

'Oh aye, the council put in a few years agan.'

'Wee's he?' she said nodding at the man at the end of the garden with a clipboard.

'He's the man from the mortgage company.'

'Der yer think he looks like Starsky?'

Mike laughed. 'He does a bit, it's the hair.'

'And the cardigan,' she laughed. 'Strite from the 70s that beaut.'

'Starsky's helpin uz get a mortgage. After thirty-seven years of rentin, me mam's buyin the house.'

'Is she?'

'Aye, ah better gan see ter him.'

'Mortgage' made her see red cards with white letters lying on blue carpet and Dad tucking pink notes under the board, having mortgaged the orange properties to fund hotels on Mayfair and Park Lane. The lies about rolling the perfect number and the tricks to make sure that his favourite properties came his way to get the came over with. Now she'd give anything to make the game last forever.

She went to see what Brooke and Chloé were doing in the long grass and found them throwing dickie darts and shouting, 'Brandon's got dickies!' at Brandon who had loads of them stuck in his hair. She scooped up Brandon and picked the dickie darts off him. '*Brandon Hasting is no good, Chop him up for fi-re wood.*'

Mike and Starsky were leaning on the fence, so being nebby, she aeroplane-zoomed Brandon in their direction.

'This is me neighbours' sister,' said Mike to Starsky.

'Hiya,' she said. 'Did yer get yer mortgage?'

'House is worth twenty thousand, that's reet?'

'Correct,' said Starsky.

'How much yer borrowin and ower how long?' she asked, slipping into Monopoly mode.

'Ten thousand,' said Starsky.

'Me mam gets the house for ten because she's lived here for thirty-seven years,' said Mike. 'You're good at maths,' he said to her, smiling at Brandon and poking his belly. 'Is two thousand payments ower twenty years a good deal?'

'Two hundred and forty monthly payments,' said Starsky. 'Twenty-year product.'

'Ah'm not good at maths,' she said, 'but forty quid every month for twenty years sounds like a long game.'

Starsky looked at her with amazement. 'You need to add 9.8% interest on to that.'

'That's easy then, ah can rund it up ter ten, then tack a bit off,' she said, buying time while she worked it out. 'That's about twelve thousand in interest, so yer mam will be payin back about twenty-two thousand.'

Mike looked to her for more, so she said, 'Yer mam will have ter pay about ninety quid every time she passes go for two hundred and forty times rund the board. Ah dinnet want ter be funny like, but is yer mam ganner live for another twenty years?'

'After five years, she can sell the house ter me,' said Mike. 'That's reet isn't it, wer the right ter buy scheme?'

'Correct,' said Starsky. 'The capital will have grown in five years.'

She remembered how the capital growth on a hotel on Park Lane was usually ten percent every time Dad passed go, and how she always had to haggle him down from twenty percent. 'Wot percent growth der yer expect ower five years?' she asked.

Starsky exhaled. 'About twelve percent.'

'That means a house that's worth twenty thousand today, will be worth twenty-four thousand in five years.'

It was funny watching their jaws flap when she added up in her head. Brandon giggled like he was in on a big joke.

'And if he sells at thirty thousand and pays back the mortgage, what will the profit be?' said Starsky.

'Hang on,' she said, closing her eyes to concentrate as Brandon tugged her lids. It took her a minute, then she opened them. 'He'll have fourteen thousand in his pocket, which from an initial investment of nothing, is a hundred percent profit, or is that an infinite percent profit? Anyway,' she said to Mike, 'yer cannet sell the house, where will yer mam live?'

Mike leaned over the fence and made Brandon giggle. 'Ah bet yer Aunty Paula was top of the class for maths.'

'Nor, ah wasn't even in the top set.'

'I thought you must work in a buildin society or somethin,' said Starsky.

'Why-nor,' she laughed, 'ah left school at sixteen, ah've got a two-year-owld bairn.'

'If I had a client with a salary of thirty thousand a year, if he can get a mortgage at three times his salary,' asked Starsky, like it was a test, 'what's the most expensive house that he can buy?'

'One ower Seaburn,' she answered.

Mike laughed. 'Is this *Mastermind* or summink?'

'I've started, so I'll finish,' said Starsky. 'He doesn't have a deposit.'

'Thirty times three is ninety, so he'll have ninety thousand to spend,' she said.

Starsky held out a business card which Brandon snatched and put in his mouth. 'I'm Frank Johnson, Managing Partner at LJ Finance.'

'Ta, but ah'm not lookin ter borra any money at the minute like,' she said.

'Our office is in Frederick Street,' he said, giving her another card. 'I need an associate with a good head for figures.'

She didn't know what he meant.

'You'd rather have a job than claim benefits?' he said.

'Eh?' she said, amazed. 'A job, me?'

'You have my card, drop in if you're passin.'

'A job deein wot?'

'How does two hundred a week sound to you? You know where I am.' He gave her another business card.

'Ah'll think about it, ta.'

She wandered down the garden, thinking about it. With her giro and family allowance and rent rebate, she would be seventy quid better off a week with the job, but then she'd have to pay for a childminder, and then there was tax. She didn't want a job. She liked being at home with Chloé from Monday to Friday, and with the eighty quid a month she got from Coralie and Ken, she could manage on what she had.

*

Chloé perched on the back of the armchair and pushed her face through the blinds. When Coralie and Ken pulled up outside, Chloé slithered down between the chair and the wall and crawled out from under the curtain, on her way to the door.

'*Bonjour ma princesse Chloé-Anne*,' said Coralie.

The Chloé-Anne version of her sweet child toddled off down the path in her pink cords, holding Grand-mère's hand and chatting away.

She face-planted on the bed. As much as she loved Chloé, it was nice waving her off on a Friday morning. She was meeting Michelle in town in Burger King that used to be Wimpy. Michelle had been taken on at the estate agents where she did her govie and her pay had shot up from £120 to £550 a month, which was more than Ally was making on the phones at Littlewoods that used to be Janet Frasers. Michelle had splashed out on some nice clothes and make-up yet was still at her mam's up Holborn Road, squeezed into a room with her two sisters.

Michelle was looking at globes in WHSmith's window, so she sneaked up on her. 'Boo!'

When the chubby lass with ginger hair and navy skirt and suit jacket turned around, it was Michelle, which was a relief.

'Hiya, is that a new top?'

'Aye, it's from ower Lisa's catalogue.'

'Wot yer wearin toneet? Yer are comin out on the hoy, aren't yer?'

'Why-aye, it's Frida. Ave yer heard owt from Ally?'

'Nor, it'll just be me and thee the neet.'

'Good wer me,' she said, linking arms with Michelle as they headed inside.

'Gan and bag a winda seat,' said Michelle, 'wot der yer want?'

'A burger and a vanilla shake,' she said, making a swift move on a window seat.

She liked Fridays when she sat in Burger King's with Michelle, watching the world go by. Glen Usher got out of a red Peugeot 106, head down, pretending like he hadn't seen them.

'Ah've shagged him,' said Michelle.

'Ah knar, at Ally's house after the fifth-year party.'

'Did yer knar that Mel Baily shagged him in a tent?'

'Neeways, did she? Bet she thought all her Christmases had come at once.'

'Aye, why, he's good lookin, but ah've had better.'

'Yer fucken slapper.'

'Aye, like yersel.'

'Yer haven't telt uz wot yer wearin toneet,' said Michelle.

'Black skirt and see-through red blouse. Yae?'

'Rust culottes and mustard and rust Western-style shirt from the Next Directory.'

'A catalogue that yer have ter pay for, sounds dodgy ter me.'

'It's a tenner, but worth it, man. Yasmin le Bon models the clays, and Linda Evangelista,' enthused Michelle. 'Yer dinnet get that in the Littlewoods catalogue.'

'The clays are nice, but yer cannet pay it off weekly.'

'Fucken-ell Paula, yer minted wer the money from the in-laws, yer should treat yersel. There's a gorgeous tweed jacket that would suit yer. It's like wot a horse rider would wear, should ah order it for yer?'

'Nor,' she said, putting the last bit of burger in her mouth. 'Ah cannet afford it.' The burger was lovely but gone too quickly. She wished she'd got chips but that would cost money which she'd rather spend on cider tonight. Then she remembered what she had to tell Michelle. 'Yerl nivver guess wot.'

'Wot?'

'Ah've been offered a job.'

'Have yer!'

'Nee need ter sound so surprised, like.'

'Ah wozn't.'

'Yer choked on yer Coke.'

'Ah didn't knar yer wer lookin for a job that's all.'

'Ah'm not. This gadgie gave uz his card ower David's back fence. Summink ter dee wer mortgages and percentages.'

'Wot's the money like?'

'Two hundred a week.'

Coke spurted out of Michelle's nose.

There was no harm in walking past to see if it looked like somewhere she could work. She could imagine the look on everybody's face if she got a job in an office. Coralie was always saying that she should get out into the world and carve herself a path, and it wasn't because of money either. Coralie said, 'Marcel will pay for Chloé-Anne no matter what.' It made her laugh how they always made out that Marcel was paying.

Frederick Street was in that odd part of town with streets of four-storey houses where the rich Victorians and Edwardians used to live, and which were now all businesses like opticians and estate agents with sewing rooms in the basement. Must not call him Starsky, not Starsky, don't say Starsky, Frank Jones, not Starsky, or anyone from the telly in the seventies. 'Frank, Frank, Frank,' she said under her breath as she followed the numbers on the doors or on the glass above the doors or on the nameplates.

She climbed the steps to the tall black door which was locked so she pressed the doorbell. A small woman with long grey hair opened it, and said, 'LJ Finance or Curtains by Debbie?'

'LJ Finance.'

'Follow me.'

Inside was like the living room of a big house with a desk at one end, shelves of files down the far wall, and bamboo chairs arranged around a bamboo and glass table in the window area with some blokes in suits sitting down. The woman with grey hair went behind the desk, and said, 'Do you have an appointment?'

'Nor, ah'm here ter see Frank Jones. He said ah should drop in if ah was passin.' She waved his card. 'He gave me this.'

The woman's face looked like she'd witnessed the resurrection. 'Okey doke, take a seat, pet. I'll tell him you're here.'

When she wandered over to sit down, the blokes looked at her like she was syphilis so she sat on the chair furthest from them and wished she had the guts to go for a magazine because she could see *Movie* and *Family Circle* on the glass table.

'Paula.'

She gave the blokes a sarcastic smile as she stood up, and her legs went all wobbly as she walked towards Frank, not Starsky, who was smiling and waving her through a white door with a green metal hinge at the top. It closed behind them with a hefty backdraught.

'You look different to the last time I saw you. You were wearin a dress,' he said.

'Ah dinnet usually wear dresses,' she said, feeling like her black jeans and shell-suit top were wrong. He was wearing a pin-striped suit and didn't look anything like Starsky apart from his hair.

She followed him down a corridor that had wallpaper like an old-fashioned house and grey lino floor like a hospital. He heaved open another double-height door with a military-grade hinge that was loaded, ready to ping shut with enough force to snap an arm off. She nipped inside as it swung closed, and he said, 'Mind you don't trip down th—' as she stumbled, '—steps.'

'Fuck, soz,' she said, bouncing off the wall and stumbling down another step.

'Sit,' he laughed. 'Safest thing to do in this dungeon.'

The room was higgledy-piggledy with shelves of files and catalogues, nothing like how she'd imagined it. All the way down on the bus she'd had the *Cagney and Lacey* tune in her head, and she imagined striding across Market Square in her knee-length tan leather boots and baggy blue jumper, ready for a kick-ass day at the office with telephones and guns and men who foolishly underestimate women.

'Thank you for droppin in. I'm so pleased to see you,' said Frank, not Starsky. He was properly smiling, it was mad.

'Tell me stranger,' he said. 'What's your full name, how old are you, and where do you live?'

'Paula Hastin, ah'll be nineteen in December, and ah live at Springwell with me two-year-owld daughter, Chloé.'

'Ah yes, the little girl in the garden. Who is it lives next door to my client in Pennywell?'

'Me brotha and his missus.'

'Have they thought about buyin the house?'

'Ah doubt it, they've got nee money.'

'You know what Paula, I've been a financial adviser for nearly twenty years, and in all that time my clients were rich people looking for business finance, but in the last five years, we've seen an increase in clients seeking finance for residential property, including local authority houses.'

'Aye, why, wer the fifty percent discount, yer'd be crazy not ter buy, apart from ower David and Lisa have arnly lived there for two years.'

'Not all our clients are lookin to buy their local authority house, some have money tucked away from the pits and shipyards and they're thinking of a large semi-detached with a double garage. There's a mortgage solution for everyone, that's our motto.'

'Wot, so yer get them ter spend their redundancy on a house?'

'Correct. And what a time to invest. In the first half of this year house prices were up nearly twenty-five percent, so tell me Paula, if a property was worth seventy-five thousand last year, what is it worth today?'

'About ninety-five thousand,' came out of her mouth and she felt her face go hot and beety as she checked her calculation.

'And if the market increases by the same amount each year, what will the house be worth in five years?'

'Ah'd say,' she said while she thought, 'about,' while she thought more, 'a hundred and eighty thousand.'

'Profit?'

She coughed and repeated *profit*, buying time. 'A hundred and five thousand, or about seventy percent.'

He sat back and smiled. 'I'll stop the numbers now. You're good, though. Where did you learn to do that?'

'Not at school, that's for sure.'

'So where then?'

'Ah think it must be from playin Monopoly, not the normal game like, Dad's rules.'

'Dad's rules?'

'It's complicated,' she said, thinking of whether to tell him. 'He had schizophrenia.'

'I see,' he said, putting his head back. 'A complicated game of Monopoly that made sense to him?'

'Yip.'

'He must be proud of you?'

She didn't want to make him feel uncomfortable, but he asked a question. 'He died.'

'Oh Paula, I'm sorry to hear that. My dad died too. It sucks. Did he teach you any more party tricks?'

'Party tricks?' She laughed. 'Nor, but ah used ter work out the odds on the nags for me stepdad.'

He smiled. 'Okay then.'

Looked like it was *Mastermind* again, so she sat up straight.

'If I put twenty pounds on a horse at ten to one, what do I get if it wins?'

'A Chinese takeaway,' she said, and he laughed. 'It's true. If he got a win, we'd get a takeaway.'

'Did he win often?'

'Nor, course not. But there was one time when he had a tenner on a horse which came in at fifty ter one.

Ah had special fried rice and me brotha had spare ribs. Soz, ah didn't answer yer question, wot woz it again?'

'It doesn't matter,' he said. 'Do you have any exams?'

'Nor, ah left school ter have Chloé, and anyways, ah wozn't that good at maths, ah never got the point of algebra.'

'Me neither,' he said. 'I failed O-level maths. Left school with an O-level in geography and a GCE in woodwork.'

'And look at yer now. Are yer the boss?'

'I'm one of them, the other boss is Kelvin Lawson.'

'The L in LJ?'

'Correct. We've got three mortgage brokers, an accountant, a client liaison officer – that's Eileen, you'll be working with her – a secretary, and Gloria, our receptionist who you've met. Any questions?'

'Wot is it exactly that yer dee? Ah mean, have yer got a vault full of money?'

'No unfortunately, no vault of money.'

'Where does the cash come from when someone gets a mortgage? And how der they pay it back? Ah cannet see nee queue of people moanin about the interest rates goin up like in the buildin society.'

'You have a buildin society account?'

'At the Sunderland and Shields on Chester Road. There's always a queue out the door. Yer can tell the ones wee are after a loan cos they've dressed up all smart like.'

He grinned. 'That's the thing, you don't have to queue at the buildin society anymore, not now that banks can offer mortgages. Have you ever used a computer?'

'Ah've had a gan on me mate's computer, she had some good games.'

'ZX Spectrum?'

'Commadore 64.'

'Have you ever used an Acorn computer?'

'Nor but ah've used a BBC, well ah say used, ah've been in the same room as one. Turned it on, but nowt else.'

'BBC computers are Acorns, so if you know how to turn it on, that's great. We can show you how to turn it off.'

'Ah haven't said ah can work here yet, ah mean, there's a lot ter think about, Chloé, me benefits, and didn't get uz wrang, ah'd rather work than claim, but wot's the point if ah'm ganner be worse off?'

'I can guarantee that you won't be worse off. How many hours can you work without it affectin your benefits?'

'Fourteen ah think, ah'll have ter check.'

'So you can work two days or there about?'

'Aye ah suppose so.'

'How are you fixed for childcare?'

'Chloé's dad's family could look after her, ah mean, her granny would love ter look after her, she keeps talkin about the Montessori, but ah dinnar about that.'

'Your in-laws said they'll pay for private nursery? Nice.'

'Aye, but ah dinnet want her in nursery, and they're not me in-laws. Is it an expensive private nursery?'

'You could do a lot worse than the Montessori.'

'Which two days would ah have ter work?'

'Any you like, how about Tuesdays and Fridays?'

'And wot would ah get paid?'

'I was thinking ten thousand pro-rata.'

'Pro-whatyer?'

'Ten thousand for five days a week, so you'll get the pro-rata amount for two days.'

'Reet, so ah'll tack home four grand?'

'Is that a yes?'

'Ah'm not sure like, ah've nivver had a job before.'

'If you don't like it you can leave, but you will like it. Go on, give it a trial.'

There was an actual bloke who wanted to give her an actual job in an office. 'Aye, gan on then, ah'll give it a try.'

He raised his hands in the air. 'Oh I am pleased.' He leaned back, opened the desk drawer and took out a metal box. Inside was a pile of notes. 'Here,' he said, giving her a wad. 'Uniform allowance.'

*

Eileen showed her how to fill in a new client form using View Sheet on her Acorn Electron. Name, address, age, occupation, income, spouse name, age, occupation.

Eileen gave her a user manual and a pile of application forms to input into the computer. 'I'm poppin out,' she said. 'If you have any problems, ask Barry, he's good with View Sheet.'

*SHEET. To switch between command mode and text mode press ESCAPE. Type CLEAR RETURN. The * characters are TAB stops. The < is the right margin stop, marking the last character position in the line. Use EDIT COMMAND CE RETURN (text to be centred). Use EDIT COMMAND PL RETURN (number of lines).

When she found a list of commands at the END of the manual, it speeded things up, but it took two hours to get one application entered and she nearly didn't save it.

SAVE (filename) RETURN records the named file on to the disc. Phew!

This was boring.

She'd spent the full hundred quid of her uniform allowance which was the only reason she hadn't quit after her first day. She'd been on her way to see Aunty Pat in C&A when she called into Next to have a look because Michelle said they do posh work gear. She'd been in when it first opened and it was full of tops neatly folded on shelves as if to say, don't touch, you can't afford me. Now she had a job, she could be the businesswoman in the window in the pencil skirt and navy blazer with stripes on the lapels. The lasses were dead canny, giving her stuff to try on, and she bought two shirts, a pair of trousers, and some court shoes that were in the sale.

*

When she got to work, there were already three people waiting on the bamboo chairs and Gloria was on the phone. The door to her office was wedged open and there was no sign of Eileen, so she took her coat off, sat at the computer, and stared into space hoping that today would be less dull than her first day.

'Penny for them.'

She looked up to see Frank and a tall bloke in a waistcoat.

'A penny?' she said. 'Me thoughts are worth more than that. How about a tenner?'

The tall bloke laughed, and Frank said, 'I told you.'

'I'm Kelvin. I hear you're our new trainee client liaison officer.'

'Am ah?'

Frank explained that today her job was to sit next to Eileen and listen to her take client details.

The first client was a bloke who was 35 and worked at Bards. He earned 16K and lived at Silksworth in a house worth 22K. He wanted to buy a house in Grangetown for 44K, and he had 13K outstanding on his current mortgage. Eileen wrote down the numbers on her pad as he reeled off what he paid for bills and loans, and she deducted this from what he earned and came up with a rough figure of what he could afford to repay each month. Eileen ripped the paper off the pad and gave it to him. She said she'd make him an appointment with a mortgage broker to which he had to bring six months of payslips.

She met Michelle in Burger King at dinnertime, and explained, 'Sam can type at the speed of light and Eileen can do the Rubik's Cube in under two minutes.'

'Nor, can she?'

'Here-man, they're all git nice.'

'Cannet believe the boss gave yer cash ter get clays. Ah've been at the estate agents for ower two years, and there's been nee thanks, kiss me arse, nor nowt.'

'Cannet wait till ah get paid.'

'Yer ganner get that dress from Dorothy Perkins?'

'Problees.'

'Aye-up,' said Michelle.

A red sports car parked outside and Sonya got out of it, her hair was still in a perfect bob, only it was dark orange, not blonde and pink like it was last week. Then Conor got out and they looked at each other and back at Conor. He was wearing jeans and a tight top, and he leaned against the car and put a fag in his mouth.

'Fuck me,' said Michelle.

'Jesus Christ, it's like watchin a Levi's advert.'

'Which one?'

'All of them.'

'Sonya fucked him yet?'

'Shhh.'

'Hiya,' said Sonya. She was wearing 501s with a cowboy belt, a cropped top, and an American baseball jacket. 'Ah'm not eatin cos ah'm meetin me dad later,' she said, grabbing a handful of Michelle's chips.

'Fuck off yer greedy bastard!' said Michelle.

'Yer comin out toneet?' she said.

'Aye,' said Sonya, grabbing more chips.

'Get Nick Kamen ter buy yer some chips, yer fucken slapper,' said Michelle.

She scrunched up her burger paper and looked at her watch. 'Gotta nash, job ter gan tee.' She wiped crumbs from her white shirt with a navy stripe on the collar. 'Bus station at half-seven?'

'Aye,' said Michelle.

*

On her next day at work, Eileen left her by herself to take the client details. First up were a couple in their fifties from Downhill who wanted to by their council house – now known as a local authority house – that they'd lived in for thirty-two years. It was worth 18K and with the right to buy discount, they could have it for

9K. She struggled to get information about where their 5K deposit was: bank, building society, Premium Bonds? Behind the clock, under the mattress, tin in the shed?

During her morning tea break, she mentioned to Derek, the mortgage adviser, that it would be easier to put the details straight into the computer rather than writing them down and inputting them later.

After eating her packed lunch with Margaret, a middle-aged mortgage broker who was nice, and Sam, the young, funny secretary, she returned to her desk to find a computer on it. She went to reception to collect her next client.

Three clients in a row were buying a local authority house, and she did as Eileen had shown her and advised they should put down as much deposit as possible to reduce the total amount repayable. All of them opted for the smallest deposit possible, leaving as much as possible to build a porch and a fancy wall to show that they had bought their house. The man from Farringdon was planning to build a two-storey extension, 'With an ensuite bathroom,' said his wife, dead chuffed.

It was nearly time to go home and she was finishing up inputting Mr White's details when Frank made an appearance for the first time that day. 'How did you get on with the subprime list?' he asked.

'Subprime?' she laughed. 'Yer wouldn't believe how much they've got tucked away. Yer should open a porch buildin company.'

Chapter 21

September 1990

'Hands up for Jesus,' she said as she slipped her vest over her head and pulled it down to her big pink pants. 'Eeee, first day at school, ower Chloé.'

'Can ah tack Thomas?'

'Nor love, he'll have ter stay here,' she said, taking Thomas the Tank Engine from Chloé's hand before slipping a St Mary's school sweatshirt over her head.

The bairn knew she was starting school today, but other than that, she was unaware that this was the first day of twelve years of torture. When she was at school, she couldn't wait until her eighteenth birthday, because that was when 'kids' becomes 'assault'. She'd knacked Hayley in their first fight, but on the second fight, Hayley's sister's mates from the fourth year jumped in and held her down and kicked her in the face, 'kids.' And then there was Lucy on the school field, encircled by the entire third year while Sandra with the pigeon shit mullet kicked the shit out of her, 'kids.' When she thought about anyone hurting beautiful Chloé, her blood ran cold. She'd kill them and their mam and dad and sisters, brothers, cousins, vicars, and cats.

Chloé couldn't be persuaded to part with Thomas, while Rainbow Dash, Applejack, Twilight Sparkle, Sugarberry Twice, Cotton Candy, and Breeze Flutter, with their curly manes, flowing tails, and pony stamps, stood on the windowsill, untouched. Thomas and Friends ruled, so today, as usual, she used the ugly plastic train and his ugly friends as bargaining chips to get Chloé to eat her breakfast and have her hair brushed. They needed to get a move on because they were being picked up at eight-thirty.

St Mary's was Coralie's choice of school, which was too far away to walk, but she was happy for Chloé to go there if Coralie could give her lifts, both ways, every day. It was great that Chloé had turned out to be Catholic because it meant she could go to St Anthony's instead of a shitty comp.

Ken parked the Volvo in a side street and Chloé laddered her bottle green tights as she got out.

'Daddy,' she said, darting towards Marcel who was leaning on his rusty blue Metro. She hadn't expected him to be here, nor his girlfriend Meredith. She couldn't understand what the fuss was about.

'How's my gorgeous girl? Are you excited for your first day at school?' said Meredith in a posh voice. She was studying drama at Teesside Poly, so had lots of voices. Chloé jumped into her arms and Marcel peeled her off.

'Isn't it yer first day back?' she asked Marcel who was now a French teacher in Hartlepool.

'Supposed to be,' he said, 'but they'll have ter manage without uz for a bit cos ah wouldn't miss this for the world.'

A child with two hands, one holding Thomas, versus five adults all competing to hold her hand and walk her into school. Madness, but nice madness. Her first memory of going to the infants was Mam shouting at David and telling him to hold her hand all the way there or else.

It was so cute at the school gates. Kids with bunches, kids who were crying, kids who were chatting, kids who were rolling on the ground. Chloé hugged and kissed Marcel and Meredith, gave Thomas to Ken for safekeeping, and then took Grand-mère and Mam's hands. Inside the school the corridor smelled of shampoo and sounded of giggles and at the end was a cloakroom with pegs.

'Which is yowers?' she said as they walked down the rows.

Each peg had a rectangle of carboard hanging by string with a name and a picture.

'Look,' said Coralie, pointing to an apple tree with CHLOÉ-ANNE HASTING below.

'Hello, I'm your teacher, Miss Dobson, and your name is?' said a young woman who looked more like a TV presenter than a teacher.

'Chloé Hasting.'

'Nice to meet you Chloé Hasting.'

Miss Dobson led Chloé into the classroom and they followed. Chloé ran off and jumped into the sandpit.

'I'll leave you to it,' said Coralie, who also dashed off.

She loved Coralie, but why did she tell the school that the bairn's name is Chloé-Anne? She didn't mind it personally, it was sweet, but in Chloé's opinion, her name was most certainly Chloé.

The desks and chairs were titchy, and the smell of wood and chalk whisked her back to her junior school days. She shuddered. She hadn't thought about Mrs Boyd for years, her teacher when she was eight who had a cyst on her forehead that looked like a baked bean. Someone had hit Joanne Mullen over the back of the head, making her gegs shoot across the floor, and Beany-Boyd blamed it on her. The class sat at their desks, and all was quiet as she was summoned to the front, and then ordered to get her gym shoes from the cage. Her gym shoe bag was stored in the second row from the top, and as she pulled it out, she wondered if she was going to have to run around the yard.

'Shoe,' ordered Beany-Boyd with her hand out.

She took a black sandshoe from the bag and gave it to her.

'Hand out.'

She did as she was told wondering why, and then Beany-Boyd took a swing and brought the shoe down on her hand, making her jump, while the whole class gasped. She stuck her stingy hand under her armpit, not that it hurt that much, not like being slapped across the face. It was more the shock and shame that stung. The nasty old bag gave her the shoe in her non-fucked-up hand and nodded for her to do the walk of shame and put it away in the shoe cage. It was a good job that teachers weren't allowed to hit kids with sticks anymore and she hoped that rule extended to gym shoes because no one was going to do that to Chloé.

Some of the other mams were saying bye to their kids and some were waiting to talk to Miss Dobson. She joined the queue for the teacher as she thought it polite to say bye before leaving her with her daughter. She kept thinking about poor Chloé being called Chloé-Anne. She was a smart kid who went along with it because she knew how much it meant to Grand-mère. She couldn't put up with it in school, it would drive the poor child nuts.

'Hello, Chloé-Anne's mother?' said Miss Dobson.

'Would it be possible to change Chloé's name on the register? Anne is her middle name, there's nee hyphen.'

'Okay, we can call her Chloé in class, but you'll need to notify the head to have it changed on the register.'

'If yer can call her Chloé, and nivver Chloé-Anne, that would be preferable. How do ah speak ter the head?'

'Ring the office and ask for an appointment with Mrs White-Edwards, or you could write, either.'

'Mrs White-Edwards, is that the headmistress?'

'A-ha.'

'Okay, thanks.'

They both glanced at Chloé who was fighting over a fire engine with two boys.

'Will yer be pickin Chloé up at home time?'

'No, her gran will be, ah told the school.'

'Yer should go now while Chloé's distracted.'

As she walked past Jesus being crucified on the wall in the main entrance, she felt like the best mam ever. Correcting Chloé's name was something that she could do to make her daughter's life better, not worse; not siding with Coralie because it was easier, not hanging her out to dry. She was definitely going to contact the headmistress and get the redchester changed.

Chapter 22

December 1990

'You still on for tonight?' said Frank.

'Aye.'

'Did you arrange a babysitter?'

'All sorted.'

'See you later then, I'll book a taxi.'

Before the birthday gathering of work people could begin, she had a full list to get through. She told her first clients of the day that it was her twenty-first birthday, and they sang, '*She's got the key of the door, nivver been twenty-one before*,' which was sweet but horrible and wrong. She remembered the day she looked under the pot of weeds, and because there was no key, she knocked on Nelly's door to ask for the emergency key. As she let herself in, in that gem of a moment, it dawned on her to put the key in her pocket, so she did. '*She's got the key of the door, nivver been nine-and-a-half before*'.

When Frank said a few drinks down the Rosedene, she expected there'd be Frank, Eileen, and maybe Derek, not everyone from work as well as Debbie and Claire from downstairs. There was a table with glasses of wine and gold balloons and a buffet with a cake. It was like they'd gatecrashed a wedding reception, and it was weird to be fighting tears when nothing bad had happened. She wafted her face and swallowed. Crying over a cake was embarrassing, even if it was the shape of a birthday present with smooth pink icenen with dark pink spots.

'Happy birthder!'

She turned to find Michelle and Ally. 'Ah didn't knar yaes were comin.'

'Surprise!' said Ally, kissing her.

'Happy twenty-first,' said Michelle, giving her a present. 'It's from both of us.'

Her eyes filled with weird tears again, so she kept her head down as she unwrapped the present, wafting her face with the wrapping paper. Under the wrapping was a white box with *Chanel* in gold letters and inside the box was a bottle of *Chanel No. 5* eau de toilette and an egg-shaped soap. As she hugged Ally, Eileen gasped, and all heads turned. It was Sonya and Conor. Sonya was wearing a long black dress and had git short, gelled-down Lisa Stansfield hair, and Conor was styled on Michael Hutchence and pulling it off better than Michael Hutchence.

As Sonya approached, they all pointed at her head.

'Der yer like it?' said Sonya.

'Suits yer,' she said, because it did. It was ellish. 'It's just, yer knar, short.'

Sonya elbowed Conor. 'Have yer got the pressie?'

He dangled a pretty yellow bag from his finger and Sonya snatched it and said, 'Eeee, happy birthder, gis a hug.'

Sonya hugged her in a cloud of perfume she'd never smelled before. She undid the ribbon and delved into the tissue paper to find a white balconette bra and French knickers, both with Gossard tags, and the bra was £39.99, which was ridiculous for a bra. She wondered how much the knickers cost and they were beautiful, and she loved Sonya. Now she was fighting back tears over underwear, for fuck's sake.

'If they dinnet fit, yer can return them,' said Sonya with a big red smile and perfect teeth.

'Do you ladies want a drink?' said Frank, extending an arm towards Kelvin who was at the bar with his wallet out.

Kelvin had already bought all the work people a drink before he ordered a bottle of champagne, which sent the bar staff scuttling for glasses and a bucket that they filled with ice for no reason because the bottle was only in it for thirty seconds. She'd never had champagne before, and it turned out to be triple-strength, perfume-tasting cider. Ally and Michelle were all over Kelvin with their glasses of champagne and he loved it. He shuffled away from them and chinked his bottle of beer off her long wine glass.

'Remember that anytime you change your mind, the offer is open,' he said.

Her body was warm and fuzzy, her head was light, and she suspected she was under attack. Frank and Kelvin had been trying to get her to go full-time since Chloé started school, and the more she resisted, the better the offer got.

'Remind me again,' she said. 'Frank said thirteen thousand and a six percent pension.'

Kelvin topped her glass up. 'And a performance-related bonus.'

'Ah dunnar, ah'll have ter think about it.'

'Fourteen thousand,' said Kelvin, adding a grand without clearing it with Frank.

Changing the subject, she said to the lasses, 'Eeee, yerl nivver guess wot happened ter Kelvin up top Ford.'

All eyes were on Kelvin. 'Little bastards.'

It wasn't funny but it was, and Ally and Sonya decked it at Kelvin running for his life as a bunch of raggy-arsed kids chucked stones at his car.

'Yer dinnet want ter park a Jag up top Ford,' said Sonya. 'Ah'm surprised they didn't have the wheels off.'

'I realise that now,' said Kelvin. 'I've had no problems in my wife's Fiat Panda.'

Everyone was keen to get the buffet going so Frank stood next to the cake and summoned her to join him and then Eileen gave her a blue bag with *Chapman's* written on it in gold. This, as well as everyone looking at her with kind faces and then singing 'Happy birthday to you', unleashed a blaze of emotion that was too fast and strong to be frozen out. Tears rolled down her face like she was as soft as clarts. She felt proper shan as she undid the gold ribbon with shaking hands and tears soaking into the pretty paper bag. In a long box was a five-bar gate bracelet and as she held it up, her shoulders were shuddering, she had a melon in her throat, and the gold bars melted into a mortifying teary blur. She was glad that after a short burst of applause, the hungry hoard left her to weep as they descended on the buffet.

The sausage rolls and quiche helped mop up the booze and tears. She'd been chemist since eight o'clock and was glad that everyone else was shit-faced, apart from Sonya and Conor. When they called last orders, the remnants of the cake and buffet had been removed from the building by Eileen and Margaret, and the girls from downstairs had their coats on and were saying their goodbyes. Sam declared she was off to her pit, and Barry offered to see her home, and everyone looked at each other with raised eyebrows, and Sam hissed, 'Fuck off.'

Michelle lifted her head from Derek's shoulder. 'Shall uz gan clubbin?'

'On a Tuesda?'

'Ku Club.'

Sonya's Seat Ibiza briefly smelled of newness before smelling of four perfumes and one aftershave that was probably from America and too expensive to name. Sonya dropped Conor off at his mate's house that was behind gates in Ashbrook. Michelle, who suggested Ku Club in the first place, declared she was too wankered to go clubbing. After dropping her off, it was nearly midnight when they parked under the road that sloped down from the rooftop carpark.

The queue for Ku Club went across High Street instead of down it, and Frank, Kelvin, and Derek were nearly at the front in their untucked white shirts like a gaggle of clergymen at a devil-worshippers' meeting. She'd never seen so many shades of black and she didn't know you could get that many holes in a pair of Docs. Sonya slotted in with her black dress, and her Lisa Stansfield look got approving nods, while Ally drew sneers in her short denim skirt, ankle boots, and cream off-the-shoulder jumper with a lace shawl that tied in a knot at the front. She was glad she was wearing a work suit and looked like she'd ended up on a night out, rather than she didn't realise it was a goth club.

As they made their way slowly up the steep stairs that had a pink swirly carpet like a bingo hall, she marvelled at a goth with a painted-on doll complexion, her eyes a work of art, like an evil Pierrot. Ally and

Kelvin were slavering on about politics while sober Sonya distanced herself on the non-queue side of the stairs, looking like she was trying to find her baby, *somewhere, somehow*. When they reached the top, the doorman asked, 'Members?'

'No,' said Frank, getting his wallet out.

It was dark and stowed-off inside. She'd never been in here before and didn't realise that late on a Tuesday, while the rest of the town is sleeping, it's all kicking off above Rumbelows. It was a big front room in a house with a wall knocked through to the big back room, with a bar down one side. Down the middle was a wooden dancefloor full of people dressed for digging the garden and dancing to a morbid song with their arms behind their backs and their shoulders down. She was squashed in at the bar behind a girl whose long black hair smelled of grease, so she clutched her Chanel No. 5 collar to her shneck.

She gave Ally and Sonya their drinks in plastic cups with no ice and mouthed, 'Where are the others?'

Ally held her cup of gin and tonic over her head as she led the way, weaving between the goths in her cream jumper. At the front end of the room, up some steps, was another bar where a handful of normally dressed people were gathered in their shirts and ties and going-out dresses. Ally chatted with Frank and Kelvin, and she stood quietly with Derek taking in the view like tourists, while Sonya stood at arm's length, all trendy and brooding, *I don't know where he can be, my baby, but I'm going to find him.*

The lights dimmed and then a fairground noise came on to a collective gasp. '*Stand in the place where you live…*' Everyone jumped on the spot and swung their arms like a student version of Agadoo. The people at the normal bar joined in like legless arseholes on a Christmas party, and Sonya jumped two footed, arms swinging in circles, onto the dancefloor, and disappeared into the sea of black.

The booth was closed, and the doormen were chucking out when they assembled at the top of the stairs, Kelvin with an arm each around her and Ally like a dad with teenage daughters. 'Are you sure you girls will get home safety?'

'Why-aye,' said Ally, shrugging him off.

'And don't forget, fourteen thousand,' Kelvin said casually, as if now was the time and place to talk about going full-time.

'Fucken fourteen grand,' gasped Ally. 'Ah'd tack his hand off if ah woz yae, Paula.'

'Driving lessons and a company car?' he added.

Ally shook her head. 'Here-man, stop fucken around and say yes will yer.'

'Go on then,' she said, regretting it, 'as long as Frank agrees ter the car.'

Kelvin was well chuffed. 'He will.'

Avoiding a weird hug, she was quick to follow Ally down the steep stairs which tumbled them out onto the cold street. They linked arms as they staggered into the wind, the fresh air multiplying the effect of the booze.

'It's fucken frozzen,' said Ally. 'Ah've had a nipple-on all neet.'

They leaned against Sonya's car and huddled together. 'Wot did Sonya say?'

'Meet at the car in ten minutes,' said Ally.

'Wee woz she gettin off with?'

'Oh man, yer should've seen him. Git skinny, all in black wer backcombed black hair and white make-up.'

'Where is she?' she said, leaning her full body against the car for shelter from the icy wind.

'Aye-up,' said Ally, nodding at the back of the shops.

She focussed her bleary eyes on the figures in the shadows. 'Fuck me! Is that Lisa Stansfield shaggin Robert Smith behind McDonald's?'

Ally laughed so much that she had to cross her legs. 'Dinnet mack uz laugh or ah'll pittle mesel.'

'They'd better hurry up, ah'm frozzen.'

It wasn't long before he mooched off and Sonya strolled out of the darkness.

'Hurry up,' shouted Ally.

Sonya got to the car and swung her keys around her finger. 'Feel bad for not offerin him a lift.'

'Dinnet worry,' she said, '*boys don't cry*.'

Ally snorted and pissed in her ankle boot.

Chapter 23

March 1991

Eileen was out on a client visit, so she did a flyer and was home by half-four. She had to be in the shower at six, so she could get ready, out, and on the bus into town. First, she nuked her cheese pasty, then put it back in the greasy paper bag for the full pasty experience. As molten cheese stuck to her pallet, she wafted her open mouth and breathed hot flakes of pastry into the air like a Greggs' dragon.

As usual for Fridays, the house was a shitpit. It never used to get this bad when she worked part-time. It's impossible to do housework without music so she brought the ghetto down from the bedroom and raked on the floor for the mixtape that Sonya did her. Chaka Khan, 'I'm Every Woman'. Full blast. She scooped toys into the plastic chest, and put the tapes in their boxes and stacked them next to the telly. She peeled back the settee cushions to reveal an underworld of half-eaten crumpets, Lego, a fork, a hoop earring, and a fifty-pence piece.

In the bedroom, she made a pile of colours and whites, and the colours pile was biggest, so she stuffed it back in the basket, and, gathering up the whites in one armful, she rammed it in the washing machine. Nowadays clothes were either on a body, in the basket, on the floor, in the washing machine, or in the fresh washing pile on the chair, yet never hanging in a wardrobe or folded in a drawer. Iron as you go was the new way.

The kitchen bin was overflowing, and the sink was full of dirty dishes. Ian and Jason liked it that she had no time for cooking as it meant they got chippy tea on Tuesdays as well as the usual Thursday. She drarked the benches in spray and wiped them down, going round the kettle, mug tree, and biscuit barrel, instead of moving them. No time for a deep clean. Overflowing bin bag out, new bag in, bin juice ignored, again.

The bathroom sink was filthy and by the amount of toothpaste on the mirror, it was a wonder that Chloé got any in her mouth. She gave it a spray and then some elbow grease, then did the same for the sink. She'd clean the bath when she was in it, but first, she'd inflate the airbed for Michelle in Chloé's room.

The bus was packed and smelled like a whore's handbag. The lass sitting next to her was wearing Samsara, and she kept getting a whiff of Eternity among the fag fumes.

As she made her way up the leisure centre tunnel, it felt ellish to be wearing light brown jodhpurs, dark brown cowboy boots with a heel, and a white blouse, left open and tied in a knot, like Cindy Crawford in the Next Directory, apart from without the brown flowery scarf, tiny midriff, and flawless beauty. She couldn't believe that riding gear was in fashion.

It was the end of the month when everyone had been paid so, as expected, the top end of town was heaving. Michelle was wearing the leather trousers that Ally got her from the catalogue with her staff discount, and Ally was wearing a skin-tight blue dress.

All the pubs were stowed-off and smoky and Ally moaned on and on about being too hot and having hurty feet. Michelle was floating because gorgeous Darren from the surveyors was in the estate agents today. He'd mentioned that he was going to Chambers and Michelle wouldn't shut up until she agreed to go clubbing. Ally couldn't go because she had work on the phones at eight in the morning.

The plan was to get to Chambers early when it was cheaper to get in, yet despite leaving Sinatra's at half-ten, the queue was down and round Mackey's corner. Her membership card was white with Chambers written in gold letters and she'd found it on a table in Boulevard. The signature on it was a squiggle.

'There's neeway were ganner get in before the price gans up,' she said. 'How much is it after eleven?'

'Ah'll pay,' said Michelle, keen to smooth things over so they could get in and she could look for gorgeous Darren.

'Nor it's alreet, ah'm not bein tight, ah woz just wonderin how much it is.'

Two lasses in front of them turned around and said, together, 'Three pund fifty.'

They were nearly at the front when the pubs kicked out and the queue got pushy and there were shouts of, 'Get ter the back!'

'Evenin lasses,' said the doorman. 'Are yers members?'

They waved their white cards and joined the inside queue on the left side of the corridor that was roped off from the right side, which was a thoroughfare for doormen dragging people out, and doormen letting lasses in for free.

'That's three pund fifty,' said the woman at the counter.

'Ha'way, let's gan upstairs,' said Michelle.

It was busy and deafening and it took ages to get to the bar. Five deep, two barmaids. Two quid for a bottle of Castaway, compared with one pound fifty in the pubs. They squashed their way into a space on the dancefloor steps, which was a good look-out position for Michelle, who wasn't going to stop moaning until she found Darren. She watched a lass in denim dungarees and a white vest with a bit of boob poking out of the side. Her olive skin was smooth and her glossy brown hair was pulled back into a messy bun with the odd strand tumbling onto her freckly face. All the men on the dancefloor tried to get close to her as she swayed her hips and glided away. The Soup Dragons came on and when boob girl glided off the dancefloor, ugly people filled the vacuum.

'Der yer wanna dance?' shouted Michelle over the ear-bursting volume.

'Nor, the dancefloor's packed,' she shouted back. 'Any sign of lover boy?' she said, knowing by the look in Michelle's eye that he was on, or near, the dancefloor.

Then the Happy Mondays came on, and Michelle grabbed her hand. 'Ha'way, drink up.'

They did indie dancing, which was all about low hips and shoulder moves. She loved this song and danced like she had no cares in the world. It went dark, then red lights came on, 'Keep on Movin–'. There was a cheer and then without warning, her arms were above her head and her hips were swaying, '*Don't stop like the hands of time–*' she didn't care that she was dancing on her own. Michelle was last seen pushing her way off the dancefloor with a bloke, who, as far as she could make out, was not gorgeous.

Downstairs, the piano bar was half empty, and it was much cooler than upstairs. No one was playing the piano, even though there was a piano. The tall white pillars, bamboo furniture, and plastic tropical plants made it look like the hotel from *Tenko* where they had their reunion after the war. The barman was well-fit.

'Wot can ah get yer?'

'Castaway, please.'

As he walked to the fridge, she watched his lovely bum in his black trousers. He poured the murky liquid into a half-pint glass and it stopped three-quarters of the way up. He plucked a beer mat from the pile and put the glass on it. 'Two pounds.'

According to the fake Rolex that she'd got from David, it was one o'clock, and she looked about to see if there was anyone she knew, and there wasn't, so she lingered at the bar like Billy-no-Mates. There was a bunch of lasses at the other end of the bar, eyeing-up the barman's sexy bum. One of them was wearing a catsuit that looked like she'd been sprayed with car tyre sealant. She had an amazing body and probably a pretty face if it wasn't for the trowelled-on make-up. Of the lasses, the one she'd most copy was the one in the baggy jeans and white bra with a red biker jacket on top, bleached blonde hair in a bob, cut sharp along her jawbone, and no make-up apart from red lipstick. The fit barman should choose her.

All eyes were on the fit barman as he served a bloke in the middle of the bar. The bloke took his drinks and came towards her.

'Castaway?' he said.

'Why are yer givin uz a drink?'

'A beautiful girl shouldn't be on her own.'

'Are yer chattin uz up like?'

'Aye, and ah'm ganner kiss yer in a minute.'

He was good-looking, early twenties probably, dark hair, brown eyes. She took the drink, had a mouthful, and then put it on the bar. 'Yer can kiss uz now if yer want.'

Soft lips, no big tongue jabbing at her tonsils, and no designer stubble scratching her face off. He was a lovely kisser. He stopped the kiss and kept her pulled to his chest.

'Ah like yae,' he said, squeezing gently before releasing her. She followed him to a table and he pulled out a bamboo chair for her.

'Have yer ever had a Singapore sling?'

'Is that a drink?'

'A cocktail.'

'Me favourite cocktail is a Black Russian. Tia Maria, vodka, and coke – it's lovely but arnly if it's happy hour on the last Friday of the month,' she said.

He laughed. 'It's happy hour ivry hour wer me. Black Russian?'

'If that's alreet, tar.'

He was called Martin, was twenty-six, and lived with his mam down Peterlee. When he left catering college, he worked making dinners in the canteen at an electronics factory in Newton Aycliffe, only he found he could earn more working on the factory line, particularly if he did nights. While he was talking, she kept thinking about lifting his t-shirt and running her hand over his chest and she wondered if it was hairy. Tia Maria always made her feel horny.

'Wot about yae? Did yer say yer work in finance?' he said.

'Ah'm a mortgage executive.'

'Yae must be git clivver?'

'Here-man, ah left school ter have a kid. Got nee exams.'

He leaned back at *kid* and she could see his cogs turn: there were two responses to this news. 1) Assume she's a slapper and pursue her in the hope of getting sex. 2) Assume she's looking for a dad for her child and leg it. She gripped her Black Russian. He could do one, but at least she had a free cocktail.

'Lad or lass?'

'Lass called Chloé, she's five.'

'Der yer still talk ter her dad?'

'Oh-aye, we're mates. She's wer her dad's family now.'

It was a long way home to Peterlee, so it was only right that she invited Martin to stay at hers. In the taxi queue she chatted with him about all sorts of stuff, he was easy to talk to, they had lots in common. Michelle and Darren were all over each other in the queue and in the back of the taxi next to her.

'Cannet yers wait until wer get home?' she said.

They kept heavy petting and she was glad when they stopped and the light came on.

'Fowr-pund.'

She went to give the driver the money and Martin pulled out a fiver. 'Ah'll get it,' he said. 'Keep the change, mate.'

Michelle and Darren headed straight upstairs, and she shouted after them, 'Chloé's room.'

She turned on the lamp in the living room.

'Nice house,' Martin said, pulling her to his chest. 'You're beautiful,' he whispered before kissing her. He was gorgeous and a nice kisser and she couldn't believe her luck, then Michelle and Darren started humping upstairs and he pulled away, decking it.

'Airbed on the floor,' she said, pointing upwards.

He swept her hair back on both sides and kissed her neck while untying her shirt, which he swept gently off her shoulders, sending a shiver down her spine.

'Will yer be me girlfriend?'

'Mebees, okay then, gan on, yerv twisted me arm.'

Her *boyfriend* kissed her and then they went to bed and had sex and then he spooned her to sleep.

In the morning, she rolled over and looked at her boyfriend as he slept. She liked the sound of that. 'Meet my boyfriend, Martin.' She'd never had a boyfriend, not a proper one, not one who she fancied. When Chloé was six months, she went out with Johnny, who she used to meet for lasts on a Friday. She fucked him every weekend for a few months, and then there was nobody for ages until Sonya's cousin Mitch who she fucked a few times. And now there was sexy Martin. She wanted to slip her hand around his hard-on, and she wondered if it was polite to wait until he woke up before going for it anyway. Not impolite, she noted, as he rolled over, groaning.

Chapter 24

June 1991

When she got home from work, the house smelled delicious, and Martin was in the kitchen wearing an apron and stirring a pot. After a week of nights, Thursday was the start of his weekend, so he always cooked tea. He lifted the lid of the pan and the smell of curry got stronger.

'That tacks uz back, funny how smells dee that,' she said.

'Where does chicken curry tack yer tee?' he said, putting his arm around her waist and pulling her closer.

'There woz this time when Mam made a curry. It smelled lovely and me and David were proper clammen. Then Billy comes in, sticks a wooden spoon in, tacks a taste, and ses *needs summink else*, so he gets a bag of peas from the freezer and stirs them in, even though he knars David hates peas.'

'Spiteful twat.'

'Anythin he could dee ter mack our lives that little bit more miserable, he'd dee it.'

She tried not to do Martin's head in talking about Billy, but her anger spilled out often. Martin didn't seem to mind, he was a great listener, a rock.

'Ah still cannet believe that Billy Hart is yer stepdar like.'

'*Woz* me stepdar.'

He laughed and she poked him in the ribs. 'Shhh, nee laughin, he woz the bairns' dad, poor little buggers.'

There was a shower of knocks on the back door.

'Speak of the devils,' she said as Ian and Jason came in.

'Smells lovely in here,' said Jason.

'Ah'm fucken clammen,' said Ian, ducking to avoid a clip from her swinging hand.

'Less of the swearin.'

As usual for Thursday, the house was spotless. She'd never seen a man do housework, or not to a standard that was useful. Martin was obsessive about tidiness, which was a bonus. She was happy with her gorgeous, funny, good-in-bed boyfriend, and he came with extras: a good job, a hi-fi separates system and loads of CDs, a video and loads of videos, a new Ford Escort that he got free because of his mam's bad heart, and a Nintendo console that Ian and Jason loved. He'd more or less moved in, not that they'd talked about it, it happened naturally.

The lads sat cross-legged in front of the telly with a joystick each. It was mad how far computer games had come since Blitz and Frogger.

When Coralie dropped Chloé off, she felt proud of her spotless house, well behaved brothers, and smell of spices wafting from the kitchen. Chloé was covered in felt-tip and ketchup after a day at school and tea at Grand-mère's.

'Why dinnet yer tack her up for a bath while ah feed the monsters?' said Martin.

'Aye, topper. If yer can get them off the game,' she said.

'Curry's ready, lads,' he said in an army voice.

They dropped their joysticks and ran to the kitchen.

The lads were back to their computer game when she came down in her half-soaked shirt and pants, with a rosy and warm Chloé in her nightie. Her beautiful girl jumped all over the lads and annoyed them while she went to check on the curry. The table was set for two and she joined Martin at the cooker and lifted the lid on the pan while taking the wooden spoon from his hand.

'Isn't it about time the lads got themselves off home?' he said.

'Aye,' she said, dipping the spoon and taking a taste. 'Needs summink else, have yer got any peas?'

'Ah luv yae,' he said, picking her up. 'Yer knar, how yer can laugh at shit.'

She pushed him away. 'Ah'll gan chase the lads, yae serve the curry, and nee sneakin peas in.'

'Ah thought it was David wee didn't like peas.'

'Ah like them, but *nivver* in a curry, not after that, it woz mingin.'

The boys were gone, and Chloé was eating a Magnum and watching *Top of the Pops*, so she propped the door open, sat at the kitchen table, and took a deep breath, happy that she'd got through another day without children going hungry and without causing an accidental death. It hadn't been the best day at work, not after she screwed up an application by putting £200,000 instead of £20,000 when she got distracted by Eileen having a barny on the phone about her gas shares. It was hilarious when she said, 'If yer see Sid, tell him ter sod off.'

She was miles away and when she refocussed there was a plate of chicken curry and rice before her eyes that looked like something from a cookbook.

'Lager?' said Martin with a can of Red Stripe in each hand.

'Well, it is nearly the weekend, so gan on.'

'Glass?'

'Nor, gis the can, save on the washin up.'

*

The new Friday night routine was to go round the town with Michelle and Ally, and sometimes Sonya, and meet Martin in Sinatra's for lasts. Then get a pizza from Street Café and a taxi from outside of JJ's, and then go home and fall asleep watching *The Hitman and Her.*

Saturdays were the quietest day in the house as there was no daughter and no brothers. Martin was frying bacon in his cowies. 'Ah woz thinkin about buyin yower Ian a slow cooker.'

'Wot for?'

'Give a man a fish, he'll eat for a day, give a man a rod, he'll eat for a lifetime.'

'The fishin rod didn't work out so well for Billy.'

Martin laughed.

'It's not funny, it woz tragic.'

'But seriously though, the arnly reason ah can cook is because it woz either dee it mysel or eat fish fingers.'

'Ah thought yer said yer learnt ter cook at caterin college?'

'Aye, ah did, but me mam wozn't much in the kitchen and she didn't mind uz hoyin all kinds in the slow cooker.'

'Ah'm not sure Ian'll be up for cookin, it's not wot lads dee.'

'There woz plenty of lads at caterin college.'

'Woz there? There were nee lads in my home economics class, the lads did woodwork.'

'Wer could gan inter town after breakfast if yer like,' he said, laying the crispy bacon on some sliced and buttered stottie. 'Der yer want ter put yer arn sauce on?'

As she slapped the bottle of HP, he slapped her arse, then cuddled her from behind, pressing his hard cock into the small of her back.

'Here-man, will yer give ower?' she said. With the sauce dispensed, she took his hands off her tits. 'Ah've got a bacon stottie ter eat, show some respect will yer.' As she squeezed the top and bottom stottie, butter and sauce trickled onto the bench.

'A bacon sarnie is better than sex, is it?' he said.

She took a bite and grease dripped down her chin. 'Yip.'

The town was busy and they parked outside of Chaplin's using his mam's disabled badge. It being impossible to walk past Durham Book shop without going in, they went in. Martin searched the old books while she twirled the rack of rude cards, the type you don't get in WHSmiths.

When they came out, Martin was fuming. 'Wot a miserable bastard,' he said, tucking under his arm an 'all colour cookbook' from the seventies.

'The woman's nice though.'

'Aye, but still. A smile wouldn't kill him.'

'Binns for the pan?'

'Aye, suppose that's the best bet.'

As they searched for the amazing one pot to buy for Ian as the first step on his culinary journey to manhood, she spotted a casserole dish with a picture of a horse on the inside. It was £39.99 so she put it down, for now.

Martin examined the base, the lid, the inside, the outside, and then after he'd chosen the perfect pan, he sent the poor girl out to the storeroom to find a medium-sized one, not large, in black, not orange.

'Never mind crockpot, more like fusspot,' she said.

'Go and look at some lady stuff,' he said, 'Ah'll meet yer near the perfume in ten minutes.'

They were making their way to the car when Martin suggested going for a drink.

'Where?'

'The Borough's on the way.'

He grabbed a booth while she got the drinks. She liked a sneaky drink on a Saturday when they were in town, drinking in the day felt naughty. When she put his pint down, he looked at her strangely.

'Wot?'

'Sit,' he said.

When she sat down, she saw the horse dish on his lap.

'Got yer a present,' he said.

'The horse dish!'

When she picked it up, his hard nob pinged from underneath. 'Suck uz off, nee ones watchin. Ah'll hide yer heed wer the dish.'

*

The trendy press-button phone warbled. She listened to a client talking to the answerphone about his mother's three-bedroom semi, and when he hung up, she rewound the tiny tape that had about a minute's recording time. She'd passed him over to the mortgage team and given him their number about three times. It wasn't long before the phone warbled again and she let it go to the robot woman, '*Please leave your message after the tone, beeeeeeep.*'

'It's me, pick up.'

She picked up. 'Hi, Michelle.'

'Get yersel rund here if yer want first dibs on a mint house.'

'Ah dinnet want ter buy a house, tar.'

'Haddaway and shite, ah knar yer secret easter egg investment has hatched. There's a repossession come on up Hipsburn Drive. It's done out git posh, mortgage company want a quick sale.'

'How much is it?'

'Denis advised they list it for thirty-four, but ah reckon they'll tack yer hand off for twenty-nine.'

'Wee's the mortgage with?'

'Lloyds.'

'And yer say they want a quick sale?'

'Aye, the dinnet want it standin empty costin them money, and they defo dinnet want ter be in a chain.

We've had that many sales fall through, it can tack eighteen months ter complete.'

'Can yer get the keys at dinnertime?'

'Aye.'

'Have yer got yer car?'

'Meet yer at the bottom of the carpark steps at half-twelve.'

It was strange to be walking across the top of the bus station where she knew there was a carpark but had never been. Michelle's car was a rusty Datsun Sunny. It took loads of turns of the key and hoofs of the accelerator, with the choke fully out, to get it started. Michelle was good at driving and weird at driving because it was Michelle actually driving. Michelle turned George Michael up and they both wound their windows down as they cruised down Holmeside.

Michelle did a perfect parallel park halfway up Hipsburn Drive outside of a semi-detached with a bay window. As she gawped, Michelle said, 'Ha'way,' and got out.

There was a white sticker on the door that said *notice of repossession*.

'Der yer knar wot happened?'

'Nor, ha'way, let's get in.'

The hallway was full of post and junk mail and there were coats hanging on pegs and shoes sitting neatly in the rack.

'Are yer sure they've gone?' she asked.

'Aye, they woz evicted two weeks agan.'

'Poor bastards.'

'That's mortgages for yer,' said Michelle, scooping up the post and arranging it neatly on the shelf.

'Did Denis say how much they owed?'

'That's the sad thing, they'd lived here for years, arnly owed six grand.'

'How come they hit the skids?'

'Ah dunnar, yer'll have ter ask Denis. Ha'way, let's start in the livin room.'

The living and dining room were open plan, with a serving hatch to the kitchen. She was glad that there was no furniture and the family hadn't been yanked from their seats while watching *The Krypton Factor*. The wallpaper was nice, looked new. It had a dark plum stripe to halfway up, then a floral border, and above that, tree branches in light plum with green buds. The curtains matched the branches, the tiebacks matched the buds, and the abandoned cushion on the floor matched them both.

The kitchen had a wall oven like Sonya's, only this one was sealed shut with striped tape and had a possession notice stuck on it, as did the fridge. There was a room off the kitchen that was painted white and had light blue lino on the floor with a dark blue rectangle and two dark blue squares in the places where, she guessed, once stood a chest freezer, a washing machine, and a tumble dryer. It made her think, what a great idea not to wash your clothes in the same room as the greasy cooker and bin full of chattie peelings. 'Wot's this room?'

'The utility,' said Michelle, as she unlocked the backdoor. 'A posh wesh house.'

The garden was small. Nana's garden was four times bigger, but Nana's didn't have a patio and sliding glass doors leading out from the dining room.

'Look,' said Michelle, 'a brick barbeque.'

Or a brick barbeque.

The bathroom was nice, the main bedroom was big with built-in wardrobes, and the smaller big bedroom was bigger than the main bedroom in Springwell. The smallest but still big room was done out in black and red wallpaper.

'It's like the eighties in here,' said Michelle.

'Can yer remember when Sonya had her room done out like this?'

'This place is gorgeous,' said Michelle. 'Yerv got ter buy it.'

'Are yer sure that Denis said Lloyds are sellin?'

'His contact is a bloke called Shoemaker. Ah remember his name cos it made uz think of the elves.'

'Wot, elves in little yellow jackets and britches?'

'Did yae have Ladybird books anarl?'

'Nor, ower Julie did, ah woz terrified of Rumpelstiltskin.'

'Ah woz terrified of the troll wer the big claws,' said Michelle.

'From under the bridge?'

'Creepy as fuck.'

'Ah thought he had a nose like an éclair and if yer bit into it, cream would spurt out.'

'Wer yer starved as a bairn or wot?'

There can't be many people in the mortgage business called Shoemaker so she reckoned it must be the same Gordon Shoemaker from WRC, a banking group that LJ Finance did business with. She'd met him when he was in the office, and she'd heard Eileen on the phone to him. Hopefully, it was him at Lloyds. She got the number from the blue book. The receptionist confirmed that they had a Mr Shoemaker who used to work at WRC and put her through.

'Gordon Shoemaker,' he said.

'Hello, it's Paula Hasting here, from LJ Finance.'

'Hello there, Paula. What can I do for you today?'

'Ah believe yer have a repossession on Hipsburn Drive standin empty, could tack up ter eighteen months ter sell.'

When she put the phone down, her ear was burning. Despite a market value of £34,000, they'd agreed on £26,000, on condition she completed by the end of November. She opened a new client mortgage application form and filled it in for herself. Deposit:

£15,000. Mortgage amount: £11,000. She rang Michelle and told her to tell Denis that she'd spoken to Gordon and that he'd call him this afternoon and tell him to take the house off the market.

She wandered along to see Barry. He was the nicest mortgage broker and the only one who didn't go on about how she could be a broker and that she should do her exams.

'Hi, Paula,' he said, 'have yer done somethin ter yer ear? It's bright red.'

Wafting her hot ear, she said, 'Got mysel a great deal on a property. Ah'd like ter apply for a mortgage.'

Barry smiled. 'Tack a seat.'

Chapter 25

November 1991

'Ah knew yer'd fill a transit,' said Martin, squashing a box of cuddly toys into the van.

The beds were still in Springwell and it looked like they'd need another two trips. It had long gone dark and cold when they hauled the double mattress out of the van. As they dragged it up the stairs, Martin pushed from the bottom and she guided it from above.

'Ter me, ter you, ter me,' said Martin as they manoeuvred the mattress into the bedroom, letting it flop down.

When the mattress was in place, she jumped on it and lay flat.

'Ah need ter tack the van back,' said Martin

*

When Martin suggested they should paint the skirting boards, she hadn't noticed skirting boards before. They were the strips of wood that went round the bottom of rooms that needed painting every couple of years with gloss paint, and the ceilings should be done too, with emulsion. Ideally this should be done before moving in.

Martin levered the lid off the tin of paint with a knife. It looked more yellow than white.

'Give it a stir,' he said, 'mack sure all the oils are mixed in.'

The yellow paint turned white and he dipped a brush into it and then smoothed it onto the skirting board. He handed her the brush. 'Off yer gan, one coat all the way rund. Ah'll gan and start on the hall.'

She'd taken Friday off work because she was dying to get fully moved and settled into their new family home. Martin was determined that all the woodwork and ceilings had to be painted before they could start unpacking most of the boxes. As she dipped and painted, she started to see why the skirting boards needed painting and wondered why she'd never noticed them before. They were invisible despite being at the bottom of every wall in every house. Now that they were *her* skirting boards in *her* house, they were totally noticeable, and it was hypnotic to see them transform from dull grey and chipped to brilliant white and shiny. When she'd done the full living room and open-plan dining room, her hand was stuck in a claw, and it took a few minutes to unfold her spine and stand up. The skirting boards made a big difference to the room.

'Martin, come and have a squiy at this.'

'They look great,' he said. 'Have yer got a shower cap?'

'Wot for?'

'Ter put on me heed while ah paint the ceilin, stop paint gettin in me hair.'

She looked up. 'Ah dinnet like bumpy ceilins, ah prefer smooth ones like at Nana's, not the colour of Nana's mind, nicotine yellow.'

'Artex, that's wot that bumpy stuff is.'

'Why did they dee that?'

'Dunnar, fashion ah suppose.'

'Does it really need paintin?'

'Yer said that about the skirtin.'

'Fair enough, but shall uz dee it tomorra?'

'Better dee it today. We've got the new settee bein delivered tomorra.'

'Wot new settee?'

'The green leather one yer saw in SCS.'

'Ah dinnet understand.'

'Ah had some savins, so ah've bought yer it.'

'Neeways!'

'Aye, the corner four-seater and a chair.'

'Ah fucken love yae,' she said, leaping on him and hugging him with her arms and legs.

'Ah'm class me,' he said, peeling her off. 'Reet then, yae get the shower cap and ah'll get the roller.'

Her job was to paint the edges, being careful not to splat the wallpaper, while he used the roller on the middle part. He was wearing jeans and a Southern Comfort t-shirt, which were both ripped and worn and now covered in white speckles. He looked like a sexy tradesman from David's porno videos. As soon as Martin was done painting the ceiling, she was going to harass him for sex.

Martin got off the ladder and when he took the shower cap off, beads of sweat dripped from his brown curly hair into the red rut from the elastic that ran across his forehead. She was about to rub the fleshy dent, when he said, 'There's a patch.' He moved the ladder, climbed up, and ran his roller over the tiny triangle of off-white that poked through the brilliant white.

His groin was level with her face. 'Mind yer dinnet get paint on yer willy,' she said, brushing his front trouser area with her brush as if painting a wall. He flung the roller to the ground, jumped off the ladder, and wrestled her to the floor.

It had got dark outside, and the streetlamp shone through the oversized window. Martin stood up then dove back down. 'Shit, yer can see strite in.'

'Gan and close the blinds then, wer dinnet want ter give the neighbour's an eyeful,' she said.

'They probably had enough of an eyeful when yer were ridin uz,' he said.

'Nah, yer cannet see in when it's light outside.'

He crawled along on his knees with his bollocks waving from side to side, then gently teased the vertical blind across the window, bringing the peepshow to an end. She didn't know if you could see in when it was daylight, she'd have to check tomorrow.

'Shit,' he said, 'here's yower Ian and Jason.'

'Fuck!' She scrambled for her tracky bottoms. 'Ah forgot they woz comin.'

She could hear them laughing and then the ding-dong of the bell.

Martin did the top button of his jeans and went to answer the door with a mass of pubes poking out. She got her top clothes on and scooped the underwear from the floor.

'Telt yer it woz massive,' said Ian to Jason.

'Yers will have ter gan in the kitchen while ah sort the livin room,' she said.

'Should ah warm this up?' Ian was swinging a placker bag that made a gloop noise.

She went to help Martin clear the living room and could hear Ian clattering about while Jason shouted 'Whoa!' at decreasing volumes as he moved from kitchen, to utility, and into the garden. Martin rolled up the dustsheets and put them in the bay window with the paint and brushes on top.

'It looks huge in here when it's empty,' she said.

'It is huge.'

'And lovely, thanks, yer knar, for all the paintin and that.'

'Nee worries,' he said, folding the ladder. 'Ah'll put this out the back.'

'Ower Jason's out there. Can yer mack sure he's not impaled on the fence.'

She hoovered, then ran a damp cloth across the horizontal surfaces, while Jason squashed his face against the patio doors. When she opened them, he ran inside, still lost for words, other than, 'Whoa!'

In the kitchen, Ian was wielding a wooden spoon, so she put her head over his shoulder and said, '*Boody-boody-boo, bork, bork, bork.*'

'Fuck off.'

'Less of the swearin.'

Ian was in the second-year seniors and was swearing much more than he did in the juniors. He'd dodged a bullet when the Bede closed and his year got sent to Thornhill. Yet sadly they'd turned the Bede into a college, instead of torching it.

As she dragged the table into the dining room, she ordered Jason to bring chairs. She opened both ends and put all four chairs around it. It had filled the kitchen in Springwell when it was half open with two chairs, yet now it looked like dolls' house furniture. Martin emerged from the blackness and slammed the patio door behind him. 'Ian said tea in ten minutes, so ah'm ganner jump in the shower and get changed.'

When she showed the lads the serving hatch, they both lost the plot. They agreed that it was a stroke of genius and pure luxury to have a window from the kitchen to the dining room. Jason insisted on handing the cutlery, one by one, through the hatch, and when the food was on the plates, they fought over who passed them through. Ian elbowed Jason out of the way.

'Gan rund the other side and ah'll pass them ter yer.'

Four plates of hot brown stew and four mugs of dilutey orange later, Jason closed the hatch then opened it again so Ian could have a go at closing it. As they took their seats, Martin came in, smelling like pine, face and forearms speckled with white paint. He wafted his hand over the steaming plate. 'Wot's on the menu, beef stroganoff?'

'Beef bourguignon,' said Ian.

'Smells amazin,' she said, wafting the steam.

Jason didn't waft or blow. He had an asbestos mouth and was four forkfuls in before anyone else took a mouthful.

'Got the recipe from that book yer got uz,' said Ian.

'Ingredients?' asked Martin.

'Beef, bacon, carrots, onions, mushrooms, and garlic.'

'Wot and Mam paid for all that?'

'Aye, she gives uz ah food allowance of twenty pund a week.'

As she shovelled Ian's stew into her mouth, she felt bad about dining on the bairn's food allowance. 'Poor Mam'll be havin fags and Aero for tea toneet,' she said.

'Nah, ah left her some of this in the fridge.'

A knot twisted in her chest. If there was one woman who didn't deserve nice food, it was Mam. She couldn't believe that, far from a begrudged tin of corned beef, Mam was shelling out on actual beef, which was a credit to Ian and to Martin for giving the boy a rod.

'She gives yer twenty pund for wot? Five meals?' she said.

'That's the thing about one pot cooking,' said Martin, winking at Ian, 'it doesn't cost much if yer knar how ter shop.'

'Here-man,' said Ian, 'the butcher did uz five pounds of diced brisket for one pund fifty. And ah usually gan in the greengrocers after school, when they're closin like, and a get the old veg that they're hoyin away. Yesterday ah got a bag of mushrooms for ten pence, fucken bargain.'

'How der yer mack it taste so—' she searched for a word to describe it.

'Rich and deep?' said Martin.

'Aye,' she agreed, 'rich and deep.'

'Ah stuck a bottle of red wine in it,' said Ian.

'Burgundy?' said Martin.

'Aye.'

She almost choked. 'Mam paid for wine ter gan in some food?'

'Nor, dinnet be daft,' said Ian, 'ah nicked it from Blaney's.'

When the blokes carried the new settee down the hallway, she stood against the living room door, sacrificing herself: they could disembowel her with the faux-mahogany legs, but they'd better not scratch the fresh paintwork. The smell of leather and cleaning fluids created a potent mix of luxury and newness. The settee looked much bigger in the living room than in the showroom, yet the four-seater fitted perfectly along the back wall and the chair was a successful divider of living from dining room. She lay flat on the four-seater and kicked her legs.

'Who'd have that thought that a lass like me would live at Humbledon Hill and have a gorgeous leather settee?'

'And a gorgeous…?' said Martin with both hands down the front of his shorts.

'Willy.'

He dove on top of her. 'Ah was thinkin boyfriend, but willy'll dee.'

*

Chloé was due anytime, and from speaking to her on the phone last night, she was with Marcel and Meredith watching television and was not going to church tomorrow. Martin came into the living room, showered and wearing jeans and a tight white t-shirt, his hair damp and tussled, his olive skin dotted with blue paint. 'Have yer had a look at the room?'

She leapt up, put her arms around him and stuck her hands down his jeans. 'A-ha, it's amazin, Chloé will love it.'

'Dinnet give uz a stiffy when the bairn's due back,' he said, pushing her away by her tits.

Martin was heading out for a takeaway when Marcel dropped Chloé off. 'How-do,' said Martin, shaking Marcel's hand.

'Not bad my good man, you?'

'Champion.'

Martin was twice the width of Marcel, who looked like a teacher in his green cords, grey sweater, and tweed jacket. Marcel gave her armfuls of toys and bags as Chloé pushed past. 'She's bathed, hair washed,' he said.

'Come in, have a squiy at the house.'

'Go on then, quickly.'

She was proud to show Marcel her living/dining room and he had tears in his eyes as he gave her a cuddle, which ended in a squeeze. 'Yer amazin,' he said, 'buildin such a great home for Chloé.'

Her namesake burst in, 'Yerv got ter see me bedroom!'

Martin had done a brilliant job. It was like a proper designer bedroom in three shades of blue with sharks and piranhas stencilled on the walls. He'd painted her pine wardrobe white and stencilled hearts on the front.

'Wow, Chloé,' said Marcel.

Chloé hugged her legs, then did a run and jump onto the bed. 'It's mint,' she said with a gappy-tooth smile.

Chapter 26

June 1992

Considering how much she was shaking and sweating, she was doing fine until her wheel mounted the kerb, and then she knew it was game over, the same as last time. She was rubbish at parallel parking, and mounting the kerb was an instant fail. She didn't give a toss after that, she wasn't even concentrating on the road, she was thinking about what she was going to wear on Saturday night. As she went down the gears, indicated, and took the next left into the driving test centre, she cringed at the thought of telling her mates that she'd failed again. She was keen to get out of the car rather than listen to the examiner read the list of errors.

'I'm happy to say you've passed.'

She walked on air out of the test centre and floated all the way home.

Martin was in the shower, so she went to tell him the good news.

'How did yae dee?'

'Ah arnly went and passed!'

He ripped the shower curtain open and hugged her, which made her so wet that she had to take her clothes off and get in with him.

She lay on the bed as he got dried and ready for work. 'Wot yer deein week startin Monda the thirteenth?' he asked.

'Of July?'

'Can yer get the week off work?'

'It's short notice, but problees, why?'

'Ah saw a holiday to Ibiza on Ceefax. Wot der yer reckon on me, yae, and Chloé garn away?'

'How much is it? Not sure ah can afford ter gan away at the minute.'

'It's arnly three-hundred and fifty quid for the three of uz, half-board. Ah better gan book it now if yer want ter gan?'

'Aye, gan on then.'

'Are yer sure?'

She dangled from his neck. 'Totally sure. Ah cannet believe that wer garn ter Ibiza, the furthest ah've ever been is Berwick-on-Tweed.'

'Better get yersel a bikini.' He pinned her to the bed and kissed her neck. 'Just wait until ah get yae on the beach.'

'Gan and book it then, wer dinnet want ter lose the deal.'

*

It was shite to be back in Sunderland and she was definitely going on holiday next year. She couldn't wait to tell her mates about snorkelling and watching the sunrise from the hotel balcony.

She rang Michelle and Sonya as soon as she got back and invited them over and they were both weird and both suggested they met for a few drinks down the Barnes as if they'd already discussed it. Seemed like hearing about her holiday was so boring that they had hatched a plan to avoid coming to the house and being bombarded with photos. She'd got Michelle and Sonya a coral ankle bracelet and Ally two hundred Silk Cut.

She had a golden tan and peeling skin over her nose. She wondered whether to wear a white top like Sonya and Ally did when they came back from Torremolinos last year. Being ginger, Michelle kept out of the sun. She had to remember that going on a plane was an ordinary thing, not a huge thing, and she was not to go on about it.

The Barnes was busy for a Wednesday and Michelle and Sonya were already there. She held her victorious brown arm against Sonya's white arm.

'Good holida?' said Michelle.

'Here-man, it woz mint. We went ter Café Del Mar. Drinks?'

'Nor ah'm good,' said Sonya, prodding her coke with a straw.

'Me too,' said Michelle, touching her cider.

She slung a Spanish carrier bag at them, said, 'Pressies in there,' then went to the bar.

When she came back with a Malibu and pineapple, they were holding up their ankle bracelets, focussing on them like they were special, avoiding her eye.

'Have yers missed uz? Any news?'

They looked at each other.

'Wot's garn on? Yers have been actin weird since ah got back.'

'It's up ter Ally ter tell yer,' said Sonya.

'Tell uz wot?'

Bleached blonde hair like Marilyn Monroe, all over each other in the Puffin Billy, May Bank Holiday weekend. Ally's mate from the call centre said the girl with Martin was a right moose, but she probably made that up to make her feel better. What if she was bonnie? What if he was in love with her? On one hand, the thought of Martin with another woman made her heart bleed and her stomach churn, and on the other hand, she wanted to kick the cheating bastard in the clems. The knot in her gut twisted and made her feel sick.

All the lasses said that she should tell Martin to fuck off, and Sonya rang on Saturday, Sunday, and Tuesday to see if she'd done it yet, which she hadn't. She couldn't face the conversation, not with Chloé in the house. All day Wednesday, the mystery woman played on her mind making her struggle to concentrate on what her clients said. She asked a bloke from Tunstall three times about his deposit and he offered to write it down for her. To top it off, on the way home, there was a man on the bus who was smoking which made her hair stink to match her mood. Nobody smokes on the hometime bus anymore, what a bellend.

The house smelled delicious, the table was set, and the patio doors were open, leading out onto a drink on the garden table. 'Tea'll be ready in ten,' shouted Martin. 'There's a vodka and lemonade in the garden.'

She downed it, which felt better.

'Come and get it while it's hot,' said Martin from the dining room.

She sat opposite him.

'Spag bol,' he said.

He never cooked proper tea on a Wednesday and his extra kindness was suspicious. He was guilty as hell, or maybe Ally's mate was wrong and there was a reasonable explanation as to why he was in the Puffin Billy with a blonde woman. Maybe Ally's mate was exaggerating about them being all over each other, maybe she was being spiteful, sticking the boot in. There was no way he would've gone on holiday with her and Chloé if he was planning to break up. There had to be a logical explanation, or worst-case scenario, he'd had a fling, which was bad, but not necessarily fatal.

'Wot's up wer yower piat?' he asked.

'Nowt. Are yer not garn ter work?'

'Aye, later.'

'How come yerv cooked proper tea?'

'Ah just thought it would be nice.'

'Ah yer seein someone else?' unexpectedly came out of her mouth. Her heart raced as he choked and coughed and cleared his mouth to speak.

'Wee telt yer that?'

'Ally's mate saw yer down Seaburn with some blonde lass.'

He twisted spaghetti on his fork. 'Melissa.'

'Yer mate or yer cousin or summink?'

'Nor,' he said, 'ah met her down the bingo.' He shovelled spaghetti into his mouth and his cheeks bulged as he gave a sarcastic smile.

Her jaw flapped, 'Like wot, yer *were* kissin her?'

He swallowed and took a drink, letting her hang. 'Kept meanin ter tell yer, yer knar, that we're done, but then there woz the holida, so ah nivver got rund ter it.'

She was reeling. She had an answer for 'went with another lass a couple of times' and for 'she's my ex who was having a bad time'. She had no answer for 'seeing someone else, we're done'. All she could manage to whimper was, 'So that's it then, yer leavin uz.'

'Suppose so,' he said, shrugging his shoulders.

If Coralie hadn't rang the doorbell, she would have thrown her spag bol at him.

'You feeling okay?' said Coralie.

'Aye, ah'm good thanks. How's Chloé been at school?'

'She's got a new friend.'

'Der yer want ter come in?'

'No, I better get going, Ken's got the tea on.'

'Bye then.'

'Au revoir.'

She got Chloé straight in the bath and locked the bathroom door. Martin would be going to work soon. She made Chloé a beard of bubbles and held up the hand mirror so she could look at it.

'Nice beard,' she said, blowing Chloé's face, making the bubbles fly off.

'Can ah have bubble eyebeards?'

'Good idea, howld still.'

When she tucked her into bed she wanted to climb in and wrap her arms and legs around her. She'd expected him to lie, or try and explain it away, and break it to her gently, or something other than come straight out with I'm leaving you for Melissa from the bingo. She thought it was sweet, him taking his nan to the bingo and sitting there with all the gannies.

She poured a vodka and paced the floor. She couldn't believe it was over. She finished the bottle of vodka and dumped his stuff in the spare room. She didn't want to be in the same bed as that cheating bastard. She'd give him three days to pack his bags and go. She had a child to look after and a job to do so there'd be no tears for

Martin, no way. There was going to be hods of room in the bedroom once his shit was gone. Every cloud.

Her head was stuck to the pillow when Chloé jumped on her chest. She put the telly on as Chloé parked herself on a cushion. Martin was in the kitchen. She took a deep breath and then went in.

The atmosphere was frosty as she poured Coco Pops into a bowl. He was leaning on the sink eating Shredded Wheat. She poured the milk and rehearsed what she was going to say in her head. She shut the fridge and picked the bowl up. 'So yerl be movin out then?'

'Nor, ah live here.'

'Not nee more yer dinnet. Ah'll give yer three days ter move out cos ah'm generous like that.'

'Ah'm gannen nee where,' he said, shovelling a spoon into his mouth.

'This is my house, so if we're breakin up, you're the one wee's leavin.'

'Like ah said, ah'm garn nee where,' he said, smug-faced.

The flames from her cheeks spread down her chest. 'Nor, it's my house and yer leavin.'

'Ah'm garn nee where, ah live here,' he said, guzzling the milk from his bowl.

Bollocks. He couldn't do that, could he?

'He can do that,' said Eileen, and Frank nodded.

'But it's my house.'

'You say that he pays the gas and electric?'

'And the phone. Seemed fair. Ah pay the mortgage and rates, and he pays for everythin else.'

'If his name's on the bills,' said Frank, 'he's got as much claim to live there as you.'

'Yer wot?'

'You'll need to apply ter the court to get him removed,' said Eileen, 'that's wot my friend had ter do when her husband had an affair and she wanted him out.'

'Shit, how long did it tack?'

'Over a year. Cost her a bomb as well.'

She felt cold and sick.

'I can point you in the direction of a good solicitor,' said Frank. 'Could have a word with him, see if he'll have a chat for free.'

'Thanks, Frank, that would be amazin. It's ganner cost uz though isn't it, ter ger him out?'

'Yer never know, he might move of his own accord,' said Eileen, backtracking on her story about her mate.

'And gan where? His mam's in Peterlee? Why would he dee that when he can live for free in my house?'

'Oh Paula, what a pickle,' said Frank. 'First step, talk to a solicitor. I'll call him now.'

*

She left most of her spicy bean burger and crushed her paper cup to pieces. Michelle did her best to listen, which must have been hard as she was ranting and making no sense.

'Wot a sneaky fucken shit,' said Michelle. 'Der yer reckon this woz his plan all alang?'

'Here-man, ah wouldn't be surprised.' She dragged her fingers across her forehead and said, 'Mug.'

'Are yer still comin out on the lash toneet? Have a laugh and that, forget about Martin.'

'Nor, ah dinnet feel like it.'

'Yae dinnet feel like comin out on a Frida? That's a first!'

'Ah cannet afford it man, fuck knars how much it's ganner cost uz ter get me house back.'

'Can yer not mack his life a misery until he fucks off?'

'Wot like mack hods of noise while he's sleepin?'

'Aye, and scrape toast crumbs in his bed and put itchin powder in his duds.'

'Ah didn't knar yer woz such an evil cow.'

'Thanks very much.'

'Solicitor said there's not much ah can dee.'

'Can yer not get David ter kick the shit out of him?'

'That'll be wot he suggests when ah tell him, but nor, Martin'll ring the police and say he's been assaulted in his own home.'

'But his name isn't on the deeds, so he's got nee reet ter live there.'

'It's on the bills and he *is* livin there, so he does have the reet, so ah'm telt.'

*

Last night Martin went to work early so she didn't see him and tonight they were going to be in the house together and alone. She was glad that Chloé was at the Wilkinsons, and it may be a good idea for her to stay there for a while, apart from she'd prefer they didn't know what was going on. The solicitor was nice and didn't charge her anything for the advice that she needs to pay three hundred quid for a letter as a first step. The second, third, and many more steps would also be expensive and not guarantee his eviction.

As she walked up the path to *her* house, she dreaded what was inside. Her plan was to hang out in the bedroom and let him have the living room. She could see him through the window, watching telly. Keep a cool head. She went upstairs, as cool as the Arctic, and then exploded. 'Arsehole!' He'd put a lock on the bedroom door. Deep breath. The solicitor said, 'Don't lose your rag, it will only act against you.'

She put the light on in the spare room to find everything of hers dumped on the bed and the floor. How could she have loved such a complete twat? Shaking with anger, she gathered the clothes on hangers and put them in the spare bedroom wardrobe and then put her underwear into the drawers. She wanted to shout, 'Fuck the fuck off out of my house!' and smash her way into the big bedroom and fling his portable telly out of the window, like what Eileen's mate did to her cheating husband. Eileen said it cost her mate five grand to get him out. It looked like she'd be kissing her savings goodbye.

She made a bold entrance and he didn't flinch.

'Ah see yerv flung me stuff out and put a lock on the door.'

'Aye,' he said without taking his eyes off the telly.

'It's my fucken house.' She could see the smirk on his face, so she bit her lip and backed out.

She sat on the stairs and rang Michelle. Her mam answered. It always took her yonks to go and get her even though their house was tiny, and she willed her to hurry up, fearing Martin would come and rip the phone out of her hand.

'Alreet?'

'Nor, meet uz down the Barnes as soon as.'

'Ah yer not comin down the town?'

'Nor. He's dumped me stuff in the spare room and put a lock on the bedroom.'

'Fuck. Where is he?'

'In the livin room.'

'Reet. Ah'll see yer in the Barnes as soon as ah can.'

'Thanks, yer a mate.'

'Bye.'

'Bye.'

Wearing her work clothes and carrying her work bag, she ran down Hipsburn Drive forcing back tears of rage. Bleary-eyed and snotty and not caring that she looked a state, she went to the bar. 'Vodka and tonic, please.'

'Is that a double, pet?'

'Aye, gan on.'

'Bad day?'

'The fucken worst, soz for swearin.'

'Here-man, there's nowt much yer can say that ah haven't heard before,' said the barmaid.

'Mother-fucken-bastard-twat,' she spat, clenching the bar and digging her nails in.

'Really bad day,' said the barmaid. She returned her glass to the optic and pumped another shot into it. 'That's on me.'

She was as surprised as the blokes at the bar to see a tall girl with windswept hair make a dramatic entrance. Ally took long strides, put a hand on the bar, bent over, and put her other hand on her stitch. 'Michelle rang uz. Ah ran all the way from home. Fuck, yae look terrible.'

'Cheers.'

'Are yer alreet?'

She exhaled through pursed lips. 'Ah dunnar. Vodka tonic?'

'Aye. Get one for Michelle anarl, Sonya's pickin her up.'

'Sonya's comin?' she said, surprised.

'Conor's on a stag do in Portugal.'

It was cold and dark and she was stotten in a spinning car. The digital clock said 23.07. She jabbed her finger at the blurry radio buttons, hitting Radio 1, then fell asleep. Next thing she knew, the radio was off and it was 23.22 on the digital clock. Sonya clicked her seatbelt into the slot.

With open eyes stinging in the light, she asked, 'Where are we?'

'Gan back ter sleep,' said Sonya.

The light went off and the engine started. Then she remembered where they were. She turned round to check, and he was there, the bloke in the Destroy top and Armani jeans from the Barnes. As they drove down the lane at the bottom of Penshaw monument, her eyes closed and her head lolled to the side, and then it was cold and light again and they were stopped halfway down Strawberry Bank.

She slowly opened her eyes to the welcome sight of Sonya's spare room. Wumph-wumph-wumph thumped in her ears and it felt like her brain had swelled bigger than her skull and was squeezing out of her eye sockets. In her bra and knickers, she staggered to the bathroom and puked.

It wasn't long before Sonya peered over her, 'Are yae blowin chunks?'

'Fuck off,' she said, grasping the bog seat with both hands. 'Ah feel like death.' As she dangled her head into the bowl, Sonya's clammy hands pulled her hair from her face.

'Yae woz shit-faced last neet, ah mean, fair enough like, wot wer Bingo Moose and that.'

She laugh-wretched. 'Did yae come up wer Bingo Moose?'

'Aye, fucken slapper, shaggin me mate's man.'

Lathered, shaking, and liften of barf, she propped herself on cushions in the middle of Sonya's double bed. Sonya lay across the end in her pink dressing gown, all fluffy and luxurious.

'Can yer remember much of last neet?' asked Sonya.

'A canny bit. Wot wer uz deein at Pensher?'

Sonya pulled her dressing gown over her face.

'Dinnet try hidin man. Ha'way, did yer shag him or wot?'

Sonya peeped out like a hamster from straw.

'Where did yers dee it?'

'Near the stile.'

'Lyin down?'

'On the grass.'

'Big cock?'

'Aye.' Sonya lay back and make the girth of his manhood in the air with both hands. 'Nee one noticed that uz left together, so dinnet say owt.'

'Are yer ganner see John Holmes again?'

Sonya sat bolt upright. 'Nor of course ah'm not! Ah love Conor.'

'Gan on then, details.'

'About wot?'

'Yer left uz by mesel in the car in the middle a neewhere at 11.07 and yer came back at 11.22 with yer knickers in yer pocket.'

'Ah didn't tack them off,' said Sonya. 'Yer better not say owt, Conor *cannot* find out.'

'Ah promise not ter say owt as long as yer tell uz the gory details.'

Sonya huffed her shoulders like she didn't want to say, yet was quick to spill. 'It woz canny dark like so ah felt about wer me feet ter mack sure there woz nee cow shit and then ah lay down and pulled me skirt up. He dropped his jeans—'

'Armani jeans.'

'He lay on top off uz and undid me bra and put one hand on me tits and pulled me knickers ter the side. Fucken-ell, Paula,' said Sonya with a face like she'd witnessed a miracle. 'Ah thought his dick was gonna come owt the top of me heed.'

'Sonya! Breakfast!'

'Saved by the dad,' said Sonya, rolling to her feet. She pulled a white fluffy dressing gown from the hook, said, 'Ha'way, put this on,' and threw it over her face.

Sonya's dad was wearing a chunky gold chain around his thick neck and a vest showing the tattoos all over his thick biceps. Sonya's mam talked posh, although you could tell that she wasn't, yet her dad was normal, or according to Sonya, common. His belly hung over his apron as he fried bacon on a hob that was sunk into the dark stone bench.

'How'd yer like yer eggs on a mornin, Paula?' he asked.

Sonya shot her a look. She couldn't resist. 'Fertilized.'

Sonya's dad laughed. 'As lang as they weren't fertilized in this house.'

'Scrambled, please Dad.'

'Me anarl, thanks.'

Chapter 27

August 1992

Saturday

She'd never been away from Chloé for more than three days since she was born and now her baby was off to Canada for three weeks. *Chloé Anne Hasting, born: 15 Aug 1986*. Chloé was proud of her passport and she slotted it into the important things compartment of her *Godzill*a bag. Marcel bought Chloé a red suitcase which she was determined to pack all by herself, which she did, five days before going, it contained: a camouflage top, jeans, three pairs of knickers, one vest, trainers, a magnifying glass, a torch, a big cuddly Sebastian the crab, a robot, and a purple folder that opened out into a stationery set. The bairn had done well, fitting it all in.

Chloé waved and held Meredith's hand while Marcel followed with baby Jacob and the suitcase. It felt like her heart was being carried away although she was excited to see her go; who'd have thought that a kid from the fucked-up family would be going to Canada?

As the car drove off, she turned on her bare heel and marched back into *her* house.

It was going to be weird with just her and Martin here. Martin had continued to be nice to Chloé, like a stepdad in a fun mask that he rips off as soon as her back's turned. It wasn't as if the bairn couldn't see the lock on the bedroom door, or see her mam in the spare room, or see her mam scowling as she plots Martin's death. The house rules were working fine up to now: the person watching telly owns the living room for as long as the telly stays on; the person in the kitchen owns the kitchen; the person in the bathroom owns the bathroom meaning she'd had a slash in the garden a few times when Martin was hoggin it like a shithead. Sonya's dad had given her a long cable so now the phone reached into the living room. She'd watch telly for a bit, then ring round later to see if anyone wanted to come over.

Martin had been upstairs all day and she had been downstairs, both of them timing bathroom and kitchen trips not to coincide. She was going nowhere. He'd taken the stereo to the bedroom and was now blasting Alexander O'Neal, and stomping about getting ready to go out, or at least she hoped he was going out. He'd been in the shower long enough and the house smelled of aftershave. She was starving and under the circumstances, deserved a Chinese.

There was some crap on BBC 1, news on BBC 2, crap on ITV, and *Brookside* on Channel 4. She rammed a whole Hobnob into her gob and watched Sheila Grant shouting at Bobby, willing Martin to fuck off out. The small comfort was that no matter what's going down, Sheila and Bobby are having it worse, and when *Brookside* finished, she felt sad to be back in her own world of shit.

The music stopped and Martin marched louder than necessary down the stairs, lingered forever in the hall, jangling his keys. The door slammed.

She wondered where Martin was taking Bingo Moose. If her luck was in, she'd be getting a bottle of Diamond White in Liberties and then eyes down for a full house at Top Rank. She'd been in the Top Rank when it was the absolutely huge Odeon cinema that Dad called the Regal. Why was *Columbo* on BBC 1 on a Saturday night? She wished the lasses would hurry up because she was clammen.

Michelle bent over and made eye contact with the lock. 'Ah'd be tempted ter boot it in.'

Sonya went in the spare room. 'Fuck, yae weren't wrang when yer said he dumped all yer stuff in here.'

'Archers and lemonade,' said Michelle, waving a placker bag.

They had a quick drink before she headed off to the China Garden with Sonya while Michelle kept guard of the living room. The queue was long and Sonya was delighted to see Ben Ellis and his older brother waiting in it. Sonya had fancied Ben at school and never managed to pull him, yet no one else saw the attraction of spotty, weedy, Ben. She could see it now. Clear tanned skin, chiselled chin, and probably a beautiful body under his tracksuit.

After ordering, Ben hovered near the window, and then their eyes met. 'Eeee, hello there, fancy seein yae here,' said Sonya, pushing her tits out and striding over to him. They chatted while she ordered and when she turned round, they were gone. She looked at his brother who was still waiting for his food. He shrugged.

Ben's brother got his food and left, and Sonya didn't show while she waited for theirs. With her bags, of Chinese she went outside to look for her. Ben's brother was leaning against the railing near the steps to the underpass and as she approached, he went off down the steps, so she walked faster after him like a mad woman. He walked all the way through the underpass and lingered on the path at the other end and watched her get closer. She was about to ask if he'd seen Sonya when she heard rustling in the bushes.

'Der yer come here often?' she asked Ben's brother.

'Arnly when me brotha pulls in the takeaway.'

'Does this happen often?'

'After the pubs aye, but not usually this early.'

'Wot, like the China Garden is a pullin hotspot?'

A man with a dog was coming down the path, so Ben's brother whistled, which echoed down the tunnel. The dog was off the lead and sniffing about all over, so she went to the bushes to shoo it away and got an eyefull of Ben's white arse going up and down.

His brother laughed when the dog made a beeline for her. She diverted it by running into a clump of trees further down, and as the dog mooched off, Ben's brother appeared. His blue eyes looked into hers. He dropped his bags. She dropped her bags. He pushed her against a tree and kissed her. As he pulled her close, she could feel his stiffy against her groin. She pulled her lips from his. 'Ah cannet have sex here, anyone could come through the bushes.'

'Can ah feel yer tit's while ah have a wank?'

Surprised not to be asked to do it, she said, 'Aye, gan on then.' She lifted her top and popped her baps out of her bra.

They didn't speak until they got onto Hipsburn Drive and then they looked at each other and decked it.

'Der yer knar Ben's brotha's name?' she asked.

'Paul,' said Sonya, 'he's twenty-seven.'

'Paul, shit. Glad ah didn't ask, ah've dreaded Paul and Paula me whole life.'

'Well?' said Sonya.

'Well wot?'

'Well woz Paul much cop?'

'Ah didn't fuck him. He had a tug.'

'Yer such a good girl,' Sonya scoffed.

'Ah dinnet think lettin a stranger spunk all ower yer tits on a bit of waste ground is Mother fucken Teresa. How woz Ben?'

'Ower too fast.'

'Aye, but yers were in a public place. He doesn't want ter be hangin about.'

'Fair enough,' said Sonya, 'but less than a minute, hardly worth tackin me draws off.'

The roar of old car slowed beside them. David wound down the window of his Hillman Hunter Estate, 'Vids lasses?'

'Have yer got *Pretty Woman*?' said Sonya.

He drove off and they jogged after him. Michelle already had her head in David's boot when they got to the house. 'Have yer seen *Ghost*?' said Michelle.

'Aye and ah'm not watching it again,' said Sonya, leaning in. 'Have yer got *Silence of the Lambs*?'

She'd let them choose. She'd seen most of his good stuff.

David lifted the box of videos and slid one from underneath. 'Have yer seen *Thelma and Louise*, sis?'

'Wot is it?'

'New out.'

He gave her a plain white plastic case, which she popped open to find a plain video. 'Is it porn?'

'Nor, it's a copy,' said David. 'It's a lass's fillem.'

'Where's yer porn?' said Michelle from the boot.

David lifted a tray of videos out of the side door and put them on the pavement. He lifted the seat off, which wasn't a proper seat, it was a piece of sponge over a tray of porn vids. 'Any of these tack yer fancy?'

Michelle and Sonya were straight in. 'Wot's good?' said Michelle, while Sonya pulled a video from the tray, and read the box, '*Necromania*.'

'That's canny,' said David, 'or if yer lookin for cock, try *Saturday Night Beaver*. Ah haven't got *Hot and Saucy Pizza Girls*, it's out til Tuesda.'

'Have yers seen *Thelma and Louise*?' she asked.

'Simone woz talkin about that, the endin's supposed ter be mental,' said Sonya.

Michelle emptied her chicken chow mein onto a plate. 'It's stone cowld.'

'Soz,' said Sonya. 'Ah met Ben Ellis in the Chinese.'

'Ah saw him the other week,' said Michelle, 'fuck me, he's changed.'

'Ah always said he was fit,' said Sonya.

Michelle forked some noodles into her mouth. 'Can ah put this in the microwave?'

'Yerl have ter put it on a smaller plate,' she said, lining up three glasses.

'So, yer let the food gan cowld while yer were chattin Ben up?' Michelle's finger hovered over the *cook* button as she waited for Sonya to explain herself.

'Ah shagged him near the underpass.'

'Yer fucken slapper,' said Michelle, pressing *cook*.

Sunday

She sat upright, held her breath and listened hard to the girl's voice in the bedroom with Martin. It was certain that he'd bring her to stay, so she was prepared: claim part of the house and keep out of their way.

It was a lovely day outside, so she claimed the utility room and the garden. They could help themselves to upstairs, the pair of twats. They could mostly keep out of the kitchen as well. She put the kettle on and was surprised to find the tea jar was empty. So was the coffee jar and there was no coffee in the cupboard. Looked like he was playing funny buggers, but surely, he couldn't be that spiteful? There was no milk, eggs, or butter in the fridge, and the bread bin was empty. The tin cupboard was empty apart from two tins of pineapple rings. Yes, he could be that spiteful. Coco Pops were fine without milk. Dry cereal and a glass of flat lemonade. The rules had changed: keep food in the bedroom. Sonya's dad was coming over this week to put a lock on the spare bedroom and she was going to ask him if he could put one on Chloé's room.

She separated a week's worth of whites and darks and then stuffed the darks into the machine. What a surprise, the big box of washing powder had vanished. After years of living with Mam, she knew how to scrape washing powder scraps from the tray, and anyway, clothes washed okay without powder. Everything was fine. He couldn't break her. She lay on the damp lawn in her cotton pyjamas with the sun on her face. She was absolutely fine.

She'd been snoozing for a while when the patio door flew open and Simple Minds came blasting out. She rolled on her side and kept her eyes closed. She could hear him raking the barbeque and then her voice. 'Shall ah ring Dave and Vicky, see if they want ter come ower?'

'Aye, could do. Ah'll get the coals from the shed, then wer can nip rund ter yowers and get the burgers. Der wer need ter get some buns?'

'Ah've got a loaf, will that dee?'

'Ah'll call in the shop and see wot ah can find.'

She rolled over and caught a glimpse of Bingo Moose before shutting her eyes and pretending to sleep. Tall, on the fat side. This was silly. She was lying three metres away from them. She jumped to her feet and straightened her pyjamas, head down. Then lifted her head and looked at him and then at her. Shoulder length, curly hair that was white and nothing like Marilyn Monroe's and neither was her face. Eyes too close together. They both gave her a sarcastic smile as she marched into the utility room. He was bad enough, but Bingo Moose had a cheek with the smugness. She put the darks in the dryer and the whites in the wash. She felt sick. The solicitor said it would take a few weeks to write the letter. She needed that letter to arrive as soon as possible, because until it did, it was war.

She watched from the bedroom window as he loaded coals on the barbeque while Bingo Moose stood inside, out of view. She needed to get out. Let them enjoy themselves. One day soon he would be fucking off and taking his whore with him.

She walked along onto Bede Bank and set off up the hill. Her belly rumbled and she laughed at the idea of going to Mam's. It was like a thirsty person going to a dessert or standing in a freezer to cure frostbite. And there it was, bolted to the bricks on the corner of the house: a big white dish that proudly announced to the street that Mam has satellite telly!

Ian opened the front door.

'Wot's wer the satellite dish?' she asked, stepping inside.

'Topper isn't it?'

'Where did it come from?'

'Walter.'

'Wee's Walter?'

'Her boyfriend.'

'*Boyfriend*?'

'Ah yer stayin for dinner? Wer havin lamb.'

'*Lamb?*'

'Aye, and puds, roasties, carrots, broccoli.'

'Mam paid for a leg of lamb?'

'Nor, dinnet be daft, Walter did. He's dead canny. And it's not a leg, it's a showlder.'

'Wee's Walter?'

'Gan and see.'

She braced herself and went in. Mam was lying down and a fat middle-aged man was sitting in the chair. 'Eee hello luv,' said Mam, sitting up. 'This is ower Paula.'

The fat man hauled himself to his feet. 'Nice ter meet yer.' He shook her hand. 'Ah'm Walt.'

It was a squash at the table and after dining like a king, she was glad to bag a spot on the settee where she could recover. Walt made the chair his own, and Ian sat between her and Mam with Jason laying across the floor at their feet like a scraggy rug. They watched a film on Sky which made her feel like a traitor to David who said he was losing video rentals because of satellite telly.

It was nearly teatime, so she decided to stay until the Cornettos in the freezer came out, even though she was still stuffed full of roasties. By nearly six o'clock, the only movement was towards the front door and not towards the freezer compartment. The two lads from over the road and two older lads that went to school with Ian, each handed Mam a bag of chocolates and crisps and cakes and pop. They sat on the floor in rows and squashed along when there was another knock.

'When yer said the lads could have some mates ower, ah didn't think yer meant the whole street,' she said.

'Aye, why,' said Mam, 'poor bairns dinnet have Sky, so ah thought ah better tack them in.'

There was a collective, 'Shhh,' followed by *The Simpsons*.

Monday

She went to work early, keen to get out while Martin was sleeping in *her* double bed in *her* master bedroom. God she hated him. She thought about sending him an envelope loaded with shit on a spring that explodes in his face upon opening and about slicing him in half on the rings of Saturn like on *Itchy & Scratchy*. Martin who painted the living room, Martin who cooked lasagne, Martin who took Chloé to casualty when she split her head open: how could someone change so much? And in Ibiza, he didn't act like he was seeing someone else; a holiday that he hadn't paid her back for. She turned it over and over in her head and couldn't solve it.

Everyone at work felt sorry for her and offered advice that they knew was useless, other than get a good solicitor. Frank popped out at dinnertime and came back with a box of Thorntons Continentals which was sweet of him.

When she got home, she claimed the living room, put the news on, and had a white chocolate with milk chocolate squiggles. When she heard Martin come out of the bathroom, she ran to claim it, then ran the bath, planning to stay there until he went to work. She'd not seen him since Sunday morning, which was a result.

After her bath, she got a glass of water, went into the living room, and jumped out of her skin to find him there. Not only was he not at work, he'd scoffed all the chocolates. He stood, put the last one in his mouth, and said, 'Shy bairns get nee sweets.'

She launched the glass of water at him, making him duck, and shout, 'Fucken-ell!' as it smashed off the wall. He ran out and she watched him stride down the path with his work bag on his shoulder. She hated him. He wasn't going to win, no way.

Tuesday

He still hadn't gone to bed when she got up for work. If he stayed in the living room, it would be fine. She didn't know how much more she could take of being in exile in her own home.

As she sat on the bottom stair and put her shoes on, he came down the hall. She kept looking down, yet she could sense him standing over her. She looked up. 'Wot?'

'Where've yer put me car keys?'

'Ah haven't seen yer car keys.' She stood up and he didn't move out of her way, so she said calmly, 'Get out of the way, bellend.'

He snatched her by the throat and thrust her backwards onto the stairs. 'If yer had a pair of balls, ah'd tack yer outside and kick the shit owt of yer.' He let go, ripping her shirt as he pulled his hands away.

She sprang to her feet, and he let her pass. She opened the door, looked him in the eye, said, 'If ah had a pair of balls, yer'd be cryin in the corner, sunshine,' then turned and fled for her life.

Panting and lathered, she sat on a bench opposite the tennis courts in Barnes Park. An old man asked if she was all right, to which she said yes, but she meant no, she was not in the slightest bit all right, everything was all wrong. She was furious and she couldn't stop shaking. Her legs were going like the clappers and when she concentrated on keeping them still, her arms went, and then her full body. She couldn't go to work looking like this, and anyway, she wasn't capable of doing anything apart from think about prick-face Martin.

She headed deeper into the park along the dark path weaving through the trees up to the back gates of the Bede, where she shuddered and then ran like she used to, all the way to the pregnant tree. She crossed into the park extension and went down the sloping path, and along the burn, her mind turning over and over what had just happened. There was no one about, so she took a deep breath, and sang Billy Ocean out loud, *'Get out of my house, get into your car, get out of my house, get out of the bedroom fuck-face, get into your car, get out of my mind, and out of my life, I say hey you, you, get out of my house.'*

When she emerged on Springwell Road she stood for a while and looked at the decaying corpse of Broadway Comp with its broken windows and seagulls pecking at the sports field. When it closed down, the next choice was Thorney Close Comp, which they changed to Sandhill View, as that'd fool 'em into thinking it's a different school.

She crossed the road and into the next park and was pleased to find that the bench was still there. Dad used to leave her and David here for hours, which they didn't mind because it was an ellish playpark, probably the biggest in Sunderland. There was broken glass scattered like in the old days, yet all that remained was the empty frame of the swings. It was a wasteland where children once ran the gauntlet of the ten-foot slide or the huge rusty seesaw with three kids on each end and one kid stood in the oily middle, trying to balance as it creaked up and down. It was incredible how many kids could pack onto the roundabout and how fast the big kids made it spin, hoping for the weak ones to fly off. They'd put rocks and sticks on the ground for those not clinging on for dear life to reach out and grab as they hurtled round – it was surprising nobody lost an arm.

Children played there for decades until Esther Ranzen pointed out what happens when a skull hits concrete. She could imagine the gut-wrenching fear of watching Chloé climb the ladder to the ten-foot slide, and she'd have to close her eyes at the top when she swung her legs over.

As she plodded on, she thought about all the ways that death could befall Martin: tie him to the climbing frame and leave him there to rot; make him lie under the seesaw and burst his belly on the saw and drag his guts out on the see; and her favourite, tie him to the roundabout and spin it so fast that his face rips off. She didn't stop torturing Martin until she got to the park at Grindon. She always walked to Pennywell this way because she loved the snaking paths and little bridges over the dried-up stream. It was here when Chloé, aged three, asked, 'Mam, where does God live?' To which she replied, 'Everywhere darlin.' Chloé asked, 'Does he live under there?' To which she replied, 'Ah suppose so.' After that, whenever they were in the park, Chloé would seek out God under the bridges. With no child in tow, she crossed the road and continued up the Sandhills.

From high on the hill, she could see the flat-roofed blocks of Sandhill View, aka Thorney Close Comp, sprawling across the park, and she wondered which bunker housed the swimming pool. When she was in the juniors they'd get taken there, which was better than going to High Street Baths where you had to swim or freeze to death. It didn't look like a school, more like a 1950s holiday camp crossed with a prisoner of war camp. It must've been easy for Dad to climb onto the roof when he did his SCHOOL SEIGE, and he couldn't have been the only kid to go up there; the flat roof was asking for it. She wondered what voices told Dad to do it, what he was thinking, how he was feeling.

Lisa answered the door with Brandon hanging off her leg. 'Paula. Wot yae deein here? Yer blouse's all ripped.'

'Can ah use yer phone?'

She rang Eileen to say that she wouldn't be going to work today and ended up having a long chat with lots of swearing in it. Lisa listened and pulled her *what the fuck* face, and when she hung up, said, 'Wot the fuck?'

'Fucken-ell Lisa, ah dinnet knar where ter start.'

They agreed that she should take David in the garden before telling him what had happened. As he came in the front, Lisa opened the back, and they both ushered him through and out.

'Wot's garn on?' he asked.

She summed it up as quickly as she could and when she got to the part about fleeing, he kicked the fence and flung a tennis ball miles over the gardens. When he calmed down he put his serious face on. 'Yer not garn back there.'

'Then he's won,' she said.

'He'll nivver win, wer'll get him out, but it'll be easier if yer dinnet live there. Dinnet give him the chance ter intimidate yer.'

'Haddaway, ah'm not scared of him.'

'Exactly,' said David, 'and that's why yer'll end-up stovin his heed-in wer a pan.'

'Ah wanted ter hit him wer a pan when he said *shy bairns get nee sweets*.'

'Did it remind yer of when Billy used to pile all the chips onto his plate and leave uz with arnly beans?'

'How could ah forget?' she said. 'He used ter say it all the time. S*hy bairns get nowt.* Oh well, in that case, yer better be a selfish, greedy twat.'

'A twat that Mam kept gannen back tee after he battered her.'

She totally and utterly refused to accept that there was any comparison between Martin and Billy. 'If we woz livin in a maisonette down Pallion, Martin would be welcome ter it.'

'Yer cannet let Chloé live wer a bloke wee's just had his hands rund yer throat.'

'He behaves himsel when Chloé's there.'

'Yer want Chloé listenin ter him shaggin his bird?'

'Shit, ah nivver thought of that.'

David was right. She couldn't live there with Chloé.

David shifted the videos from the back of his car and Lisa made him stack them neatly next to the telly. He was determined to go and get Chloé's things now and he wouldn't let anyone go with him. There was no way Martin would dare come out of the bedroom and face David. The plan was to take Chloé's things to his lock-up and then go back tonight to get her things.

'Dave said that yer mam got a satellite dish,' said Lisa.

'Aye, she loves it.'

'The movie channel,' huffed Lisa. 'We've lost hods of customers. It'll not be lang before nee one's hirin videos.'

'There's nee hardcore porn on Sky and none of the excitement of pickin a fillem from under the seat of a Hillman,' she said cheerily.

'Ah dinnet mind the porn, Paula, but ah dinnet like him mackin money from video nasties.'

'Have yer got *Texas Chainsaw Massacre*?'

'It's good,' said Lisa. 'Ah'll get Dave ter put it on after the bairns are in bed if yer like.'

David did an ellish job of getting in and getting Chloé's things out. He said Martin didn't come out of the bedroom. David tried to persuade her not to come when he went to get her things, but she got in the car and refused to move. Martin should be at work and she hoped that Bingo Moose wasn't there.

She put the hall light on. There were girl's shoes on the floor and a girl's coat on the hook.

'She's problees in bed.'

'Fuck her,' said David, stomping up the stairs.

They moved everything from the bedroom into the car. Clothes, bags, shoes, toiletries, towels, pillows, the car was full, and the room was empty. She reached under the bed and got Milly-Molly-Monkey and the tin of Dad's things.

'Fucken-ell, Paula, ah aven't seen that monkey for a lang time.'

'Can yer remember when Billy punched her across the room?'

He laughed. 'Aye and can yer remember how much uz laughed? Stupid twat, punchin a toy monkey.'

'Poor Milly. She didn't like it,' she said, hugging Milly.

'Wot's in the tin?'

She opened it and handed him the photo.

'Ah remember this. When uz woz livin up Thorney,' said David.

'Nineteen seventy-four, the Christmas that Dad went ter Cherry.'

He emptied the tin on the bed. She could see the Beach Boys tape and the tin of creamed rice. Then she panicked. Where were the rest of his things? 'Fuckin bastard.'

'Wot?' said David.

'There woz some other stuff in the tin.'

'Wot other stuff?'

'Stuff from a bag that Dad hoyed in next door's garden when he was fleein the fire.'

'There was a bag?'

'Aye. Ah didn't say owt cos ah woz shittin mysel that he'd go to prison for arson.'

'Wot der yer mean?'

'There's nee way he could've grabbed the stuff in the bag as he was escapin from a fire. He filled the bag before the place went up.'

'Yer sayin he torched the house?'

'Ah knar he did.'

'Nor, nah,' David shook his head. 'He'd nivver let his precious *Echoes* burn. He'd have saved them.'

'Yer mean the *1973 FA Cup Echo* and the *1937 FA Cup Echo* and *Shipping Gazette*?'

David's face turned grey and still like concrete.

She cowered slightly, 'And the Cup final programme from Wembley in 1973.'

'They burned in the fire,' he said.

'They didn't. They woz in the bin bag.'

'The *1937 FA Cup Echo* woz in the bag?'

She winced and half turned away, 'The footy *Echo* about Bobby Kerr shootin down the Mags woz in the bag anarl. Soz ah didn't tell yer, but ah woz scared because ah knew that Dad had torched the house.'

'Ah've fucken cried ower those papers burnin!'

She couldn't tell if David was overjoyed or angry.

'They're here somewhere,' she said.

He glanced at the stuff on the bed and then at the empty tin. He turned in a flash and she moved fast behind him onto the landing. He took two steps forward, and on the third, he booted the door handle on the main bedroom. The door flew open, and he disappeared into the darkness, followed by the sound of louvre strips snapping like matchsticks.

Bingo Moose shot out and down the stairs.

She shouted after her, 'Go on, fuck off.' Then she heard the phone dial clicking so she went down to the hall and ripped the extra-long cable out of the telephone socket.

In the bedroom David had booted the shite out of the fitted wardrobe. She rummaged on the bedside cabinet for the phone and took it off the hook. 'That'll stop her ringin anyone.'

David went along each top cubby hole, clawing the jumpers and sports gear like a mechanical digger, dropping them onto the floor.

'Hope the twat put them in a box. Any damage and ah'll fucken kill him,' he said.

'It would've been better if yer hadn't booted the crap out of the wardrobe.'

'Is that chicken soup?' he said. 'Fucken-ell man, wee is this dick? Tins of soup in the wardrobe?'

'Yer've nee idea how much of a dick Martin is.'

'Ah cannet see nowt in here,' he said.

'He's that much of a dick, he problees stashed them under the bed,' she said, moving some louvre strips and kneeling down. And there they were, under the bed on the dusty carpet with the socks and nob wipes. She hooked them out with her foot, blew the dust off, and gave them to David.

He clutched the bundle to his chest and looked to the heavens. She'd never seen him so happy or so much like he was going to kill her later.

'Ah'll get the tin.'

He was standing in the same position when she brought the tin, and as she gently teased the *Echoes* from his palms, the clippings fluttered out, settling on the wreckage.

'Wot are those?' he said.

'Clippins about Dad.'

He grabbed one. 'Man rescued after FA cup glory high jinks.'

'Grandar give uz them when Dad died. He kept them in the shed.'

'And yer didn't think ter tell uz, man?'

'Ah can hear yers, ah can hear yers,' came out of the telephone receiver on the bedside table. They both shouted down it, 'Fuck off!'

With all the loot in the tin, which David had hold of and was never going to let go of, he said, 'He's got a nice hi-fi.'

'If the house is as much his as it is mine, then the hi-fi is mine,' she said.

'Champion,' said David, unplugging it. 'Need somethin ter listen tee. The problem with CD players is that CDs are fifteen quid a go.' He emptied Martin's sports bag and started filling it with CDs.

She picked the telephone receiver off the bedside table and could hear Bingo Moose still on the line, so she said, 'We're off now. Enjoy *my* house.'

On the way out, she pulled the long cable out of the telephone socket again.

'She'll ring Martin's brother the minute we're gone,' she said, squashing the bag of CDs into the Hillman.

'Nor she winnet,' said David, wielding a tool.

'Wot's that?'

'Ah'll gan snip the outside line.'

She loved David sometimes.

Chapter 28

September 1992

Last night she dreamed she was hitting Bingo Moose in the face over and over until her neck snapped, making the biddies raise their eyes from their bingo books and glare as if she were the Devil. She'd decided not to do Michelle's head in. Nobody wanted to hear about Martin. There was nothing anybody could do. She had to wait and see how he responds to the notice to vacate the property that was costing her three hundred quid, that hadn't been sent yet, and would be the first of many letters before they would get anywhere near court. If it did get to court, she'd have to prove a legal reason for Martin to move out, and the only thing they had against him was not paying rent; he'd likely tell the court that he's happy to pay rent, and the court would tell her to go away and charge him rent, which he won't pay, so back to square one.

Michelle parallel parked into a tiny space to show off. 'Wot der yer think?'

She thought it was a rental on Mount Road while Martin was in the house that she was paying the mortgage on.

'It's nice rund here,' said Michelle. 'Private lets, that's the way it's gannen. We've got a section for rentals now. The wifey wee owns this place is git canny.'

'Why's she rentin it out?'

'Proper good story,' said Michelle, 'her husband had an affair wer her sister and they fucked off ter live down Leeds. The ratbag gives her everythin for an easy divorce, not that they had owt, big mortgage, hods a debt. Anyhow, she arnly gans and wins eighty grand on Spot the Ball.'

'Nor!'

'Aye!'

'Ah bet her husband woz gutted.'

'She moved ter the Lakes. Put this place up for rent last week. Ah've been puttin people off lookin at it, so yer better fucken like it.'

'Der yer swear in front of all yer clients?'

'Nor, arnly the fucken charvers like yae.'

It had high ceilings that made the two reception rooms feel huge. The kitchen had a low ceiling and went back for miles. 'This has to be an extension?' she said.

'Aye,' said Michelle, 'galley kitchen leadin onto a conservatory. Yer could have mint parties in here.'

'Wot did yer say the rent is?'

'Two hundred and fifty a month, but ah woz thinkin, wer could rent it together, if yer fancy like.'

'Wot, both of us live here?'

'Ower Lisa's movin out, so ah reckon it's time ter leave home.'

'Yower Joanne'll be pleased ter get the bedroom ter hersel.'

Michelle stared at the floor. Michelle adored Lisa and loathed Joanne, and after twenty-two years of all sharing a bedroom, it was surprising they hadn't killed each other.

'Three bedrooms?' she asked.

Snapping out of her stare-on, Michelle said, 'Three and a loft room that wer not allowed ter say is a bedroom. Wait till yer see it, it's massive.'

'Suppose it's better than where ah woz ten years agan.'

'Eeee, talkin about the maisonettes down Pallion,' said Michelle, 'have yer heard wot the deein ter them?'

'Nor, wot?'

'Turnin them into student accommodation.'

'Shit! Ah wouldn't like ter be the student wee gets number 34 Peacock Street West, yer knar, bump, bump, bump in the neet, the ghost of Billy's heed rollin down the stairs.'

Michelle laughed. 'It's either that or knock them down like they have up Gilley Law.'

'Knock em down,' she said. And grind every drop of evidence into the soil, she thought.

'Ha'way, let's gan in the garden before ah show yer the upstairs,' said Michelle.

*

The main reason for being given a company car was to drive brokers to properties on occasions when an expensive car would alert too much negative attention. It was Kelvin's wife's old Fiat Panda, which was free wheels, even if it was shitty. Kelvin got it out of the multistorey and drove it to Frederick Street. Frank, Eileen, and Sam came out to see her receive the keys. When she turned the keys and revved the engine, they all clapped, then waved as she pulled away.

Her first stop was the Wilkinsons' to get Chloé. It felt great that, at last, she wasn't reliant on Coralie and Marcel to give Chloé lifts. When Chloé came out of Grand-mère's, her face dropped at the tin-box car, and as they drove away, the bairn pressed her palms on the window and looked wistfully at Coralie like she was being carted off to the cottage homes. Next stop was Mam's to get Ian who was babysitting tonight. Ian loved the kitchen in Mount Road because it had a flashy double oven and a double sink. He was going to make a dessert for her to take to Sonya's dinner party.

Ian gave her the horse dish full of chocolate pudding with foil over the top. 'Have yer got the custard?'

'Michelle's got it,' she said. 'Dunnar why wer cannet tack a tin of custard.'

Ian put his hand on his forehead. 'Mack sure it's hot when yer serve it. Go.'

Sonya had a jet-black, ultra-short, flicky-out bob and was wearing black leather hot pants, big black boots, and a short black leather jacket with a zip up the front. She'd come in Conor's minibus car to pick them up.

'Eeee, yer could get six kids in this, Sonya,' said Michelle.

'Fuck off,' Sonya replied.

'Wot is it?' she asked.

Darren was quick with the info, 'Mazda MPV, four-wheel drive.'

Sonya had moved yesterday and on the phone earlier she sounded like she'd been marooned, far from civilisation. After seven years of living at home like a pampered princess, as well as staying at Conor's family mansion that had a swimming pool, he had finally persuaded Sonya to move in with him. Sonya had specified that she wasn't leaving Sunderland, so despite it being Conor's house to which she was contributing nothing, Conor obeyed with a five-bedroom house in Offerton.

'Shame he couldn't find somewhere even more on the edge of Sunderland,' moaned Sonya.

'The posh edge with views over the countryside,' said Michelle. 'We've got instruction on a house rund here that's worth five hundred thousand.'

'Ower David and Lisa live less than half a mile away,' she said, pointing in the direction of Pennywell.

From the outside, Sonya's new house looked like an old folks' home, and on the inside, it was an upside-down luxury labyrinth. They went upstairs to the living room that had a green three-piece suite and a big telly. At the other end was a wood-panelled den with a bar, green leather stools, and an old-fashioned jukebox. On the wall was a picture of Louise from Eternal and a Helena Christensen calendar.

'Welcome,' said Conor, shaking Darren's hand.

'Nice gaff,' said Darren. 'Wurlitzer, 1940s?'

'Replica,' said Conor. 'Needed somewhere to store dad's collection of singles from the fifties and sixties.'

Conor left Darren to ponder which record to play and went behind the bar. Conor's hair was long and swept back and he was wearing a white vest under an open denim shirt. He laid out some long-stemmed, triangle glasses. 'Cosmopolitans fine with everyone?' As he twirled the silver shaker, he looked like Brad Pitt playing Tom Cruise in *Cocktail*.

'Ha'way, ah'll show yer upstairs,' said Sonya.

'Yer mean downstairs?' said Michelle.

They rolled on the super kingsize bed while Sonya shouted from the ensuite, 'Come and see in here, lasses.'

There were oversized beige tiles on the wall and floor, two gold sinks with gold taps, and steps up to a shower that was built into the pine panelling like it was a sauna.

'Piss de résistance,' said Sonya, referring to the gold toilet.

'Dinnet mind if ah dee,' said Michelle, pulling her knickers down.

When Michelle had done her wee, they went with Sonya along a corridor of doors and slit windows.

'Ta-da!' said Sonya, leading them into the room at the end. 'Wot der yer think?'

There was a tent for people who sleep standing up. Sonya aimed a spray paint gun at them. 'Ah'm leavin the clinic. Ganner have me own spray tan salon in the back room of the hairdressers.'

'Like in case wifeys wee come in for a wesh and blow want ter get blasted wer brown paint?'

'All of the tan, none of the cancer,' said Sonya. 'The rich bitches at the clinic cannet get enough of it. Ah haven't waxed a chin in months.'

Michelle stood in the tent and put her arms out, 'So like yer tack yer clays off and stand in here.'

'Aye, gan on then,' said Sonya.

'Wot?'

'Get yer clays off, both of yers,' said Sonya, pointing the gun at Michelle's face.

It was worse against the glossy white kitchen units and white marble floor.

'Ah look like an Oompa Loompa,' said Michelle.

Conor pulled a can of Tango from the fridge. 'Drink, lasses?'

They laughed so hard that even Sonya joined in, although she wouldn't laugh for much longer after this beauty disaster. This was worse than when she waxed off Michelle's entire eyebrows.

'How long till it wears off?' said Darren, wiping his eyes.

'A couple of days,' said Sonya.

'More like five,' said Conor.

Sonya screwed up her face at Conor, who swapped the Tango for wine.

'Ah'm ringin in sick for the rest of the week,' said Michelle.

The deck at the back had a view of fields lined with hedges shimmering in the setting sun like something from a postcard. The table was under a pergola that had plants growing over it that looked like placker but were real.

They chinked glasses. 'Cheers!'

'Thanks for comin, lasses,' said Sonya.

They didn't speak as they sipped the wine that was probably expensive. They listened to the gentle flow of water from the cherub's spout into the pond.

The peace was broken when Conor asked, 'Where's Ally tonight?'

'She couldn't come because she's workin as a trolley dolly for Air UK,' said Sonya.

'It's arnly a shitty little airline that gans ter Amsterdam, it's not like she's flyin rund the world,' said Michelle. 'The way she's been actin recently, yerd think she woz a pilot.'

'Here-man, did yer hear her last Frida,' said Sonya, 'she wouldn't shurrup about Newcastle airport.'

As they bitched about Ally, the men retreated.

'She doesn't get paid much,' said Michelle, 'she was better off at the call centre.'

Conor placed a big round metal pan in the middle of the table. 'Seafood paella.'

Michelle looked at it with horror. 'It's got eyes!'

'And legs,' said Sonya. 'Langoustine and baby octopus.'

'Octopi,' said Darren.

'Or Octopuses,' said Conor.

'Yer can pick the seafood off and eat the rice,' said Sonya.

Michelle's face was like an orange slapped arse. 'Is there any ketchup?'

While they cleared their plates of claws and tentacles, Darren and Conor were deep in conversation about music. Sonya kept bitching about Ally working as a waitress in the sky, and she joined in, as did Michelle. She liked Ally, but yeah, recently, she'd disappeared up her own backside. There was a lapse in girls' talk and the boys' talk filled the space. "Close to Me', 'In Between Days',' said Conor, 'their early stuff is much better than 'Friday I'm in love'.'

Michelle perked up, a smile spreading across her face. 'Yer talkin about The Cure?'

'Yeah,' said Conor, 'you into them?'

'Eeee, ah love them,' said Michelle, while Sonya gave her a death stare.

'Ah didn't knar yer were into indie music,' said Darren.

'Ah've got reet into them since ower Lisa leant uz her tape.'

'Ah'll put them on later,' said Conor. 'Favourite track?'

'Boys Don't Cry,' said Michelle, laughing and inhaling her wine so she couldn't stop coughing.

The men cleared the dishes and when they were gone, Sonya said, 'Yer total fucken cunt.'

'Ah dinnar wot yer mean?' said Michelle.

'*Eeee, ah love The Cure*,' said Sonya, doing a topper impression of Michelle.

Conor put the chocolate pudding down and took off his oven gloves while Darren brought the custard that had been transferred from the glass measuring jug to a silver jug. Conor gave her a spatula. 'It's portioned, you serve.'

She felt like a dinner lady as she scooped up the chocolatey-spongey pudding portions, dispatching each with a schloop. They held out their bowls as she poured the custard, except for Michelle, who was allergic to eggs.

Sonya smirked at Michelle. 'Yer can see the horse in the dish now it's empty.'

Catching on, Michelle said, 'Nice *nosh*,' with the tone of a statement and the eyebrows of a question.

'Yeah, nice nosh, defo,' Conor agreed. 'Vanilla custard, yummy. Hats off to your brother.'

'It's hot so wer'll need ter *blow*,' said Sonya.

'Mack sure yer chew before yer *swallow*,' said Michelle

'Ah'm ganner have a good *gobble* on this,' said Sonya.

'It brings me out in a rash,' said Michelle, 'but ah've heard it's satisfyin ter *clear the custard*.'

That was it! She snatched the horse dish with both hands and knocked the chair over as she turned and flung it, hard and high across the garden. It glinted in the sun as it hurtled through the air, then it bounced off a fence post onto the spouting cherub, exploding on impact.

'Well,' said Sonya, 'that's well and truly fucked!'

Chapter 29

January 1993

Chloé was at Marcel's and Michelle and Darren were asleep. It had been a quiet one for New Year's Eve. She nearly jumped out of her skin when the phone rang and then panicked when she saw the time. Something had happened to Chloé. Why else would anyone call at 6:07 am on January 1st?

She snatched the phone up. 'Hello, is everythin alreet?'

'Hello, Paula, it's Walt.'

'Me mam's Walt?'

'Aye, ah'm afraid ah've got some bad news for yer, pet.'

Her heart sank. Jason had done something.

'Yer mam's passed away.'

'Wot?'

'In the early hours of this mornin.'

All Mam had to do was eat a box of chocolates and not die. Walt said that he tried to howk the Brazil nut out of her throat, but it was slippery, and he couldn't grasp it. When he came back from ringing the ambulance Mam was unconscious. She didn't know why Mam was eating a Brazil nut in the first place and reckoned she must've been sucking the chocolate off it when she inhaled it.

Frank gave her the week off work to sort the funeral. Organising everything took her mind off Martin for hours at a time, and the past two days had been a blur of phone calls and running around picking people up and dropping them off. The lads had been little troopers like kids who were scared of being taken into care, even though they knew she would never let that happen. They were moving in here with her and Chloé and they could have the loft room. Michelle had been amazing, cleaning the room and talking to the lads about where they should put their beds, finally deciding on Ian at the back and Jason at the front, separated by a sheet hanging from the mid-point. The loft room was wass and the lads didn't mind stooping under the sloping ceiling. They loved it up there, happily distracted from having no mam by the Sega Mega Drive Darren gave them.

Ian and Jason took everything in their stride, as if it was normal for a parent to die, which it was for them, the fucked-up family with dead dads and now a dead mam. 'We're all orphans together,' said Jason to Karen, the Hart family's new social worker.

It was weird that Karen wasn't much older than she was and that she had a lot to say about looking after children despite not having any herself. After the umpteenth time of being called a foster carer, she said, 'Ah'm their sister.' She didn't say that looking after her brothers would be the same as usual, only as a fosterer, she'd get paid for it.

There were lots of forms to fill in before she could be their legal guardian and she would've preferred to fill them in herself rather than dictate the answers to Karen who wrote everything in bubble writing.

Among the hundred questions was, 'Do yer have a care record?' for which Karen ticked yes before she'd answered.

Seeing the look of *what the fuck* on her face, Karen said, 'Don't worry, there's nothin on yer record that suggests you're unsuitable to look after yer brothers.'

'Wot der yer mean, *me record*?'

'Erm,' Karen squirmed.

'Ah knar wot happened when ah was a kid, but ah thought the records were destroyed when ah woz eighteen.'

'Nor,' said Karen, 'cradle ter grave.'

The permanence of her *record* from the bad old days sparked a cauldron of rage.

Karen said cheerily, 'This house is much bigger than wot it looks from the outside.'

Clicking back into smiley face mode, she replied, 'It's good here, handy for school, plus the bairns have the top of the house ter themsels. Would yer like a tour?'

'Ah was goin ter suggest that,' said Karen. 'Ah need ter make sure that it's suitable.'

As they went upstairs, Karen said, 'Yer said that this is a private rented house?'

'Aye, but ah own a house as well.'

'Do yer?' said Karen, clutching her leather zip-up file to her chest with surprise.

By the time Karen was done, the poor woman must've been glad to get out of there. She hadn't bitched about Martin since New Year's Eve as her resolution was not to do everyone's head in. Anyway, Karen deserved it after lecturing her on how to look after children.

It had been five days since Mam had died and she was yet to have an attack of breath-stopping grief. She couldn't believe Mam was gone. It was surreal that she had no parents, yet all that she felt was a bit sad. After Dad died, she counted the days. Wednesday 9th November, 14 days since Dad died. Saturday 4th June, 221 days since Dad died. Mam's funeral was tomorrow, and she was at a loose end, so she thought she might as well get on and sort out her things.

Chloé was keen to come with them to her 'Nana in heaven's house,' which was a change in name from 'Nana who smells of smoke.' Walt had been at Mam's all the time since she had died and was in pieces about losing 'Beautiful Marie.' The boys were at Nana Hart's the night Mam died and hadn't seen Walt since he dropped them off in Hetton on New Year's Eve.

Walt was gaunt, a shadow of his former self. The lads hugged him as he wiped tears from his eyes, and then he handed Jason a cotton handkerchief for him to dry his eyes. Ian's spotty face grimaced the same way as David's did when he was holding back pain, which was enough to bring a tear to her own eyes.

Chloé said, 'Don't cry, you people. Nana who smells of smoke will be watchin Corrie with the father, the son, and the holy spirit,' and she was confused when they laughed.

She left Chloé to help Walt put Mam's ornaments into a box to go to Aunty Pat's, and while Ian and Jason sorted out their rooms, she made a start on Mam's.

In Mam's underwear drawer, there were knickers that were older than she was. Under the everyday scruds, were some black lace bikini pants with matching bra and suspenders, and red, silky, fluted pants and cami top. The sexy stuff looked new; Walt was a lucky man; no surprise he missed her. Next drawer down was jumpers and below that socks, mostly unpaired, and some stuffed with money.

She sighed as she squeezed another roll of twenty-pound notes from a novelty Christmas sock. She counted out six hundred and forty pounds on the bed.

That would help pay for her part of the funeral. Her and David were giving eight hundred quid each and Aunty Pat was putting the rest. Lisa was fuming about spending their holiday fund on a coffin and said that they should let the council pay for it.

*

There was a decent crowd down the crematorium and Aunty Pat and Mam's mates from the bingo cried when 'Wind Beneath My Wings' played, whereas the lads were bored, and Chloé was annoyed because she wanted Kylie. The Wavendon put on a good spread and Mam's mates didn't let any of it go to waste. Family-wise, as well as Aunty Pat and Uncle Bobby, there were a few cousins from Mam's mam and dad's side, as well as Uncle Jack, Mam's dad's brother who, at the age of seventy-nine, was the last one standing: Georgie was carried off by a German shell in 1942, Albie by Japanese dysentery in 1943, Ernie by a German torpedo in 1944, Joe went under a coal truck in 1947, and Arthur and Pat were carried off by heart attacks in the 1970s.

The lads were enthralled by Uncle Jack's lost brothers.

'Is dysentery when yer cannet stop shittin yersel?' asked Jason.

'Did me Grandar Joe's guts pop out when the wheels went ower him?' asked Ian.

Despite forking out three hundred quid on food, she didn't get a bite, and when she put a pizza in the oven, everyone decided they were also hungry, so she had to put another two in. Ian was watching *Star Trek* with Darren, Chloé was playing a game of small stuffed toys being held hostage among the shoe pile by big bunny, aided and abetted by Jason's Action Man. Michelle was having a bath, which she deserved after being an absolute legend, helping with the funeral and looking after the lads.

She went up to check on Jason, pausing and knocking, hoping that he wasn't cranking one out like Ian was the other day when she walked in. Jason was probably too young, though.

'Enter.'

Jason was lying across his bed playing on the Game Boy that Nana Hart got him, so she sat next to him and waited until he died and flicked the tiny screen in disgust.

'Wot yer up tee, me little orphan?' She ruffled his hair and he batted her off.

'Playin, or ah woz like.'

'There's pizza in ten minutes.'

As she was on her way out, he said, 'Paula, ah've got summink ter show yer.'

'Wot?'

He reached an arm down the back of his bed, then gave her a small blue book with Yorkshire Bank in gold writing on the front. Inside, it said Jason Hart. The first entry was a deposit of five pounds in 1982, then a deposit of a tenner, then withdrawal of a tenner, and then in 1986, there was a £5,250 deposit from cheque 100238.

'Dad's money from the pit,' said Jason. 'Mam used ter hide the book in her jumper drawer and when ah got back from Nana Hart's after she died, ah went strite in and nabbed it before Walt could.'

'Did he knar about it?'

'Dinnar.' He shrugged then smiled, flashing his yellow teeth. 'It's yowers now.'

She flicked through the pages that showed years of a tenner out here, twenty out there, leading to the current balance of £3,180. Mam could've blown the lot on cheap holidays like her mates did, so it was good of her to leave a decent wad for her sons. She patted the bank book. 'Ah'm ganner put it away for yae and Ian ter have when yers are eighteen.'

Jason shook his head. 'Nor Paula, it's yower money, ter buy a horse.'

'A horse?'

'Aye,' he said, eyes wide, 'as long as ah can ride it.'

'Ah cannet gan buyin nee horse, man, lovely idea though, thank you.' She gave him a death hug and kissed his ear. 'We'll be alreet, won't wer? All orphans together.'

Chapter 30

February 1993

The woman at Penshaw Riding School said that it would be best for her and Jason to have a couple of private lessons as a taster. She decided to pretend she was a total novice, which she was given it had been six years since she'd been near a horse. She was glad that Jason had gone on and on and on about going horse riding because it reminded her of how much she wanted to go horse riding and how much she could do whatever she wanted now that she was a grown-up.

On the way to the first taster session, she bored Jason with how, in the holidays, her and David would go on a walking adventure all the way from Pallion to Penshaw and how she thought she could see the whole world from the top.

'How owld wer yers?' asked Jason.

'Oooo, about seven and eleven.'

'Where woz Mam?'

'Watchin telly.'

'Where woz yer dad?'

'In Cherry knocker.'

Penshaw Village was made of pretty cottages, modern bungalows, a tiny stone church with a graveyard, and a mock Tudor pub. Her spine tingled as she pulled into the riding school and parked the car; as a grown-up, she could drive to the riding school, and no one could slap her into the gutter when it was her turn to ride.

The riding school owner woman and the younger lass who was doing the lesson were canny and not at all snobby. She acted nonchalant like it wasn't a moment she'd dreamed of all her life.

'We don't have any boys,' said the owner woman, eyeing Jason up and down.

'Ah've nivver seen a lass ride a winner at Aintree,' replied Jason, eyes firmly down as he made a semi-circle in the dirt with the toe of his welly.

Two horses were led to them by two lasses that looked about twelve and who were wearing flimsy tops despite the biting wind. 'Treacle and Monty,' said the riding school owner woman, referring to a sleek chestnut with a swishy tail and dapple-grey shire with muddy legs. 'Liz will look after you.'

Liz, the instructor, got her on Treacle and Jason on Monty. They clip-clopped towards the riding arena that she'd looked down on from the top of the monument, watching the ant-sized horses trotting up and down and cursing the lucky gits that were riding them. Now she looked up at the Victorian Ancient Greek temple on the hill in the distance and would've punched the air if she didn't have tight hold of the reins. There's nothing to dislike about horse riding. Jason's face agreed. They were going to have to drag him off Monty.

As they walked a lap of the training arena, she felt happy. As she kicked and cajoled Treacle to walk the diagonal, she noted how horse riding wasn't like riding a bike unless the first bike was a tricycle and the next one was a unicycle.

'Leg on!'

'Hands down!'

'Straighten your back!'

'Stop bobblin about!'

Jason wasn't having the same problems or any problems.

'Nice job!'

'Good, good!'

'Give your horse a pat!'

There's one thing riding along with the wind in your hair and another thing riding along with the wind in your face and snots coming out of your nose without a free hand to do anything about it. She also had cramp in her hip.

A week later, on the next and last taster lesson before deciding which group they should join, the humiliation continued. Treacle was less than enthralled to be assigned to the riding idiot, so instructor Liz had to coax her to trot, which she did occasionally with the attitude of a teenager being made to run around the field in PE. To be fair, she'd take a moody mare over a good-as-gold gelding any day. The romance between Jason and Monty flourished.

'Nice job!'

'Good, good!'

'Give your horse a pat!'

She stepped aside and let her teenage helper lead Treacle away, whereas Jason reluctantly dismounted and refused to surrender the reins. After a tussle, instructor Liz stepped in, ordered Jason to lead Monty to the stall, and told the helper to teach him how to untack.

She felt like a spare part hanging about the yard waiting for Jason, so she wandered down to the training arena, then along the intriguing path she'd spied while on Treacle. She reckoned it was a bridle path, and as she walked, her suspicions were confirmed when horses emerged from the mist up ahead. She quickened her step towards them, and as they got closer, she recognised the gorgeous bay horse with the black mane. And then they were in focus, and she could see Maddy on his back, so she turned and sprinted to the stables and across the yard. She slowed at Monty's stall, hissed, 'Jason, car, now,' then sprinted, sweating cobs, to the carpark.

It took Jason ages to meander to the car, then he started to kick mud off his boots.

She leaned across and opened the passenger side door, 'Get in, *quick*.'

'Why the hurry?'

'For fuck's sake, Jason, get in or ah'll leave yer here,' she rasped, dipping her head below the dashboard.

'Ah'll get in when yer tell uz wot's garn on,' he said, smirking like Billy used to.

She was the one in the driving seat now. She revved the car. 'Get in *now* or that's the last horse ridin yae'll ever dee.'

He got in slowly. 'Why yer actin so funny?'

'Shut the fuck up, will yer! Ah'm drivin.'

She booted the car along the main road, Jason silent and sulking. She didn't regain control of herself until she was parked on her road. 'Soz about that Jason, it's just there woz someone at the stables that ah need ter avoid.'

'Why?'

She told him what had happened as they whacked their boots on the front step.

'So yer cannet show yer face at the stables because yer nicked some posh lass's jacket seven years agan?'

'Aye, me Burberry one.'

'She'll problees not remember.'

'Oh aye, like yae would forget about the skanky lass wee yer gave a go on yer horse, and then she nicked off in yer five hundred quid coat.'

Jason's sock came off with his welly and his long toes were filthy.

'It's a matter of time before the gossip spreads ter the stables that we're Billy Hart's kids,' she said.

'So?' said Jason. 'Nowt ter dee wer them.'

'Fair enough, but if they get wind of me thievin, we'll be shunned.'

'So wot yer sayin?' he said, sock in hand, bottom lip wobbling. 'Nee more ridin?'

'Ah'm ganner give it a miss for now, at Penshaw, or anywhere near here. Yae can gan though.'

'Can ah?'

'As long as yer dinnet tell nee one wee yer sister is and yer get the bus there.'

'Here-man, ah'll walk there,' he said, planting his mucky mouth on the side of her face. 'Can ah have some proper boots?'

'Pushin it now, son,' she said.

He pulled his other welly off and wanged it into next door's garden. 'Ooops.'

'Dinnet dee that,' she laughed. 'Ah'll get yer some boots.'

He unbuttoned his jeans. 'And some britches?'

'Dinnet hoy them into next door's.'

'Ah winnet as lang as yer buy uz some britches.'

'Mind ah expect yer ter win hods of rosettes if ah'm payin for lessons.'

'Ah will,' he said, 'ah totally will, ah winnet let yer down, and they're called ribbons.'

Chapter 31

July 1993

Jason had told everyone at the stables that his sister was buying a horse, so people kept suggesting animals that were for sale. The 'horse money' was in a high-interest account to divide between the lads in five years, yet Jason kept coming home with torn-out bits of notepaper: 14-year-old mare, bay, 16.3hh, good all-rounder; 5-year-old-gelding, Irish sports horse, 16.1hh; 7-year-old gelding, cob, 16hh.

He whacked his boots off the front step sending clarts everywhere. 'Yer knar that bloke ah woz tellin yer about wee owns the factory?' he said.

'Aye, daughter wer a Carmelo geldin called Sidney?'

'Daughter's up the duff.'

'Nor, how owld is she?'

'Siventeen.'

'If ah had a horse at her age, there's neeway ah'd have looked at lads.'

Jason laughed. 'Have yer seen her? Reet blimp. Feel sorry for the horse.'

She sighed. 'Wer not buyin a horse, Jason.'

'He'll tack nine hundred.'

'Even if yer look after it, there'll be livery fees, vet's fees, and shit,' she said. She knew he knew the score about looking after horses now that he helped out at the stables all weekend, offering his services in return for being near the horses. He'd then come home smelling of horses, which made her feel proud as she pressed her face into his shoulder and sniffed. He batted her off.

'At least gan and have a look.'

*

She'd consulted the map and memorised where she had to go: stay on Durham Road all the way past Houghton, turn off at Rainton (if hit A1 gone too far), then get on road that goes across to and under the A1, after gone under A1, turn right and the stables are halfway up the road that goes to Great Lumley. Her road atlas was free with some petrol coupons, so it wasn't great for the smaller roads. As the single windscreen wiper left a line of crud down her line of vision, she wondered, as usual, who the heck designed a car with one wiper?

Like most days, she couldn't stop thinking about Martin or concentrate on anything. It was over a month since he'd had the second letter telling him to get out.

David and Uncle Jimmy were doing their nut, and she didn't know how much longer she could persuade them not to drag him out and change the locks. The solicitor said that anything like that would likely result in never getting him out. She was so angry thinking about all the shit that she almost missed the turning at West Rainton.

She weaved through the village and popped out in the countryside like she remembered on the map. She turned left onto the road that led to the road with the stables on it. She reckoned it was posh round here because Cocken Road hadn't been changed to Cockend Road. Not far along, she could see horses grazing, so she tried her luck with the next turn. At the end of a muddy lane was a yard and a large stable-looking barn, surrounded by fields and lined by hedges.

She parked and wandered into the barn, looking for signs of life and kicking herself for not changing into some boots. There was a man in black wellies grooming a coal-black horse with a white star on its head. She smiled at him as she made her way down the stalls looking for Sidney, the blimp daughter's Carmello gelding that she wasn't going to buy. At the end of the stalls was an office, and at the sound of her court shoes click-clacking, a stern woman with a weathered face came out and gave her a full body up-and-down look.

'Ah'm here ter see Mr Benton about Sidney. Could yer tell uz if he's about?'

The woman smiled, activating every wrinkle. 'He was here and then his daughter ran her car into a ditch, so he's gone to rescue her.'

'Did he say when he'll be back?'

'No. Would you like a cup of tea while you wait?'

'Thanks, but ah better get back ter work, ah popped out in me dinner hour.'

On her way out, she stopped to stroke the coal-black horse, as it would've been rude not to. The horse lowered its head, so she pressed her face onto its cheek. The man came out of the stall and said, 'Ah hear yer lookin ter buy a horse?'

'Not really,' she said.

'Shame,' he said, pulling his baggy trousers up. 'This lady is for sale.'

She stroked her nose and drifted off into a dream of riding across a meadow with the wind in her hair. When she returned to the world, he was smiling at her.

'Beautiful, isn't she?' he said. 'Ah'm Des, by the way, this is me sister's horse.'

'Paula, nice ter meet yers both,' she said, stroking the horse's nose.

'Fifteen-year-old thoroughbred, 16.2 hands high,' he said. 'What type of ridin do yer do?'

She felt her face go beety. 'Not much at the minute.'

He smiled. 'She's a great all-rounder, likes jumpin, great in a canter, comfortable ride.'

'Why are yer sellin?' she said, running her hand along the horse's side.

'Me sister can't look after her now she's got two baby boys.'

'Twins, shit. One's hard enough, ah'm not surprised she hasn't got time for a horse.'

'They're not twins, well, Irish twins ah suppose.'

'She's Irish?'

He smiled. 'Me sister had two boys with ten months between them, like what Irish Catholics do because they don't believe in birth control.'

'That's Irish twins?' she said. 'Ah've nivver heard that before, but ah knar wot yer mean. My kid's dad is an English Catholic, and he doesn't believe in birth control either.'

He laughed. 'Are yer from Sunderland?'

'Why der yer think that like, cos ah've got a bairn?'

He shook his head, 'Nor, it's not that.'

She wanted to dig him in the ribs and ask, 'Wot is it then?' but she remembered that he was a strange man who was trying to sell her a horse that she couldn't afford.

'Der yer want ter ride? Ah can tack her up,' he said.

She gave him a theatrical look of, *of course I want to ride*, then tapped her watch. 'Ah'm on me dinner break from work.'

'Where der yer work?'

'For a mortgage company.'

'Ah, so that's how come yer buyin a horse?'

'Nor, ah'm not loaded or owt.'

'Me sister's lookin for twelve hundred. Ah could have a word with her. Give uz yer number and ah'll see what ah can do.'

She knew she could never own this beautiful creature, but if there was a test ride in it, she could play along. She got a pen and a scrap of paper from her bag and gave him her number.

'Mebees ah could come back when ah'm not at work and ride out?' she suggested.

He waved the scrap of paper, then tucked it in his back pocket.

As she stroked the black mare, her insides tickled. 'So does she have a name?' she asked.

The horse licked his hand. 'Yeah,' he said, 'Mayfair.'

*

When Jason shouted up the stairs that a bloke called Des was on the phone, she couldn't think who it could be until she heard his voice.

'Oh, hi, Des with the horse. Hang on.' She went out of the bedroom and shouted, 'Jason, put the phone down.'

An hour and a half later, she lay back and stared at the ceiling, trying to take in what had just happened. She was upfront that she couldn't buy Mayfair, and when he said she could ride her anyway, she had to bite the pillow. Des was ten years older than her, grew up on Ferryboat Lane, and left St Tommy Akkers in 1975 to work as a ship fitter. He said it was crap getting up in the cold and dark to go to the shipyards, so he was pleased when he was made redundant. He used the cash to buy tools and a van and now he mostly fits kitchens and sometimes wardrobes. He told her about how his dad died so his mam moved to Great Lumley, which is where she was from, and then she got cancer, so he moved in with her, and although she's had the all-clear, he still lives with her. She didn't tell him about Dad. Where would she start? She told him about Mam choking and about fostering the boys, yet was vague on the details of how their dad died because she didn't want to soil a nice conversation.

When she closed her eyes, his face gave her fanny flutters. He was tall with dark hair and blue eyes, and she wished she'd paid more attention to everything else. She could hear Michelle huffing and puffing, and instead of using her bedroom phone, she used the hall phone and talked loudly, 'Hi Donna, sorry to call so late, but the phone's been tied up for over an hour.'

*

Des rang again tonight at the same time as last night, and if this was the routine, she liked it. When she heard his voice, the blood rushed to her nethers, making it difficult to concentrate. He was so easy to talk to that she decided to tell him about Martin, to get it out of the way, even though the weird thing was that since she'd met him, much less of her headspace was taken up by the scumbag. Fitting in hatred for Martin was difficult between the sexual fantasies and dreams of romantic weekend breaks with Des. As she slavered on about Martin, Des made sympathetic noises, which made her feel tragic. He said that she shouldn't feel like an idiot and that Martin probably wasn't planning it; rather, he saw an opportunity and took it. Des said that if she gave him the keys, he'd call in and keep an eye on things. He also said he'd like to kick Martin's head in but promised not to.

*

It had been nine days since she'd met Des. She'd taken the afternoon off work to meet him at the stables. She was wearing a new knicker and bra set in case her clothes fell off.

She parked next to a van with *Desmond Butcher Carpentry* on the side with his phone number. As she got out of the car, Des came running towards her, arms waving. Her insides melted, and it wasn't just the britches and knee-length boots, he had a good body, broad shoulders. He'd scrubbed up since she was last here. She was expecting awkwardness, not for him to go straight in for a lift-off-her-feet hug, which turned into a kiss that gave her butterflies. He pulled away.

'Mayfair's tacked up, yer ready?'

Too many happy things were happening to speak, so she smiled, and grabbed his hand.

'Yer okay?' he said, opening the stall.

'Ah'm more than okay.'

'That's wot ah mean,' he said, 'are yer sure yer can cope wer all the excitement?'

He led Mayfair out, and as he handed her the rope, the horse flicked her ears. Des opened the next stall, and led out a huge bay. 'This is Duke.'

'He's lovely.'

'Wot was it yer said about flyin across the sky on a magic creature with the wind in yer hair and no troubles in yer soul?'

'Did ah say that?'

'On yer get then,' he said.

'Is there a step?'

'Nope.'

He said that he'd taught himself to ride and that he was hopeless at it, although there was nothing hopeless about how he mounted and took up the reins. 'Ready?'

The beautiful man on the beautiful horse made her entire body flutter.

Trying to use her heel, not her whole foot, she gave Mayfair two taps with both feet. After clawing a front hoof, the horse started walking. When Des saw that they were moving, he pulled Duke's rein back on one side, gave him a dig, and clip-clopped off across the yard. They followed Des and Duke down a path to a hedge. Des got off, opened the gate, and lead Duke through.

'Wot der yer reckon, Mayfair?' he said, stroking the horse's nose. 'Should wer take Paula for a run?'

They walked in single file across the top of the field. It was ellish to be riding in peace – no instructor and brother to tell her she's rubbish, no Maddies and Minties to sneer at her commonness, and no sexual predators lurking in full view. Also, it was brilliant that no one could stand in her way because this horse belonged to her boyfriend.

Des stopped. 'Ready?'

She pulled the reins and Mayfair stopped and tossed her mane. 'Wot for?'

'Canter to the trees,' he said, turning Duke to face down the field that disappeared off into the distance. He kicked his heels and was gone.

She tapped to walk, and then to trot, which was elegant, not bumpy like at the riding school. She got her 'Leg on!' and Mayfair went faster and smoother. She was cantering! Her heart flipped and her legs jerked, and then she could feel the power of the horse's hind legs pushing forward, and then they were hurtling at full speed, and she was leaning forward, hooves thudding, muscles pumping, the world was a blur as she swung between joy and fear, tugging at her 'spaghetti reins'. This was galloping, this was flying, this was freedom like she'd never felt before. Mayfair slowed to a canter, then a walk, and when the field came back into focus she sat tall as if she hadn't been clinging on for dear life. Mayfair walked over to Duke and stopped.

'Didn't fall off then,' said Des, dismounting.

'Shit, man. We accidentally galloped.' When she got off, her legs were like jelly. 'Will yer get wrang?'

'Wot for?'

'Lettin uz gallop.'

He laughed. 'Nee one's ganner get wrang.'

'Ah thought yer weren't allowed ter let just anyone loose on a horse.'

'Wot, like ridin without a licence?'

'Aye, ah suppose. Yer cannet drive without passin a test and ah reckon Mayfair can shift faster than my shitty car.'

'Aye, well, anyone can ride a horse, and if it's my horse, it's my rules.'

Like a pair of cowboys, they tethered Duke and Mayfair to the fence under the trees, then he helped her over the stile. She trembled as he undid her chinstrap and gave a little yelp as he pulled her to his chest. They kissed for ages, his hands all over her boobs, her hands all over his bum.

'Ha'way,' he said, leading her out of the trees.

'Will the horses be okay?'

'Why-aye man, they'll be munchin on the nettles.'

He led her into the long grass of the field on the other side of the trees.

'It's lovely here, peaceful,' she said. She wondered where he was leading her as she looked at the sky.

'Mind the dip,' he said.

'Wot's a di—' she said before skidding on her back down into a sandy, grassy hole.

Laughing at her sprawled in the sandpit, he jumped down and whipped his top off. No belly flab, no weird moles, only smooth skin over pecs and abs. His body looked like it was off a poster. He was much fitter than anyone she'd pulled before. She was trembling so much she could hardly grip the zip on his britches.

*

Des dropped by after a local job and despite telling everyone not to call him her boyfriend, as she welcomed him into the hall, Ian shouted from the kitchen, 'Is yer boyfriend stayin for tea?' Then two heads popped out of the living room.

'Hi,' he said. 'Des.'

Chloé looked him up and down. 'Are yae Indiana Jones?'

'Yep,' he said, picking her up sideways. 'Ah'm here ter save yer from the eyeball soup.' When he let her down, she clung to his arm like a limpet.

'Can ah ride yer black mare? How many hands high is she? Does she jump?' said Jason, keen and unsubtle.

'Less of the million questions. Let the man breathe,' she said, pulling Chloé off him.

It wasn't much better in the kitchen with a three-pronged attack from Michelle, Darren, and Ian.

'Ah'm Michelle, long-sufferin friend and housemate.'

'Ah'm Darren. Welcome ter steak Thursda.'

'Der yer want ter stay for tea, ah've got an extra steak?' said Ian.

'No thanks,' said Des, 'mebees next week.'

'Why-aye man,' said Ian. 'Let uz knar yer favourite cut. Ah'll dee it wer me secret recipe sauce.'

While the men talked about cuts of beef and the best way to cook steak, Michelle winked and mouthed, 'Phoar.'

Des had to get back to Great Lumley to take his mam to a cards evening, bless him, and he wasn't dressed for steak night. He was sexy in his hanging-off jeans and black hair peppered with sawdust. She took him into the dining room to speak in private, and he pushed her against the door and kissed her. She considered a quickie despite the feet running down the hall and Ian shouting at Jason in the background. He took her hand off his cock and stepped back.

'Knock it off, ah've got ter talk ter all the old ladies later.'

'If yer turn up at me house lookin like Indiana Jones, ah will molest yer.'

He laughed. 'Ah like yae. Yer funny.' His eyes twinkled and her insides melted. 'Can yer get the afternoon off tomorra? Got yer a ridin lesson sorted.'

'Aye,' she said, thinking, sickie or late notice leave. 'On Mayfair?'

'Nor, Mayfair's with Heather,' he said, 'showjumpin at the weekend, best leave them to it.'

'Heather?'

'A teenager from the village. Always mackin herself useful at the livery yard.'

She laughed, 'Yip, like ower Jason.'

'Ah said that if she woz prepared ter muck her out and look after her, she could treat Mayfair like her own horse. If ah'm honest, Heather has been great since Janis lumbered uz with a Thoroughbred. Bloody sisters, eh?'

'Soz about Jason earlier, ah telt him that wer not buyin a horse. Wot about Heather's family, any chance they'd buy a horse for their darlin daughter?'

'Mayfair's not for sale.'

'Janis changed her mind?'

He shook his head in disbelief.

'Wot?' she said, confused.

He put a hand on her shoulder and a waft of fresh sweat made her swoon. 'Ah made Janis a good offer.'

'Yer bought Mayfair?'

'Aye, for yae.'

*

She decided on a sickie for her riding lesson, which was going to be on a horse called Buttons. She was watching out for Des's van and thinking about asking if he could sacrifice his manly pride and be seen in a Panda when the doorbell made her jump out of her skin.

'Where's the van?' she asked.

'Ah've got Janis's car,' he said, pushing her inside and scooping her up against his white t-shirt. She was going to lead him to bed, when he broke free.

'Let's get gone.'

Janis's car was an electric blue Honda Civic. He kissed her before putting his seatbelt on. She leaned back and relaxed.

'Did yer pull a sickie?' he asked.

'Women's problems.'

When he turned down Durham Road, she wondered which way he was going, then he turned onto Seaforth Road. 'Why have yer come this way?'

He exhaled. 'Don't go mad, but somethin's happened.'

Her heart started to pound. 'Wot? Is it summink ter dee wer Martin?'

He smiled. 'Yer were reet when yer said he wouldn't have changed the locks, fucken twat.'

'Yer've changed the locks?' She kissed the side of his face. He hadn't mentioned Martin since she'd given him the keys. 'Cheers, but that won't get rid of him.'

When he stopped outside, she could see from the road that there was a poster stuck on the door. 'Wot's that?'

'Go and see,' he said.

LEGAL WARNING. *This house has been occupied by squatters. Entry into this house without permission of the squatters is a criminal offence under Section 6 of the Criminal Law Act of 1977. If you want to get us out you will have to apply for a court order for possession.*

'Nor, nah!'

'Looks like Martin'll need a court order.'

Her mouth was open and there were so many things she wanted to say that nothing came out.

He rang the bell and a fat man wearing a Sunderland footy shirt opened the door. 'Hello Desmond,' he said. He had Borstal dots on his cheek.

'Paula, meet Norm.'

'Hi Norm. Can ah come in?' she said, stepping forward.

Norm blocked her. 'It's a criminal offence ter enter without permission.'

She turned to Des.

'Okay,' said Des, 'my mate Norm here is squattin. Ah've changed the locks, so Martin'll have ter break in, and—'

'He'll be committin an offence,' she said with a smile. Now she got what was happening. This was amazing. Des was amazing.

'When's he back from Tenerife?' said Norm.

'He's in Tenerife?' she exclaimed. 'Is he with Bingo Moose? Bet they're havin an ellish time at my expense.'

'That'll change when he gets back tomorra,' said Des. 'When he finds out he has ter apply for a court order ter get into his bedroom.'

Her bitterness melted into laughter. This was all too good to take in. She said to Norm, 'When yer see Martin, tell him ah can recommend a good solicitor. It'll tack months, cost a wad, and there's nee guarantees.'

'Here-man,' said Norm, 'they'll need a bulldozer ter to get me owt of here.'

'Best wer clear his stuff onto the garden,' said Des. 'Then he'll have nee reason ter come in. He can tack wot's his and bugger off.'

Inside hadn't changed. She pointed Norm and Des at Martin's things in the living room: video recorder, telly, framed picture of a Ferrari.

'The settee is his, but wer cannet put that on the street,' she said.

Norm and Des looked at each other. 'Ha'way,' said Des to Norm as he took the end of the four-seater, 'get that end.'

While the men were doing the heavy lifting, she danced around *her* kitchen, clapping her hands. Let's see how Martin likes this!

There was nothing left belonging to Martin and Bingo Moose inside because their stuff was piled on the front garden including his stereo, telly, video, and all his clothes in a heap.

'Is that the lot?' said Des.

'Shame we cannet get into his car,' she said.

'Why?'

'Café del Mar tape that wer bought when uz woz there.'

'A one-off?'

'Aye, on a TDK C90.'

Des strode over to the car, and she thought he was going to try the handle, not stick his foot through the driver's side window, then open it from the inside. He leaned in and grabbed a hand full of tapes. 'Gypsy Kings, nor,' he said, flinging it on the pavement, 'The Eagles, nor.'

'It's a yellow tape.'

'This it?' he said, holding up a yellow tape.

'Yip.'

He put it in his pocket. 'Reet then, gorgeous, that's us done.'

She lingered and read the squatters' notice one last time. 'Ah'm strugglin ter tack it all in. It's like ah'm ganner wake up and it's all been a dream.'

He kissed the top of her head. 'It's all real,' he said, 'especially this.'

'Wot?'

He dropped his jeans and pissed in an arc, soaking Martin's clothes and making her laugh so hard that she had to drop her pants and take a waz on the armchair.

Chapter 32

May 1994

It was weird going into Thornhill with Ian in his dark red blazer, which wasn't as bad as the purple blazers of Monkey House or the shitty brown of Southmoor, yet it was worse than all the other schools. The Thornhill motto, *learn to live,* was on his badge next to some wheat, which was a bit shit compared with the Phoenix on Bede's badge. Bede's motto was *post tenebras lux* – after darkness light – which had turned out to be true. The sun hadn't stopped shining since she left that shithole.

When Ian had his options interview, Mam made him take Uncle Harry Hart. It was a good move as it gave the impression of a normal family, and the father figure looked the spit of his actual dad. Uncle Harry Hart often phoned to talk to the lads, and he took them out sometimes. It sent a shiver down her spine when he mooched in the hall, jangling his car keys like the ghost of Billy jangling the keys to her prison cell. Ian had chosen history, geography, art, PE, and home economics, as well as the compulsory subjects, maths, science, and English. Since when could you do an O-level in PE? Ian said it was a piece of piss that you can't fail and that it was GCSEs now.

Ian was a good lad who went to all of his lessons, and was top of the second set for maths. Ian was good at history and Nana Hart helped him do his coursework about the Easington Colliery Band for which he got a B. The only lesson he'd skipped was home economics and only six times, yet to be fair, he found the cooking easy and boring, and the class was full of lasses who talked about lads. When she got a letter from the head of year asking her to attend a meeting, Jason spilled the beans that some of the lads had called Ian a puff, so he gave one of them a fat lip. Jason said that they left him alone after that, thus proving, she noted, and Jason agreed, that gobshites are softshites. She hoped that Ian's handy reputation would filter down to Jason's year and serve a warning to any kid who had a problem with lads riding horses.

As she made her way with Ian down the walkway next to the concrete spaceship, she reminded herself to be on her best behaviour, to act like Ian's *mother*, not his *sister*. She'd got Des to have a talk with Ian about not going to his cooking classes, as anything she said would be hypocritical, given how much she didn't bother with school. Now Ian had missed a critical number of lessons, there was a procedure.

As the head of year let them into his office, Ian did his best to look sheepish. She relaxed her face and tried to look serious while giggling like a schoolgirl on the inside. The head of year warbled on about Ian not passing his GSCE because he hadn't been to the lessons or done the coursework, although noted that, to Ian's credit, his pastry was the talk of the staff room.

When the head of year stopped talking, she looked at Ian. 'Tell him how ter mack good pastry.' She looked the teacher in the eye with a hint of smugness, then sat back and folded her arms. Oh, how long Ian could talk about making pastry. It was enough to make a glass eye weep, in a good way, and Ian knew it, and he didn't let her down.

After ten minutes of the joy of choux, the head of year looked at his watch, then sent Ian back to class.

*

Norman had lived at Hipsburn Drive for free for months, which was helpful while she was selling as he looked after the place, including doing odd jobs that Des never got around to. Despite wanting rid of the bogey house that had drained her spirit like a curse from the evicted family, she'd turned down a few offers, and after six months on the market, she caved on £40K. Des decided that they should have a party before they sold it, thus getting some use out of the poisoned chalice. The plan was to get Ian to do the cooking, thus re-igniting his love of catering, which was bound to get him running back to the crusty, old school ovens in a room of bitchy lasses.

Having a barbeque meant they would use the brick barbeque at least once before selling, and a neighbourly gathering would be a good way to get information about what happened the day that Martin and Bingo Moose found Norm the squatter. Norm's feedback wasn't full of details. 'The twat tried to get in, then he packed his car and fucked off.' The meagre description she got from Des was that Norm was watching the telly with the curtains closed while Martin rang the doorbell, then he banged on the front windows, then he stood on the drive with Bingo Moose and shouted swear words until the snakes next door took them in. She managed to grab a quick chat with Mr Murray from two doors down, yet he was cagey other than there was some argy-bargy in the street, then Martin drove away. She didn't press Mr Murray for more info because she didn't want to come across as a mad woman, which was an inevitable consequence of talking about Martin, even after he'd slung his hook.

The weather wasn't too bad, cloudy and sunny, and likely to stay dry. Des, Ian, Jason, and Darren got the barbeque going, while she went to Asdas with Michelle.

As they emptied the car, Sonya parked her Suzuki Samura and unloaded two boxes of beer and a good-looking middle-aged bloke.

'It's weird in here,' said Michelle, heaving three placker bags into the empty kitchen. 'Bad vibes.'

'Yae were the one wee selt uz it,' she said.

'Nor, ah woz the one wee conducted the viewin, yae were the one wee got on the phone ter Lloyds.'

She cringed at how naïve she'd been calling a random director to make him an offer on a house. Blind confidence worked though. She'd never do that now.

'Are the steaks in that bag?' she asked Michelle.

'Dinnet ask me, yae packed them.'

'This is Dave,' said Sonya. Her bleached blonde hair was long, and she was wearing her white embroidery Anglaise with blue lace trim dress from Leaf in Newcastle, a shop for rich people, and a Valentino denim jacket from Sisters in Newcastle, another shop for rich people.

Sonya said to Dave, 'There's a bucket of ice in the garden for the beer.'

Dave kissed Sonya on the cheek and went to join the men in the garden.

Sonya pierced the film of the mince with her false fingernail. 'Ah though it woz a barbeque? Won't the mince fall through?'

'Wot der yer think burgers are made of?'

'Cows.'

She shook her head. 'Lay the food on the bench while ah fetch ower Ian.'

Outside, Des was assembling the manky trestle table from the shed while Darren and random Dave hovered next to the crackling coals. Ian was at the white plastic table with his two mates. She was the coolest sister ever when she gave them a beer. Then she summoned Ian to the kitchen. As he washed his hands, she explained, 'Ah got everythin, but there were nee avocados, and ah got normal mushrooms instead of Portobello.'

Ian shook his hands over the sink. He inspected the produce, picked up a pineapple, kissed it, then kissed her on the side of the face. 'Paula, yer the best.'

Sonya and Michelle each gave her a double thumbs-up.

'Yer'll need ter tell the girls the menu so they can tell the guests.'

'Can ah mack it first, there's hods ter prepare,' said Ian.

'Ah yer tryin ter say yer want uz out of the kitchen?' said Michelle.

'Nor *yae* can stay,' he said, 'ah need an assistant.'

'Ah'm not fucken helpin,' said Sonya, 'not wer these nails.'

Ian gave Sonya a pitying look. 'Michelle der yer mind givin the mushrooms a rinse?'

'Nee problem,' said Michelle, rolling up the sleeves on her white jumper.

She left them to it and went with Sonya into the garden. Darren was poking the coals while Des was throwing a dustsheet over the trestle, transforming it into a banquet table.

'Mam!' shouted Chloé. She couldn't see where the small, big voice was coming from, then was distracted by Marcel, Meredith, and Jacob coming in the side gate. There was a rustle, a crackle of branches, and then a thud.

'Chloé's landed,' said Marcel.

Chloé's rosy face popped out of the undergrowth, followed by her body which was wearing a Spider-Man outfit. Fair enough outfit, who wouldn't if they could get away with it? But it has to be Wonder Woman or even the Little Mermaid, not an animal that you can wipe out with a slipper. Spider-Man Chloé shinned up the twisted tree and lay across the branch, while Jacob, dressed as Batman, tried to climb up. Marcel and Meredith were on the patio and Jason handed them each a beer from the ice bin like the perfect host.

Then there was a flurry of neighbours coming in the side gate. Mr and Mrs Murray from two doors down headed straight over the grass, and Mr Murray shook her hand while Mrs Murray held out a bowl of salad. From the corner of her eye, she could see Mandy and her husband from across the road with their two daughters, which made Ian's mates' heads turn.

Cornered by Mr and Mrs Murray, she said, 'Thanks so much for trimmin me hedge, can ah get yers a drink? Beer, spirits, pop, tea?'

'It woz nee bother, pet,' said Mr Murray, 'ah'll have a beer if there's one goin.'

'Orange juice, thanks, pet,' said Mrs Murray.

'Jason,' she shouted under her breath. Jason came striding over. 'Can yer get a beer and an orange juice and tack this lovely salad ter the kitchen,' she tussled Jason's hair. 'There's a good lad,' she said and he punched her hand away.

She made small talk about the garden and told Mr Murray what she'd got for the house because she knew he was gagging to know. As soon as Jason placed a drink in their hands, she asked, 'Ah've been meanin ter ask yer for ages about wot happened when Martin came back ter the squatters' notice. Wer yers home that day?'

Mr Murray said that it was about midday when he heard raised voices, and went outside to find Martin shouting, 'Get the f— out, yer filthy parasites.'

She was amused to find out that after banging on the door and the window, Martin gave Bingo Moose a bunk-up onto the porch to climb in the open bedroom window.

'Ah was shoutin, get down, yer'll break yer ruddy neck, but ah didn't want ter set foot on the property, antagonise him like,' said Mr Murray. 'Then the squatter closed the bedroom window while the woman was bangin on it, shoutin *get outta me house yer f— b—*.'

He said that the 'folks' next door came out and helped Martin get 'the woman' down from the porch. An hour or so later, the police arrived who were there for five minutes and left. The day after, Martin loaded his car, then came back later that afternoon with a van for the furniture. Mr and Mrs Murray hadn't seen him since. Mr Murray changed the subject to the buddleia in his garden that attracts hundreds of butterflies, so she listened patiently, keeping one eye on Mandy who didn't look old enough to have two teenage daughters.

Ian's mates were all over the oldest daughter, while Darren and Des had faraway looks of being fifteen again. She had perfect skin and big brown eyes with smoky lids and smudged eyeliner, grungy like she was a drug-addicted prostitute. She was wearing a biker jacket over a skin-tight cropped top that showed her pancake belly, and rolled-up jeans with high-heels and socks, which was ridiculous yet cute.

Mr Murray enthused about her purple flowers and when his beer was empty, she took his can and handed him another. The drinks and nibbles area was busy and Mandy offered out a Victoria sponge.

'Has no one given yer a drink yet?'

Mandy shook her head.

'Ha'way in the kitchen.'

In the kitchen, Mandy glanced at the vodka. 'Have yer got any tonic?'

She'd only spoken to Mandy a few times before, and as she fixed her a drink, she couldn't be arsed with small talk, so she said, 'Gan on then, tell uz wot happened wer the squatter.'

Mandy smiled as if realising why she'd been invited. As she tipped vodka into a red beaker, then rifled in the bags for some mixer, Mandy didn't disappoint. As it turned out, everyone in the street had taken a stroll up the path to read the squatters' notice, so when Martin and Bingo Moose got out of the taxi, everyone was at their window, door, or gate. Mandy said Martin shouted and banged and kicked the front door, then the snakes came out and they went inside. The next day it all kicked off when Bingo Moose lobbed a half-brick at the living room window, which missed and bounced off the frame.

She sloshed tonic into the beaker, 'Gan on.'

It was after the failed brick attempt that Bingo Moose scaled the porch, and according to Mandy, the big window was open, and she actually got inside before Norm threw her back out onto the porch roof.

'That food smells mint, man,' said Mandy, keen to end the interrogation.

She led her guest outside where the delicious air was full of grilling burgers. She noticed that the snakes next door had shut their upstairs windows. Ian was busy tending the grill and directing salad and bun traffic. She was determined that he would make it to catering college and grow up to be a man who was nothing like Billy.

Des had encouraged Ian to cook by jotting down his menu, which he stuck to the fridge. Ian then added to the menu 'kebab hell' next to which he drew a picture of his big sister with a sad face. She couldn't think of two worse things to be skewered on a stick than pineapple and prawns. Everything else on the fridge list sounded topper and she wondered how she was going to eat it all with only one stomach.

As Ian flipped the first batch of burgers onto a metal plate, Des shouted, 'Grub's up, folks.'

They didn't need telling twice. Mandy, her husband, and younger daughter were first to the banquet table, collecting a paper plate, plastic cutlery, and a piece of kitchen roll, before advancing to the pile of burgers and pyramid of twenty-four buttered buns, with twenty-four more in the kitchen. Jason, Meredith, and Marcel joined the queue, all drooling. As host, she hung back, and anyway, there were kebabs to come. She didn't want to fill up on burgers. She decided she'd ask for a bite of Jason's burger, as a sample, a starter, leaving room for one of each kebab, which, excluding 'kebab hell', were 'Steak Taco': steak, marinated in olive oil, crushed garlic, and finely chopped jalapenos, and skewered with corn, and red onions. 'Balsamic Mushrooms': grilled mushrooms with balsamic-soy glaze. 'Balsamic Steak': steak marinated in olive oil, crushed garlic, and rosemary, skewered with red onions, small round tomatoes, and bell peppers. There were eighteen lamb burgers made from expensive lamb mince with onion, garlic, and coriander, and there were twenty kebabs, of which only twelve were steak, versus the hungry mouths of seventeen people.

Mandy's family had reached the buns and were moving on to the sauces and salads, not including the older daughter who was at the white plastic table, her chair facing away. Also at the white plastic table was Ian's fat mate, who rocked back on his chair, and his fit mate, who touched the older daughter's stick-like arm as she talked.

Chloé hadn't moved from the tree and Jacob was running feral. She made her way across the garden, the plan: gather children, get burgers for children, deposit children on picnic blanket, take a bite of Chloé's lamb burger.

'Ha'way,' she said to Chloé, holding her arms up, 'jump.' Chloé slung both legs over the twisted branch. 'Ha'way down and have an Uncle Ian burger.'

With Jacob on her hip and Chloé by the scruff of her neck, she dragged and plonked them in the middle of the lawn, then sprinted to the utility room to get the tartan blanket. She was so fast that they hadn't moved, so she threw the blanket over their heads.

While they giggled and wiggled under the tartan sea, she went to the table, pushing in for plates and kitchen roll, before assembling a lamb burger in a bun on each plate. She covered one with yoghurt and mint dressing for Jacob and left the other one neat for Chloé. She'd taken a bite of Chloé's burger before she put it on the plate, and as she crossed the garden, she had a nibble on Jacob's.

'Mine's got a bite missin!' said Chloé.

'So's mine!' said Jacob.

'Aye, it wer the Lambton worm,' she said, wiping juice from her chin.

She found Michelle and Des conspiring in the kitchen with the kebabs and two cakes.

'Wee brought the chocolate cake?' she asked.

'Black Forest Gateau,' corrected Michelle. 'Meredith.'

'Ah wish yer hadn't been so quick ter sell the fridge,' she said to Des.

'Wot, turn down a good offer so wer can keep a couple of cakes cold for one afternoon?' said Des. 'Yer'll ah've ter mack dee wer *ye olde* fridge.'

Ye olde fridge was a sink of cold water with beers bobbing and a bottle of vodka standing in it. No good for cakes. Anyway, she was thinking about where to put the kebabs she was about to hive off the main tray and cook separately once she wasn't busy with bairns and guests and cakes. She put three kebabs onto a plate and hid them in the oven. She gave the main tray to Des. 'Can yer give these ter Ian?'

As she wiped Chloe's hacky face, she watched it play out at the food table. When the kebabs went on the fire, the drooling guests watched each drop of fat splash onto the coals.

Ian lined a plate up, then used a fork to scrape the food from the skewer, forming a pile of sizzling morsels and solving the mystery of how you eat kebabs without poking your eye out on a scadden metal prong. Then the locusts swarmed from both sides of the table and picked the kebab plate dry in a fork frenzy. When they drifted away, plates full and mouths stuffed, she got her hidden kebabs out of the oven.

Ian was busy eating the one steak kebab that he'd kept for himself.

'Still hot enough for these?' she said to him.

'Where did they come from?' Ian said. He put his food down and raked the black coals, churning up glowing embers. 'Be ten minutes.'

She went to see to Spider-Man and Batman, who were sat crossed-legged on the blanket like a pair of scruffy urchins. Chloé had made them another burger each and applied the top half of the bun to Jacob's and the bottom half of the bun to hers. She wiped yoghurt sauce from all over the blanket with kitchen roll, then folded the blanket in around them like a shrinking continent.

Mr and Mrs Murray were holding empty plates and empty drinks when they caught her eye and made their way over. Her knees clicked as she stood up. Chloé wiped her greasy hands on the leg of her jeans. 'How woz yer food?' she said to Mr and Mrs Murray.

'Ah've never had owt as nice as that off a barbeque before,' said Mr Murray, while Mrs Murray nodded. 'How old is yer brotha? Ian, isn't it?'

'Aye, Ian, he's sixteen, about ter dee his GCSEs.'

'Does he know what he wants ter do when he leaves?'

'Ah woz hopin he'd gan ter caterin college.' She opened both arms to encompass everyone's happy, greasy faces as evidence of Ian's ability.

Mr Murray smiled, rocking forward on his toes. 'He should have nee problem with those burgers.'

'If he applies,' she said. 'Some of the lads at school have been callin him a puff for cookin, so he chinned one of them. That's why ah wanted him ter dee the food today, ter relight his interest.'

'Ah work for Bass and there's plenty of blokes in the kitchen, most of our top chefs are men.'

'Yer work at Bass, the brewery?'

'Aye, for ower thirty years,' said Mr Murray. 'Ian should apply for an apprenticeship as a cook.'

'How does he dee that?'

'Ah could ring personnel, get them ter send him an application form, and look nee further for a reference. Ah'd be happy ter recommend him.'

She wanted to kiss Mr Murray. 'Did yer try his kebabs?' she said, knowing that he hadn't been quick enough.

'No,' he said, 'they smelled delicious.'

She could see Ian taking *her* kebabs off the fire and fork them onto a fresh plate. 'Yer luck's in,' she said, 'give uz a minute.'

She took the plate of steak taco, balsamic mushrooms, and balsamic steak from Ian and gave it to Mr Murray.

'These kebabs are heaven. Try them,' she said, assuming that they were.

While salivating for a feast she'd never taste, she thought about how good it would be if Ian got an apprenticeship at Bass.

After she cleared the meat-smeared plates into a bin bag and replenished the banquet table with Mr Kipling Bakewell tarts and fondant fancies, the guests descended like a pack of crows in *Hungry Horace*, pecking the lot to crumbs. Luckily, she'd stashed Meredith's home baked with love Black Forest Gateau in the oven away from the greedy bastards.

It was 8:04 on the oven clock. The hidden cake was the only edible thing on the premises. Chloé was asleep upstairs on a pile of quilts, Marcel and family and the grown-up neighbours had gone, and Sonya was shagging random Dave, hopefully not on a pile of quilts. Michelle and Darren left early while Jason, Ian, and his mates were listening to sweary music with the youngest daughter from over the road. The oldest daughter from over the road was standing warily against the kitchen wall, eyeing up the gateau like it was an unexploded bomb.

'That empty feelin inside yer belly that echoes up the hollow of yer neck and macks yer heed lose sense of everythin. It woz worst in the winter,' she said, as the soft cream and sponge yielded to the flimsy plastic knife. 'Like a hollow, shiverin, no one.' She slapped a slab of cream-slopping, booze-soaked cake onto a fresh paper plate. 'And that's why ah'm ganner eat this like a massive fucken gissy. Want some?'

'Aye, gan on then, ah'm fucken clammen,' said the sunken-eyed waif.

She turned the lights off in the house and went into the garden. Des was knotting a bin liner.

'Mates gone, lads upstairs,' she said, marvelling at the completely cleaned-up garden.

'Sonya and lover boy?'

'Gone.'

'Oh,' he said, remembering something important like he does. 'Forgot ter tell yer about me mam.'

Her heart thudded with dread. 'Wot about her?'

Seeing her stricken face, he blurted, 'It's not cancer.'

She exhaled, dropping her shoulders. 'Thank fuck.'

'It's worse than that. She's got a boyfriend.'

'Nor! That's mint, good for her.'

'She's a sixty-seven-year-old woman with one boob and a false hip.'

'Doesn't mean she can't enjoy herself. Who's the lucky fella?'

'Kenny.'

'Kenny the compere at the club?'

'That's the one.'

'Bless them. He must be, ooo—'

'Seventy-three.'

She lay on the damp grass, spreading her limbs like a starfish. Des lay next to her.

'Can yer hear them humpin in the next bedroom?'

'Ah might be spendin more time at yowers if that's okay?'

Her top was soaked so she rolled onto his warm chest. 'It's more than okay, why don't yer move in properly?'

He kissed her and stuck his cold hands down her jeans. He gazed up and said, 'Wanin gibbous.'

'Wot?'

'The moon, wanin gibbous.'

She didn't need to turn her face because she could see the whole of the night sky reflected in his eyes. 'Ah love you.'

'Ah love you too.'

Chapter 33

August 1995

The house was quieter now that Michelle and Darren had bought a three-bedroom semi at Chapple Garth, yet the middle floor was nosier now that Ian had moved from the attic to the back bedroom, with his stereo and horrible rave music. She missed Michelle's rent and now that Ian was sixteen, she missed his foster money. She'd also stretched the finances to buy two cottages in Millfield. It was good to get the brown properties 'under the board,' and it wasn't like she was going for Trafalgar Square and Fleet Street. In a market that was rising much faster than £200 every time you pass go, it would be mental not to buy.

Des was doing well with his kitchen business so was keen to buy an 'off-board' family property such as the one at Middle Herrington that had four bedrooms and stables. While Jason was delighted at the prospect of Mayfair living close to him, it would be unfeasible to move Mayfair from Great Lumley where she was being trained to showjump with Heather and used by the riding school. In return for letting them use Mayfair, she got lessons on horses suitable for, in Jason's words, a 'placker rider' on 'happy hacks' that 'tacks nee skill.'

When Eileen said that she was living vicariously through Jason, she looked it up in the dictionary to find that she had indeed spent her life imagining herself doing what Jason was actually doing. He was top of the class at Penshaw, or as he put it, 'made the lasses weep,' and went to Great Lumley to ride Mayfair as often as he could. Unlike Jason, she didn't have a competitive streak so was content with being the shittest rider in the less-able adult group, not that she got to ride often. Jason said that she shouldn't care if Maddy tells everyone that she nicked her coat, and that all the posh twats call them the Addams Family anyway. She'd heard them clicking their fingers as if being common made her deaf and stupid. Des said that he was chuffed to be Gomez while Jason decked it, and said, 'More like Lurch.'

*

Chloé was in bed, Des was on a job, and she was processing the mound of washing on the dining room table, when she sensed a ghostly presence that made her shiver. She looked up and saw Ian standing there. The snarl on his lip and his pin-hole eyes made him look like

Billy, risen from the grave. Ian was nothing like Billy mostly, but when it came to money, he was a chip off the old block. Thanks to the glowing reference from Mr Murray, he'd gone straight from school to the kitchen at the Barnes, where he lasted for eighteen months before going to a pub in Durham to cook gastro food, whatever that is. She'd given him the Panda so he could drive there, and she was forever giving him money. As good as he had it, his half of Mam's money in the savings account was gnawing away at his soul. Ian had picked up the scent of notes, turning him from nice little brother into an asshole who wasn't going to back down until he got what was rightly his.

'Ah'm movin in wer Lynsey,' he said in a low, I'm angry, you're in the firing line voice.

'Lynsey? Yer've only been seein her for a few months. Is she pregnant?'

'Nor,' he bit.

'Eeee, ower little Ian movin in wer a lass.'

Ian pulled his self-pity face, bowing and shaking his down-trodden head. 'Here-man, ah could really dee wer that cash reet now mind.'

She sighed. 'Yer not ganner shurrup until yer get it, are yer?'

'Nope.'

In the kitchen, he stood over her while she got her cheque book out of the drawer. 'Yer'll have ter find a pen.'

She'd never seen him move so quick.

As she scraped the food scraps into the bin, she felt sick and had to take her foot off the peddle to stop the bin stink.

Ian returned with a navy felt tip, which worked fine: two thousand, four hundred pounds. She ripped the cheque from the pad and he whipped it from her fingers.

'Dinnet cash it till next week, ah need ter transfer some funds ter cover it.'

'Are yer alreet?' he said.

'That bin hums, made uz want ter yark.'

'Yer face's gone all mottled like Mam's used to when she woz pregnant wer Jason.'

Chapter 34

May 1996

They found the perfect house in a field near Shiney Row, or rather they'd seen the plan for the exclusive development with four detached properties, all of which were expected to sell before being built. After weeks of debate and calculations, they decided to wait until after she gave birth before making plans. When she had Edward Jordan, everything was cancelled for the foreseeable.

When people said that she was lucky Chloé was an easy baby, she'd think, looking after a baby isn't *easy*. EJ was ten weeks old and now she realised that Chloé was as easy as Sunday morning. With Chloé, she got six hours of sleep, broken by one or two feeds that took a minute, then she'd go back down. Her beautiful boy EJ cat-napped for forty minutes here and there, and she'd tried her best to breastfeed, but a friggin' blue whale couldn't produce enough milk to fill him. Between naps, he liked to play. He wasn't a screamer, he'd settle easily on Mam or Dad's shoulder, always with his eyes open, ready for cuddles and nursery rhymes.

'What do you do if you cannot find a loo, in an English country gar-a-den? Pull down your pants and fertilize the plants, in an English country gar-a-den.'

EJ liked this one and so did she because it had lots of verses, meaning she could have a half-sleep while singing it.

'Look out for the nettles as you're watering the petals, in an English country gar-a-den. Then get a leaf and wipe your underneath, in an English country gar-a-den. Make them hold their noses as you duck behind the roses, in an English country gar-a-den. Then get a spade and bury what you made, in an English country gar-a-den.'

Before she had EJ she'd lie in bed and listen to Jason get ready to go out to Penshaw. Last winter, he'd leave before sunrise, and as the wind lashed rain against the windows, she'd snuggle into Des, feeling bad about Jason mucking out before school, although she would've done the same given the chance. Now she slept downstairs with EJ, or rather, she stayed awake. The sun had been streaming round the edges of the shite blackout blind for over an hour when the first sleeping git emerged. It was always Jason, 6:10 out of bed, 6:20 kitchen, 6:25 quick EJ cuddle, 6:30 out of the door. The waking of Chloé used to be the start of her day, so she always willed her to sleep for another five minutes. Now Chloé's waking was the end of the nightshift, so she willed her to wake up.

When at last Chloé came clattering down, shouting, 'Mam, breakfast,' she took EJ up and passed him to Daddy in the big bed, her eyes burning in anticipation of sweet sleep.

Once she had Chloé stationed at the bench with Coco Pops in the blue bowl with a small spoon, she mined the clean washing mountain to find the bairn some socks. When Coralie arrived, she sent Chloé out, trying not to seem excited to wave her off despite singing, 'Hallelujah, Hallelujah, Hallelujah,' on the inside. She'd dreamed about this moment since yesterday. Des now had EJ until 10:30. Two whole hours of luxury sleep.

It took until midday to get out of the house. EJ had screamed at the top of his tiny lungs for an hour, then filled two nappies. No sooner had the pram wheels touched the pavement, his tiny eyes closed. Bless him, he was worn out, he needed to recharge his tiny baby batteries ready for when they got to Nana's. She went to Nana's three mornings a week for some lovely golden sleep and sometimes she could get four hours.

As she yanked the pram backwards up Nana's steps, Gavin's girlfriend Gemma turned into the square in a Polo with baby Jamie who was two months older than EJ. She hadn't seen Gemma for over a year, although she'd seen Jamie when he was first born when Gavin brought him to Nana's. His name was James, changed to Jamie to avoid being Jimmy. That was when she decided to call her boy bump Edward because Nana would be chuffed with James and Edward, the next generation.

'Eeee, how's me bonnie lad?' said Nana to EJ, who had his eyes open. Nana lifted EJ out of the pram.

She carted two bags of EJ stuff inside, which was an increase on the one bag she had for Chloé. EJ needed so much more gear, what with him shitting and puking more, and then there was the stuff for bottle feeds. Instead of sprinting up the stairs, she went into the kitchen. She'd give it five minutes before she sloped off to bed. She lay her head on the bench, and closed her eyes. When she opened them, Gemma was next to her with her head on the bench, eyes closed, twitching. She gave her a prod.

'Gemma.'

Gemma jumped, drool dripping from her lip. 'Am ah alive?'

As a fellow living dead, she nodded. 'Jamie not a sleeper?'

'Fuck,' said Gemma, 'when Laura-Jane was a babbie, ah woz torn apart by guilt when ah woz workin on the cruise ships. With Jamie, ah dream about six hours kip in a hot cabin. He never sleeps.'

'Wot did he weigh?'

Gemma put her head back on the bench. 'Second baby'll be like shellin peas they said. Eight pounds he woz, three pounds heavier than Laura-Jane.'

'Here-man, Chloé woz tiny, she woz four months before she woz the weight that EJ woz when he woz born. Thank fuck for the epidural.'

'Twenty stitches. Yae?'

'Fifteen.'

'Ah pittled mesel in the Co-op yesterday,' said Gemma. 'Next ter the breakfast cereal.'

She put her arm around Gemma. 'Der yer think yer can mack it upstairs?'

'Is there a bed free?'

'It has ower names on it.'

'Might be safer ter stay here than ter cross a room wer EJ and Jamie in it.'

She peeped into the living room and reported, 'Jamie's squashin his slavery chops onto Grandar's belly and EJ's on Nana's shoulder.'

'Run or stealth?' said Gemma.

'Both, ha'way.'

She closed the bedroom blinds as Gemma flopped on the bed.

'This is new,' she said, lying next to Gemma on Nana's quilt. 'When wer woz bairns, she'd bind us under layers of striped cotton sheets like mummies, then put a candlewick bedspread on top that was tucked in tight.'

'Yer couldn't dee that ter ower Jamie. He's Houdini escapin from a swaddle.'

They watched each other's heavy eyelids close.

*

She was in a police cell, but only it was the Bede school bogs, which was thick of fag smoke with graffiti all over the tiled walls that said *shop at Binn*s next to an Empire billing for *Bobby Thompson Tonight*. She was perched on the edge of a sink that was full of bloody fanny pads, so she swung her legs so she wouldn't fall in. Fitz from *Cracker* was perched on the end sink and behind the smoke she could see Mrs Watson's wizened face. It was as if they hadn't noticed the pyramid of used tampons or the diarrhoea splats up the walls; it was like it was fine, normal. 'I can read you like a book,' said Fitz, 'little Paula sat in the corner, eating her curds and whey.' She wanted to shout, 'It was an accident,' but the smell of shit blocked her voice, and still Fitz smiled as if he hadn't noticed the stench. She tried to wake up, but EJ was in her arms, tumbling, tumbling, tumbling, she stooped to catch him and he turned into Billy's head. There was something on her face and she woke with a jolt to find Des dangling stinky EJ over her.

Short, hot, weird sleep was better than no sleep. She pressed the dirty washing into the overflowing basket and positioned the baby bouncer chair on the bathroom floor. With EJ strapped in, she had about three minutes before he started screaming.

'All of a sudden, a great big puddin, came flyin through the air; it missed me mar, and hit me dar, and knocked him

off the chair,' she sang as she got dried. She put a damp flannel on his big bald head, buying a minute to put on some pants and a bra that were both too big. Her maternity leggings were fine if she ruffled the belly panel down, adding a new top from Des that she wouldn't be seen dead in, yet she wore it every time she went out. She was too tired to care about standards.

She suspected that EJ barfed his bottle of highly processed milk substitute because he enjoyed being sung to and rocked in his bouncer with her foot while she made another bottle. The health visitor laughed at the suggestion that a newborn could mastermind extra nursery rhymes and bottles. The big squishy had a fresh nappy, a clean babygrow, and a dummy stuck in his mouth. Dummies are genius. She loved dummies. And disposable nappies.

When she was a kid, the worst day of the week was Friday because that's when she was born; her logic was that if Friday didn't exist, then neither would she, and that would be helpful to everybody. Having EJ made every day a happy day, even Fridays when there was no sneaky sleep plan and she had to go out to collect the rent. As she pushed the pram, she admired her boy as he waved his tiny fists across his face, gurgle smiling as he made the light appear and disappear. She monitored the dangers as she battled the pavements, manoeuvring her wheels around dog shit – if a car mounted the kerb now, she'd heroically throw the pram into a garden while taking the force of the blow; if a rottweiler leapt into the pram, she'd gouge its eye out with her finger. She cursed the booming exhausts that made EJ jump out of his skin: my loud car exhaust makes me? A) cool; B) a cunt.

Most times when she passed Peacock Street West, she pushed on down the main road because, 'The murderer always returns to the scene of the crime.' They'd moved Margaret out to Astral House and the last she knew, Gail and Dawn were living at Ford Estate. She wouldn't put it past Margaret to stalk the scene, still watching, waiting to put the pieces together: the sound of the bath running, the wet towel on the bedroom floor, yet the body was filthy and unkempt; the impossibility of Billy to tie a noose never mind construct a web of fishing lines. Today she decided to wander down Peacock Street West to look at the maisonettes-come-student accommodation, hoping perhaps this would set her demons to rest. As she passed Steels, fear ran down her spine as she thought about the clever new guy in Sunderland CID going over the case in a Scottish accent. 'There was no misadventure in Billy Hart's death – it was *mur-der*.'

She kept going past the tyre place with curls of barbed wire across the roof. Nothing had changed on that side of the road. On the other side, the gloomy bricks of the maisonettes had been cheered up with squares of white render. She stopped outside of her flat.

In the recess above where the kitchen had been, they'd built an extension up to the top floor, and the front door was a window. She wondered if they'd taken the stairs out and made them all one-level flats. 'These are the artefacts found under the stairs at the murder scene.'

Yesterday, she'd dreamt that the man from the post office found a blood-stained sword under the kitchen floor. When she tried to flee, she couldn't move her legs, so she had to bite the floor and drag herself along with her teeth. Dreaming confirmed that she'd been properly asleep, which was good, she supposed. Not so good were her deepest fears being dredged up so vividly that she couldn't tell if she was asleep or awake.

She regretted spending valuable energy observing a building with a couple of students kicking a ball about in the carpark. It didn't look like a murder scene. Life had moved on.

A chippy who Des knew and his missus Christine had rented the Ravensworth Street cottage from the beginning. Christine was always welcoming, keen for her landlady to come in and see how spotless the place was. She hadn't put the rent up like she had with Milburn Street because she liked her tenants and wanted them to stay. As usual, Christine counted out forty-two quid in cash and offered her a cup of tea, which she declined. The man renting Milburn Street was a weirdo who left his rent cheque with the woman next door, who was mostly vexed at being part of the arrangement. Mr Weirdo didn't want to pay monthly or by standing order, so she'd decided that when he moved out, she'd put in the contract that rent was to be paid monthly by standing order only.

After bagging the rent, she made her way to David's video rental shop.

She hadn't been in the shop since before EJ was born, so she cast her mind back, trying to think if there was anywhere to lie down for ten minutes. As she struggled inside with the pram, Lisa put her nail file down and came from behind the counter.

'Eeee, ha'way in, how's me bonnie lad?'

She gave her a mother's look.

'Ha'way baba,' said Lisa, lifting EJ from the pram. 'Come give yer Aunty Lisa a cuddle.'

Lisa perched on her stool behind the counter with EJ on her shoulder. At the side was a telly next to two video players stacked on top of each other. Lisa un-paused the bottom one and the blokes on the telly started to move. 'Have yer seen *Pulp Fiction*?'

'Nor.'

'It's got John Travolta in it.'

'Has it?'

'Aye,' said Lisa, waving for her to come watch.

There was a black dude with mutton chops talking about cheeseburgers with John Travolta in the background, who had put some weight on since Danny Zuko. Then the black dude shot the kid, making her jump. *'I'm sorry, did I break your concentration.'*

Lisa patted EJ's back.

'So, there's nee singin and dancin in this then?' she said.

'Nor,' laughed Lisa, feeding a tape into the other video machine. 'They nivver rewind them, lazy bastards.'

'Is David here?'

'Aye, he's out the back, gan through. We'll be fine, won't wer?' said Lisa, jiggling EJ.

David had expanded his video enterprise well beyond an estate car. He had thousands of films – everything from *Bambi* to *Driller Killer*, you could find it at Dave's Video.

'Aye-up, sis,' he said.

He was sitting in a high-backed leather swivel chair in front of a huge screen surrounded by expensive-looking computers, like a supervillain at the helm of downfall headquarters. Along the wall were shelves stacked with cardboard boxes with music names written on in felt tip. In every other space there were boxes with TDK CD-RW printed on them.

'Nice kit, man,' she said.

He pressed a button on the tall black box and five CD trays popped out. He plucked the CDs from the trays, then flung them at her one at a time. 'Put them in the Joshua Tree box, there's a luv.'

'Are they full of copies?' she said, casting her eye across the top shelf, 'Portishead, Dummy, Pulp, Different Class.' She reached up and plucked a disc from each. Leftism, Leftfield, Debut, Bjork, Faith, George Michael.

'Fuck me, David. This is amazin; it's like supermarket sweep meets HMV.' She stuck her hand into Screamadelica, then moved along. 'Nor, nah, not The Lighthouse Family, and on the same shelf as Snoop Dog, shame on you.'

The next shelf down was best of albums. Best of UB40, Best of the Sixties. 'Is yer entire best of shelf copied from the CDs yer took from Martin?'

'Here-man, they're a reet money spinner. Four quid for an album, six quid for a best of, and double that for a double album.'

'Have yer got any cases for these?' she said, clasping the silver discs that were smiling rainbows.

He nodded to the box of plastic cases under his desk.

'Yer'll end-up in trouble, yer knar that?'

'Trouble,' he said, swivelling to face her. 'Ah'm already in trouble.'

'Alreet,' she said, 'dinnet bite me heed off. In trouble, how like?'

'The world-wide-web has halved me porn sales.'

There was a screeching noise, then a ship's steering wheel appeared on the screen. David typed *sex*.

'Look,' he said, as a list of sex stuff came on the screen, *Hot babes, SEX, Soapy tit wank!*

'Is that the world-wide-web?'

'Aye, watch this.'

The screen went blank, then an image rolled slowly down: hair, face, mouth open, tongue out, big knockers, and then she couldn't work out what she was seeing. 'Is that her blurt or her cervix?' she asked, putting her head sideways.

'Exactly.'

'Where der the pictures come from?'

'A server.'

'Wot's that when it's at home?'

'Like a telephone exchange but full of mega-computers called servers that store the webpages.'

She'd heard Eileen bending Frank's ear about how they should network the computers and upgrade the hardware and software. Eileen mentioned that the world-wide-web was good for watching interest rates, yet had said nothing about a mega-computer full of porn.

'How der the webpages get there?' she asked.

'Anyone can put a webpage on a server for people ter see.'

'Where's the server?'

'In a room on an industrial estate somewhere.'

'Who owns it?'

'Pipex.'

'Since when did yae knar so much about it?'

'Since ah lost all me pervy customers,' he said, clicking his mouse. The lady parts disappeared, and the ship's steering wheel reappeared. 'All yer need is a computer, a modem, and a phone line. Goodbye Dave's

Videos, hello sex dot com.' He put a CD on his little finger and blew the dust of it. 'Ah'm arnly deein the bootlegs ter get some cash together for me cyber room.'

'Cyber room?'

'Desks wer computers where people come in and ah charge them ter gan on the world-wide-web.'

'Wot? They have a ham shank in the shop?'

'Nor,' he laughed, 'they dinnet look at porn, they gan in chatrooms and send messages, hods of stuff.'

He pushed the keyboard towards her. 'Search for whatever yer like.'

She wiggled her fingers.

'It doesn't have ter be sex. There's horses and stuff.'

She typed *interest-only mortgage.*

Chapter 35

August 1996

It felt strange walking through town, like she'd left some major organs at home. With no baby to push and no chatty ten-year-old hanging from her elbow, she swung her arms and skipped, uncaring that people were giving her funny looks – they didn't know that if she walked normally she'd fall asleep standing up. The training day was at the Mowbray, so she thought about going for a lie down on a bench in the park.

Since she went on maternity leave, Frank had called every other week to keep her up to date with work things, apart from she knew he was mostly trying to make sure that she came back. He was in no danger of receiving her notice anytime soon. She couldn't wait to get back to work for a rest. On the phone last week, he said that everyone in the company was going to a training day and there would be dinner and coffee.

As she rounded the corner, she could see Harry and Derek going into the Mowbray. Over the road was the pebble-dashed multistorey carpark that stood where the Victoria Hall had been before it was obliterated by a Nazi parachute mine. It was built in 1872 by Mr Backhouse, as in Backhouse Park, and was a grand theatre where all the famous people performed. It was a shame about the health and safety failure of 1883 when a generation of the town's children were crushed to death. It was impossible not to imagine 183 twisted bodies laid out in the dress circle, Walter aged ten, Margaret aged three, the father looking for Isabella, James, and William, his full brood, gone. As she went up the grubby white steps of the Mowbray, she was weeping for the lost children like the crumbling statue in the cemetery.

'Paula,' said voices across the ocean on which she was floating. Through burning eyes, she saw Eileen and Frank, smiling and waving at her like people on a lifeboat.

'Good to see you,' said Frank, giving her hug.

'Good ter see you, or it would be if ah could see properly.'

'Caffeine,' said Eileen. 'Are yer drinkin coffee?'

'Ah'm totally drinkin coffee, cold mainly.'

Nana still called the Mowbray the Palatine and said that it was full of 'down and outs.' There was nothing shabby about the leather Chesterfield in the lobby and she thought that if everyone was engrossed in training, she could sneak out and have a lie down.

The first session was more of a sales pitch than training. A new product was coming in September where landlords can get a mortgage to buy a property to let. The strong coffee perked her up for half an hour, then her eyes started to wibble-wobble and her sight and hearing went slow and blurry. She made it to the break, then decided to go for a sleep, all she needed was a twenty-minute powernap. Her prayers were answered with a chaise longue in the ladies. She lay down, tucked her knees up, and closed her eyes.

She was sound asleep and drooling when Eileen nudged her to say that food was being served in the restaurant. She had quiche and salad, then as much coffee as she could drink before they were put into groups and taken to a huge bedroom of faded grandeur that had been set up with desks, chairs, and computers with 15-inch monitors.

'Welcome everyone, I'm Janet,' said the IT trainer from *Re:mark*. 'In front of you is a personal computer with an Intel Pentium processor, which is running Windows 95 on an NT operating system.' She had a Yorkshire accent and tits that could conquer the world. 'What machines do you have at LJ Finance?'

'Everyone has an IBM, some of them are knockin on a bit though, the computers that is, not the staff,' said Frank.

'Windows 3.1?' asked Janet.

They all laughed. The poor woman must've been confused.

Eileen explained, 'We didn't get IBMs until three years ago, and most of us are still runnin Windows 3.0 on a 386.'

'You might be,' Alex chipped in. 'I'm still on a 286. MS-DOS. No mouse. Imagine that? It's ridiculous.'

'At least we've got Excel 2,' said Eileen, 'which is an improvement on ViewSheet – one small step for mankind, one huge step for LJ Finance.' She chuckled and everyone stared like she'd returned from the dead.

'Yer not wrong, Eileen. ViewSheet wasn't even a spreadsheet, it was like squared paper from the juniors.'

Frank scowled like he regretted inviting the revolution. 'Those computers were a big investment for a small company at a time when a pencil and a calculator would've done.'

'The late eighties were a time when everyone was using Lotus 1-2-3 and WordPerfect on MS-DOS systems,' said Eileen, 'and we upgraded our typewriters and ledgers to shitty 8-bit Acorns with 2 megabytes of RAM.'

'I remember that the Acorns cost a *shitty* 1,800 pounds in 1987 and that's without the peripherals,' said Frank. He addressed Janet directly, holding his arm up to Eileen to block her input. 'We're upgradin to Intel chips.'

Janet was quick to regain control. 'That's good because today we are going to learn about what's new in MS Office, starting with Excel 5, then Outlook.'

'We're gettin email?' said Eileen.

'Eileen, we've been discussin this for months, let the lady continue with the trainin,' said Frank.

The final session was in the dining hall with everyone gathered round one computer. 'Has anyone heard of the world-wide-web?' said Janet.

There was a murmur, then Kyle, the young new financial advisor, said, 'Is that computer connected?'

'Yes, you'll all get a go in a minute.' Janet continued. 'Using the Netscape browser, you can access all the information stored on the world-wide-web. Can anybody tell me what a search engine is?'

Kyle raised his hand. 'Like a Yellow Pages that uses meta-tags.'

'Can you give me an example of the type of thing you can search for?' said Janet, with a hint of, 'anal fantasy, Kyle?'

Frank jumped in with, 'Interest rates,' making everyone groan.

'Like Kyle said,' said Janet, 'the world-wide-web is a Yellow Pages that links to webpages. Anyone know how it works?'

She put her hand up like being at school. 'It's like a telephone exchange, but full of mega-computers called servers that store the webpages.'

Janet looked impressed. 'Have you used it before, Paula?'.

'Once.'

'Why don't you sit here and search for something, anything you like.'

She knew what to put and she knew how to spell it, *schizophrenia*. She expected there to be nothing because it's not something that people tend to talk about, so was surprised when a list appeared. Janet gabbled about modems as a website scrolled slowly down. As each sentence appeared, she read it, absorbing as much as she could. *Compared with the general population in the UK, life expectancy among people with schizophrenia is reduced by an average of 14 years.*

'Right then, who wants a go next?' said Janet, ousting her from the place she'd been searching for all of her life.

Chapter 36

December 1997

The childminder called her out of work at three because EJ was exploding at both ends. She got stuck in traffic with him screaming and reeking so bad that she had to open the window. Then there was no consideration for not parking outside of the home that contains a mother and monster child. Most of the people on the street knew not to vex a sleep-deprived woman with a bag of toddler turds, but not Mr BMW from *nine* doors down. Luckily for him, she had her hands full.

She clattered inside with EJ on her shoulder, and peeled off his shitty joggers straight into the kitchen bin. She ran the bath with him on her hip, and he perked up a bit in the water, then crashed face-down in the middle of the big bed. Her heart burst as she watched him sleep. She would've curled up beside him if she wasn't so freakin' busy. If she relaxed, the whole house of shit would collapse, so she kept going, walking from room to room wondering which to tidy first.

It wouldn't be long before Jason would be home, shedding hay and treading clarts into the carpet. Today was netball so Chloé wouldn't be home until five and Marcel insisted on picking her up and dropping her off even though he had to drive from Spennymoor. Before Christmas, Chloé didn't want to go to Marcel's for a couple of weekends in a row because there was so much going on with her friends, in each other's bedrooms, listening to music, going into town, hanging about in shops and trying on clothes. There was nothing to do at Marcel's and she'd long since tired of Meredith's overenthusiasm for baking, dance, archaeology, knitting, *The Sound of Music*, etc. Since starting at St Anthony's, Chloé had got the bus with her mates from round the doors rather than get a lift from Coralie. Heck knows where they would've ended-up without the Wilkinsons' kindness, yet she was glad that the school lifts had stopped. The money had stopped too, or at least the direct payments had. Ken let everyone know that he was putting money away for Chloé's future, bless him.

She kicked the mound of shoes against the wall and transferred the washing from the computer desk to the dining room table. She'd bought a Pentium 200 through her property business. Everyone at work told her to set up a company to manage her houses, and now PHDB properties Ltd had a portfolio worth £264K gross and £41K net. Her mates called her 'Paula and her properties' as a funny nickname with undertones of bitterness. She'd used her sales bonus and the equity in her brown properties as deposits on a couple of three-bedroom houses near the ski slope. Symington Gardens and Scarborough Road were her orange properties. Des was long-suffering of her Monopoly-based approach, even though it made perfect sense. Every month the tenant pays your mortgage and with a buy-to-let mortgage you can use the equity in one property as a deposit against another. What's not to like?

When she dialled-up AOL, the modem whined like an electronic cat being strangled. As she waited for Netscape to load, she folded clothes. She wasn't surprised that David's cybercafé had a queue on evenings and weekends. David had sold his stock of videos and dodgy CDs, and Des had helped him to refit the shop with six computer bays. The backroom was stacked with cans of pop from the cash and carry, and at 150% mark-up, David was raking it in. He was right about the world-wide-web being popular. She was obsessed with a chatroom where people from America talked about their mental families. She loved the bulletin board. It was like Eamonn Andrews with his red book, 'Paula Hasting, *This is Your Life*.'

Suzy23: when I was thirteen my father decided to go to Russia to be a spy and I remember him walking out of the house in his black coat, carrying his briefcase. A month later he was caught shoplifting Wieners from Walmart in San Diego. Mom and me had to drive 600 miles to get him.

Goatboy: when I was a kid all the adults would act strange around me and not talk about my pa's illness. They'd joke and make out that it was normal to think that baseball scores were a secret code from Che Guevara. He had so many insane ideas, one linked to the other, it was hard to keep up.

Boston_JRX: my big brother was smart at math, captain of the football team, etc. In his final semester at Dartmouth, he walked into a police station and confessed to the murder of a kid in Maine. He was released after two hours on account of there being no evidence. My brother begged his friends to stop him from committing murders and he barricaded himself into his room – that's when they called my father to come and take him home. Before my father got there, my brother took the bus to Norwich, walked into the police station, and confessed to the assassination of Kennedy. Next day, his body was pulled out of the Connecticut River.

> Joanie_Queen_of_Scots: my sister was sectioned after voices told her to set fire to our school.

She was busy reading about other schizo families when the gang appeared in a cloud of noise. She welcomed Marcel inside as Chloé and her mate dumped their bags and clomped up to her room.

'Coffee?' she said to Marcel, her heart sinking.

'Have yer got time?' he said.

'Ha'way,' she went into the kitchen, thinking *go away I'm up to my eyes in it.* She put the kettle on, then pulled the biggest saucepan and the frying pan off their hooks and plonked them on the hob. Marcel took a stool, bedding in for a moan.

'How's Jacob gettin on at school?' she asked, bracing herself.

After tea, Jason put EJ to bed, then mooched off to his bedroom, and Chloé spent half an hour on the phone to a mate from down the road, then spent an hour in the bathroom. After tidying the kitchen, she flopped in the messy living room and half-watched the nine o'clock news, trying to enjoy a moment of telly despite half-listening for EJ signals. When Des's keys jangled, she prayed for EJ not to wake up, get up, and go his ends.

They tip-toed into the kitchen where Des molested her against the fridge until the lobster magnet clattered to the floor. There was a rumble from above. 'Ah'll gan check on him,' said Des. She put a pie in the oven and opened a tin of peas.

Des reappeared, having had a shower and changed in less than three minutes. 'Ah wouldn't worry about him, he's flat out.'

'Ah woz called into the nursery today. Sickness and diarrhoea. He cannet gan back until he's two days clear.'

'How woz he toneet?'

'He was champion at teatime, shovelled it in, then crashed.'

'Good news,' he said with furrowed brow, implying bad news. He set down a piece of paper on the bench. 'It's a plan.'

'Ah can see that,' she said, looking at the plan of a house.

'Ah quoted on some carpentry work for the extension, next thing, ah hears on the grapevine that the bloke's decided ter sell. Not on the market yet, but ah've got the keys if yer want ter have a butcher's.'

'Where is it?'

'And that's the great thing,' he said, the same way he did when he said they were viewing a 'great' house in Houghton that was in Washington. 'It's off Cocken Lane.'

'Great Lumley?' she said, trying to act excited while feeling disappointed.

'Three bedrooms and needs some renovation. There's plannin permission for a kitchen, utility, and downstairs netty, and upstairs, a triple aspect master bedroom with walk-in wardrobe and ensuite, and another double bedroom.'

'Room for a stable?'

'There already is stablin,' he said, switching the architect's drawing for an aerial flat plan of boxes in fields. 'There,' he said, pointing at a shaded square that was half a mile away from the rectangle that was the house.

'That's part of the property?'

'All of this is part of the property.'

'Wot? All of that land?' she said, marvelling at the size of the fields compared with the size of the rectangle.

'Forty-two acres.'

*

The reason she'd never seen 'Nettle Lodge' during the many times she'd drove down or rode a horse down Cocken Lane is because it was a quarter of a mile down a dirt track that wasn't meant for cars. There was a fly-tipped mattress in the hedge, and as the track narrowed, the hedges got denser until it was like being in a hedge carwash.

'On foot from here,' said Des.

She got scratched to buggery as she squeezed along the side of the car and onto the dirt track. She let Des unload EJ as she strode off in search of a pretty country lodge with horses in the paddock. The dirt track ended at a padlocked gate that was bordered by six-foot high bushes with thorns that could have your eye out. She climbed over the gate and into an empty field. In the distance on the other side of the three-foot thick bushes was a house. Unlike the stonework on the house down the lane, or any of the traditional cottages around the Finchale Priority area, 'Nettle Lodge' was built of what looked like council house bricks.

EJ laughed at the squeak of the gate as Des pushed it open.

'Wot der yer think?' said Des.

'Ah didn't expect it ter look like an abandoned council house.'

'It'll be rendered the same as the extension. White like a country cottage.'

'The dirt track isn't big enough ter get a car down.'

'Wait till ah've hacked down the hawthorns and brambles. The car's parked six foot from the front door.'

'Is it?'

'Here-man, with all the bushes gone,' he said, waving his arm along the deforestation project, 'wer can put a driveway in.'

EJ sat on Des's shoulders as they clomped through the long grass, stopping at the edge of a swamp that stretched to the gable end of the 'cottage.'

'This is where the extension will be,' said Des.

'Where from?'

'Here,' he said, stamping his feet.

'Wot, from here to the side of the house?'

'Aye.'

As she squinted, a vision of the future emerged from the bog. 'That's *massive*.'

The front was so overgrown with hawthorns that they had to go in the back. First was a tiny kitchen with green units from the 50s, brown wallpaper from the 60s, and a rusty boiler from the Grim Reaper. Beyond this was a hall with bushes pushed against the glass porch creating a *Day of the Triffids* vibe. The staircase was probably rotten under the disgusting carpet.

'Rip this out,' said Des, 'and tack down the ceilin ter mack the hall double height.'

'And yer said wer could have wooden floors and painted walls – absolutely nee carpets or wallpaper.'

'Why don't yer gan see the bedrooms and ah'll stay here wer the bairn,' said Des. 'Careful on the stairs; they dinnet look safe.'

The first bedroom was huge with pink striped wallpaper and bare floorboards that were in good nick and would probably polish well. The next bedroom was huge with green painted walls and a sink that was hanging off the wall and covered in cobwebs. Des said that the owner's dad bought the place in the 40s and lived here until he died five years ago. She ventured into the bathroom, wary of the walking frame, pile of ashes, and charred leg wearing a black slipper. It was that type of house. There were no spontaneously combusted body parts in the huge bathroom; only a loo, bath, and sink on opposite walls, miles away from each other. The last bedroom was down a dark corridor that smelled of fish. She looked through the missing window across the field that stretched into the fog. She had to own this strange country estate. This was the extra dark blue property, a bonus that's available to those who play the game for long enough. She turned her face to the heavens, 'Hey Dad, ah'll buy it.'

The living room was long with an entire wall covered in stonework surrounding a small gas fire. In the middle of the opposite wall was a French door that was so filthy, they couldn't see out.

'Tack this scabby thing out,' said Des, handing over EJ, who was keen to be let loose. He flicked the lever and hauled it open. 'Conservatory here, then a patio. Wer could fence some of the field off and mack a lawn, wot der yer think?'

'Wot is this place? Wot's it deein here?'

The surrounding field was mostly head high with nettles that were making a good comeback against the lodge. Des did his best Indiana Jones, beating a path with a stick, getting stung to bits, much to her and EJ's amusement, until EJ got a slug on his face, and she had to flick it off.

They followed as hero Daddy hacked his way to the brick outhouse rising from the tall grass.

'Wot is it?' she said.

'Dunno,' said Des, taking EJ from her arms.

She kicked the rotten door with excitement at the prospect that they'd stumbled across a stash of things that gain value in an abandoned outbuilding such as whisky or a Picasso. There was a rusty motorbike and some tins of paint.

They pressed on through the long grass until they reached a tumbled down stone wall which they scrambled over. Beyond the wall, the grass was shorter and there was a path leading into the fog. The sound of wet tyres on the A1 hummed in the distance and the squawk of crows made the bleakness feel eery.

'Shame it's foggy,' said Des. 'It's hard ter appreciate the size of the place.'

'Me legs can appreciate the size of the place. Ah dinnet fancy a half mile hike ter the stables every day.'

In the distance the stables looked like a nuclear bunker. Close up the stables looked like a nuclear bunker.

'Wot der yer think?' asked Des.

'We'll be sorted if there's a war.'

'Aye, it's a bit bunkerish.'

'A bit! It's made from concrete.'

'Four stalls and a tack room, wot more der yer want?'

'Doors.'

'Picky cow.'

'How long der yer reckon it'll tack ter dee the work?'

Des sucked air through his teeth. 'Eight months, max.'

Chapter 37

June 1999

Ten months behind plan, she was glad to be leaving Mount Road, not least because her family had wreaked such havoc that she'd become, as Chloé said, 'A pariah.'

Her thirteen-year-old daughter was quick to reassure her, 'Dinnet worry Mam, Jesus woz a pariah and look how much joy he brought ter the world.' She looked up *pariah* in the dictionary and was unsurprised to learn that she was 'A person despised or rejected by society: an outcast'. In her defence, as she pointed out to the nebby cow from over the road, Jason was her brother, not her son, and it takes two to tango.

While Jason was still at school there'd been a rumour he'd got a lass pregnant. Along with a few other lads, he sweated it out until she popped the sprog and named a lad who denied being there when seven lads shagged her, or as Jason said, 'Gave her a roastin.' This got him a clip from Des, 'Dinnet be so disrespectful ter lasses.

Yer supposed ter love someone before yer shag them, and next time use a condom, *bellend*.'

Chloé didn't pretend not to know what was going on as she danced about, singing, '*Who's that gigolo on the street, gigolo, huh, sukka*.'

Jason sat all his exams because he was being paid twenty quid each time he put his name on a paper. It was good of Des to bribe the lad, yet unnecessary as Jason went to his classes and he wasn't thick. It was just a shame that he was mostly interested in horses and lasses. He got a 'C' in English and a 'D' in everything else, apart from PE, for which he got an 'E' even though his riding skills were beyond the grasp of the failed-footy-player-not-even-bright-enough-to-teach-geography PE teacher who marked his coursework. It was better when there was only an exam because at least you failed on your own lack of merit. Jason didn't need exams to earn two hundred quid cash-in-hand for various horse jobs, plus a grand through the books labouring for Des.

Not long after starting work on the house, Jason got a lass pregnant, then decamped to the rickety damp bedroom. Pauline was a free-spirit and Jason would've supported her if she hadn't had an abortion and moved to Scotland, leaving him heartbroken. He fled to Great Lumley, happy to use the hanging-off sink and the bucket-flush toilet rather than face the gossip of the Mount Road Mothers' Union. He was keen to learn the trades: carpentry, plastering, bricklaying, starting with the tumbled down outhouse. It was only ten by eight foot, yet in a Tardis transformation, Jason crafted a room called 'a space,' and built a bunkbed called 'a mezzanine.'

The last of the boxes were packed and she was down to the nitty-gritty. She ran her hand over the anaglypta that EJ found irresistible; every petal and square motif had a semi-circular nail print pressed into it. As low and as high as he could reach, EJ had made his mark in the squashy paper puffs. She'd let the bairn do it, kept him busy. If he was methodically annihilating the wallpaper, he wasn't diving off a chair or rolling sidewards off the kitchen bench, practicing for a career as stunt man. Or shouting, 'Fat pig!' at the woman three doors down. Despite pushing the family further into pariah territory, EJ had an irreverent sense of adventure that she would never try to tame, and anyway, the woman clearly liked a pie, so fuck the fat pig. There's no need to snarl at a three-year-old.

Chloé was a different type of workie ticket. Rather than doing crazy things without thinking about the consequences, she did crazy things because she *knew* what would happen. She was in the second year and had already been put on report and threatened with suspension, not that they'd go through with it, and Chloé knew it. She was top of the year for Spanish and could speak French better than the teacher. The art teacher loved her, and said that she, 'Wouldn't be surprised to see Chloé win the Turner prize,' on account of a goldfish with its eyes poked out and pickled in turpentine, presented in a marmalade jar, and called 'The physical inconvenience of death in the mind of a blind fish.'

On the dressing table was a mishmash of hair slides and nearly empty bottles of perfume. She tipped out the box that once contained a watch and was now a reservoir for buttons, hairgrips, odd earrings, colourful paperclips, a broken kids' watch, twenty-three pence of loose change, and a folded-in-half photo of her in a classroom in the third year at Bede. She had greasy hair tied in a ponytail, Michelle had the same ginger frizz and her freckles on show, having not discovered foundation yet, and Sonya had hair like the Nolans and Baby Oyster lipstick. Ally wasn't in the picture because she'd taken it with her Olympus camera. When she'd boxed her photos for the move, it was like the fossil record stopped at the point when Ally left town. She put the crumpled photo in her address book. Who'd have thought that a bunch of slappers would turn out so well? They were all thirty this year. THIRTY. Where did the time go? From birth to sixteen felt like an eternity, but from seventeen till now had zoomed.

Chapter 38

December 1999

Even though it was going to be a busy day, it was suspicious that Des was up at sparrow's fart. He turned down morning sex, which was unheard of, and then evaded her non-suspicious questions about why he was getting dressed before he'd had two coffees. It was still dark when he left the house. What was the sly dog up to? She said she didn't want flowers or a choir. For the occasion, she'd treated herself to a long, red, belted coat, high-heeled, black leather boots, and black leather gloves. If Des wanted to book her a surprise trip to Saks for a wash and blow, that would be acceptable.

EJ was at Gavin and Gemma's and had been for two sleepovers which was in return for his partner in crime, Jamie, staying at hers on Millennium's Eve. She wasn't bothered about going out tonight. Everywhere would be expensive and stowed-off, and she didn't want Chloé to have to mind EJ until the early hours. She pressed her head into the pillow. At midnight the clock would turn from the twentieth century to the twenty-first century like a magnificent version of staying awake to watch the digital alarm clock flicker from 11:59 pm to 12:00 am.

When Des returned from wherever he'd been, he spent ages in the bathroom, and came out all damp and lovely. He battered her hands away as he wrestled with his jeans, so she left him to it and went to check the weather on the computer.

When aftershave drifted in from the hall, she shut the computer down. He took his gansey from the hook.

'Yae smell nice,' she said, bending over and zipping up her boots.

'So der yae,' he said, feeling her bum.

She put her red coat on and tied the belt. 'Shall wer off?'

'Got the tin?'

She swung her Fiorelli handbag at him. 'Yip.'

The label was tatty and faded, and the best before date was July 1986, yet the tin of Ambrosia creamed rice was in good condition. She disagreed with Des that the tin could burst at any time, exploding with enough force to blow the cupboard doors off. She'd kept it in the utility room after moving here, out of harm's way. Des, however, would be more comfortable if she chucked it in the bin. Since David had seized the *Echoes* and the Beach Boys tape, all she had that Dad had once touched was the photo and the tin of creamed rice. Throwing it in the bin would be like throwing Dad in the bin.

It wasn't the crisp winter day that she was hoping for. The sea wasn't sparkling in the sun. It was overcast, dull, and blarn a gale. As they drove down the bank behind the café, Des said, 'Did yer knar there's a tunnel under the pier?'

'Is there?'

'The pier took eighteen years ter build, opened in 1903, and there's a tunnel all the way underneath it.'

'Did yer Ask Jeeves about Roker Pier last neet?'

'Google,' he said. 'A new search engine.' He pulled forward into a space so they could see out to sea.

'Not be gettin down the pier today,' he said, referring to the giant swells that were lashing the pier to a whoop of voices as each grey wave burst into a tower of white spray. 'Problees be shut.'

'No shit,' she said as another wave hit, spewing a smooth white cloth of froth across the dark bricks. With the pier out of action, her first thought was where else would be a good place to hoy a can of creamed rice into the sea? At high tide, the sea's up to the wall at Seaburn promenade, so that would be a good place. She could take a run up and brace herself against the railing as she launched the tin into the deep.

'Yer didn't happen ter look at the tide times?' she said.

'High tide, one o'clock, low tide, seven-thirty. Wanin crescent moon.'

'Is that all from wadyamecallit?'

'Google. Fuck me,' he said, 'ah spent ages readin about the guillotine.'

'Sounds cheery.'

'Ha'way,' he said, 'ah've got a plan.' He headed off towards the river rather than the promenade and she had to jog to catch up. She threaded her smooth woollen sleeve through his fisherman's rib elbow and pulled him to slow down.

'It's nice rund here now,' he said, nodding at the swanky new houses. 'Can yer imagine the view from that winda?' He skimmed his arm as if to flatten the gleaming estate. 'All this used ter be a sawmill.'

'Did it? Ah thought it woz the block yards.'

'Nah, the block yards were along next ter the old north pier. Over there was a sawmill; made pit props and telegraph poles. Closed in the early nineties.'

She couldn't remember what it was like before the new estate was built even though she'd gone past it loads of times on the bus as a kid. The road that went from the town bridge to the seaside had gloomy houses on one side and smoke and iron and grime on the other. She'd never taken any notice of the industry on the river because she was mostly trying to see the sea while thinking about strawberry bonbons from the old-fashioned sweetshop at Seaburn.

They reached the end of the road next to the old north pier where a yellow brick building had appeared. The sea-facing side of the upper deck had tall windows with a blue balcony that ran along the front. The words on the wall, *Sunderland Yatch Club,* made her think of Simon Le Bon in a white suit, sailing down the river in a yacht singing, *'Across the Wear Grande,'* with Andy Taylor playing guitar on the concrete jetty.

'That road and carpark were all concrete,' said Des, sweeping his arm to include the clubhouse and boat yard, 'and all of this was the block yards.'

'Ah came down here once in a car wer Ally and her boyfriend. It woz full of boy racers revvin their engines and pumpin out shitty rap music.'

'Ah came down here once after the Blue Monkey chucked out. That was a neet ah'll nivver forget. Should've seen it, hundreds of ravers off their tits.'

'Yer never telt uz yer woz a raver.'

'Ah wasn't. Ah was the man with the van.'

She nodded. 'Kev?'

'Kev, decks, amp, speakers, hooked up to a generator that some gangsters from Stockton had brought. The music quality was shite.'

'The gangsters organised an after-club party ter sell drugs and shit?'

'Es for fifteen, ice pops three quid, can of pop a fiver.'

'Didn't the rozzers break it up?'

'Ah only agreed ter gan cos ah thought it'd get broken up straight away, yer knar, it'll last ten minutes. Flatties leaned on their cars and watched; don't think they'd seen owt like it, everyone dancin and shakin hands.'

'Wot like, nee violent drunks?'

'Honestly Paula, it was mental. They woz rockin ter Hooligan X when the generator cut out and it went quiet apart from a ship's horn in the distance. Then, nee word of a lie, this sweaty raver in a bucket hat starts singin, *you shall have a fishy on a little dishy*, and they all start dancin and blarn whistles.'

'Can yer remember the early days of the Blue Monkey? Coach loads of ravers pilin up ter Sunderland.'

'Aye,' he said, kissing the top of her head. 'Ha'way, ah've got a surprise for yer.'

She reckoned that the top deck of the club house had a bar and hoped that the surprise was a vodka and tonic with a sea view. 'Wer need ter get ter Seaburn for high tide,' she said.

He grasped her gloved hand and kept walking in the wrong direction, past the new apartment block with a view of Hendon, and along the edge of the dock that was lined with a white handrail and fancy paving. She knew this area had been renovated because Michelle had just sold a two-bedroom flat for sixty grand.

As they walked the path along into the main harbour, she recognised where she was. She'd been here last when she was eight, when Dad had the idea that they'd catch a boat home up the river rather than get a bus. It was miles from Seaburn to Roker and she had bare feet because

David had buried her flip-flops and didn't know which rock he'd used to mark the spot. They couldn't believe their eyes when Dad led them off the road and down some steps to a secret dock with small boats.

'It's smaller than ah remember,' she said, leaning against the railing, looking into what was now a smart marina with lines of small boats bobbing. 'The Cortinas and wood huts are gone.'

Des hugged her from behind and stuck his head over her shoulder. 'Did yer come here with yer dad?'

'Oh yes,' she said, 'to hitch a ride on the magic boat. Must've been 1977.'

He hugged her tighter and she closed her eyes, listened, and breathed in through her nose, hoping to catch a memory of that day with Dad. It was a long way back to the bus stop with everyone staring and tutting at the dad with the kid with no shoes. She wanted to tell them, 'Me brotha buried me flip-flops, it's nowt ter dee wer me dad.'

Des moved next to her and leaned over the railing. 'It would've been different in Brunel's day. There would've been tall ships, and all where those houses are now, would've been piles of coal.'

'Isambard Kingdom Brunel?'

'Aye, he designed the North Dock in the 1830s.'

'Ah thought he built bridges.'

'And harbours.'

'Did yer read that on the web?'

'Nah, everyone knars that.'

'Do they?'

'Ha'way, we're meetin a man wer a boat.'

'Strites!' she jumped up and down like a child. 'Wot type of boat? Is that why yerv been sneakin about?'

'Wot der yer mean, *sneakin about*?'

'Ah mean where did yer gan first thing this mornin?'

As they neared the carpark, Des greeted an old gadgie with a tangly grey beard and a leathery face. They shook hands, Des said, 'Choppy today.'

She surveyed the boats and hoped it wasn't going to be a small one with no roof.

As she pulled the manky life vest over her gorgeous coat, she made a face to tell Des that whereas she appreciated the effort he'd gone to, he'd overlooked some things. The metal gangplank was pleasingly connected to a biggish boat with a roof. Her vex about the life vest disappeared when she stepped into an actual sitting room with white leather seats. She sat down, got the tin out, and put it on the walnut table, smiling at Des to say, 'I'm fine, you go and drive the boat with your crusty seadog mate.'

There was a smell of diesel and then they were moving. She held the tin to her cheek and thought about Dad's ashes lying under somebody's fireplace in the new estate they'd built where Roker Park had been. It was sweet of Des to get tickets to the last competitive match to be played at the ground in its ninety-nine-year history. In the first half, Sunderland got a penalty, and she held her breath as Paul Stewart put the ball on Dad's head. As they made their way out after the match, she liked to think that the men and boys were crying for Dad, lying alone on the penalty spot. She wished she'd put him on the centre spot because they dug that up and took it to the Stadium of Light. She'd laughed when she heard the name of the new ground, which was to do with it being built on the site of the old mine shaft where miners would look up and see daylight. Suppose it was better than calling it 'the stadium of two hundred metres down and three miles out under the sea,' which was a horrible thought, particularly the pit ponies.

She was enjoying chugging along in the luxury quarters with the smell of diesel in her nostrils, the growl of engine in her ear, and the hint of lighthouse out of the side window. Then the engines went louder, the boat went faster, and she wondered how far out they were going; here would be fine, near the lighthouse, looking down the Wear. She looked out of the back of the boat, and watched the lighthouse go from small to speck to gone. All her life she'd looked out from the shore and wondered what was beyond the horizon and now the mystery was solved – more sea and sky, and no sign of Germany.

They spewed fumes for ten minutes before it went quiet and still. Des said, 'Ready?'

She took the tin outside. The sea was grey and choppy, the sky was grey and cloudy. Des kissed her head. She kissed the tin. '*My feet will want to walk to where you are sleeping, but I shall stay alive.*' She lobbed it as hard as she could and watched it plop into the swell.

It was good to be back on dry land. Des was acting strange and she wondered if it was because she had a sulk about him letting her put her new coat on when he knew that they were setting out to sea. Her red coat was spotless, and Dad was drifting in the currents, so she wished she hadn't acted like a dick about putting the life vest on.

They took a direct route across the new housing estate, walking in silence. She squeezed his hand a few times to say sorry about the life vest hissy fit. When they got to the carpark, he let go of her hand. His neck was all red like when he's annoyed.

'Ha'way,' he said, striding off towards the beach.

He stopped on the promenade looking out to sea and as she walked up behind him, he spun round. She braced herself for a rollcall of errors, yet he locked his soft eyes on hers and tilted his head like when he's totally in love with her. Now she was confused.

'Ah've got somethin ah woz gonna hoy off the boat, but it didn't seem reet; too good for that cunt.' He pulled a brown paper bag from his inside pocket and inhaled.

'Wot is it?'

He produced a saveloy and she gasped with horror, so he grabbed her with both arms, hauling her to his warm body. She pressed her cheek against him while cold milk poured down her arms, curdling round her wrists. She knew he was hugging hard to buffer the pain, but all it did was leach toxic old life into her perfect new life, tainting everything forever. Feeling vile, she shrugged off the pity hug, glad that the wind was lashing her hair across her face, covering her shame. She could hardly look at Des as he dangled the sausage in the air.

'It was the *colour* of a saveloy, the size of a thumb. Poor bastard only lasted ten seconds, hardly worth the effort. Ah wozn't sure wot woz happenin cos ah couldn't feel owt and then it woz over.'

Des dropped the saveloy on the ground and scrubbed it into the concrete with his foot. He took a few steps backwards with his arms open and she walked forward into them. He kissed her head and the pit of her stomach churned as she thought about what she'd just said out loud. She was furious with Sonya for blabbing. He grabbed her shoulders and turned her around. 'Look.'

He nestled his chin on her shoulder as they watched two massive herring gulls squawk and squabble over the tip of the saveloy while another jabbed at morsels in the bumpy concrete. The screeches and long yelps were deafening as hods of gulls circled and swooped to take a peck at the rapist's splattered dick. It wasn't beyond her wildest sadistic venge dreams, good enough though.

As they watched the feeding frenzy, she said, 'Go on then, when did Sonya tell yer? It had ter be Sonya. Wot did she say?'

'Dinnet be angry wer Sonya, she woz tryin ter help.'

'Ah'm furious with her for blurtin me secrets.'

'Ah woz worried about yer, wer both were.'

'Worried, why?'

'It woz when yer were havin a phase of sleep talkin.'

'Sleep takin? Wot sort of things?'

'Couldn't mack out wot yer were sayin, it was more how loud yer were shoutin, and the violent kickin that got uz worried.'

'Why didn't yer say owt ter uz?'

'Yer had enough on yer plate wer two bairns and a job. Ah didn't want ter stoke it up, whatever it was that was lurkin in yer memory. When ah ran it by Sonya, ah thought she was gonna say it was Billy, or yer dad, or somethin shite from down Pallion. Didn't expect her ter tell uz about Saveloy Dick.'

She cringed when he said his name. 'What *exactly* did she tell yer?' She could feel his body sigh against hers. 'Dinnet be shnidey, spit it out.'

'Just that yer were in some pub and a bloke went ter show yer the way out, but it was a cupboard, and that he pushed yer against the wall and that.'

'And that's all she said?'

'More or less.'

It was good work of Sonya telling Des it happened in a pub. She'd probably forgotten where it happened, or got confused with her own catalogue of pub shags. 'Why didn't yer say owt ter uz?'

'The freaky dreams stopped, so ah thought best not ter upset yer.'

'When woz this?'

'When yer went back to work after havin EJ.'

'Wot! That woz *years* ago. Yerv knarn all this time and yer didn't tell uz?'

'Didn't want ter stir things up.'

As horrific as it was, at least his faulty sleuth work had sent him down the wrong alley. She lifted his hand to her mouth and kissed it. She'd rather be a rape victim in a cupboard than a murder culprit in a cell. Thank fuck not one single person knew how Billy met his end. The foghorn bellowed like a warning never to tell, and she shuddered at the thought of being thrown into prison.

'Have yer dreamed about it recently?' said Des.

She hadn't thought about it for years, yet here she was, talking about it all because of her sleeptalking Billy dreams. The asshole still sticking the boot in despite being dead. 'Why like? Have ah been sleep talkin?'

'Nor, well, mebees now and again like.'

As her body tensed with fear, his arms grew tighter around her. He said, 'Once those seagulls have destroyed the last of the saveloy, ah'll never mention the cunt again, so if there's owt yer want ter tell uz, yer better dee it now.'

'Sonya already telt yer everythin. Haven't thought about it for yonks.'

'It's not too late ter gan ter the police.'

She looked Des in the eye and said, 'A drunk slapper in a pub? They'll get vice squad strite on ter it, *not*.'

The saveloy was gone and the seagulls had moved on to some chips.

'Ha'way,' he said, lifting her off her feet and dropping her facing in the other direction. 'Let's gan and see ter the bairns and the horse.'

It was an odd atmosphere in the car and she willed him not to squeeze her leg and smile like everything was going to be fine now. The three o'clock news came on the radio as they went down Houghton cut. Already there was the constant crack of fireworks. They gave each other a worried look. It wasn't going to be an easy night for animals.

As he turned down the track, the house was lit up like Blackpool illuminations. When Des got out, she ordered him to tell Chloé to turn the lights off and the heating down before seeing to Mayfair. She got in the driver's side and headed off to get EJ.

Gavin and Gemma had a lovely new build in Ryhope. As she parked in the drive, the uPVC front door opened, and EJ and Jamie ran out and started scrapping on the perfect lawn. Gemma had her hair in rollers and was wearing a towelling dressing gown with orange make-up round the collar. 'Eeee, ha'way in,' she said, with the face of a woman who'd spent two days with EJ and Jamie.

She hugged Gemma. 'Yer smell lovely, are yer lookin forward ter toneet?'

'Here-man, ah've been lookin forward ter it since ah booked it in 1997.'

'Ah dunnar how yer can be bothered,' she said, going into Gemma's show home. 'Fifty quid to get into a pub for the honour of singin *Auld Lang Syne* wer a bunch of armpits in yer face. Bet the drinks'll be extortionate anarl.'

'There's a meal and a band,' said Gemma, zipping up Jamie's bag. 'Thanks for this, Paula,' she said, giving it to her. 'Ah'm proper grateful ter have a babysitter on Millennium's Eve.'

'Bloody fireworks,' she said, 'it's like the Western Front out there. Ah've got nee choice but ter stay home and keep watch on Mayfair, so havin Jamie's nee botha.'

Gemma looked guilty, then confessed, 'Jamie winnet shut-up about havin a gan on the horse. Ah telt him it's ower big for him like, but he'll problees hassle yer nee end.'

'Ah can handle Jamie.'

'Eeee, Aunty Paula,' said Laura-Jane, also with her hair in rollers and wearing a dressing gown, 'ah like yer coat.'

'Ta, it's new.'

‘Nice boots,’ said Laura-Jane. ‘Mam, they’re like the ones ah woz tellin yer about.’

The bairns sang ‘Jingle Bells’ from Ryhope to the Rainton Lodge, then sparked out. She was pleased for the peace even if it was a catnap before the next stint of mayhem.

The main road was full of speeding taxis and the country roads past West Rainton were lit up with bursts of fire shooting into the dark sky. There was a horse transporter turning right onto Pithouse Lane, so she stopped back from the junction, giving the driver enough room to turn the tight corner. It was too flash for anyone she knew at the stables and *EJK Equine Transport Services* suggested it was a transport company.

As her tyres hit the track, the bairns’ eyes opened, and they were out of the car before she’d properly stopped. They ran off towards the bushes and she left them to it as she scooped bags and shoes and Game Boys out of the car. When she went inside, it was like walking into an oven and all the lights were on, including the downstairs loo. She signed, dumped the stuff, then went to fetch the little monsters.

There was giggling from the bin store, so she tiptoed across the gravel and then did a two-footed pounce, cornering them as she pointed her finger gun, yelling in an American accent, ‘Any of you cheeky sticks move and ah’ll execute every toad-lickin last one of ya!’

They stood, terrified, backs against the wall. She pointed her gun at EJ's face. 'EJ Butcher, get off yer horse and inter the house before ah blow yer brains out.' He ran and Jamie waited for his turn looking down the barrel of a finger. 'Jamie Hasting, get off yer horse and inter the house before ah mack yer eat lead.' He ran. She blew on her fingers and put them back in their holster. It was going to be a long night.

She always knew where Chloé had been because she left a trail of light. She went to see what she was doing, flicking switches as she went.

'It's Mam,' she said, knocking.

'*Entrez*.'

Chloé was at her dressing table, brushing her long brown hair, a hint at her desire to dye it black. There was no way she was letting her do it, and not because it would make her look like a witch, but because thirteen is too young to ruin your hair – a lesson she learned when she was fourteen and sprayed Sun-In all over her long brown hair. Instead of a golden glow, it went gingery-brown and as dry as sticks. It's a mam's job to protect her daughter from this fate, so she was not going to be persuaded.

Chloé looked Gothic enough with her powdery white face, thick black eyeliner, and blood-red lips without topping it off with black hair. She wished she'd said no to the make-up the day she got back from her summer holiday in Canada. She'd waved off Britney

Spears and welcomed back Siouxsie Sioux. Marcel said that his cousin's kids were 'Emos' and that she'd picked it up from them like she'd caught chickenpox, not gone from colourful and cheeky to black and tortured.

'Wot time is Kat comin over?'

'Dunnar.'

Now that Chloé had been 'forced' to move to 'the middle of nowhere' the only person she could possibly have as a friend was Kat as she was the only person who also had a mobile phone. The Nokia that she'd got her as a bribe to move to 'the middle of nowhere' had been upgraded at Christmas for a Motorola flip phone, which was better than her own, in Chloé's words, 'Brick phone.'

'Are yer joinin us for pizza later?' she dared to ask.

'Can wer eat it in me room?'

'Ah suppose so, but it would be nice if wer can have a bit of a party.'

Chloé laughed through her unpierced nose. 'We'll eat in me room. Pepperoni for me and Margherita for Kat, and bread sticks, and coke.'

'Any more requests?'

'Nah.'

The bairns had unpacked their bags in the hall, so she followed the path of detritus – shoe, sock, half-eaten chocolate orange segment, the jumpers that they were wearing in the car. The trail led to the conservatory, where she found them in their Quinn and Phillips footy tops that she'd conspired to buy with Gemma after being swept up in the euphoria of Sunderland's 4-1 defeat of Chelsea. Fair play to the bairns, they were doing good keepy-uppies, only it wasn't great that Quinn was using an apple, and Phillips, a clementine.

It was cold outside, and she didn't care. She opened the conservatory and ordered, 'Oi, Quinn, Phillips, out!'

As they disappeared into the darkness, she lobbed a real football after them. Des appeared covered in hay and smelling of horse. 'How's Mayfair?' she asked.

'Settled for now. Ah've put the radio on in the stall.'

She said, 'Quinn and Phillips are in the garden.'

She had a long list of things to do before she could relax in front of the fire with the telly on and a pint of Baileys, starting with sweeping the fire and getting some logs in. It was pizza for tea and whatever she could forage for a Millennium feast later.

Des was busy drowning the lads in the bath when Kat's folks dropped her off. Kat, who had also been infected with Emo, was wearing black clothes, a white face, grey eyes, and jet-black hair with a middle parting.

'Are yer absolutely sure yer don't mind havin Katarina?' said Kat's mam who was dressed for a night out on the basis that the answer to this question was, yes.

'Nee probs, ah'm stayin in anyways.'

'Beautiful tree,' said Kat's mam, tipping her head to see into the hall.

'Ha'way in if yer like.'

'No, no thanks, need to scoot, we're off to a party.'

'Come and see me tree, have yer got a camera? Could get a pic of the girls in front of it.'

Kat's dad came in from the car with a professional-type camera and they cooed over the seven-foot silver tree with red and green baubles, and the garland wrapped round the sweeping bannister. The finishing touch to the Christmas card scene were the twinkling lights hanging from the high atrium. The girls refused to smile and did their best to look like Tim Burton characters. Chloé, a zombie in a tartan dress and fishnets, and Kat, a beetle in purple and black striped socks.

'At least there are no boys on the scene,' said Kat's mam.

'There's Justin.'

'Justin? Who's he? Is he at Aiden's?' asked Kat's mam, thrilled.

'Lad from the village down the road.'

'Katarina hasn't mentioned him. Is he her boyfriend or Chloé's?'

'Neither by the sounds of things.'

'Is he a goth?'

'Aye, but he's not very good at it. More grey than black.'

She was watching Hypno-Disc obliterate Robogeddon pending putting the oven on and sorting the disaster zone kitchen when Des came down.

'Hacky boys all clean?' she said.

'They're in bed and the little twats better stay there until at least seven tomorra.'

Des was a fastidious arsonist, and she watched his bum as he leaned into the hearth to place the scrunched-up newspaper first, then a shaving of firelighter, and logs on top, chopped by his own swinging axe.

'Is that the *Radio Times* yerv put on the fire?'

'There's arnly one day left and there's nowt on.'

'Pizza? Cheese, pickles, and leftover bacon joint for dessert?'

'There's a reason ah love yae.'

'Beer or bourbon?'

The fire was almost out, and Des was gone. It was gone half-eleven and she'd been asleep on the rug since stuffing her face. She could hear Des whistling in the downstairs loo, a sure sign that he was up to something. He was still whistling when he came in, all showered and changed.

'Yae look nice,' she said.

'Thought ah'd mack an effort for the Millennium.'

'Ah thought the plan was ter stay wer Mayfair.'

'Can still look nice and pretend wer at a party. Ah've put a bottle in the stables.' He flung a placker bag at her. 'Quick, get this on.'

'Wot is it?'

'That dress yer like in Kookai. Yer cannet see the Millennium in wearin a jumper wer tomato stains down the front.'

The dress was gorgeous, so it was a shame about the scabby fleece. The sky was clear earlier, so it was going to be nippy out there.

As the glow of the house faded into the pitch-black of the field, she could see lights twinkling on the stable block. She squeezed his hand. He'd been so sweet today, sorting everything out. Fireworks cracked in the distance.

'Poor animal,' she said, walking faster.

The fairy lights on the stables were dazzling. She kissed Des and stood back to admire them.

'Ha'way,' he said, 'ah've summink ter show yer.'

In the empty stall, he'd set up a table, complete with tablecloth, candles, a bottle in a silver cooler, chocolates, and a red rose. They kissed until a boom made them jump.

'Fuck,' he said, 'that sounded close, better check on Mayfair.'

She lifted the champagne bottle from the ice and took it outside. 'Der yer want ter open this?'

Des came out of Mayfair's stall. 'Aye gis it here.' He took the bottle and said, 'Gan and see in there.'

He pointed at the stall that was used as a store, so she suspected he'd been up to something. 'Have yer made a bed from hay?'

'Nope,' he said, going in.

She followed him. Her jaw dropped.

'Meet Alby Dallas,' he said. 'Ah thought wer could call him Ambrosia.'

'Oh my god!' she gasped at the ivory horse with an ivory mane and ivory tail that had appeared in the storage stall, which had been cleared and painted.

'He's a seven-year-old grey Connemara geldin, 15.3 hands high.'

Shocked and unsure which beautiful creature to kiss first, she stroked Ambrosia's neck. He whuffled.

'Came over from Ireland today,' said Des. 'Registered Thoroughbred.'

Her belly did summersaults. With one arm around the horse's neck, she pulled Des in for a three-way. 'Ah cannet believe it,' she said, kissing them both.

'Ah still feel bad that last time ah bought yer a horse, yer hardly got ter ride it,' he said. 'Ambrosia is easy ter ride, a good boy, nee attitude.' The horse whinnied and Des patted his backside. 'Nee more ridin school nags for my Paula.'

'Nee more bein telt wot ah can and cannet dee.' She hugged Ambrosia's neck with both arms. 'Ah can dee anythin ah want on my horse in my field.'

'Wot's the matter, mate,' said Des, 'somethin in yer shoe?' Des pointed at the horse's front leg. 'Ah gave him a trot earlier and he woz limpin on that foot afterwards.' He took a hoof-pick from his pocket. 'Here, give it a rake.'

As she stooped to lift Ambrosia's foot, he nuzzled her face with his velvety lips and lifted a hoof like the best-behaved horse she'd ever met. She scraped away the top layer of muck to reveal a hoof and then she gently sunk her pick into the clarts in his collateral groove. She felt her metal hook hit something hard. 'Ah think he's got a stone; hope it's not wedged in.'

As she cleared more muck, something sparkled in the light. 'Shit! Looks like a piece of glass.' She picked at it like an archaeological dig, revealing gold. 'A ring!' She howked it out with the hoof pick.

'Gis a look,' said Des.

She dropped Ambrosia's leg and gave Des the hoof pick with a filthy ring hanging on it. He rubbed the ring with his fingers.

'Is it a diamond?' she said.

He held it up to her. 'Paula, will yer marry me?'

Ambrosia stomped his hoof and the ground trembled.

'Yes, Desmond, ah'd love ter marry yer.'

He slipped the ring onto her filthy finger. 'Thank goodness yer said yes,' he said, looking at his watch, 'ah've ordered some fireworks ter start in sixty seconds.'

Chapter 39

May 2000

After refurbishing the stables with handcrafted wooden doors, a tack room, and a wash bay, Jason progressed to getting the grounds in order. He was meticulous about the cross-country field and the pasture paddock and didn't mind looking after the main field but not the garden lawn. It was Saturday so she leaned out of the bedroom window and gave him a wave as he sped by at 8 mph on the ride-on lawn mower. She turned her face to the sun, closed her eyes, and took a deep breath of freshly cut grass. This week had been horrible. Work was manic, EJ got a red card at nursery, and the tenants at Symington Gardens flooded the bathroom, again. Money was as tight as a gnat's chuff.

The horses were turned out and knocking about under the tree in the far corner of the paddock, plotting how to get into the neighbour's field that was overgrown with cow parsley and other delicious treats. She was halfway across when Ambro raced over to greet her, tail up, nostrils flaring. She gave her best mate a scratch.

'Mornin, gorgeous.'

As she led Ambro to the stables, she told him about booking Lumley Castle for a non-religious ceremony. Ambro was a great listener, his ears flicking back and forth. He never judged, unlike Mayfair, who would listen to Jason moan about his girlfriend but pinned her ears flat and moved away whenever Paula mentioned the price of apples. Mayfair mostly enjoyed a life of pasture having voted with her hooves. She couldn't jump on grass so wasn't suited to the cross-country course that Jason had cultivated in the top field, and after throwing Heather while on a hack, Jason decided to retire her. Every day, Jason rode Mayfair along the perimeter of the estate like a park ranger. She loved her new role as patrol horse.

Jason was training Ambro for cross-country and was smashing his training goals. The Nettle Lodge course was set in an eight-acre field with a three-mile path through the woods, including a wide water-filled ditch and jumps that were fallen trees. There were certain jumps she was permitted to ride, the ones that Jason reckoned she could manage without ending up in hospital. Despite Ambro being her horse, she was still being told when she could ride, what she could ride, and how she could ride, yet she couldn't complain at Ambro's work with Jason.

Ambro nibbled her collar as she put his bridle on. They watched Jason on the lawn mower in the distance and gave each other a head bump. Ambro nickered. He was so cute.

Down the gradual dip, with a steady gait, faster and faster, boof, boof, his feet hit the soft earth. Ambro took the oil drum and pole jumps that were set at the lowest height and at distances that, in Jason's words, 'Mack the transitions easy for someone as shite as yae.' Then Ambro cantered, tossing his head, and as he got near, he adjusted his stride, then jumped the hessian sacks stuffed with dirt excavated from the water-filled ditch beyond. He landed short of the edge on purpose, splashing and soaking her, his guilty pleasure. He powered on to the next jump that was built from weathered planks and looked like the village stocks, in which she'd imagined many an offender clamped by their testicles, as she flew over them on her steed. After the stocks, Ambro was like a coiled spring, waiting for the signal, then she leaned into the gallop, and they hurtled down the straight.

Slowing to a trot, she pulled the rein, turning away from the high jump that Ambro could nail with Jason, which was made from box hedge that Lisa's dad said he should take from his dead neighbour's garden, 'Before the council massacre forty years of pride and joy.' As they rounded on the lesser ability side of the course, Ambro snorted. She patted his wither, then they were off, over the tractor tyres jump, the pallets jump, and the old prams jump, cantering between adequate transitions, before dipping down into the woods.

They walked along the track, detouring into the stream, Ambro's favourite where, unlike when he was with Jason, he could frolic, stamping his feet and sticking his nose in and splashing water on his face. 'Having fun?' she said, tussling his mane. It was cool and calm in the trees and she loved the solitude. As they walked, the snap of twigs and crunch of leaves beneath his hooves rooted her to the earth.

They wandered off the path and she made Ambro promise that he wouldn't tell Jason they'd been in the trees. And definitely no telling Jason they'd stopped in the clearing, a great spot for Ambro's favourite, wild garlic. This was confession corner, a place where she could say things out loud. She'd told Ambro about how Billy died and how glad she was that he was dead. Ambro also knew about how she'd 'negotiated' with Michael, although so did Des now. She'd been quietly Googling Michael Smith FRCS when her cry of 'Neeways!' alerted him. Shocked to see that Michael was a surgeon in Australia, she blurted out what had happened, immediately regretting it. Des laughed when she said she thought he was an accountant. He said, 'The nonce deserved to be ripped off,' and hasn't mentioned it since. Today she bent Ambro's ear about the rude woman from the marquee company, which wasn't a revelation, but everyone was sick of her going on about it, so she'd saved the latest installment for confession corner.

Back on the track, they walked around the fallen tree jump and down the dip. When Ambro saw the path stretching ahead to daylight, he picked up pace in anticipation, so she gave him a kick, and he powered up the steep hill with determination. At the top was a jump with logs piled like mortgages, one on top of the other, ready to roll from beneath them with one wrong move. Surefooted, he cleared the mortgage logs, proving that there was nothing to fear on a horse with heart and spirit.

Chloé was waiting at the wash bay with the hose poised and potions lined up. In Chloé's entire life she wasn't interested in horses and there was no way her daughter would ever get on a horse. Now Chloé had struck up a sweet friendship with Ambro, which she reckoned was because opposites attract – contrary and stubborn versus eager to please and easygoing.

She took Ambros's saddle off and he pranced and rolled in the dust, making sure he was filthy in preparation for his brush, shampoo, hose down, rub down, hoof clean and oil, and mane and tail plait. Chloé was methodical and had it all covered from reading the web, having refused to be told anything by her or Jason. As she mucked out the stall, she could hear Chloé fussing over Ambro as she groomed, '*Out, out damn spot.*' Then she talked gibberish like from a book, '*The Thane of Fife had a wife–where is she now?*' She could hear Ambro whuffle, answering her question in horse language.

Chapter 40

May 2001

Getting the bridesmaids to the wedding dress boutique for their final fitting was a right clart on, and everything about this wedding cost a fortune or involved hours of planning. A year ago, when she showed Chloé a dark red corseted dress, she hoped that it was vampy enough for her to suffer for one day. When Chloé tried it on, her boobs popped over the top and Kat and Justin decked it. The more tortured than usual expression on Chloé's face made her feel like a bad mam. She knew Chloé didn't want to wear a dress and it wasn't worth the drama of trying to persuade her.

Today, when her ladies came out of the fitting room looking like the bridesmaids' version of *Reservoir Dogs*, she knew that Chloé's refusal to wear a dress had paid off. Silk trouser suits, crisp cotton shirts, and silk ties with tiny diamantes. Michelle: primrose yellow. Sonya: soft pink. Chloé: powder blue. The wedding dress lady said that a bride in an ivory tuxedo was the only other time that she'd fitted a suit, and she lined the bridesmaids up for some photos.

It was a shame about Chloé's skinhead, which she hoped would grow a bit before the wedding. Chloé said it was a feminist fashion statement. She wouldn't say which hairdresser merrily gave a teenage girl a cueball. As far as she could see from her mates, either the fashion hadn't caught on, or they weren't feminists. Des reckoned it was Chloé's way of getting attention, what with EJ consuming everything and the wedding consuming everything else.

The prospect of a wedding had kept Nana and Grandar alive for another year, and although Grandar could walk, they decided to put him in a wheelchair. She'd taken Nana shopping to Fenwick's for an outfit and would never forget the pride on her face when the lady placed the pillbox hat with netting on her head. Des was in charge of the men's suits, including eight friends and family, as well as EJ and Grandar. They'd agreed on dark grey with waistcoats and cravats to match the bridesmaids.

Ian was doing the catering and was happy to miss most of the wedding for the chance to cater a large event in her oversized kitchen. In an unexpected move, Ian quit his job at the pub where he'd worked for years and went travelling with a mate to Thailand and Vietnam. When he returned, he moved in temporarily and seven months later, he was still here. Ian put the double ovens and cold marble worktops to good use, waking the household at six-thirty each morning with the smell of pastry and Southeast Asia. Des gave Ian his old van so he could deliver his wares, mainly to a company in Darlington and to some pubs. After the wedding, Ian was planning to go travelling to South America with his girlfriend from Gateshead, who he met in Hanoi.

When she said a buffet would be easier than a sit-down meal, Ian laughed. 'Cheaper, not easier, and not necessarily cheaper.' Ian decided it was best to keep the pissed-up wedding crowd sitting down and to put food in front of them. Starters: cantaloupe melon with or without Parma ham. Main course: Ian's cow pie, new chatties, and green beans, or vegetarian lasagne. Dessert: cake, ice cream, cheese board.

The final guest list was confirmed, including forty-nine on her side and thirty-seven on Des's. She was hoping that some guests would decline the invitation, reducing the numbers, but the only people who couldn't make it were Marcel and Meredith as they would be in Orlando.

*

She agreed to let Sonya and Michelle dress her up, and she expected them to do better than a bin liner dress covered in L-plates and dildos plus a top hat made from cardboard covered in scrunched-up tissue paper.

She'd been dropping hints about how she'd always wanted to dress up as Elizabeth Taylor playing Velvet Brown in her jockey silks, yet she reckoned they'd put her in stockings and suspenders, hopefully a devil, probably a nun.

She had a little black dress and heels in her bag, just in case it was a bin liner – she could slip it over her dress, then after Luciano's, she could take the bin liner off and go clubbing without shame. She'd keep the veil on that she hoped they'd made her, and she didn't mind if it had *sheaths* on it.

Darren was staying at his mam's with two-year-old Oliver because the hen party was leaving from and returning to Michelle's. She parked behind Sonya's BMW Z3 that Conor got her for her thirtieth birthday, which they all reckoned was strategic. It was as if he knew how many gentlemen Sonya had entertained on the spacious back seat of the Jeep.

She hauled her bags into the open porch. The front room was full of gold balloons. She could hear voices and shuffling, then Sonya and Michelle burst in wearing dressing gowns, each holding a short blonde wig. They put the wigs on and whipped off the dressing gowns. Sonya was wearing a mink coat and silver dress, and Michelle was wearing a cerise skirt and matching jacket with shoulder pads, straight from 1985. Sonya and Michelle said, '*Fr-aa-nk*,' explaining the clobber, pink eyeshadow, and dangly penis earrings.

Her sides knacked from laughing – she was going to be Mrs P Butcher, so it was a fair theme and hilarious, apart from she wasn't changing her name. Des was hurt until she explained that Hasting was all that she had left of Dad, although she didn't explain that Mrs Butcher was bad taste given she'd slaughtered someone.

She was laughing so much that they could hardly get the blue eye shadow and pink blusher on her. They dressed her in a short, leopard print dress, black stilettos, a blonde wig, and dangly penis earrings.

As they waited for the taxi, people in the cul-de-sac came out to see the Pat Butcher trio, some of them using it as an excuse to get close to Sonya's car.

The taxi driver said, 'Cab for Mrs P Butcher?'

It was a balmy evening, and the top of town was stowed-off with people dressed to party and already well on their way. There was another hen party spilling out of a minibus on the taxi rank down the side of Idols, the bride in a bin liner dress covered in dildos and her mates in as few clothes as possible.

Michelle adjusted her stockings, and they did a round of '*Fr-aa-nk*' to the amusement of the passers-by. Sonya said they were meeting in Luciano's and that nineteen people had confirmed. She could hear shushing as she reached the top of the stairs, so she braced herself. And when she went in, there were screams and cheers and a crowd of familiar faces. Everyone was here and they were all in fancy dress! Even Nana was wearing a wig and dangly penis earrings and was chuffed to see her grandchildren rocking her outfits. Ellie-May was wearing Nana's suit with the nasty black and white swirly pattern, and Laura-Jane was wearing her purple chiffon blouse and string of pearls. She doubled over when she spotted Eileen and Sam who looked like Nora Batty and Cupid Stunt. No one expects twenty Pat Butchers on a night out.

Michelle and Sonya guided her to the long table and sat opposite. To the right, the non-family end, was sister-in-law-to-be Janis, Eileen and Sam from work, and Heather and Diane from the stables. To the left was the family, Gemma, Julie, Nana, Brooke, Laura-Jane, and Ellie-May, Lisa and her sisters Fiona and Angela, and as far away as possible were Chloé and Kat. Chloé raised her hand to double-communicate *hello and don't hug me*, and she really wanted to hug her because with a wig on she looked normal.

The booze was flowing, the pizza was on order, and she didn't get a look in with the garlic bread and dough balls because she was forced to talk to everyone, which was good, but she needed to eat because she hadn't eaten for months. She didn't know how many more times she could explain that they were delaying the honeymoon until October and that they had two minibuses to serve each side of the river with pickups from the Board Inn or from Hepworth's, and then drop at Lumley Castle for the ceremony and then drop at the house for the reception. There was a big bus to take them back to Park Lane, leaving from the end of the track at ten. Everyone said that it was an early close until she pointed out that the reception started at midday and there was a free bar.

By the time the pizza came, she was bladdered, so she concentrated on eating and not talking. She only managed to stuff three slices down before her plate was taken away because everyone else was finished. Michelle was gulping down water while Sonya was at the bar sorting out a round of tequilas. Without the fur coat and wig, Sonya looked normal as she stalked the hot waiter.

'Ah'll help Sonya,' she said, squeezing her way out.

'Get some more watter,' said Michelle.

'Aye,' said Lisa, 'a couple of jugs.'

While the older Italian man found the shot glasses, Sonya leaned against the bar like a cat waiting for a fish to swim by.

'Can ah get some jugs of water ter the Pat Butcher table please?' she asked the bloke behind the bar.

Sonya was delighted when the hot waiter came over.

'Hi there,' he said, 'were yer at a weddin at the Hallgarth Manor last summer?'

'Aye,' said Sonya. 'Denise and Clint. She was in my class at school.'

'She got an invite and ah didn't,' she said, poking Sonya in the arm.

'Me girlfriend's family are friends with the groom's,' said the hot waiter. 'It was a good day.'

'Aye,' Sonya agreed, moving closer to him, undeterred by *my girlfriend*. 'Ah had a proper three-day hangover.'

'So you are, ah'm guessin, Conor Spencer's sister?'

'Sister?' said Sonya, wrinkling her entire face. 'Do ah look like him?'

'Nor,' said the hot waiter, 'although he is good lookin, defo a James Dean thing garn on.'

'How der yer knar Conor?' asked Sonya.

'Ah dinnet. Me girlfriend's brotha went on a birthder weekend that Conor woz on, so she sort of knar's him, if that macks sense. So, if yer not his sister, how do yer knar him?'

'Ah'm his girlfriend,' confessed Sonya.

He stepped backwards with his head tilted to the side, then said, 'Oh reet,' shook her hand, said, 'Patrick, nice ter meet yer. Better get on, busy-busy,' then split.

'Why did yer tell him that?'

Sonya shrugged and took the tray of tequilas.

When Sonya lowered the tray, arms flew in, hands grabbing at the glasses, so when she put the tray down, it was empty except for one glass. They clapped as she necked the tequila that was bad and not made better by licking salt off the back of her hand.

The dishevelled and de-wigged hen party gathered outside of Luciano's, glad of the cool breeze. The staying-out crowd wandered up to the corner while the rest waited for their lifts. On the other side of the road, Chloé thumbed her phone while Kat hung on her shoulder. Her heart sank to see Chloé's bald head. Kat had hair down to her tiny waist. Chloé's punishment was to have 'Nothing Compares to You' sung at her by everyone over the age of twenty.

A good-looking lad got out of a gleaming Primera, kissed Laura-Jane, then let Julie and Ellie-May get in the back. Laura-Jane had done well for herself. She was at college and Gemma said that her handsome boyfriend worked at Nissan. Chloé was staying at Kat's and Lisa said that David could drop them off, or she thought that it was going to be David picking them up, not Lisa's brother-in-law in a VW campervan. It was a crowd-pleaser. Lisa's brother-in-law got out and chatted to the revellers. Brooke and Angela didn't hesitate to jump aboard, whereas Chloé was mortified and had to be dragged by Kat.

Gemma, Lisa and Fiona, Janis, Heather and Diane, and Eileen and Sam were up for Idols, so Sonya and Michelle led the charge to the front of the jostling queue. The general belief was that it was the power of eleven Pat Butchers that had got them straight inside, even though there were hens and stags galore, all in fancy dress and waiting in line. It was the power of one Sonya who had fast-tracked the party; she'd fucked a couple of the doormen, and they knew they'd get lucky if they let her jump the queue.

They squeezed into the hot, steamy, heaving pub, Sonya leading the way to the corner bar. Heather and

Diane had never been in Idols before, and their eyes popped out of their heads at the barmaids in bikinis and the barmen in denim shorts with the arses ripped out. She'd seen many hens gang-banged on the stage by the barmen, and she was glad that it was too late and too busy to be dragged before the baying crowd for ritual humiliation. As they waited five deep to be served, she watched Michael Jackson on the tellies hanging from the ceiling all along the main bar, and then the moonwalk cut to a barmaid's norks. The DJ laughed as he zoomed in on her cleavage before moving the camera onto a lass bending into the fridge, her bikini bottoms disappearing up her crack across twenty screens.

'A Smirnoff Ice and two watermelon Bacardi Breezers.'

'We've arnly got Hooch,' said the barman in denim shorts and a chopped-off t-shirt.

'Wot flavours?'

'Lemon.'

'Three of them, and a half a cider, and a glass of white wine.'

'Wer haven't got any wine.'

'A gin and tonic then, and half a lager and lime, and a Southern Comfort and lemonade, please.'

They clutched their drinks to their chests and squashed into the smoky crowd in search of a space and ending up in a mosh, with elbows in tits and fags in faces. The girls from the stables weren't impressed with being pulled and pushed and soaked or with the arm that knocked Heather's cider out of her hand. She shouted over the shouting and the music to Diane, 'Wer nivver usually come in here.'

She would've gone outside if she wasn't rammed face to face with Gemma as they endured 'Mustang Sally' and then 'Everybody Needs Somebody'. The DJ called lasts, then played 'Nutbush City Limits', which did nothing to halt the party. It was well gone eleven when they stopped serving and the doormen pushed their way through the crowd, shoving everyone away from the bar while the bar staff clambered onto it. The bar staff kicked their legs to 'New York, New York' and then did the Timewarp. It was like *Coyote Ugly* but with fewer clothes, no choreography, and a thousand pissed Mackems who were making the most of missing the last bus home.

At last, the music went off, the lights went on, the bar staff clambered off the bar, and a doorman shouted, 'Drink up lads and lasses!'

The crowd thinned to reveal a claggy carpet of broken glass and shattered dreams.

'Reet then you sheep, FLOCK OFF!' shouted a doorman.

The staff who were dancing two minutes ago were now shifting glasses and stacking ashtrays for the lass in the silver bikini, six-inch heels, and rubber gloves, to wash in the tiny sink. Before emptying each ashtray into the bin, the lass carefully extracted the focus point coupons, which she dropped into a clean glass – looked like enough for a CD and she still had tons of ashtrays to clean. Sonya chatted to one of the barmaids while the rest watched the doormen dragging mortal people out of the pub.

They were the last people in the place when Sonya finished her chat with the manager and three doormen. Sonya led the charge upstairs to Annabel's that had no queue. They were down to six Pats which was well within Sonya's ability to get them in for free, not least because, far from its heydays, it was empty. All the tables in the café area were free so they sat and looked through the arched window at piss artists running all over the road. When Sonya returned with the DJ from Idols and a tray of shots, she escaped for a wee.

She'd been in the bogs for ages, talking shite with some lasses from Washington when Michelle came in. 'Where the fuck yer been?'

'Chattin.'

'Ha'way,' said Michelle taking her hand, and leading her out of the bogs and into Aiya Napa, 1995.

'Love life and laughter is all that I believe.'

They danced like everyone was watching and thinking *sad cows*, but she didn't care. She could almost smell the Cabotine and taste the Archers.

'These sounds fall into my mind.'

When the Bucketheads came on, Sonya swaggered onto the empty dancefloor waving her arms.

She hugged Eileen, Sam, Heather, and Diane, waving them off pending seeing them, 'On the day,' like it was a day that was as significant to them as it was to her. She leaned on the cloakroom counter waiting for Michelle to have a slash and for Sonya to have sex with the manager. All three emerged at the same time, righting themselves in different ways.

'Taxi outside High Street baths in ten, tell him ter put it on the Annabel's account,' said the manager, kissing Sonya.

Free taxi, no queue. Sonya was the best type of friend, and having played her part for the team, she flopped in the armchair while she helped Michelle fetch some vodka and crisps. The night wasn't over yet.

'Ah fucken reek of smoke,' said Michelle. She undressed then flung the whole lot into the garden.

She copied, pulling her nylon dress over her head, making her hair stand on end and crackle.

'Ah'm puttin me nightie on,' said Michelle.

'Can yer throw mine down?' she said, 'it's in me bag.'

Sonya stuffed crisps into her mouth. 'Top neet.'

'Here-man, it woz a mint neet, much better than ah thought it woz ganner be. Cheers.'

Sonya swallowed a gobful and straightened her back. 'Ah reckon Conor's havin an affair.'

She wanted to sound surprised, but it was too much of a stretch. 'Well yer've had yer suspicions in the past, and let's face it, if he's not interested in yae, he must be gettin it somewhere; either that or he has a lot of wanks.'

'Aye, but now ah have evidence.'

'Der yer?'

'Yer knar that barmaid ah woz talkin tee?'

'The waiter's girlfriend from the weddin?'

'That's her. Anyways, she doesn't knar Conor but her brotha was on a birther neet out in Manchester and he saw him in a pub. They didn't talk or owt, but he recognised him as,' Sonya made air quotes with her salt and vinegar fingers, 'the fit man from Sunderland with the Porsche 911.'

'Woz he with a lass?'

'Nor, on his own, apparently,' said Sonya. 'She said he only saw him from a distance.'

'That proves nowt. Thought yer said he gans ter Manchester on business. Yer dinnet expect him ter sit in the hotel room.'

'He doesn't sit in the hotel room,' Sonya slurred. 'Dry Bar, Ten Bar, The Castle. He's nivver mentioned The Village.'

'He must gan ter hods of places that he doesn't tell yer about,' she said, stumbling out of the room to collect her night clothes that were strewn down the stairs. She was glad that Sonya was opening her eyes to the cracks in her relationship, so she was keen to encourage her despite Conor having done nothing exciting. When she wiggled into her pj bottoms, everything got all tangled and the next thing, she was face down on the floor, then she was lying face up, the artexed ceiling spinning.

Michelle appeared in a silky dressing gown and fluffy slippers, 'Yer alreet there, Paula?'

'Aye, champion,' she said, crawling into the living room.

Michelle took her vodka and tonic from the glass table and the suede settee farted as she plonked down.

'Sonya reckons Conor's havin an affair.'

'Wee with?' said Michelle.

'Dunnar,' said Sonya, passing Michelle the bowl that had five crisps in it.

She filled in the lack of details. 'He was spotted in a pub in Manchester.'

'Wee by, wee with?' said Michelle, like a game of Cluedo.

Sonya explained, 'So the lass from Idols said that her brotha went on a birthder weekend ter Manchester and spotted the fit man with the Porsche 911.'

'So? He goes there all the time for work,' said Michelle, solving the crime.

'Not to The Village, he doesn't.'

Michelle spat her vodka out.

'Wot?' said Sonya.

'The Village,' said Michelle, wiping her chin. 'Have yer not seen *Queer as Folk*?'

'Nor,' said Sonya, 'why?'

'Ah've seen it,' she said. 'Reet eye opener into the lives of gay men.' And then she clicked, gasped, 'Neeways!' and put her hand over her mouth, her mind whirling. It made sense. Why else would the only man in town not having sex with Sonya be in a gay bar?

Sonya was none-the-wiser, so Michelle looked her in the eye and said, 'The Village isn't a pub, Sonya, it's an actual village with gay bars.'

Sonya's mouth was opening and closing as her head was nodding. Michelle crawled over to her and put her arm around her.

'Lyin cunt,' hissed Sonya, holding her glass out.

'Yer dinnet knar nowt yet,' she said, filling it. 'It might not be arnly gay people wee gan there.'

Sonya took a gulp of vodka. 'The lass said her brotha wandered off to The Village on his arn because he didn't fancy the strip joint.'

'That'll be why the waiter thought yer wer his sister,' she said.

Sonya was staring into nowhere, gurning, and shaking her head. 'Cannet believe how blinnd ah've been. It's fucken obvious.'

'It's not obvious,' said Michelle.

'Nivver in a million years would anyone guess,' she added.

'Not wer yae by his side,' said Michelle.

Sonya's shoulders slumped. 'About five years agan, ah found a gay porn mag. He said the lads at work put it in his newspaper for a laugh. It was down the side of the reclinin chair.'

'Could be true,' said Michelle. 'Garn ter a gay bar doesn't mean yer gay. Yer need ter talk ter him before yer jump ter conclusions.'

Sonya knocked her knuckle on her head, '*Drrrrrr,* that'll be why wer nivver have sex.'

'Ah knar that it's not very often like, but yer have had sex wer him,' said Michelle.

'Here-man, we must've had sex, erm, ten times.'

'In sixteen years!' she said.

'Fuck,' said Michelle, 'me and Darren dee it all the time.'

'Strite up?' said Sonya, surprised.

'Ah've had sex fifteen times in a week wer Des.'

'Have yer?' said Sonya.

'When uz first met that is,' she clarified. 'It's more like once a week now unless ah can palm EJ off on Gemma.'

'Then how many times?' said Sonya, keen for more information.

'Six times, mebees.'

Sonya hung her head. 'Conor always had an excuse, man flu or any virus that was garn rund, he'd have it, or he'd have eatin summink dodgy, or he woz workin and exhausted.'

'And yer didn't think it woz odd?'

'It didn't cross me mind, man. He like persuaded uz that ah woz abnormal cos ah wanted it so much.

Yer knar, made excuse after excuse until ah stopped tryin it on.'

'Der yer love him?' she asked.

'Nor, course ah dinnet!' Sonya hissed. 'He's a borin prick.'

'Yer gonna dump him then?'

'Why-aye,' said Sonya. 'Fucken lyin cunt.'

'Are yer gonna out him?' asked Michelle.

'Nee point, nee one would believe uz. He'll have another lass on his arm by next week, guaranteed.'

'Ah bet he will,' said Michelle.

'Oh yes,' said Sonya, 'he's got all the bases *well* covered.'

'Is that your plus-one off the weddin list then?'

'Fuck off is it, ah'm bringin someone.'

*

Des didn't believe that Conor was gay on account of his stash of porn mags and his obsession with Louise from Eternal, which he fleshed out with how he'd get her in the shower and lather soap all over her tits and arse.

'Have *yae* got a stash of porn mags that yer show mates?' she asked.

'Nor,' said Des.

'Do any of yer mates?'

'Nor.'

'Exactly, because they've got nowt ter prove.'

'Ah'd dee Louise in the shower though.'

Sonya went to ground, collecting her assets and boxing her life, and enjoying breakfast with a view one last time. Conor didn't know what was happening. He was going away on Saturday when Sonya would move to her mam's, leaving him a note saying that it was over. No reason, no apologies, nothing to talk about, not even a picture of a stickman with a nob on his head. Sonya wasn't bothered about the furniture or the appliances, and she couldn't be persuaded to walk with the coffee machine from Italy or the painting of a bloke in a field with a dog, which was worth five grand.

Des reversed the van onto the drive. Earlier, he'd questioned whether a van was needed for some clothes and make-up.

'Did everythin go okay?' she asked.

'Lad alive ow! She's got more shoes than Imelda Marcos. Couldn't get everythin into her mam's so ah said there's room in ower wardrobe.'

She helped Sonya unload her clothes onto the empty rail in the walk-in wardrobe. She'd often wondered who had enough time to wear enough clothes to fill a wardrobe that was the size of a bedroom. Now she knew.

'Put these on,' she said, flinging some breeches and a top at Sonya.

'Why?'

'Yer gannen ridin.'

'Nor, nah, ah dinnet like horses.'

Sonya protested all the way to the stables.

Mayfair was the horse of choice, and as she tacked her up, the fussy mare put her head back and curled her lip and Sonya did the same. They were like two peas in a pod with their fiery temperaments, loving souls, and fashionable hair, yet unlike Sonya, Mayfair was picky about who could ride her.

She plonked a hat on Sonya's head and Mayfair snorted.

'Is the horse laughin at uz like?' said Sonya.

'Shurrup man and get yer leg ower. Yer dinnet usually have a problem wer that.'

'Fuck off, yer cheeky bitch.' Sonya did as she was told, then wiggled her bum in the saddle.

As she led Mayfair to the perimeter path, Sonya was beaming. 'Ah can see the whole world from up here.'

'Wot does it look like?'

'Ellish.'

As she'd hoped would happen, Sonya and Mayfair's loathing for each other backfired into respect. Mayfair didn't veer off and refuse to move until she had a mouth full of dandelions, rather she was sensitive to the needs of her idiot rider, walking steadily and staying on the path.

'Sixteen years wasted,' said Sonya.

'Nor, not wasted, yer had a good time wer him.'

'Nor Paula, yer dinnet knar the half of it. There's so much that woz wrang that seemed normal at the time.' Sonya put her head down and bobbed it theatrically in rhythm with Mayfair's steps.

'Such as?'

'Like when uz woz ski-in and stayed in a chalet wer his cousin and his mate Henry. Honestly Paula, out of the times we've had sex, half woz on this holida.'

'Is Henry gay?'

'Why-no, but lookin back, Conor fancied the pants off him.'

'How like?'

'His eyes lit up when Henry spoke, and he had a hard-on the whole time. He jabbed it at me in weird places.'

'Wot like?'

'Oh man, ah was comin out of the bog, and he accosted uz and dragged uz into the cloakroom and shagged uz against the ski jackets. He'd nivver been so horny or spontaneous.'

'Wot's that got ter dee wer Henry?'

'Ah thought the black run had pumped him up and that he woz lettin off steam. Wrang!' said Sonya. 'It was because Henry woz nearby, the picture of his face not far from Conor's mind, the sound of his voice in the next room, it figures. It woz like he had a hard-on, so he thought, *ah'll shag Sonya, get it ower with for another year or two.*'

'At least now yer can have sex in a bed every neet with the same man,' she said, excitedly. 'How good will that be?'

Sonya twisted her face. 'Sounds borin.'

As she listened to the crunch of hooves, she listed in her head all the places that Sonya had had sex: Penhsaw, on a Metro between Cullercoats and Whitley Bay, on the beach, carparks, pubs, parks, and she laughed as she remembered, the boiler room of the eye infirmary with the gadgie from the League of Friends trolley.

'Wot's funny?' hissed Sonya.

'Nowt,' she said, stopping at the gap in the hedge where Mayfair could reach her muzzle into the neighbour's overgrown field. In the gap, Jason had built a high fence, which Mayfair had jumped twice, able, it seems, to cope with grass if there's an all-you-can-eat buffet on the other side. But then, as everyone pointed out to Jason, if you build a fence that looks like a jump, a showjumping horse will jump it.

'Yer better get down for now,' she said, pulling the lead rope to stop Mayfair from poking her head between the struts in the fence.

Sonya swung onto her belly, slid off, and patted Mayfair. 'Cheers for that.'

'Horses help yer see things as they really are.'

Sonya stared at the ground in brooding silence, digging her toe into the gravel. 'Ah keep rememberin stuff, hods of it, that macks sense now.'

'Wot like?'

'It woz problees about five years agan and we'd had a proper barney, so ah telt him it woz ower.' Sonya put her hand to her face and shook her head.

'Wot? Gan on, yer can tell me.'

'As usual he talked uz round. After a load of slavver, he ses, ah knar ah nivver want ter have sex with yer, but ah will.'

She laughed. 'Soz, that's not funny, but *ah will*, like, if ah have tee, that is.'

'Aye,' said Sonya, 'not *ah want tee*. Then he booked a holida ter Portugal.'

'Is that when yer shagged the waiter?'

'Fuck off,' Sonya hissed, 'he was the head chef.'

'Worked out topper then.'

'No it didn't!'

Mayfair swished her tail and stomped her legs to shift the flies.

Sonya patted her lips, then said, 'Wot's that song that gans, *ah once woz lost but now ah'm found, woz blinnd but now can see*?'

'That's 'Amazin Grace', a hymn.'

'Is it?'

'It's about when Grace finds out that her boyfriend likes penis.'

'Ah really hate Conor's guts. Is that bad?'

'Nor Sonya, or ah hope it isn't, cos ah'll be burnin in hell with yer, all the people ah hate.'

Chapter 41

June 2001

The day before the wedding, the marquee went up. It was like a circus big top made from peaches and cream. It had an opening onto the patio at the back and covered the entire lawn. She wasn't sure how the far side was going to work until the marquee blokes took the fence down. They did it before she had time to defend the expensive sticks of wood that were pegged into the ground. She was furious and stormed off to get Des. She found him fixing the house name sign, which she'd been asking him to do since EJ belted his football off it months ago.

'Can't welcome guests with a broken sign,' he said, tapping his handiwork with a screwdriver.

'Come and see this,' she said, trying to calm down.

He hid a withering frown of *what now?* 'It's garn well with the marquee then?'

She took the opportunity to tread the route that the guests would be taking down the drive and round the side of the house and onto the patio that was currently chaos.

She strode huffily into the marquee, summoning Des to follow, keen to show him how the tent monkeys had ripped down the fence, but as she stepped inside her mood changed, and Des looked at her in amazement. Through the gap at the far end of the marquee was a green field stretching to a wildflower meadow that shimmered and swayed into the distance, tiny cars beyond, glinting in the sunshine as they rumbled down the motorway. Above the strip of green soared a crystal blue sky. Des kissed the side of her head. 'Fuck me. Ah wasn't expectin that.'

Des took Ian in the van to the wholesalers to get the food, while she guided the lorry with the portaloos down the track to a spot that was twenty metres from the house. Chloé had created some cardboard arrows with *gents* written on them and a picture of Cartman to stick on the portaloos. She also did some *ladies* arrows leading to the inside downstairs loo and stuck a hand-drawn picture of Medusa on the door, which Chloé and Kat argued looked totally like a woman.

Then the catering event van went too far down the track and had to reverse onto the grass.

'Fuck me, this kitchen is *massive*,' said the bloke, wheeling his trolley of plates.

She led the bar gadgies along the route that the guests would be taking to the patio, avoiding the inside of the house. They put fridges and a bar across the back of the conservatory in the space where there weren't boxes of champagne from a booze warehouse in Calais and crates of Smirnoff Ice from Makro. They were connecting the keg of lager when Michelle and Darren arrived with the men's suits.

Darren put the suit carriers over the back of the chair while Michelle took her hand. 'Ha'way, let's leave him to it. Can ah see in the tent?'

Michelle ran into the marquee waving her arms. 'Fuck me, Paula! This is beautiful!'

She ran after Michelle to the opening, and they looked out across the glowing countryside.

'Yer knar that yer ganner have people pissin and runnin all ower the field,' said Michelle.

'If they want ter get savaged by midges, that's fine by me. Ah'll be dancin ter Wham! wer a glass of fizz in me mitt.' It was kind of Kev to do the disco for free. He was bringing an amp that was good enough to keep the village awake.

Michelle slapped her arm, splattering a midge. 'Ah reckon this view deserves a drink, der yer knar if there's a bar rund here?'

'There might be. Hang on, ah'll see wot ah can muster up,' she said, heading off to find the drink wagon.

The gadgies had finished setting up the conservatory as a bar area. It was ellish. Pub Paula, *le conservatoire*, The Thieving Crow, The Butchers' Arms. She was spoilt for choice for free drinks that she'd paid for, and with champagne on offer, she chose champagne.

'Mother!'

She turned to see Chloé.

'There's a man at the door with a van full of tables. Could yer kindly oblige?'

She led the table company into the marquee, then left them too it. She joined Michelle in the opening of the marquee, and said, 'Race yer,' running off, waving the bottle of Chateaux warehouse above her head.

She ran down the field and at the end, and out of breath, she leaned on the fence in the gap. Michelle was miles away, hauling her carcass down the field. At the fence, Michelle bent over and clutched her side, her face glowing red.

She pointed the bottle in the air and thumbed at the metal stuff covering the cork.

'Wait, man, dinnet open it,' said Michelle. 'It's all shaken, yer dinnet want ter lose half of it.'

She sat down cross-legged, and Michelle sat, legs splayed, next to her. 'Shouldn't yer gan supervise wot they're deein in the marquee?'

She sighed and flopped back on the cool grass. 'Ah'm sick of talkin about weddins. So wot's garn on with yae?'

'Nowt much, the usual.'

She unfocussed her eyes on the spotless blue sky and exhaled the fear.

Eventually, Michelle thought of something that was going on. 'Did ah tell yer that ower Joanne saw Ally in the Bridges?'

'Nor! When?'

'Couple of weeks agan, and get this.'

'Wot?'

'Up the duff.'

'Neeways!'

'Aye. Joanne reckoned about seven months.'

'Last ah heard, she was flyin from Newcastle and livin with the air traffic controller she met in Luton.'

'When did yer last speak ter her?' said Michelle.

'Rang her ter invite her out on me thirtieth. Left a message and she didn't reply, so ah thought, fuck her.'

'Aye, fair enough,' said Michelle grabbing the bottle. 'Reckon this'll be reet now.' She winced as Michelle eased the cork out. As it fizzed, Michelle caught every drop in her mouth, then passed the bottle.

She took a swig and wiped her mouth on her bare arm. 'That's lovely.'

'It's so peaceful here,' said Michelle. 'Ah hope there's nee horse shit.'

'There is on the path, should be fine on the grass.'

Everyone in the family agreed that this was a peaceful spot. From here, the house looked like a matchbox at the top of the hill, and fields stretched into the distance in all directions. Chloé would often set up camp here with a sketchpad or notebook. Last month she got a poem put on the wall for Parents' Day at school: *The emerald field yawns at sunrise; The daisies smile, make a chain; The petals fall, make potpourri; The path tumbles, falling away; At the edge of creation, a fence.*

She lay in a boozy haze, watching the aeroplane trails as a gentle summer breeze wafted over her face. She could've stayed there forever if she didn't have to get married tomorrow. 'Better gan see ter the chabble people.'

Michelle downed the last of the champagne, then dragged herself to her feet and belched.

The gadgies from the table company were lying on the field with what must have been lager, fresh from the keg. As she got closer, she felt her stress levels rise, and despite her angry charge toward them, they kept lying in the sunshine and supping. She didn't want to swear like bridezilla, so, avoiding eye contact, she picked her way among the lounging workers and into the marquee.

'Fuck!' she said, clamping her hand on her mouth.

'Fuck!' said Michelle.

The marquee was full of round tables facing a long table down the side. The tables were covered with crisp white cloths and the white satin-covered chair backs were wrapped in soft pink sashes tied in big bows. Each centrepiece was a bouquet of roses in pastel shades of pink, yellow, and blue. She was glad Chloé had saved her from a red and white theme. They did the rounds, inspecting the tables, and the top table, and the cake table, and the sashes on the chairs, and the silk drapes. It was like a photo in a magazine.

'Eeeeee,' rang out across paradise, followed by Sonya with a wedding dress carrier slung over her shoulder. 'It's canny in here.'

Her dress and bridesmaids' suits were hanging in the walk-in wardrobe, with shoes laid out beneath. She could hear all hell breaking loose below, but the lasses blockaded her in the bedroom.

'Gan ter bed and the next thing yer knar, wer'll be here wer the hair and make-up woman. Wot time's she comin, Sonya?' said Michelle.

'Ah telt her eight so she can dee the bridesmaids, then start on the bride,' said Sonya, as if she wasn't there.

'Ah'm not garn ter bed at nine o'clock, man,' she said, her mind reeling with the things that needed to fall into place. She was glad that EJ was at Gemma's and she could show Gemma her appreciation with a free bar, cow pie, giant pink slice cake, and a dancefloor with a postcard view of rolling fields.

'Yerl arnly be in the way downstairs,' said Sonya, peering out of the window.

'Wot's happenin? Ah'm garn down.'

Michelle pushed her onto the bed and signalled to Sonya to come over. 'Wer'll gan get some booze. Dinnet move.'

She balanced the crystal-encrusted hair slides on her greasy hair and held the matching dangly earrings to her ears making a glitterball effect on the magnolia walls. She couldn't believe she was getting married tomorrow, it felt surreal. The weather forecast was for sunshine all day, and, most importantly, she was marrying the right man. It would be Des at the altar not some random gadgie, or woman, or animal, like in the dream where you can't decide whether to go through with it or leg it. 'Do you take this walrus to be your husband?' And then there's the any known impediment part where she braces herself for someone to shout, 'She's a murderer!'

After downing a few glasses of fizz, her bridesmaids tucked her in, and ordered her to sleep. It must've been gone midnight when Ian's kitchen went quiet, and it was after one when Des turned in.

Des was up at six, showered, shaved, and he pressed his toothpaste lips on hers as she lay with her eyes closed. He whispered, 'See yer at the altar,' then in a waft of mint, was gone.

She sat bolt upright. Wedding day!

The cavalry arrived at 7:39 wearing dressing gowns, armed with champagne and make-up bags.

'Eeeeee,' said Sonya, hugging her, followed by a pile-on cuddle from Michelle, 'Eeeee, Paula, yer gettin married.'

They smelled of mouldy outhouse. 'Good neet in the Tardis?'

'It's properly nice in there, like a new age country lodge or summink. Bed's comfy, ah woz out like a light,' said Michelle. 'Then an owl woke uz up.'

'Woke me up anarl,' said Sonya, 'hooty cunt.'

'Shower,' said Michelle.

'Me too,' said Sonya.

They went in the ensuite together, leaving her to welcome the flustered make-up lady with her pink sports bag and diamante-encrusted vanity case.

'How are yer feelin?' she said, laying out her palettes and brushes on the dressing table.

'Not bad, to be honest. Ah'll gan get me daughter, best do her first.'

As she crossed the landing, she could hear banging and swearing and men's voices, loud and happy. She knocked. 'Chloé, are yer awake?' She heard stirrings. 'Jump in the shower, will yer, luv? Make-up in ten.' She would've said hair and make-up, but she still didn't have hair, bless her. She wouldn't change her weird Emo for any other daughter.

The bridesmaids looked like gangster princesses. Michelle's spiteful frizz was a mass of soft, gentle curls, and she'd been transformed from blotchy ginger lass to a lardy version of Nicole Kidman. Chloé had dewy skin, and her big eyes had soft, smoky lids, a hint of liner, a wisp of mascara, and thick eyebrows brushed neatly. It was like the make-up lady had seen a picture of Sinead

O'Connor. Sonya hadn't changed much, and it was a miracle that she'd trusted someone else to do her hair and make-up.

At last, it was her turn to look the best she was likely to look in her whole life ever. The lady curled her hair with tongs, piling the curls and twists into layers, held together by a million hair grips and a can of Elnett. Then the lady painted her face and pencilled her eyes like on the picture of Priscilla Presley ripped from a magazine. Everything would be fine as long as she didn't shed a tear.

Sonya laced up the ribbons on the back of her ivory silk dress, pushing her boobs out, pinching her waist in, and crushing her spine. It was nothing like what she'd imagined she'd wear when she was little, back when wedding dresses had puffy sleeves, and skirts with layers of netting, or worse, a hoop. Her top half was strung tightly into the strapless corset and as she walked, the bias-cut silk hugged her legs making a glamorous swish with each statuesque step. She had white cowboy boots and a cowboy hat for the photos of her on Ambro.

Chloé unboxed the ivory satin shoes with the cluster of diamantes on the front and a line of diamantes down the six-inch heel. She slipped them on and stood warily, finding her balance, before practicing walking in them while wearing the dress. For once in her life, she was in a state of perfect hair, perfect make-up, perfect dress, perfect jewellery, and perfect shoes, and she had to stay perfect until the photos were perfectly taken, after which she was going to get perfectly hammered and fall disgracefully over.

'Ready?' said Michelle.

'Let's get hitched,' she replied.

Sonya went to tell the wedding party that the bride was ready as Michelle and Chloé faffed with her bodice. She could hear movement and voices and then Sonya said, 'Go,' and Michelle picked up her skirts and she walked out of the bedroom and down the sweeping staircase. At the bottom was a crowd in white tops and black bottoms and Ian in a suit with a powder blue cravat and matching rose buttonhole. They clapped as she descended and on Ian's command, mooched back into the kitchen, leaving Lisa in a floral dress and hat, Brooke in a skin-tight blue dress, and Brandon in a suit with a cravat that matched David's.

David stepped forward and said, 'Yer beautiful. Dad would've been proud.' He offered her his arm. 'Shall wer?'

She took a deep breath and exhaled. She must not cry. She had no choice but to think about Billy in charge of food. 'Open yer mouth and close yer eyes,' he'd say, 'if yer dinnet dee it, yer cannet be hungry.' It was a shame to contaminate her wedding day with bad memories, yet necessary to stop her heavy eyeliner from running down her face and dripping onto her dress.

The dam nearly broke when Lisa lifted her stunning bouquet from the hall table. 'Yer look like a princess,' said Lisa, giving her the flowers, tears rolling down her face.

David led her to the vintage Bentley with white ribbons. She noticed that the track was already chocka even though Ian said he could get all the staff there in four cars. The Bentley glided off the paved drive and crunched gracefully down the track. She hadn't seen David for yonks and there was little scope for a conversation anytime today except for now.

'How's it garn wer the cybercafé?'

'Aye canny, man. Busy, queue on most days.'

'Turnover?'

'Seventy-four.'

'Profit?'

'Fifty-two.'

'Fuck me, bro, ah hope it's legit.'

'Wot der yer mean?'

'Ah mean yer a tax dodgin charver.'

He went to kiss her, and she batted him off. 'Nee emotion, not wer this make-up.'

He looked out of the window in his grey suit with pink cravat and matching buttonhole.

'Wish Dad woz here,' she said.

David put his hand on hers. 'Yer knar wot, Paula, ah dinnet usually say owt cos emotions wer nivver allowed.'

She nodded.

He breathed in, pushing his ribs out, his eyes filling up. 'Ah'm git proud of yer, and ah knar Dad would've been gutted that yer've got a mansion when the best he could dee woz a burned down house in Pennywell.'

She squeezed his hand and would've said something if she wasn't choked.

They turned off the tree-lined road and onto the sweeping tree-lined drive of Lumley Castle. Behind was a black Jaguar full of bridesmaids, and she waited for them to assemble before swinging her luxury legs out of the luxury car. The photographer appeared from nowhere and arranged them on the steps.

There was coughing and rustling as David offered her an arm and led her into the drawing room. As she stepped forward, she could hear violins, real ones, rather than track four on the *Best of Classical* CD. They were playing Pachelbel's Canon in D. Heads turned and voices gasped as she walked slowly down the aisle. As she walked further, she could see young lasses on violins under the window, including Heather with a cello between her knees, having kept the string quartet a secret.

When she reached the flower-covered table, Des and EJ stepped forward in matching suits. David let go of her arm and winked at EJ, who let go of Des's hand. They took their seats, and she took a deep breath, holding it in until she could see stars. Misery was easy compared with this hardcore bliss, and there was no point freezing her heart; not breathing was the only way to survive this onslaught of dreams coming true without weeping.

She took Des's hands. He was shaking more than she was. The lady with the book came from behind the table and said, 'Ready?'

Her voice was well wobbly when she had to speak, 'I take you Desmond John to be my husband.'

'I take you Paula to be my wife.'

The outward music was Handel's Arrival of the Queen of Sheba, which she tried to savour over the cheers and camera clicks. Des led her out onto the steps. It was quiet. She was married. They kissed. The cheers started again, and everyone came outside. The photographer appeared and snapped as the guests defined the casual shots.

With everyone in a photo, the newlyweds legged it into the garden, and once out of view, Des grabbed her tits. 'They belong ter me now that wer married.'

She looked about, scoping a public place suitable for performing a lewd act, until the photographer walked quickly down the path, waving his camera at a sunny spot next to a colourful border. While she posed, she wondered if they could nip behind the bushes. Des didn't have to drop his kecks far and she could hitch her skirts up. When the photographer left them alone, they managed a kiss, then all chances of sex were quashed when EJ and Jamie ran across the lawn. Gavin wasn't far behind, and Des joined the chase while she collected

EJ's shoe, which had come flying off. She stood at the top of the weathered steps, enjoying a moment of solitude while she waited for Gavin and Des to retrieve the monsters. Today had been brilliant so far.

Des held her hand as they made their way out of the garden.

'Ah hope that everyone's started ter get in the minibuses,' she said.

'Dinnet worry, it's all under control.' As they turned the corner, she heard hooves on tarmac. 'Sounds like your lift is here,' he said.

She couldn't believe her eyes. Jason was in a top hat, driving a buggy drawn by Ambro with feathers on his head. Jason clearly hadn't discussed it with the hotel as the staff were running about all flustered, torn between kicking up a fart and fussing over the cute horse. Jason opened the buggy and Des helped her aboard. As Ambro set off, everyone waved and cheered. Soon they'd left the mob behind and were trotting along Ropery Lane.

'Today keeps gettin better,' she said. 'Ah love yae.'

'Just as well cos yer stuck wer uz forever.'

They held hands and listened to the clip-clops that were soon drowned by the sound of impatient diesel engines until Jason turned down a side street, letting the wedding entourage pass. It was a pleasant detour of the village with people waving as Jason doffed his top hat and Ambro held his handsome head high.

It ended too soon as they turned off the road and down the track, wheels churning up yellow dust and rocks as they were thrown from side to side.

Jason pulled on Ambro's rein to stop. 'Yerl need ter walk the rest of the way,' he said, taking off his hat and rubbing his brow. 'The buggy won't get past the cars, so ah'll tack Ambro in the top gate.'

She wasn't expecting a hike down the stoney track in her wedding dress. She thought she'd be gliding down it in a Bentley with a glass of champagne gliding down her throat.

'Der yer think everyone will be at the house by now?' she said.

'Enjoy this quiet moment while yer can,' said Des.

She did, it was glorious. The sun was shining, and the birds were singing, nice ones, not squawking crows. The peace was broken by a car of string quartet lasses, which stopped behind them. There was no way she was squashing into the thorny hedge to let them pass, so she kept walking to the gap and slipped into the field. There wasn't a person, or a building, or a vehicle to be seen, and Des's eyes flashed as he hauled her to his chest.

'Here-man, dinnet ruin me flowers,' she said, pulling away. 'Ah could still have the marriage annulled.'

'We'll see about that,' he said, taking the bouquet and flinging it down.

There was no danger of a romantic wedding night in a house full of wankered guests, yet she didn't expect to consummate her marriage against a tree in next door's overgrown orchard.

Des went to face the guests while she went to the bedroom to touch up her hair and make-up and to change her spunky knickers.

It wasn't long before she heard, 'Eeeeee!' Sonya had a bottle and Michelle had three glasses.

'Champagne on a walnut stomach before midday?' she questioned as they poured.

'Why-aye, it's yer weddin day.'

'Aye that's the point, ah dinnet want ter end up face down before the disco.'

'Dinnet worry, we'll keep yer reet,' said Michelle, giving her a brimming glass.

'Did yer hear the string quartet?' said Sonya.

'Did yer knar about it?'

'Nor,' they said together.

'There'd better not be any more surprises, ah dinnet think me nerves can tack it.'

'Yer ganner faint when yer gan in the tent,' said Michelle.

'Wot's garn on?'

'The string quartet are here, they're settin up,' said Sonya, stealing Michelle's news.

'Ah knar, they were behind us in a car when we woz walkin down the track.'

'Wot were yer deein walkin down the track?'

She took a long gulp. 'More like, wot were we deein in the orchard.'

'Nor!' they said together.

'Aye. Properly married. Can't get it annulled.'

'Ah'm impressed,' said Sonya.

'Thought yer would be.'

'Ha'way then, yer fucken slappers,' said Michelle, 'let's gan join the party.'

She would have stuck her nose in the kitchen had Ian not been in the hallway in his white chef's jacket, sweating like a man in charge of feeding eighty people. The patio was a sea of floral dresses and hats, and the men were so smart that she didn't recognise some of them. Uncle Jimmy and the rest of the family had populated one end of the patio and were enjoying the free bar and canapes in the sunshine. It was great to see them all together, but not at a funeral.

'Have yer seen EJ?' she asked Gemma as Uncle Jimmy hugged her and said, 'Yer look like a princess. Yer dad would've been proud.'

Gemma clutched a bottle of champagne that she was keeping to herself. 'The last ah saw of EJ and Jamie, Des and Dave were draggin them out of the marquee.'

She made slow progress as she said hello to all the people who had made a big effort to turn out in their finery to celebrate her day. Sonya's plus-one was the doorman from Annabel's. 'Last time ah saw yae, yer were dancin rund dressed as Pat Butcher,' he said.

'Last time ah saw yae, yer wer in the court round-up,' she replied.

'For jumpin a red light, that's all,' he protested.

'Ta for comin, there'll be nee trouble wer yae here.'

He stuck his chest out. 'Nee worries, ah'll keep an eye on things.'

EJ and Jamie were standing like guards at the closed flaps, and EJ said, 'No entry.'

They were so cute in their suits even though they'd both untucked their shirts and had knees covered in grass stains. Gemma had gelled their hair into spikes; bless her, she'd looked after EJ loads lately.

She made a parting action with her hands. 'Open for the bride.'

It was cool and calm in the marquee and she couldn't keep her eyes off everything. The plinths had amazing flower displays, and the top table was like the Garden of Eden.

Des was hot on her diamante heels. 'Ha'way out of here.' He grabbed her middle and spun her to face him. 'It's photos with the horses before we receive the guests.'

Her feet were killing, having covered more ground than planned. She sat down on a chair with a blue bow. Her swollen feet bulged like puddings, and after prising the satin shoes off, there was no way they were going back on. 'Ahhh, that's better. Can yer send Michelle ter get me boots and hat?'

By four o'clock she was glad to be propped up by a table. Keeping the cowboy boots on was a good decision. She'd managed to eat all the starter and half of the main course, and everyone else managed to eat everything. Just when she thought they were going to start foraging for cake, Ian summoned the bride and groom to stick a knife through the wass pink slice.

The catering crew were clearing the dessert dishes and dispatching fizz, EJ and Jamie were running feral with the disposable cameras, Janis was sleeping sitting up, and the rest of the adults were sloshed, including Aunty Pat. Chloé had fled the top table during the starters, causing chaos as she squeezed a chair in beside her mates who were actually dressed as if attending a wedding rather than a gothic exorcism. Kat was sporting a wispy blue dress, heels, and normal make-up and hair, and Justin was wearing a normal suit.

Lisa hit a glass with a spoon and the chatter hushed as chairs swivelled to face David, who slowly got to his feet. He cleared his throat, stroking his chin the way Dad used to when he was nervous.

'Ah'd like ter thank yer all for comin here today ter celebrate me little sister's weddin,' he slurred. He took a slug of red wine and wobbled. 'Wot yer might not knar is that ower dad Eddie had schizophrenia and he died in the Wear after being turfed owt of Cherry. Anyone who knew me dad would knar how proud he'd have been of Paula.'

She put her head down and listened. It was sweet and mortifying.

'She used ter be a raggy-arsed kid wer nowt, and now look at her proper smart kip. Please join me in raisin a glass,' he said, raising his glass. 'Ter Paula and Des from Eddie in heaven.'

The guests obliged with a rousing, 'Eddie in heaven,' and surprise tears jerked from her eyes which she dealt with using the tablecloth.

Des squeezed her hand and said, 'Love yae.'

EJ had done a great job of presenting the rings at the ceremony, leaving Craig to sign the register and do the best man's speech. As expected, Craig told the story about when they were at St Tommy Akkers and Des launched a freshly cooked pie from the top stairwell. It spun in its foil tray and exploded off the floor, covering everyone with steak and kidney like a scene from *Carrie*. He also made the same old joke about how the bride had wandered into the livery yard looking to buy a mare and ended up with a stallion.

Then Des thanked everyone: the string quartet, the chefs, the waiters, the bridesmaids, Jason and Kelly for looking after the horses, Gemma for looking after EJ, and EJ for not causing the tent to collapse yet. The string quartet had disbanded after the main course and now she watched them sneaking back to their instruments. It took Des yonks to get through the thank-yous and then he talked about his regret that his deceased mam couldn't be here.

'So, to my beautiful wife, wot can ah say? Ah'm a lucky man.' Des nodded at Heather and the string quartet started to play. After a few seconds everyone recognised the music and sang along, '*Wise men say, only fools rush in, but I can't help fallin in love with you.*' Her tears rolled, plopping onto the tablecloth. She was done. She couldn't fight this.

With wet eyes and dry glasses, most of the guests stampeded to the bar. Too pissed and emotional to deal with her panda eyes, she pushed her way into the conservatory.

'Here, lasso, are yae jumpin the queue?' shouted Michelle.

'Get ter the back yer bride-pusher-inerer,' said Gemma.

'My weddin, my pub.' She elbowed her way between the Walker sisters' husbands.

The fridge was full of Breezers. 'Is there any champagne left?' she said to the bar girl who was pulling a pint of lager.

'Nor, that went ages ago. There's nee white wine either.'

She lifted her silk skirt off the wet floor and flattened an empty box under her boot to make a dry mat. Behind the bar, she decided to be Bet Lynch. 'Wot can ah get yer, cocker?'

People were milling around, and Des was helping Kev set up the disco, hopefully warning him not to play 'Cheer up Peter Reid' or 'Who the Fuck is Alice?'. She stood in the middle of the empty dancefloor and looked out over the fields. Her jaw was aching worse than her feet, so it was nice not to talk or smile. She could see EJ and Jamie pushing Grandar across the grass in his wheelchair and felt arms around her waist.

'Yer alreet, wife?' Des kissed her.

'Nivver been better, husband.'

He brushed hair from her neck and fixed her smudged lipstick with his thumb. 'Is it everythin yer imagined for yer weddin day?'

She laughed so hard that she nearly popped her corset. 'Much better.'

'First dance in ten minutes,' he said.

'Ah'll wait here,' she replied.

It wasn't so much of a first dance to Shola Ama's 'You Might Need Somebody'; it was more of a sway with all eyes watching. The song always reduced her to mush, so she put her arms around her husband's neck and pulled him close like shelter. As he nestled his head into her neck, she whispered into his ear,

'Ah'm gonna spend the rest of me life blowin yer mind.'

He put a hand on each butt cheek, which fit perfectly, and said, 'Oh, Paula,' in that way where tone is everything.

They were swaying as Sonya led her doorman onto the dancefloor, followed by all of the couples. Then Kev played 'Islands in the Stream', and everyone took a side, Kenny or Dolly, for a mass singsong.

Des kept EJ and Jamie under control while she danced like a mortal bride in a circle with her best people: Nana, Julie, Gemma, Ellie-May, Laura-Jane, Brooke, and the full set of Walker sisters. Even Chloé and Kat were doing Emo dancing to Abba.

'*One, two, three o'clock, four o'clock rock!*' Nana's boobs were a force to be reckoned with when she was jiving, and Julie's old guy was swinging Aunty Susan like they were at The Rink in 1959. When the twist came on, Sonya's doorman handed Nana to Uncle Jimmy, who had the moves but not the knees, unlike Frank's wife, whose ass was an inch from the floor.

When the oldies were paggered and went for a sit down, Kev put a CD on and went to the bar with Uncle Jimmy and Frank.

Outside the Medusa loo was a gathering of women, hopping from barefoot to barefoot, grabbing their crotches, desperate to go. They all pondered the Cartman latrine and decided to wait for a porcelain bowl, except for Sonya who was having a slash on the Fig Tree.

'Here-man,' she said, dangling over the side of the terracotta pot. 'It'll be like a beanstalk tomorra wer all this fertilizer ah'm supplyin.'

'For fuck's sake, dinnet have a shite,' said Michelle.

'Wot der yer think ah am, an animal?'

She spent ages talking to the Walker husbands about the notorious wedding of the sisters' cousin when there was a murder. Then she went to the kitchen to tell Ian and Jason to get out of the kitchen and rescue their girlfriends from Uncle Jimmy's stinking patter. Then, like a bridal snow plough, she pushed folks off the patio and into the marquee where Kev was playing Rod Stewart to an audience of EJ and Jamie spinning Grandar in his wheelchair. The bride from hell marched onto the dancefloor, dragging the groom with her, and Kev responded with The Stone Roses, which was the right answer.

After dancing like wankers, the men retreated, replaced by women and Frank and Des because she was clinging to him and not letting him leave. She was giddy and Des propped her up, stroking her hair.

Ha'way,' he said, pulling her out of the marquee.

On the grass, a crowd had gathered to admire the view as a waxing gibbous moon rose in the pink twilight. It was perfect for three minutes until a biblical swarm of midges sent them fleeing. Des and Darren had to close the flap, making the inside darker, the disco lights brighter, and Level 42 louder.

Sonya was dry-humping her doorman in the middle of the dancefloor, Michelle and Darren were at a table, arguing, Gemma was absolutely mortal, so Gavin was holding her up, and Laura-Jane, Ellie-May, and Brooke were dancing with Frank and the Walker sisters. David was unconscious under the top table.

In a state of happy everything, she was spinning, watching her skirts flair out, until she was derailed by her husband, who cajoled her into the corner behind the cake. He pulled her close, 'Ah knar yer dinnet like slavver, but from the first time ah saw yer stridin down the stables in yer high heels, me heart skipped a beat and ah knew yae were the one.'

'And there yer were, handsome with a gorgeous smile, a ray of sunshine through the cesspit of my life.' she replied.

By quarter to ten, EJ and Jamie had crashed out, and Des had put Nana and Grandar in a taxi. 'We're gettin ter the end of the evenin folks,' said Kev. 'The bus will be leavin promptly from the end of the track at ten, so now would be a good time ter find yer shoes.'

She went to drag the groom onto the dancefloor for the last few songs. It was dark outside and those not dancing had gathered in the conservatory, which had full lights on, attracting all the insects. Des was laughing with Rich, and she was making her way over when a cold hand gripped her arm. It was Justin, his face white, eyes wide.

'Flippin heck, Justin, yer look like yer've seen a ghost. Where are the lasses?'

'In Chloé's room, yer need ter go and see.'

'See wot?' she said, slightly worried by the look on his face and continued grip on her arm.

'Kat's with Chloé, yer need ter see her,' he said, '*urgent like.*'

'Is she drunk?'

He shrugged.

As she did a fast walk through the kitchen, she said to Ian and his buddies, 'Last couple of songs folks, then we're lockin the bar.'

She took the stairs two at a time. If Chloé was pissed, she'd put her in the recovery position, then get back to the party. This is all she needed. She knocked and slowly creaked the door open, not an angry burst in, yet not waiting for a reply.

The room was dim, the bedside lamp on its side on the floor, and as she focussed her bleary eyes on the powder blue jacket that was stabbed to the wall with Ian's kitchen knife, her heart raced. Chloé was standing on the bed in her underwear clutching a crucifix to her chest, with Kat clinging to her ankles, 'Ah'm tryin ter stop her from climbin up the bookshelf.'

'*Je n'ai pas peur. . . Je suis né pour faire ça!*' Chloé rasped, swiping the crucifix at the ceiling. '*Mon Seigneur est avec moi et je ne crains rien!*'

She kneeled next to Kat, who was clinging to Chloé as if trying to stop her from being dragged off to heaven. She put her hands over Kats's. 'How long's she been like this?'

'She disappeared for ages and then ah found her in here, talkin ter God.'

'Is that wot she's deein?'

'Dieu j'entends ton message, je vaincrai l'armée Anglaise!'

'I got a message from God,' Kat translated, 'to defeat the English army. She's quotin Joan of Arc.'

'Then wot happened to Joan of Arc?'

'She got burned at the stake for heresy,' said Kat, slinking her hands out of the loop.

'Je ne me rendrai jamais!'

She let go of Chloé's ankles, then launched herself onto Joan of Arc, dragging her in a motherly love slam down onto the bed. Chloé crumpled like a ragdoll, glassy-eyed, drarked with sweat.

'Wot's the matter with her?' asked Kat, white and shaking.

'She's havin a psychotic episode, like me dad used to.'

'Is she gonna be okay?'

Is she going to be okay? Now, tomorrow, forever? Yes, maybe, probably not. 'Wot's that song?' she said, stroking Chloé's furrowed brow, 'the one about Joan of Arc?'

Poor Kat looked terrified.

'When me dad had a psychotic episode, singin woz good ter keep him calm. How does it go? *Joan of Arc had a heart,'* she sang.

'It's OMD. Dad's got the tape in the car,' said Kat. 'Shall ah sing it?'

'Der yer knar the words?'

'*Little Catholic girl has fallen in love*,' Kat nodded as she counted the beats, '*A face on a page, a gift from above—*'

As Kat sang, she teased the crucifix from Chloé's clenched fist and mopped her top lip with her dress. 'Back in two ticks. Keep singin.'

As she came down, Justin was hanging about in the hall, and she could hear Fat Larry's Band ring out the last song. 'Wait there,' she said to Justin as she ran past.

In the dark utility room, she reached into the top cupboard for the medicine box. When she was clearing out Des's mam's things, she'd found some Mogadon.

On her next pass of Justin, she said, 'Kat's comin down now. Mack sure she gets on the bus.'

He nodded, 'Yes, Mrs Hastings.'

'Wot's heresy?' she asked.

'When yer say bad things about God.'

'*Is it*?'

'Yeah, why?'

'Nee matter, just mack sure Kat gets on the bus.'

She could hear Kat singing louder and more desperate, and she went in to find her against the wall as Chloé jerked back and forth, rasping in French, shaking the crucifix at an invisible demon like Linda Blair and Father Karras rolled into one.

'Thanks, Kat, yer a star,' she said, 'great voice.'

Kat stopped singing and nodded, pretending like she wasn't about to run a mile.

'We'll be good now,' she said. 'Justin's waitin. Get yersel on the bus.'

'Night,' said Kat, splitting the scene.

She swirled the dregs of water in the glass on the bedside cabinet. 'Open wide.'

She waited for a downward rock, then face grab, mouth open, Mogodon in, water slosh, wait for the gulp.

She righted the fallen lamp and yanked the knife out of the wall. She climbed into bed and pulled the covers fully over Chloé and half over her. Chloé was muttering and shivering so she spooned her and sang 'Twinkle, Twinkle, Little Star' like she used to when she was a baby. The miracle baby who saved her from stitching pockets in a factory and who got the ink flowing on chequebooks. Her squishy little girl who sang 'Away in a Manger' in a wonky tinsel halo and her teenage weirdo who made the nuns wish they'd never evolved. She felt her baby's breathing deepen, then a leg twitch. The party was over.

It was 23:33 on the clock when the squeaky floorboard jolted her awake. Des was leaning over her.

'Are yer comin down? Sonya and Michelle are lookin for yer.'

'Sorry ter flake. Can yer flick the landin light off?'

'Yer cannet sleep in yer dress.'

'Course ah can. Ah'm nivver tackin it off.'

'Top day.'

'The best.'
'Night-night wife, see yer in the mornin.'
She whispered, 'Night-night, husband.'

Her hip was aching, and hairgrips were digging into her head. Chloé was sound asleep, eyeballs flickering under her soft lids. She rolled out of bed and to her feet. Her bodice was still strapped in place. The rest of her dress was mostly creased. It was 4:48. The birds were twittering as a dusky light filled the room with morbid stillness. Her soul bled. Life had changed and would never change back. She closed the blinds to stop the sun from rising on her sleeping girl. She licked her finger and ran it under each eye, then put her boots on.

There were sleeping bodies in the living room and the patio was strewn with glasses, bottles, and a man's suit. She was disappointed to find that the marquee was empty of fully dressed people who'd slept where they'd dropped like a wedding in Pompei. There were more trousers on the side lawn as well as a trail of shoes. The Tardis was open, so she stuck her head inside, saw Sonya's white veiny wabs, then withdrew.

As she made her way across the field, the fading moon was high in the orange sky. Ghostly dew rolled across the grass as a woodpecker's drumming echoed from the misty woods. With layers of sodden skirts hitched above her knees, she marched and sang, '*Morning has broken, like the first morning, blackbird has spoken, like the first bird.*' She'd always stand in assembly and postpone the misery with hope, singing her lungs out so that God would make today different, *better*.

Ambro greeted her with a toothy yawn. 'Hello, lovely,' she said, kissing his nose. When she let him out of the stall, he rolled in the dust and snorted like he does when celebrating another day on planet earth. That's it with horses. There's no bitterness for yesterday and no fear for tomorrow. He shook himself down, then sidled over and licked her face. She stroked his forelock as he slobbered down her dress.

As he munched on haylage, she tacked him up with the saddle and bridle that she'd got for the wedding photos. 'No child of mine hidin from voices under the bed,' she said to him, tightening the girth. 'We'll look after her, won't we? Not my Chloé dead in the river.'

She hoisted her skirt to her waist as she mounted, then let the silk flow down his sides as he clawed the ground like he did when he knew something was brewing. They trotted towards the cross-country field, and when she steered him in the other direction, he pricked his ears, eager to know more about this adventure.

They stood at the top of the field in the hazy glow of sunrise. His head was high, hot breath steaming in the fresh morning air. She patted his ivory neck, 'Today and forever will be different, *better*.'

They set off, muscles pumping, his powerful legs fast and fearless on the glistening grass. As they sped down the field, the long meadow beyond the fence at the edge of creation swayed and whispered, 'Jump Ambrosia, jump!'